KINGDOM OF BLIGHTED
THORNS

A Kingdom of Bitter Magic

ALAYA WELLS

A KINGDOM OF BITTER MAGIC

Kingdom of Blighted Thorns, Book 1

Copyright © 2024 Alaya Wells

All rights reserved.

No part of this book may be reproduced in any form or by any electronic or mechanical means, including information storage and retrieval systems, without written permission from the author, except for the use of brief quotations with prior approval. Names, characters, events, and incidents are a product of the author's imagination. Any resemblance to an actual person, living or dead is entirely coincidental.

Cover Art: Silvermist Cover Designs

Editing: JA Wren and Owl Eyes Proofs & Edits

Enchanted Star Press

No AI was used to write this story or create the cover

*Special thanks to
Alex, Stephanie, & Jessica
for making this book the best it can be.*

A KINGDOM OF BITTER MAGIC

A dragon rider seeking revenge for the death of her brother.
A ruthless fae lord with his own agenda.
A love that will drive the fae kingdom to its knees.

I'm nothing but an orphan, a dragon trainer in one of the many border fortresses. When beasts attack the villages, I ride, driving them back to the hellscape they crawled from.

When my adopted brother's killed during battle, I discover who's controlling the invading beasts—the brutal ruler of the neighboring fae kingdom. A gruesome plot is brewing beneath the glimmering fae surface, and he's responsible for it all. Now vengeance is all I live for. No matter how powerful or well-guarded the king is, I will avenge my brother. This I swear.

To infiltrate the king's court, I'm forced to make a deal with Vexxion, a devastatingly beautiful and equally malicious fae lord. In exchange for getting me close to the king, I'll allow Vexxion to collar me at the upcoming Claiming. He'll train me, and I'll give him access to my supposedly dormant magic. Little does he know I have no power for him to harness.

Surrendering to Vexxion's seductive allure could fracture what little remains of my heart. Falling for him could destroy my wounded soul.

But learning his wicked secrets could shatter me completely.

A Kingdom of Bitter Magic is Book 1 in the Kingdom of Blighted Thorns trilogy. Expect spice, suspense, a ruthless, determined woman, and a fae lord with stalker-like tendencies who will stop at nothing to claim her as his own.

This book ends with a cliffhanger.

Trigger warning: stalker-like, morally gray hero, creatures licking blood, blood, killing beasts, battles, danger, death, fire, many trying to murder Tempest, touch her and die (sometimes he does so on the page).

Look for the rest of the
Kingdom of Blighted Thorns Series
A Court of Wicked Fae
A Crown of Cursed Hearts

1

VEXXION

The weathered gray stone of the border fortress loomed ahead, perched on the mountain peak like an enormous bird of prey. Below it and stretching across the top of the cliff, I could just make out the dark openings of the aerie where the fortress's dragons roosted when they weren't training or flying riders on patrols across the valley below. The empty stables on the right were for me and the two men I traveled with.

Some might say I was the true predator here, and they wouldn't be wrong. When I was sent on a mission, there was nothing–and no one–who could stop me from completing it.

Today's mission would change the course of someone's life, deviating them onto a path many others had been placed on already. Did I like that I played a part in such a horrifying plan? No, but I was granted few choices myself. Like the game of

Wraithweave, each game piece had one role. In today's game, *I* was the master.

"How long will you need with the fortress commander?" Zayde asked from where he flew to my left on his own dragon.

"Not long," I said.

I still wasn't quite sure why I, in particular, had been sent, but I hadn't asked questions. I never did.

A gust of wind swept up the tall cliff, bursting across us, and I changed my dragon's flight with a subtle touch of my heel on Glim's side. He responded by angling his body, accommodating the air currents with a sweep of his massive wings and the twisting of his scaled spine. For a dragon as large as mine, a few spurts of air like this were nothing. Like all those bred in the fae realm, our dragons were huge, much larger than those I'd find at the fortress.

Zayde had come on this mission by choice, and I trusted him as much as I could anyone.

Farnoll, flying to my right, grunted. He'd said almost nothing while we traveled, but my cousin had never been one for conversation, especially with me. He rode with us as assigned, and he needed watching.

With a light touch of my heel, I flew Glim lower. We'd leave our mounts in the fortress's stable while I met with the commander. It had been a long journey, and they were eager to return home.

As Glim slowed the pace of his blue scaled wings and extended his forearm-length claws to land on the edge of an open stable, I felt *her*.

She was an eerie scrape across my skin. A shifting of the world beneath me.

A sudden *stilling*.

I froze, suddenly, inexplicably shattered. Before now, I'd barely existed. On this journey, I'd played the role of the Wraithweave master, the one controlling every other piece on the board.

But now that I'd found *her*...

I was the one being lifted and placed on a new path.

I became the shield.

The weight of Farnoll's gaze landed hard on my spine. Zayde only shot me a lazy look before focusing again on our destination.

My wrist... I reinforced the concealing spell before it gave me away.

Stifling the hoarse cry slicing up my throat, I changed Glim's course, shooting him upward sharply, aiming for the large open area in front of the main building instead. Every part of me ignited with urgency, the feeling nearly overwhelming me.

She was the coming storm and I, her protector.

"Vexxion?" Zayde asked, noting the change in my demeanor. He shifted in his saddle, his hand snapping to the hilt of the long blade strapped to his side, his gaze sweeping the area for threats. "What—"

"We'll land in the courtyard." I kept my voice as neutral as possible. If I revealed *anything*, it would be over.

They knew I had only one task to complete here, that I was eager to get it over with. As far as the commander and the

Nullens working at the fortress were concerned, I was a mere messenger. Revealing my true identity could get me killed, or worse. If I'd learned nothing else while growing up among those who'd taken great pleasure in trying to destroy me, it was how to mask myself completely. With magic, of course, something forbidden among the Nullens, but rampant among my kind.

Now that I knew she was close, my plan had just become complicated.

One of my men probed my mind, determined to discover what had changed, why I'd deviated now when I hadn't over the past three days of flying. I snapped out my threads, my lips twitching upward when Farnoll hissed in pain.

"You're mad," he whispered.

I huffed, rubbing the back of my neck. I still maintained *some* control. Control that was slipping with a razor's edge through my fingers, but control, nonetheless.

With a light touch of my heel, I sent Glim soaring above the enormous stone structure that served as one of the first and last barriers keeping the dreg hordes from overrunning the Nullen territory.

Six round guard towers were evenly spaced along the tallest part of the central building, and high walls jutted away from there like arms, encircling smaller buildings used as residences and for administrative tasks. As I passed over the wall, men bristling with weapons looked up before returning their gazes to the valley. They'd give the signal if a flight of riders was needed to defend the villages below. Dreg hordes were swarming across this part of the continent with increasing frequency, though the Nullens didn't know why.

Glim finished our descent, hitting the rough, gray ground hard. I jolted forward, making it clear I was distracted, that the façade I projected wasn't as solid as I'd hoped.

It was all I could do to focus. I *felt* her still in the flood of warmth across my cold soul and the pool of heat shooting to my groin. The closer I got to her, the more thoughts of her consumed me.

The muscles in my thighs bunched, and I remained in my seat when all I wanted to do was leap off Glim and rush to the central building where I'd demand the commander bring her to me now.

I didn't know her name or anything about her, but one stunningly exquisite thing was clear.

She was *mine*.

Like a serpent hypnotized by the trill of her flute, I remained locked in my seat, peering around as if she'd appear beside me, hold out her hand, and urge me to claim her forever.

Someone barked out a laugh on the wall, and though it wasn't directed at me, it shook me, dragging me back to the present I needed to remain in. One slip, and this would be over.

I made myself start breathing again and slid off Glim, giving him a pat to thank him for the smooth ride, nodding to a rider walking past us. Without making it obvious, I scanned the open compound, dismissing one black leather-clad rider after another. Something would give her away. But no one in the vicinity had the glow that would identify her as the one.

"Take our mounts to the aerie," I told Farnoll. "Zayde, tell the commander that I'll be with him shortly."

Or much later.

"On it," Zayde said.

Farnoll dipped his head forward. When his gaze narrowed on mine, the lines in his face deepened. "You won't see him right away? I thought—"

"Don't," I bit out, then pushed again for restraint. I flashed him a smile.

He grimaced.

"I need to stretch my legs," I said.

"Very well." He and Zayde exchanged confused looks but held in their questions. Zayde slid off his mount and strode toward the main building. Farnoll's face tightened, and his intent gaze scanned the big open courtyard. Had he noticed me looking?

Riders jogged by with purpose, but something deep inside dragged my attention to the fenced-in area beyond the entrance to the aerie, the netted cage rising many stories and arching over the top to keep the dragon being trained inside from bolting.

I was *compelled* in that direction.

While Farnoll flew our mounts to the cliffside entrance of the aerie, I walked right up to the fence, barely stopping myself from pressing my face against it like a child peering into a castle yard where everything was beautiful while he remained on the dingy street outside in squalor.

A petite female trainer worked with a youngling dragon,

carefully grooming each scale on the skittish beast's hide. The dragon was like any other in need of breaking, but *she* ...

As I stared at her, vibrant colors scorched through my mind for the very first time. Before her, everything had been shades of gray.

She had the darkest, richest hair, nearly as black as my own, though with a few strands of gold woven in that matched the dragon. The strands caught the sunlight, reflecting it. Freckles speckled her pale cheeks and marched across the bridge of her slender nose.

But her green eyes. They rivaled the beauty of the rarest pabrilleen stone.

No, the rarest pabrilleen stone rivaled her eyes.

As she worked with the dragon, her lush lips spread in the prettiest smile. The dragon, his gaze full of mischief, kept swinging his head around to butt her side with his snout.

Like a rough, hardened warrior, she wore simple black leathers that hugged her deliciously lush frame. I scoffed with dismay. She should be dressed only in the finest silken gowns. *I'd always* adorn her in pabrilleen green.

The surface of my cold heart that was as bleak as my world cracked. I swore a shudder rocked across the fae and Nullen realms combined, tearing them apart.

Tearing *me* apart.

When she slanted a glance my way ...

My world stopped spiraling.

My ragged breathing tamed.

Only my heart kept beating in a furious rhythm, thundering behind my ribcage.

She was the blaze of a shooting star across the inky night sky. A vicious scream gouging at my soul. A solitary, achingly glorious blossom trapped within a maze of bristling thorns.

And only I could free her.

My heart quaked as I struggled to absorb this new reality.

She ... was *everything*.

2

TEMPEST

"Someone's watching you," my best friend, Reyla, said as she sidled up behind me, keeping me between her and the golden dragon I worked with, Seevar. If she got too close, he might butt her belly playfully. Or he might strike out with his claws. It was hard to tell with this one. The long scab on my left arm would attest to the latter. I'd never worked with such an amazing creature before, and I'd trained enough dragons I'd lost count.

"There's often someone at the fence." I continued grooming the beast's hide, making sure I polished each fist-sized oval scale. "*Watching*, as you say." Fortress visitors weren't that uncommon, though they were more often riders or trainers like us. Perhaps a commander from one of the other structures built along the mountain range to protect the villagers.

Reyla and I had been raised together here, me from the time I was dumped here at four and her after her parents were taken during a dreg attack in the valley below. She wasn't much older than me at the time. Someone found her crying near one of the villages, high in a tree, and brought her to the fortress. It wasn't uncommon for orphans to be raised in one of the many compounds like this sprinkled at regular intervals along the border between Nullen territory and the wasteland. We were killed too quickly. Despite our extensive training, much too easily. And village orphans carrying anger in their hearts could be trained.

As soon as we could toddle, they put us with the dragon eggs, tending them until they hatched. The dragons grew fast, and we worked with them, gentling them to touch until they were ready to begin their training. We gave our labor in exchange for food and a roof over our heads. We should be glad about it. That's what the commander said, anyway.

And once we'd turned eighteen? Then we became fodder for the ongoing battle, joining one of the many flights tasked with defending the villages from the ravaging dreg hordes.

"I've never seen a watcher like *him*," Reyla said.

"Oh, really?" My hand holding the stiff bristled brush stilled on Seevar's left flank, and I glanced toward the gate. The angle of the netting blocked my view, making it impossible to see anything over there but shadows.

Seevar slanted me a miffed look, and I got to work again before he smacked me with his long, spiked tail. Grooming soothed him. Standing around doing nothing resulted in the slash of his claws or a bite from his fangs. He'd hatched this way, and his wild spirit reminded me so much of myself, I had to work with him. Four trainers had said they'd no longer work with him, rubbing their wounds and declaring he would never willingly take a rider, never be safe enough to fly against the hordes.

I disagreed. After all, many had said the same thing about me.

I wasn't one to give up on any creature. If that was the case, I would've let Drask die when I found the fallen crow near the eastern wall of the fortress with one wing half torn off.

Drask, sitting on my left shoulder like always, fluttered his wings as if he knew I was thinking of him. I'd healed him like all the other creatures I'd befriended from the time I was little. He could fly now, though at a crooked angle. Rather than leave when I'd deemed him healthy enough to care for himself, he'd remained with me. He brought me presents every now and then. A bit of metal. A rusty ring I wore on my pinky finger until I lost it. Sometimes, just a pretty feather.

To my few friends and I, he was part of the family.

"This man feels different," Reyla said. I wasn't sure why she kept going on about this. "He's not from around here. Two more just joined him at the gate. Their backs are to the fence; they're looking around the compound. Only *he's* interested in you."

I kept my mind focused on my work.

"As soon as you've relaxed, my beauty," I crooned to Seevar. "I'll climb on your back, and we'll see what you can do."

"He'll buck and shoot toward the sky like he did yesterday, the day before that, and a month ago," she said with a low laugh. "You, *my beauty*, will tumble onto the ground and complain about your sore ass for the rest of the day."

"Not this time." Soon, we'd soar above the valley, and it would be the purest, most wonderful flight imaginable.

"Wait until he gains his fire."

Only fully matured dragons could blast, a good thing for us trainers.

"He'll be rider-worthy long before that happens," I said softly.

Kinart, Reyla's lanky boyfriend, slipped through a gap in the fence and came over to join us. He and Reyla kissed—for a very long time.

Finally, they broke apart, all sunny smiles. He came over to nudge my shoulder. "Tempest! How ya doing, sis?" He called me that, just like I called him brother, though we weren't related by blood.

He'd been gone on a training mission for days, and this was how he greeted me on his return? I bowled into him, nearly knocking him over before rocking him in a hug, both of us laughing. Leaning back in his arms, I ruffled his hair. "I'm fine. You? You're looking kind of messy there. Might want to comb your hair. Or maybe shave it off and you won't need to worry about Reyla snarling it up anymore."

"Hey, I like him dirty and snarly," she said with a laugh, joining us.

Kinart rewarded my tease by running his fingers through my own strands, though most remained secured in my long braid. "Beast." His smile warmed me right through my bones.

I loved this guy more than anyone. I was going to stand beside him when he married Reyla, and I was going to be an amazing auntie to their children.

"How'd it go in the city?" I asked.

"I almost met the king," he gushed. "Saw his daughter, though. Brenna. Rumors are flying around that the king's going to marry her off."

"He just got married himself." The first queen, Brenna's mother, died years ago. The king had mourned her. So had the entire country. She was sweet and adored everyone. You couldn't find a queen better than that.

"We saw her too, though only briefly. She kept smiling at the king. As for Brenna, she's pretty."

"Don't tell Reyla that. She'll get jealous." Probably not, but she knew how much Kinart loved her.

"Nah. Brenna has dark hair like you. She wears frilly clothing, though. Unlike you." He smirked. "The city's not all that wonderful. Boring, actually, though the buildings are tall like the fortress and there are so many of them. Lots of Nullens there too."

"Fae?"

He shrugged. "How could I tell? They don't look any different than us."

"True."

"We finished up early, and they made us sit while the legislature was in session. It was all I could do not to fall asleep. It finally ended, they fed us in a big banquet hall, and we flew back home."

Home. I guess that's what we all considered the fortress.

"I'm glad you're back," I said.

"Me too." He moved away to lock his arms around Reyla from behind. She melted into his embrace.

Their love was so pure, so special, it hurt to see them together. They reminded me of stories I'd heard of the rare fae who'd bonded with a fated mate. But Nullens weren't fae. Our people fled the fae ages ago and carved out a home in a stretch of scraggly land between the fae realm and the dregs' wasteland. Back then, my people served them. Now we served ourselves.

When I was feeling down or at my most vulnerable, I ached for a love like Kinart and Reyla's. There was no chance for anything like that for a person like me. I'd be lucky to live long enough to celebrate my twenty-fifth birthday.

Kinart shifted Reyla's hair to the side and kissed her nape. Her eyes slid closed. They'd been together from almost the moment he arrived here. How could something so perfect survive in this rough, wretched border fortress when we all knew everything could fall apart within a heartbeat?

"Later?" he whispered.

She tipped her head to the side to look up at him. "Always."

The feeling of being watched persisted, and as Kinart strode toward the gate, I turned that way again, seeking the men. They remained in the shadows of the netting, though as Reyla pointed out, only one of them faced in my direction.

The sun stabbed through the clouds, seeking the ground, lighting it up as if the man stood beneath a torch.

My eyes locked on *his* and the world came to a complete stop.

I gaped at his coal-black hair with a shocking streak of silver spiking through it at his left temple. It hung loose around his shoulders, long enough to cling to, but not long enough to make him look messy. He wore a blue tunic that matched his sapphire eyes, snug black leather pants, and scuffed boots. He was bigger than the other men, taller than anyone I knew. His broad shoulders fit well with his muscular chest and narrow waist and hips. His lips thinned as I watched him as intently as he gazed at me.

I vaguely noted Drask squawking, whipping his wings against my head, one of them drilling my ear. Seevar's tail snapped around to smack my ass, a warning I could barely absorb. Even when a cold gust of wind burst up over the fortress walls and barreled into my right side, I still couldn't find the will to look away from him.

It was said the fae could lull you with one look, that you'd then belong to them forever. I'd always thought stories like that were made up. Titillating tales crafted to make orphans like me quiver with fear in their beds at night.

Tales told to make me behave.

The fae controlled the largest part of this continent and their border was on the opposite side of where I stood now on the western border between Nullen territory and the dreg wasteland. We'd locked the fae behind their veil, and few dared to challenge the treaty we'd made ages ago when Nullens split from their rule and fled. If any of the fae traveled across our land for official reasons, though I'd heard that was rare, they were forbidden to use more than rudimentary magic. Certainly not a lull. The penalty for breaking the rule meant death.

They looked a lot like us, though I'd heard many were prettier. They could walk among us glamoured to look plainer, I supposed, and no one would know the difference. But they wouldn't. They respected the treaty, and our king enforced it. Only those on specific missions were allowed to pass through the veil and walk among we Nullens.

The only time any of us saw the fae was during the annual Claiming, an event where fae lords could pluck a servant from among us lowly Nullens. Soon, three Nullens would be sent from the fortress for the Claiming and thank the fates my friends and I would not be among them. The events surrounding a Claiming were sketchy, but since I was not being claimed, I hadn't made the effort to find out.

The man watching me couldn't be fae. He was not lulling me.

So, then why couldn't I look away?

The other two men kept talking, though I couldn't hear what they said. *His* attention remained on me. As if life and everything mundane he should be paying attention to no longer mattered.

"Who is he?" I asked, inexplicably desperate to know. "He's gorgeous. I'll admit that. But one man is the same as any other."

Drask cawed and flapped his wings in agreement.

Reyla snorted, moving closer to stand beside me, lowering her voice. "Maybe he wants to roll around with you inside the aerie."

"He'll have to at least say hello, not stand by the gate, gaping."

"You'd turn him down. You're too picky." She huffed, though not with malice.

"Men enjoy gossiping, and I refuse to give them fodder."

"Actually, you don't like it when they cling."

Very true.

With Drask rocking on my shoulder, I tossed the brush into the grooming basket and grabbed the bottle of claw oil and a cloth. Humming softly, I cautiously approached Seevar, watching his eyes that would give away his intention before he acted. When he stared at me blandly, I lifted his front leg, carefully inspecting his claws. He allowed me to apply a coat of oil, something he wouldn't have done months ago. I'd earned a new scar on my left thigh for my efforts that day, adding one more to those I couldn't remember receiving. At least the new wound didn't make me limp any worse than the others.

"You're too gentle with youngling dragons," Reyla said. "The best way to prepare them for a rider is to force them to do whatever you ask."

"Break them, you mean."

She shrugged. "That's how it's always been done."

Not by me. Kindness and a gentle manner worked better than force, but I was different. Even I couldn't quite explain why.

I released the dragon's front leg, pausing to inspect his tail on my way to his other side. It wasn't uncommon for a dragon to turn up with an injury that needed tending from a random squabble in the youngling pen.

As I was rounding his back end, the spiked tip of his tail plunged toward me. Drask squawked and bailed, flying up over us. I dove to the side and rolled, coming up in a crouch, rubbing my weak thigh.

Drask cawed and returned to my shoulder, his claws digging into my leather tunic.

I hobbled toward Seevar as best I could with pain shooting down my left leg. But rather than smack him for misbehaving like any other trainer would, I cooed and stroked his cheeks.

He grumbled, which I'd take as an apology, and lowered his head for more pats, gently nudging my belly as I scratched his long ears. This beauty would take a kind hand to fully tame him, but he'd never betray the one he trusted.

However, it was time.

Watching Seevar's eyes, I strode to his left side and tapped his knee. As I'd taught him, he crouched, turning his head my way as I scrambled up his leg and leaped onto his back.

Reyla reeled away, her arms lifting. "Go, girl. Show this golden dragon how it's done."

"You might want to find another place to roost," I told Drask. He squawked and took off again, landing near Reyla, his head cocking as if he was as interested in seeing what happened as her.

The dragon burst from the ground, his wings snapping out and flapping, taking us close enough to bump the upper netting. As he dove down, he bared his long fangs. Smoke blasted from his nostrils. Before he impacted with the rocky gray soil, he banked to the right and twisted, trying to dislodge me. I clung with my thighs and a hand on the spike between his shoulders.

Another burst took us back up to the netting, and he coiled his body as he spiraled back toward the ground.

I lost my seat and fell, landing hard on my back. I blinked at the clouds churning across the sky. It was a fine day. Not too cool. Not too hot. Too bad I couldn't breathe.

Someone clapped, and my body heated with mortification. This wasn't the first and it wouldn't be the last time this dragon had tossed me from his back. He'd get used to a rider eventually and then we'd begin his final training.

"Well done. Well done." My other friend, Brodine, strolled over to stand beside me.

"Shift to the left," I gasped out.

Frowning, he did as I asked. "Why?"

"Now you're blocking the sun. It's highlighting you, Bro." I gingerly sat up and rubbed my left elbow that had taken the brunt of the impact.

"It's showing off all my muscles, right?" he said with a smirk.

"Definitely."

"Makes you pant for me, doesn't it?"

"Don't push it."

He grumbled but offered me a hand. When he tugged me up, my brain started spinning like I still rode the dragon. I grabbed onto the front of Brodine's tunic, waiting for the world to stop tumbling around.

"See?" He grinned; his brown eyes sparkling. Every woman swooned about those eyes—except me. I'd known him most of my life. There was no way I'd ever crave him the way he wanted. "You're dying to land me, aren't you?"

"Fates, get over yourself." Scrambling for a laugh, I played his comment like a joke and shoved against him while stepping backward. "If I took you up on your offer, your jaw would drop, and you'd swoon on the ground."

His gaze darkened. "Try me and see."

He needed to stop liking me this way. Just because Reyla

and Kinart had paired up, that didn't mean that he and I had to do the same. The four of us were family. I'd always thought nothing would break the bond we'd formed while growing up in this shithole of a fortress. But if he kept at it, I'd walk away and avoid him after that.

"Never," I vowed.

When my skin prickled, my smile faded. Reyla and Bro sucked in sharp breaths. Only one thing gave us that spine-clawing feeling.

The horns mounted on the highest peaks of the fortress erupted with a long bellow, a high-pitched, jarring scream that pulsated through my bones.

Reyla snapped her teeth together, her wild gaze meeting mine. "Dregs."

Seevar would wait here until I returned.

"Wait at the fortress, Drask," I bellowed as we bolted for the gate. Well, my friends bolted. I hitched behind them. They climbed through slats in the fence while I scrambled to the gate and wrenched the two-story metal monstrosity open to stumble through the gap.

I smacked into a wall of a man and looked up. And up. And up. My eyes locked onto twin orbs of sapphire ice.

My heart floundered.

Gasping, I took in his thick black hair—maybe it was a touch too long, though I still itched to run my fingers through the strands and tangle them up.

A few years older than me, he appeared infinitely harder, as if me being ditched as a toddler and raised by my peers was a paltry thing when compared to the torturous world he'd grown up in.

A network of scars twisted from beneath his shirt collar, snaking around the right side of his neck to the back. For a heartbeat, pure sympathy roared through me. I knew how painful it was to be injured badly enough to carry scars like that for the rest of your life.

As I stared, pretty much panting, his rocky jawline tightened. His full lips twitched upward as if he could taste my emotions going wild from this simple contact. As if he could expose my every secret, my every desire, and lay them bare for the entire world to see.

His nose had been broken, but instead of detracting from his jaw-dropping appearance, it merely made him look . . . dangerous. I suspected it would only take one stab from those piercing blue ice eyes to kill.

He was stunning. Gorgeous. So breathtaking, he'd make conversation come to a halt when he entered a room. And from the darkening of his eyes as they fell to my mouth, he knew it. Women swooned when they saw him. I bet he had to watch where he walked to avoid stepping on them.

My swallow went down hard, making me cough, but finally waking me from the trance I'd fallen into.

I yanked my hands off his chest and backed away with my hands lifted. Burned. I'd been utterly, completely burned, and I'd barely touched him. Thank the fates I hadn't made contact with his skin.

"Sorry," I gulped, realizing long moments had passed while we said absolutely nothing. "I didn't see you there."

Reyla and Brodine had stopped on their way to the aerie to wait for me to catch up and were looking this way. I waved for them to continue, glad they did so without a word.

As for the two men who'd been with this one? They were no longer around.

"Not a problem . . ." The man's intent gaze slid down my front. When his lips curled into a sneer, I stiffened. "Do you always dress like this, tiny storm?"

"My name's *Tempest*, not storm." I drew myself up tight. "And I'm not tiny."

"To me, you are."

"Yeah, well, not everyone is over six feet."

"Six-six, to be exact," he bit out.

"Leave it to a man to be fixated on the measurement of things." I rolled my eyes. "I don't wear ballgowns when I'm training dragons." Or any other time for that matter.

"A shame." His sneer didn't fade.

"Well, I'd say it was a pleasure to meet you, except it wasn't." I shuffled around him and hurried to the bale of hay where I'd left my weapons.

"The pleasure is all mine, tiny storm," he called after me. "Just like you soon will be."

I snorted, not even trying to figure out what that meant.

With his gaze so intent on me I literally *felt* it, I secured my long sword in the harness I wore along my spine from before sunup until well after sundown. I strapped my main sword belt to my waist, making sure both of my medium length blades were secure inside their sheaths. My daggers followed, one for each calf. I slid my final four knives into the slender sheaths strapped to my thighs.

Then I hitched my stupid, useless leg forward, making it take me toward the aerie as fast as it could. I crossed the big open yard, my boots mating with the wind to stir gray dust devils toward the sky.

Entering the aerie, I hurried down the wooden hall with dragon stalls on the right opening to the enormous valley below. As I passed dragon equipment hanging on the left, I snagged my saddle and bridle and aimed for the pen near the end.

My friends were already mounted and flying. I could hear their calls echoing along the wind outside.

I grumbled at my stupid leg that continually slowed me down.

My regular dragon, Fawna, huffed when I unlatched her gate and stepped inside. She fluttered her wings and shot me a steady look. After dropping the saddle and bridle, I released the outer gate, letting it swing wide, before hurrying over to give her a quick kiss on her forehead.

"Gotta fly, sweetness," I said, my sleeves scraping across her scaled ruby hide. She accepted the bridle easily, but I'd trained her myself. This little lady never balked.

I tapped her left side, and she dropped to the sand-strewn floor, allowing me to climb up enough to swing my saddle across her spine. She rose, and I slid beneath her to fasten it. I didn't pause but scrambled back up and settled my ass on the worn leather.

One nudge of my heels on her ribs, and she scrambled to

the opening and erupted from her pen. She plunged down into the valley, my heart and belly gobbled up along with her. As the wind stole my gasp, her wings snapped out, snagging the air and leveling out her flight. No matter how many times we did this, the glorious wonder of it still amazed me.

Behind me, other mounted riders flew out of aeries on the backs of dragons, diving quickly into a battle formation with one goal: to protect the defenseless who'd settled in the valley. They'd settled here ages ago, after their ancestors fled the fae realm, and it wasn't their fault the dregs had started swarming across the wasteland to kill them. Should they pack up and leave, move further into the continent where they'd be safer? Sure.

But this was their home.

I understood. Despite the dangers, the fortress was my home, the only place I'd ever belonged. I rode and trained dragons, and the fates knew I didn't savor killing dregs despite how I shouted with excitement along with the others. It was dirty work. Sucky work.

But it had never occurred to me to leave the only life I'd ever known.

Spying my flight of dragons banking toward the right, I guided Fawna in that direction.

As I drew my long sword, a deep blue dragon speared down from above and leveled out beside Fawna.

The man who'd watched me sat astride the dragon's back—no saddle—his seat as steady as if he'd slipped from his mother's womb and onto the back of this magnificent beast and had remained there since. Frankly, the blue dragon put Fawna to shame. Huge. Bred in an exclusive stable, no doubt.

His dragon was perfectly trained for his prissy, pristine rider.

He could know our king. Even pretty Brenna who I'd only seen once in my life myself and from a distance.

He might even work for the king and that would explain why he'd come to the fortress. Rumor had it the king had ordered an assessment, that he planned to start sending us better supplies.

I wouldn't hold my breath while waiting for them to arrive.

The man's frosty gaze met mine. "Turn back, fury, and stable your dragon in her aerie." Even with the buffeting wind, scorn came through in his cultured voice. "*I'll* handle this."

3
TEMPEST

"Are you out of the fates damned mind?" I barked his way, urging Fawna to fly beneath him and bank to the right. "What do you think we do at the fortress, hold tea parties?"

"You need more training," he said simply. "You're not prepared."

"I've done this before."

Flames leaped into the air to the right, evidence of the dregs' attack. I brought my dragon down fast and furious. While the dregs were stupider than a clod of dirt, their controlling Lieges were clever. Born from the wasteland like the dregs, they would've heard the horns and knew we'd ride for them, that we'd be armed to the teeth and determined to slay every single dreg we came across.

Dregs had erupted from the wasteland ages ago. Their Lieges channeled the very fumes from the pits below to turn them into mindless, eight-foot-tall beasts that were nearly impossible to kill. They were monsters, craggy, beastly things with long gray hair and claws on their fingers and toes, plus sharp tails they were eager to drive through your heart.

They'd recently kicked up their attacks on the valley villages with an almost feral urgency, but no one could say why. It wasn't like the dregs could talk or explain. The most prevalent theory was that their increasing numbers had resulted in less food in the wasteland. The dregs hungered for our flesh.

My private suspicion was that their controlling Lieges who gorged on our energy—our lifeforce—were thirsty. They'd drained every Nullen they could easily find, tossing aside the empty husks for the dregs, and they needed more.

If we didn't stop them, they'd not only burn what was left of the village, but they'd take as many Nullens as they could find. Once captured, few were seen again and those we rescued blubbered and shrieked. They were never the same. We didn't want to speculate about what happened to them after they were taken, but our nightmares featured numerous horrifying options.

"I told you to return to the aerie," the man bit out, his dragon tailing mine. Despite me guiding Fawna in what most would find a series of difficult maneuvers, he easily followed, soaring up to hover beside us again.

He might be gorgeous, but I didn't have time to cater to his whims.

"You can shove that idea up your ass," I snarled.

Under my direction, Fawna shot down toward where the

dregs were stomping through the burning village. Nullens wailed.

Their children screamed.

Tossed over the dregs' shoulders, Nullens were quickly carried to the barred carts driven by the black-cloaked Lieges.

As I leveled Fawna a few feet above the ground, I swiped out with my long blade, cutting down a dreg with one pass and gutting another with the second. Gray blood stained my tunic, my dragon, and everything around me.

The infernal man followed, his own blade stabbing freely. Under any other circumstances, I might hold back and watch him, because he fought a deadly dance unlike any I'd seen before. He was amazing.

And under other circumstances, I might also beg him to train me.

Instead, I was going to finish here and find a place to hide from this man. He irritated me, but he also unsettled me. The itch on my spine told me that while his gaze might not be focused my way all the time, he hadn't stopped watching. And my body *liked* it.

My friends and fellow riders fought around me, their grunts ringing out as they swung their blades, the thick swish of gray dreg blood spattering the ground, the walls, the dragons, and the riders' grim faces. With each pass, dregs leaped toward me, their finger-length claws slashing.

One scored a swipe on my right arm, and damn, did it burn. Before I could plunge my blade into the monster's chest, the man did it for me.

"This is why I told you to return to the fortress," he grated through clenched teeth, his hair a wild mess around his face, the silver streak shocking through it like a bolt of lightning. His sapphire eyes were dark. They rivaled the ice buried far beneath the mountain range supporting the fortress. "You're going to get yourself killed."

With my hand clenched over my wound, I rolled my eyes. "Too many dregs left to gut before that happens."

"You're not prepared!"

Why did he keep saying the same thing? He didn't know anything about me or my training. I'd survived more dreg battles than I could count. Killed Lieges.

A cry tore through the air on my right, dragging me away from the jerk. I had better things to do than argue with him. With a nudge of my heel, I drove Fawna toward the last cage in the chained column where a dreg had a child.

The boy flailed, his ruddy face streaked with tears and terrified screams pouring from his mouth.

Fawna dipped lower; her claws outstretched. As she soared over the dreg, snatching the boy from its grip, I stabbed the monster in the back, severing its spine. It toppled to the ground as I lifted my blade in victory.

Fawna landed on her hind legs and released the child behind a long series of thick bushes.

"Wait here," I hissed as she swooped upward. "Don't come out until it's over." If it was ever over. One attack followed another. I'd begun to believe we'd never drive the dregs away for good.

As long as he stayed silent, dregs wouldn't find him.

Sweeping Fawna away from him, I flew her back across the

village, looking for the next dreg to challenge, but I found them either moaning on the ground while dismounted riders stalked toward them with blades lifted or unmoving enough, they'd already been finished off.

I landed my dragon and slid from my saddle, picking my way through the carcasses to reach Brodine's side. He was cleaning his blade with swipes through the tall grass, and when he turned a grin my way, I shook my head at the gray blood splotching his face.

"Did we get them all?"

"I think so," Bro said.

"We're all good?" I didn't see Kinart, but Reyla was rushing toward us.

She smacked her arms around us both, squishing us close. Blood trickled from a gash on her cheek that needed stitching, but her eyes gleamed with adrenaline forged by battle. "Kinart?"

Brodine and I shrugged.

Panic widened her eyes. "I need to find him."

"I'll make sure the dregs leave the valley." I pivoted and hobbled toward Fawna.

The stranger had landed his dragon beside her, and I ignored him as I mounted and took flight once again. Under my guidance, she flew furiously after the carts, passing low enough overhead I could see if they carried anyone in need of rescuing.

Grateful to find the front line empty, I banked her to the right and flew her up along the steep cliff close enough I could kick out and make the ledge crumble.

"You're too damn cocky," the man said.

"What are you, my evil shadow?" I asked. "You act as if you have some say in how I live my life."

"I will," he said.

"Threats, threats, threats." I groaned and turned Fawna toward the dull gray fortress perched at the top of the cliffs, in the juncture between two of the tallest mountain peaks in this area.

"Yes, return to the aerie." His attention traveled past me to another string of carts rattling from the valley. Giving chase, his dragon shot ahead of mine, proving his was bigger, faster, and likely stronger than Fawna.

Following, I patted her shoulder, grateful for how steadfast and loyal she was. Other mounts had been known to jerk back if a dreg got too close. Never Fawna.

We gave chase, catching up to them. She preened her neck, and I swore she batted her lashes at the man's dragon, though she didn't have eyelashes; just segmented lids that, when closed, protected her eyes from dragon fire blasts.

"Don't even think about it," I chided her. "His rider's obnoxious. Controlling. Demanding."

"I heard that." The man turned and looked down his crooked nose at me.

I just crinkled my face and dragged my gaze away from his muscular ass.

Since I never followed anyone, I urged Fawna to bolt past his mount, sending him a sneer as she soared by him. Then I flew low over the carts.

I shuddered when I spied a child locked inside the last one, wailing as she clutched the metal bars.

Flying low over the carts in the opposite direction, I leaped from Fawna's back, and pain rocketed through my leg. I ignored it like always, though I'd pay the price tonight when I tried to sleep. Landing with a thud on the ground, I raced toward the chain of cages.

Reaching the last, I wrenched on the gate with the child's wild eyes locked on mine.

Dregs roared, rushing from the front of the column to challenge me. Killing them while mounted on Fawna was one thing. Hand to hand combat was another, but this was why we trained all the damn time.

"Stay there. Duck down," I told the child.

Releasing a feral cry, I gutted the first dreg to reach me and with a spin, sent one of the blades from my thigh sheath at another, impaling him in the right eye.

More churned toward me, and I was contemplating backing away to gather help when a guttural howl rang out behind me. I spun to find the tip of the man's long blade jutting from a dreg's chest. He shoved it off with his boot and it toppled to the ground, dead before it hit.

The man saluted me with a gorgeous grin so different than the slick one he'd given me when he said I would be his. I didn't know how to handle him when he treated me like this, so I only gave him a nod.

Side by side, we took on the rest of the dregs. Soon, we were surrounded by gray-stained dreg bodies lying on the ground.

"Mia. Mia," a woman cried, racing toward the carts that had continued clambering toward the border. She picked her way among the bodies, then raced to the side of the cart and struggled to rip off the gate while the little girl screamed inside.

As I wrenched my leg forward to help, the man strode past me, reaching the cart. He sliced through the leather fastenings along one corner, and the side of the cage fell to the ground with a clatter. The child sprung into her mother's arms. She raced past us and toward the village with her daughter.

The line of empty Liege carts gathered speed and rumbled through the pass and out into the wasteland beyond.

After swiping blood off my long blade in the grass and sheathing it, I leaned against the cliff to catch my breath. The man came over to stand beside me.

"I don't even know your name." Despite his cocky demeanor, I felt a strange camaraderie with him. We'd faced the same foe and came out victors.

My friends and I would celebrate tonight, and at this moment, I wasn't opposed to inviting him to join us while we did it.

"Vexxion," he rasped, his gaze locking on mine.

"I already told you mine. Tempest."

"Who are your parents, pretty *Tempest*?" he asked.

Hearing my name on his lips was both devastating and intriguing, as if he was tasting it and finding it to his liking. Flames licked down my spine, and my skin rippled. Just by speaking my name, it felt like he knew everything about me. As if he recognized all the parts of myself I'd spent a lifetime trying to hide.

Why did he care about something like that? "I'm not actually sure who they were."

He stepped toward me so fast, I stumbled backward, jarring my shoulder against the jagged cliff. Tiny hairs on the back of my neck prickled and rose.

"Tell me who your parents were," he growled. "Now."

My rapid heart rate collapsed. Ah, there was the sardonic ass I'd interacted with already. I huffed and barricaded my heart.

"I don't know much of anything about my past, and I have no idea why you think it's any of your business." With that, I raced to Fawna as quickly as I could on my cursed, throbbing leg. She thankfully saw me coming and crouched for me to scurry up her side and settle in my saddle. With a nudge of my heel, she took flight in a burst of speed.

Vexxion remained on the ground, watching as intently as he had while I worked with Seevar back in the training area.

So much for inviting him to join us tonight.

4

TEMPEST

I could still function decently enough after two cups of wine, but three was usually my limit.

Tonight, I'd already had four.

My friends and I sat around a wooden table in the fortress's only bar, celebrating our day's victory. You never knew when one battle could be your last, which meant you needed to raise the cup and praise the fates, the might of your sword, and the heart of your dragon as often as you could.

Four cups of wine made me silly. And when I felt like this, I enjoyed singing.

"Please don't," Brodine slurred when I started to sway in my seat and hum.

"What?" I asked. "I've been thinking up a song."

Reyla groaned, leaning into Kinart's side, and I was grateful he was as safe as us after the battle.

Our eyes met, and we both snickered. Yup, he was my

brother even if we didn't share blood. We were almost as in tune as he and Reyla.

I liked it.

"Sing, Tempest," he shouted, lifting his mug. He tipped it toward Reyla's mouth then frowned, staring down at it. "We need another bottle because I'm still not as drunk as I should be."

I expected they'd be leaving the fortress soon for good. Riders and trainers were allowed to marry, but after that, they often chose to leave the fortress to settle in one of the villages down in the valley. Sure, they'd still have to fight dregs, but at least they'd have some prior training.

"I'm going to sing, then." I drank some wine and called for more. "In the glow of the moon's caress," I bellowed. "A lass met a rider, and that was it."

"It?" Brodine's face scrunched. "What kind of song is that?"

"A quickly made up one. Close your trap and listen to my lovely, lilting voice as I compose the next passage."

He hooted. "I'm going to need more wine for that."

"Hey, she sings better than her bird," Kinart said, smiling my way.

I patted Drask's back and dipped my head toward my brother. "Thank you, kind sir."

Bro sniffed. I took another sip of wine.

"I have a wonderful voice and my songs are pure poetry, right Reyla?" I asked.

She and Kinart had locked lips and there was no stirring them from that, so I turned back to Bro and continued my song.

"With his dragon shooting a fiery dance, he whisked her away for a night of romance."

Brodine rubbed his hands together. "Now it's getting good."

"A twist and a twirl, the woman sang with delight. Dragon wings unfurl, we soar through the night."

"This could get hot." Brodine scowled down at his mug. "Definitely need more wine."

"Eyes locked in thrill beneath stars agleam," I shouted.

Someone across the other side of the room cheered.

See? I had supporters.

"Her laughter wove around his stiffening steam," I sang.

"Stiffening steam?" Brodine frowned. "You mean his cock, don't you? Why not just say it?"

"Cock doesn't rhyme with agleam."

"At this point, I'm not sure it matters. Use it. It's the best word for his ... *steam*."

I snorted. "Allow me to finish, my kind gentleman, and then you can go to your bed and take care of your own *steam*."

He pouted, his gaze shooting toward the door. "Sure you won't do it for me?"

I shook my head and continued with my song. "And when he laid her on his blankets so pure, he ..." My head tilting, I followed Brodine's intent gaze to find the man—no, make that too-gorgeous, too-masculine *Vexxion*—standing a short distance away from our table. My song ended in a squawk echoed by Drask, his shrill voice ringing in my left ear.

"You've had too much to drink," Vexxion rasped, his gaze sweeping from Kinart and Reyla still kissing, to Bro, who'd sidled closer to me to follow up on his offer with a hand landing solidly on my thigh.

"What of it?" I asked Vexxion, lifting my empty cup while digging my nails into the back of Bro's hand. He hissed and yanked it away.

"It'll mess with..."

I lifted my eyebrows. "With what?"

He leaned close and whispered for my ears alone. "Your magic."

"Are you out of your mind?" I jerked my thumb toward my chest. "Nullen. No magic. The fae stole it from us long, long ago, and we're happy enough to live without it."

"As I already pointed out," Vexxion said with a shake of his head, "you're definitely not prepared."

"For what?" I stood, not liking how I swayed, but grateful for Bro rising with me and putting his arm around my waist to hold me in place. At least I wouldn't fall face forward onto the table. "You keep harping on me about not being prepared, but you never explain what it means."

Why in the world did I find such an infernally irritating man so attractive? I'd like to think it was the wine playing with my head, but if nothing else, I was always honest with myself.

He was too attractive.

His gaze lingered on Brodine's hand gripping my right hip. Kinart and Reyla continued to kiss, oblivious to the furor going on around them. "This isn't the place to discuss anything."

"Don't you have a life?" I asked loudly enough to make Drask flutter his wings before settling on my shoulder once more.

"Not much," Vexxion said.

"If it's not what you want it to be," I flicked my hand toward the door, "then go fix it."

"Not without you, tiny fury," he huffed.

Yeah, I'd had enough of his innuendos. His nicknames that made my heart beat too fast. And cheap wine.

I shifted away from Bro and stumbled around the table. Kinart and Reyla remained lost in each other. I doubted they'd come up for air until morning. If tonight was like most nights, they'd wind up in his bed inside the residence he shared with Brodine.

Vexxion tapped my arm as I passed him. "I'll walk you to your residence."

"No help needed. When are you leaving the fortress?" It couldn't be too soon for me.

"I'm here for an undefined span of time."

Wonderful.

"I can find my own way to my residence." I held out my hand to Brodine. "Come on, Bro. After all that wine, it'll take both of us to make up two legs. We might be able to walk to the residential buildings without tripping over something." Me tripping, that is. Even as drunk as my friend was, he could still propel himself along a straight line. I could barely do so when I was sober.

Brodine hustled over and slid his palm across my lower back.

"I said *I'll* escort you," Vexxion said.

Let him touch me? He smelled too good. Looked too tasty. And I couldn't seem to control myself whenever he was around.

I stumbled away from them both and nearly fell on my ass. Drask, fed up with me, took flight, landing on our table. He cocked his head, his gaze going from me to Vexxion.

One look from Vexxion and Brodine froze. Frowning, he shook his head and collapsed into a chair, staring blankly at Reyla and Kinart.

What the fuck . . .? Why had my friend suddenly backed away and why were his eyes blank? He stared down at his hands as if he hadn't just been trying to help me.

While I gaped back at Bro, Vexxion urged me toward the door. Outside, I stumbled again.

With a sigh, he swept me up in his arms that were too warm and cozy for my liking. Why, oh, why, did my heart trip over itself when he touched me?

"Put me down." I said, smacking his chest, finding that it was no different than hitting the cliffs.

Pausing, his brows wedged together in the same way they had when he glared at Brodine inside. "You should be quiet. You should no longer be moving." A tic bloomed in his left temple, and he turned his icy gaze on me once more. "Why are you still hitting me?"

"Because I asked you to put me down and you're not doing it," I said.

Drask soared out the door behind us and flew toward the residences.

"I'll take you to your room," Vexxion said. "Sleep this off, and I'll find you in the morning."

"I can't imagine what you have to say to me."

"I'm not telling you anything tonight."

I grumbled and resigned myself to letting him carry me. I also reminded myself that it did *not* feel good to be held in his arms.

"Why are you following me around everywhere?" I asked.

"I'm not following you."

"Hovering, then. Watching. Whatever you want to call it."

"I don't do that, either," he purred. I truly wished he wouldn't talk like that. It made my skin flame and the last thing I wanted was to heat up due to his voice.

"Tell me what you plan to say tomorrow. I'm sober enough to listen, although I make no guarantees about my behavior after you've spoken."

"You're not sober enough," he said. Pausing, he took in the rows of squat buildings nestled near the wall. Each had two bedrooms, a bathing room, plus a small sitting area. I shared a residence with Reyla.

"Last on the left," I said when he paused. "Back row."

With a grunt, he continued toward it, booting open the front door. Drask soared inside and landed on the perch I'd made for him near the far wall in the living area.

"You know we have knobs. *Knobs.* We turn them and the door magically opens."

He snapped his teeth together and strode into the small sitting area, turning left and right. "Which is your room, may I ask?"

I deepened my voice, mimicking his courtly tone. "No, sir, you may not ask." I loved teasing him.

He growled, his boots digging into the thin carpet as he moved across it. "Don't call me sir."

"What should I call you, then? Plain old Vexxion?"

"Some call me Vex."

"I can see why."

One of his dark eyebrows lifted. "And what do you mean by that?"

"You must vex everyone you meet."

He flashed me a smile that made my pulse surge up my throat and my heart flip over. "A few find me quite charming."

"That's hard to believe."

"Where is your room?" His voice echoed in the small seating area.

"Right side."

He carried me over to my door and stopped, gnashing his teeth as he grabbed the knob and turned it.

"Put me down here. I can walk the last few feet to my bed." Yeah, I needed to stop thinking about him lying me on my bed. Following me down...

"You should take care of your teeth."

"Are you suggesting I have bad breath?" I asked in mock horror. Truly, it was a pleasure to tease him. Why hadn't I thought of talking to him like this earlier? Oh, yeah. Right. I was sober back then.

"I believe I'll need to stay drunk as long as you're visiting the fortress," I declared as he strode inside my room.

"Are you always this irritating?" He stopped beside my bed and laid me on the blankets in a surprisingly gentle manner.

"I believe I am. I've found that a snarky demeanor keeps

people at a good distance."

"I can understand the need to maintain walls."

"Not exactly the same thing, but sure."

He braced himself over me, caging me with his palms on either side of my shoulders. His dark gaze locked on my mouth, and for one second, I thought he'd kiss me. Then do a whole lot more than that.

If he did, would I kiss him back? Let him climb into bed with me?

"Don't look at me that way," he growled.

"Like what?"

"Like you want to eat my mouth."

My laugh snorted out. "Now isn't that romantic?" I lowered my voice, deepening it to make it sound like his. "I want to eat your mouth, my luscious one."

His face softened. "You fight hard and play equally hard, don't you?"

"Doesn't everyone?"

"Not me."

With that, he lifted himself off me, though he remained beside the bed, staring down at me.

I stretched, teasing him, really, because I couldn't help it and he *was* gorgeous. What would it be like to kiss this man, to drag him down to my bed and crawl all over him?

A raw, aching need scraped across my skin.

Everything inside me shouted beware.

This man could shred me badly.

After he was done, there wouldn't be enough scraps left to sew me back together again.

5

VEXXION

*B*efore I made a colossal mistake, I backed away, striding to her open doorway.

"Leaving already?" she asked.

I wanted to turn back, to look at her one more time. I yearned to wrap her thick braid around my hand, coiling it until I could draw her close. Then I could claim her mouth with my own.

"Are you sure you don't want to . . . have a seat?" she said. "We can chat."

Absolutely not.

I lifted a hand as if I planned to run my fingertips across her lush lips but yanked it back. If I let myself lose control, I'd become the beast many had already named me.

"Until tomorrow." I stepped out into the tiny hallway.

She sighed.

I forced myself to shut her door. Then I leaned against it, spearing my fingers through my hair.

Never in my wretched, torturous life had I felt emotions this sweet. So sweet I'd do *anything* to possess her. Own her.

Have her gaze at me with complete adoration.

Damn the fates for shoving me in front of the one woman who made me gloriously vulnerable.

I wasn't sure I could handle my chest cracking open like this. If I didn't take care, the wild feelings would rip away the tenuous control I'd wrapped around my mind long ago. With the slightest touch of one finger, she shattered the barricades I'd encased around my soul.

With a muffled curse, I raked my hands across the top of my head and pawed the back of my neck.

It wasn't supposed to be like this. I was supposed to deliver the message to the commander and leave for the fae realm. Instead, like a blundering fool, I'd remained here, as if being close to her might thaw the ice engulfing my heart. Because of her, it now thrived, gorging itself on the riot of blazing colors only she could give me.

The crow watched from his perch with his beady black eyes fixed on me no matter how he tilted his head.

Now that I didn't have Tempest in my arms, I could finally look around the house, taking in the simple seating area with a dark blue sofa holding a spattering of color in the cushions so bright I wanted to shield my eyes. The lighter blue carpet. And on the narrow table in front of it, a vase holding a solitary, shriveled pink flower.

Everything was vivid now when I'd always wallowed in

shades of drab gray. I wasn't sure how to process the overwhelming sensations. The colors. The feelings.

I made my legs carry me across the room and out into the chilly night. Even the sky had changed from endless darkness to a blue richer than the Moorellian Sea. The stars remained unchanged, pristine flashes of white. And the moon, a sickle slice in gray, peered down at me with what I knew was a deep frown.

Striding away from the residence, I passed through the spindly grove of trees between the squat rider residences and the wall, where I turned and leaned against the cold stone, hoping the chill would sink deep enough to resolidify my heart.

I squatted down on my heels and stared at her building. Waiting, though I didn't know what I was waiting for. Watching while the woman who'd changed everything slept.

"Stop lurking, Farnoll," I said.

He strode over to join me. "The commander is still waiting for you to speak with him."

I straightened. "Yes, I'm sure he is."

"But you haven't gone to him. This is why we came here, isn't it?"

Me, yes. Farnoll? His motives remained unclear.

"Where did you go?" Zayde asked, joining us with huffed breaths. "We looked for you everywhere."

"I took care of a few things."

Zayde nodded.

Farnoll watched me as intently as I did Tempest's residence.

"The commander's miffed that you've kept him waiting this long," Zayde said.

"He'll wait until I say it's time to talk with him," I bit out, though I had no true reason to be angry with the commander of the fortress. He was as greedy as everyone, and he'd have to restrain his need.

"I thought you were supposed to meet with him, then leave," Farnoll said in a reasonable tone, his gaze following mine to Tempest's building.

Yes, I shouldn't be hanging around, seemingly moonstruck over a simple rider. Yet I knew deep inside me she was anything *but* simple. How had she ended up in such a desolate place?

"Very well," I said, striding through the grove and past the buildings. "Prepare our mounts to leave immediately after I've spoken with him."

"Excellent," Zayde breathed. "I always did enjoy traveling at night."

Farnoll cuffed Zayde's shoulder, and the other man smacked him back. I ignored their antics and walked toward the central building where the fortress commander had an office. Inside, I took the stairs two at a time, not slowing until I reached the third floor. My boots made soft thuds on the marble tiles as I continued down the hall to the end. The commander's office hosted a wall of windows overlooking the valley and the dreg lands beyond. Some said this allowed him to see them coming long before they descended on a village, that he was the one who sounded the alarm.

I entered the room without knocking and shut the door in Farnoll's face. So much for him going to prepare our mounts.

"Ah, yes," the commander said. "Finally. I was beginning to believe you'd never come to me. And may I say that . . ."

I ignored his blustering and walked over to stand in front of his desk.

"He said no," I said.

"But..." His eyes widened, and he started to rise. "I need it. I've been—"

A sweep of my hand, and he slumped in his chair.

"Your needs mean nothing," I said. "Did you truly think he'd care? However..."

He gasped with eagerness, the shake of his hands giving away his addiction. "Yes?"

"If you do one thing for me, I'll talk to him again. Try to change his mind."

Nothing would change his mind, but the commander couldn't know that. I would try, however, because the commander now had one thing *I* needed.

"Anything," the weathered man said.

Leaning over his desk, I told him precisely what I wanted him to do.

His breath caught. "That's... interesting."

"Why?"

"Because..." His eyes shot to the door.

Was Farnoll listening?

"Because what?" I growled.

"Nothing. Consider it already done."

"Already?"

"Yes, well, yes."

With a nod, I pivoted and stalked back to the door, opening it and slipping out into the hall, finding only Zayde waiting.

"Our mounts are ready," he said.

"Where's Farnoll?"

"He was here. I don't know where he went. I'm sure we'll meet up with him at the aerie."

"Let's go."

Farnoll waited in the lobby.

I shot my threads at him, lifting and pinning him to the wall, randomly noting my threads were silver, not the white I'd always believed. I held him against the wall while his heels thudded against the stone surface.

Stalking toward him, I tightened other threads around his neck. "What did you tell the commander?"

Farnoll's wild eyes shot away from mine, and he gurgled. "No . . . thing."

Nothing? No, he'd done *everything*, and I'd pry the information from him now.

Zayde laid a restraining hand on my arm. Only he was allowed to touch me, to intervene. "Put him down. Deal with whatever this is later. We need to go."

I released my threads and as Farnoll slammed onto the stone floor, I strode outside, not looking toward Tempest's residence. I continued toward the aerie with the two men following.

Shouts rang out to the right, but I didn't see anything of concern and continued into the aerie and down the hall, preparing Glim for flight.

I was about to urge him from the aerie when more shouts echoed in the courtyard.

Cold dread rushed through me.

I left my dragon and bolted back out into the courtyard.

Pandemonium rained down on this world. Shrieks and cries rang out as riders streaked in every direction. Another dreg raid on the village?

My gaze was trapped by a flickering light in every shade of yellow, orange, and red.

My heart... shuddered.

Flames engulfed Tempest's building.

6

TEMPEST

I woke with my arms pinned above my head and the world on fire.

Gasping and groaning, I tried to suck in air, but smoke clogged the world, snaking around me to form a deathtrap.

As flames licked along the ceiling and engulfed the walls, I bucked and strained, trying to break the ropes tying me to the top of the bed. The last thing I knew, Vexxion was carrying me. He'd laid me in my bed so sweetly.

Had he followed it up by tying me and . . . I didn't want to think about what else might've happened.

And now he was burning me alive to destroy the evidence.

Drask smacked about the room, shrieking each time he slammed into the wall.

"Get out," I cried. "Leave, Drask. Leave!" My scream was sliced off by a throaty cough. Each breath I took pulled in smoke, and it burned. Burned so much.

Like I would soon.

This was wrong. I blubbered, tears stinging my eyes and driving the smoke from them for only a heartbeat.

"Get out, Drask. Please."

Something silver, like long threads of oily light, flashed across the window on my left, and it burst outward. The fire fed by the lovely cool air wafting in through the opening churned and jutted around, eager to consume everything in sight.

Drask landed on the bed beside me, shrieking, flapping his wings as if this bit of air would keep the flames away from me.

As ashes rained down on us, I cried out for him to leave and thrashed on the bed, jerking up before collapsing down. I screamed and gasped, desperate to suck air into my scorched lungs.

The silver strands of . . . something wrapped around me, trying to lift me, while a leg clad in fabric as black as the night jerked through the opening, followed by Vexxion. I swore the silver threads were attached to him, but I couldn't be seeing this right.

His wild eyes locked on me.

I groaned and flailed, yanking on the ropes hard. My wrists stung, wetness telling me they bled.

Vexxion crouched, his eyes pinning me in place. The silver bands jerked me one way, then the other. I must've been seeing things, but they appeared to extend out of him.

Fuck, he'd come back to make sure I didn't escape.

Hauling in spurts of air laden with smoke and heat from the flames, I wrenched away from him.

"Fly, Drask," I croaked. "Fly free!"

Bent forward, Vexxion stalked over to me, confusion filtering across his face. His gaze landed on my wrists still secured to the bed, and his snarl ripped out. He tossed Drask toward the opening, and my little friend soared through.

Wrenching a blade from the sheath at his waist, Vexxion plunged it toward me.

I released my final scream, a peal of pure terror.

Hold still.

He sliced through the ropes binding me to the bed and after stuffing his blade into a sheath at his side, he lifted me and raced back to the window.

We tumbled out, falling hard on the ground, and he rolled us away from the flame-gutted building. It collapsed with the groan of a dying beast, and the fire engulfed what was left, sparks flinging themselves toward the night sky in a wild rage.

I whimpered as Vexxion sat up with me in his arms.

"You're all right." His fingers rushed feverishly up and down my back. "I've got you. You're safe. I promise."

Heat seared across my wrists, and the pain ... ceased.

People rushed around us, crying out in dismay. Others had created a chain and were slogging buckets of water from one to another, the last one flinging it onto the fire. The building was gone, well beyond gone.

And only my building was burning.

I stared around blankly. Shock. That's what this feeling was. I'd barely survived a traumatic experience, and now that I was relatively safe, my mind couldn't take it any longer. I needed to be alone where I could think.

No one came near us, but maybe they couldn't see us sitting

on the ground beyond the ruins of the building. Everything I had, everything I was, had been consumed in a flash.

Drask landed on the grass nearby and fretted his claws in the soil, releasing soft chirps of distress that broke my heart.

I stroked his back, and he stilled beneath my hand.

Then I remembered how I woke, and what Vexxion must've done. He'd tied me and . . . I reeled around on his lap and started smacking him, my eyes shedding tears I despised and my voice croaking out the same words over and over. "Bastard. You fucking bastard."

He grabbed my wrists and trapped them together with one of his big hands, stretching them up over my head until I wrenched one free and hit him squarely in his rocky jaw.

"You fucking bastard!"

"Is there any reason you're calling me *that* in particular?" he asked with a dryness that cut through me with a dull blade.

I struggled to break his hold.

He was too big. Too strong. And too fucking determined to subdue me.

"If you don't stop," he said with a sneer, "I'll lay you on the dirt and pin your body to the ground with my own."

I stilled, though my stupid tears kept tracking down my face. Swiping them away with my sleeve, I glared up at him.

"You're a fucking bastard," I hissed.

"That's already been established but why bring it up *now*, precisely?"

"You tied me to the bed."

"If I wanted to do something like that, you'd be whimpering for another, more delicious reason."

Bastard. "So says the man who takes what he wants and calls it passion," I growled.

His face tightened. "I. Never. Force. Anyone. I did not tie you up."

Staring up at him blankly, I tried to remember what happened, but everything was scrambled in my mind. The alcohol or for a more sinister reason?

There was no way magic was involved in all this.

I didn't trust this man. But I saw the stark honesty in his face, and it deflated me all at once. "You must've done something."

"I did nothing but leave you," he growled, inner flames flashing through his dark eyes. Or maybe it was the smoldering ruins of my life I saw reflected there, not real flames. "Why would I bother to tie you?"

"But . . . someone did. I assumed—"

"You assumed wrong." One of his dark eyebrows lifted. "Tell me, tiny fury. Who's trying to kill you?"

7

VEXXION

Farnoll and Zayde rushed over, both winded, stopping beside us.

"Guard," I said, and Zayde pivoted sharply, drawing a weapon that should already be in his hands. Farnoll remained at my back, staring at Tempest while Zayde stalked around us in widening circles.

I tightened my arms around Tempest as if that would somehow protect her. A fierce need to take her from here, to hide her nearly overwhelmed me, but I stomped the feeling flat. There was too much at stake to do something like that. I was already exposing myself by holding her this long.

With that thought in mind, I lifted her off my lap and placed her on the ground. As the crow hopped up and landed on her shoulder, I got to my feet.

She blinked up at me, looking lost. And fuck if it didn't make me want to drop to my knees and hold out my arms.

The male from the bar ran over and dropped down beside her, yanking her against his chest. While the crow clung to her shoulder, the male encircled her in his embrace. Did he think this spitfire needed *his* protection? She had while inside the building, but not now. Already, I could see her processing what had happened, studying everyone in the vicinity, and analyzing how best to handle my question.

"Shit, Tempest, are you alright?" he grumbled, his wide gaze taking in the smoldering ruins, all that was left of the building in which she'd slept.

"I am." To my relief, she eased out of his arms and stood. She stroked the crow nestling on her shoulder, who flapped his wings and cawed.

"What happened?" the male asked, jumping to his feet. His attention narrowed on me. "And who are you? You were hanging around here yesterday, watching Tempest. You were at the bar last night."

I lifted one eyebrow at his impertinence.

"He's Vexxion," Tempest said, shooting me a look I couldn't define. Her anger had fled but something like resolution had taken its place. She'd sheltered in my arms, drunk in the comfort I offered, but now she was pushing me away. I still couldn't believe she'd pretty much accused me of something that might be common where I came from, but what I'd never do to another. "I don't know anything else about him." She stalked over to stand in front of me. "Who are you really? Why were you conveniently here when the building was burning down around me?"

"I saved you," I said dryly. "You should be thanking me, not questioning me."

The male took her hand and pulled her away from me, trying to wrap his arms around her again.

My low growl ripped out.

He paused, frowning.

Tempest snarled. "Don't act like that." After sucking in a breath and shooting it out along with a long series of coughs, she turned to the other male. "I'm fine, Brodine. My throat hurts and my lungs ache, but he . . . I . . ." She shook her head, making her long braid dance across her spine. "He got me out in time."

"I should've been here for you," Brodine said. If nothing else, I could tell he cared for Tempest, though it was clear he wanted more than the friendship she offered.

Seeing that she didn't want him in return calmed my beast —for now.

When I saw her building aflame, something inside me snapped. All I could think of was saving her, of making sure she lived. If she died . . . it was unthinkable. I'd sacrifice myself to make sure it didn't happen. As long as my blood roared through my veins, and my lungs could suck in bitter air, I'd save her.

There would be no softness left inside me if I lost her. She was the only thread of sanity in my cursed, wretched world. The only one who could save *me*.

Farnoll said nothing, though I felt the scrape of his magic, poking away at my mind.

"Farnoll," I barked. "Do not." A snap of my threads in his direction made him back down quickly.

Zayde came over and spoke quietly by my ear, his back facing Tempest and Brodine. "I found something." He tilted his head to the side of the smoldering structure. "Ignite spell."

Of course. That was why the building caught fire so fast. "Keep that to yourself."

Zayde nodded.

Farnoll grumbled. "The mounts are still waiting."

"I'm not leaving yet." How could I leave her when she was so painfully vulnerable?

"We've already stayed too long."

"I need to speak to the commander again."

"About what?" Farnoll asked.

"Nothing you need to concern yourself with." Another piece to position on the Wraithweave board. Farnoll, I suspected, battled on the opposing side.

Zayde studied my face for a moment before nodding. "I'll let him know." He sheathed his blade and stalked toward the central building.

I sought Tempest, my gaze meeting hers. Even with grime on her face and her hair in disarray, she still stunned me. It was all I could do to breathe when she was near.

I'd have to be incredibly careful. Everything had changed once more. It would take a cutthroat plan to win this game. I couldn't allow myself to give in to the emotions clogging my throat and making my heart burst into flames. Could I suppress them, hide them?

I'd find a way to do it.

If anyone discovered I harbored even a touch of warmth for this glorious, achingly perfect slip of a woman...

They'd rip her apart.

Not only that.

They'd torture her until screams scraped her throat raw and her mind had shattered.

8

TEMPEST

"Let me take you to my quarters," Brodine said, his hand on my arm. If I let him, he'd sweep me up, carry me there, and place me in his bed. Drown me in emotions I didn't want or need from a friend.

Reyla and Kinart rushed over.

"Jeez, Tempest. Are you alright?" Reyla looked from me to Brodine to Vexxion.

"Who do I need to kill?" Kinart roared.

"No one, no one," I croaked, following my words with a chesty cough.

Kinart stroked my forehead, tilting my face toward his. "You're sure? Because I'm all over it if you need me."

That was my brother. I adored him. I hated to see him worried.

"I'm fine. No burns. Vexxion saved me." Why did the words taste bitter on my tongue? I was grateful he'd broken the window and risked his own life to get me out, but I still felt unsettled around him.

Of course I knew why. I was attracted to him, something I didn't like admitting to myself. Attraction to a man like him would be my doom; I just knew it. If only my spine didn't tingle whenever he was around.

Vexxion sent Brodine such an odd look, I couldn't tell what it might mean. Jealousy? No way. Vexxion and I only met today —yesterday.

Yet he'd saved me. I couldn't stop remembering him plunging inside my room, his face stark with desperation, the way he'd sliced through my bindings and carried me outside. He'd held me, soothed me. He'd acted like he cared.

I needed to get over my stupid hero worship and recognize this for what it was, gratitude.

Maybe.

His sharp gaze met mine. Always so intense. Did he ever relax or laugh? I felt a twinge at the thought that he didn't. "If you don't need me any longer..."

"I don't. Thank you," I said.

"You're welcome."

"I'm not sure what would've happened if you hadn't gotten me out."

We turned to the ruins of the building, and every one of us knew exactly what would've happened. There would be nothing left for a funeral pyre.

Was he right that someone had tried to kill me?

If only I could remember who'd tied me to the bed. The realization that I had no memory of it happening was as terrifying as the fire. I'd had a lot to drink, but I'd never blacked out before. Why hadn't I seen or heard someone enter my bedroom and tie me to the frame?

Next time, I'd stick to no more than one mug of wine. I needed to find another way of dealing with my emotions scraped raw after fighting off a dreg attack. I'd long since learned sex didn't make me forget any better than wine.

After a long look at me and what I swore was a sneer directed Brodine's way, Vexxion left. His two men followed, one studying my face as if he wanted to make sure he remembered everything about me. They stopped enough distance away I couldn't overhear them while they spoke, though with the uproar ebbing and flowing around me, I'd have a hard time hearing them even if they shouted next to me.

"What happened?" Reyla asked, and I explained what I remembered.

"Tempest." Kinart put his hand around the back of my neck and hauled me against his chest. "You could've died." His gruff voice gave away his horror.

Reyla nodded; her eyes shadowed with fear.

"You smell smoky," Kinart added. He was teasing me because he wanted to cheer me up. We'd been closer than siblings for years. It was only natural either of us would freak if the other one got hurt.

A glance at the moon showed me only a few hours had passed since I'd left the bar. With all the wine floating through my veins, I should still be staggering, not stone-cold sober.

"You need to see the healer," Kinart added. "I'll drag you there myself if you don't do it under your own effort. You inhaled smoke. I'm sure you're still hyped up from what happened, but you could have burns you don't even feel." His urgent concern draped across me like a warm blanket.

There was no harm in seeing the healer. "I'm taking Drask to the animal healer first."

"You should be seen before your crow," Brodine bit out. "I insist."

I'd relent on this. "Right after, then."

"Lean on me," Kinart said.

Brodine picked me up and started carrying me in that direction, Drask rocking on my shoulder, scrambling to hold on.

"I can get there on my own." Truly, he had to stop being touchy-feely. Every time I allowed it, he took it to mean we were one step closer to being a couple like Kinart and Reyla.

"Your leg must be killing you," he said softly.

It was, but still. "Put. Me. Down."

With a growl, he did so, but he kept his arm around my back. "Lean on me, at least, would you? I want to help. You don't know how horrible it was to see your residence covered in flames and think you were still inside, burning."

Yet he hadn't broken through my window to rescue me. No, a stranger had rescued me instead.

I didn't like feeling irritation toward my friend, didn't like that I was comparing them. Brodine was a decent person. He'd make some woman incredibly happy one day. She just wouldn't be me.

"Thanks," I said gruffly, letting him help me.

When Drask took flight, soaring beside us, Kinart slipped

his arm around me from the other side, kissing my temple. "You okay, sis? I mean it. Really?" Reyla fretted by his side.

"I'm going to survive, and that's all that matters."

His concerned gaze met mine, seeking a lie in my words.

Hating to worry him, I held everything back. My fucking leg ached like crazy. Pain blazed across my lungs. You'd think I'd gone for an hour-long run or something, not lie in bed with my wrists pinned to the bedposts while smoke churned around me.

"Wait out here, Drask," I said when we reached the healer's. I'd bring him inside, but the last time I did that, after taking a gash in my arm courtesy of Seevar's fangs, she'd scolded me, saying animals didn't belong there. They weren't Nullen.

I didn't agree, but I also didn't argue. Good healers were hard to find. I'd need her again soon.

Drask landed on a light fixture mounted by the door, and we went inside the main building, taking the hall to the healer's office.

Inside, she leaped up from her desk, and with concern creasing her face, she waved to a low bed near a wall. "Put her over there."

"I'm fine. Really," I said as my friends carefully guided me over to the pristine blue surface and made me sit. Before I could protest, Brodine lifted my legs and made me lie down. "Enough. Really. I'm fine." He gave me such a dragon baby look of dismay that I sighed. "I'm sorry. I don't mean to snap at you. I know you're only trying to help."

"Bro," Reyla said, edging in between us, her back facing me. "Come stand with me and Kinart near the door. Let the healer take a look at Tempest." While he listened to her and not me,

Reyla pivoted to face me. She rolled her eyes and mouthed, "Boys."

Yeah, if only he looked at me like a boy who was a friend and not like a man.

When she joined him, Kinart put his arm around her shoulders.

The healer checked me over and pronounced me fit. "Relax for a few days," she said, her stern gaze meeting mine. "No fighting dregs and no training."

I couldn't let Seevar take a few days off when he was only making tiny steps of progress. To please her and my friends, however, I nodded. I could do what I wanted tomorrow.

"You'll stay with me," Brodine said when we returned outside. His arm went around my waist again while Drask took his place on my shoulder, his claws digging in enough to make me wince.

I peeled myself away from Brodine and stroked Drask to soothe him. "Sorry. Thanks, but nope. I can't stay with you."

His baby dragon expression turned sullen. "I meant as friends. You're hurt. You know I'd never push for more at a time like this."

Yet he was.

My wan smile rose as I aimed for the animal healer. He'd helped Drask when I first found him, told me how to care for his wing. He was one of the good guys.

As I hobbled along, I spoke to Reyla. "We both lost our home tonight."

"I had a few things in there I'm going to miss." The realization must've struck her, because her eyes watered with tears. So did mine, but that was from the smoke, not dismay over lost possessions. "A picture of my little sister and mom. Some clothes. My stuffed dragon. But I'm alive, and I've got Kinart."

Truly, to her, he was everything that mattered. I got it. She loved me just as much.

I'd lost . . . nothing, really. It hadn't taken too many of my fellow orphans stealing what little I had before I decided not to cling to a thing. I *had* liked my blankets, though. I'd saved up my earnings to buy them from the weaver, and he'd made them with pure flooferdar, a fabric many coveted—including me.

I could buy more with my next wages.

Thankfully, the healer was still inside. He must've been roused along with everyone else because of the fire.

He examined Drask, who preened under his touch. As I said, he was a good guy. "He appears to have come through it unscathed. I know you'll watch over him well. Bring him to me if there's a change." His penetrating gaze met mine. "How are you?"

I shrugged and another cough wracked my frame. "I survived, and that's all that matters."

His hand landed on my shoulder. "*You* matter. Remember that."

Uncomfortable with his affection, I eased away. Drask flew up and landed on my leather tunic, clinging.

"I'm going to go change and wash," I said.

He grunted. "Make sure you see the healer."

"Already have. I'm doing as well as Drask." Or not. My soul felt like someone had slammed through it wearing heavy boots. My stupid eyes kept seeping, but that had to be from the smoke.

As for my emotions . . . I wasn't going to examine them too closely right now.

We left and started across the compound, though I wasn't sure where we were headed. I had no home to go to, no bed with a decent pillow to lay my head on and fluffy blankets to slide beneath.

Brodine hovered by my side, his arm stretched out to catch me if I fell. Sadly, I might. I gave him a wan smile that did nothing to dispel the concern clouding his eyes. Like the animal healer, Brodine was a good guy. I loved him as much as I did Kinart.

"Can I borrow some clothes?" I asked Kinart.

"You could wear something of mine," Bro said.

I shook my head and stifled my cough. "Too big."

"Of course you can," Kinart said from Brodine's other side.

Reyla clung to his arm; her face full of the same devastation flooding me.

"Everything I have is yours and Reyla's," he said, though his gaze met mine. "Always will be."

"We can stay with the guys," Reyla said. "They'll assign us to another residence tomorrow, though I doubt we'll be put in the same place."

I'd miss sharing with her. She didn't steal, and she spent more of her time at Kinart's place than with me. I liked being alone. The silence didn't ask questions or judge me.

"Alright," I reluctantly agreed. "We'll stay with the guys."

Brodine grinned.

9

TEMPEST

Drask clung to me, coming into the bathing area while I washed and changed into Kinart's clothing. Then he perched on the sofa and groomed his feathers, apparently coming through the event unscathed.

I wasn't so sure about myself, though I was able to sleep—mostly. The sofa was hard, and the guys snored. Nightmares chased me. A shadowy figure grabbed my wrists and tied me to the bed before flicking their hand out to light the world around me on fire.

Come dawn, I slipped off the sofa and limped to the bathing area where I used the guys' tooth cleaning powder. I massaged my leg that kept spasming, as if I were the one climbing through windows to rescue damsels in distress last night, not Vexxion.

Ignoring the pain in my thigh, I tiptoed into Kinart's room to raid his wardrobe again, studiously avoiding looking too closely at my friends entwined together beneath the blankets. I'd borrowed Kinart's stuff on and off for years. He wasn't a big guy like Brodine.

Dressed in loose pants and a tunic, I stepped out into the living area, Drask soaring past me to land on the scarred table spanning the front of the sofa.

A vase sat in the middle of it, holding a rose. It . . . wasn't there when I woke. I would've noticed the rose if nothing else, because it was unlike any I'd seen before.

I tiptoed closer while Drask looked from me to the flower. Stooped down beside the table, I stretched my fingers toward the inky, black-as-a-tortured-soul rose, its silver tips shimmering in the low light.

Such a thing couldn't exist in real life. Where did it come from?

I touched the rose, delicately stroking the smooth, silky petals, sighing at how gorgeous it was, how soft. I even traced the tip of my finger along the silver streaks etching the tips.

It was a bed of black velvet sprinkled with crushed silver jewels.

I moved my fingertip down to the stem and cried out when I pricked myself on a thorn, jerking my finger into my mouth. The bitter, metallic tang of my blood gave way to an odd sweetness. Pulling my finger out, I stared as another drop welled.

Drask cawed and flapped his wings.

Grimacing, I wiped the blood off on my pants.

I glared at the rose as if it had purposefully hurt me, which was silly. Kinart had probably plucked it for Reyla, and she'd slid it into the vase last night.

No one would leave such a beautiful thing for me.

Hearing movement in Kinart's room, I went to the tiny sink and filled a glass with water. I sucked it down, washing away the strange tang still lingering in my mouth.

A short time later, I walked across the central compound, aiming for the dining area. Drask rocked on my shoulder, his claws biting through the thinner fabric of Kinart's tunic. My skin was a network of tiny scars there, just like my thigh, only these were gifts from my interactions with my crow friend.

I sucked on my finger, though it no longer bled. My cough kept wrangling up my throat, making riders nearby jump when I released it. I had to keep swiping at my stinging, watering eyes.

"Wait." Reyla caught up and skipped along with me, a sleepy Kinart skulking behind her with his hair slicking up in all directions. She paused at a low, swooping sound overhead and tipped her head back. "Huh."

Was Vexxion gone? "Talk about making a girl's day." I grinned as a dragon flew toward the mountain pass.

"One of Vexxion's team," Brodine said with the same satisfaction pouring through me. He walked over to join us. "Flying to catch up with him, I hope."

Same, bud, same. "Don't come back," I shouted for good measure, but the male didn't glance back.

"Maybe he's just out for a ride. A patrol." Kinart put his arm around Reyla's shoulders, and she gazed up at him with complete adoration.

Sometimes, I wasn't sure they were aware that anyone else was around.

"Truly, you two should get married today and leave the

fortress," I said. "Go build a house. Have a bunch of cute babies."

"What do you think, love?" she asked, her eyes sparkling. "How many babies should we have?"

"At least ten."

"Ten?" she shrieked.

He swept her up in his arms and kissed her while spinning around. They tumbled to the ground, and he rolled until he could brace himself above her. "How about twelve, then?"

She smacked his arm. "One, maybe. Two. Not twelve."

"We'll start there." With a heavy sigh but a sappy grin on his face, he levered himself up and off her, pulling her to her feet.

"When we get married, you're going to stand with us both," Kinart told me. "Be my man and her woman. Bro too. I can have more than one, right?"

Since he sounded concerned that I wouldn't do this for him, I nodded and slapped his shoulder. "After you get married, I'm coming to visit all the time. I'll cook you both meals—"

"Please don't," he said. "The one time you tried . . ." Grimacing, he rubbed his belly.

"You didn't get that sick."

Reyla snickered. "I'll cook. You can hang out and sing for us."

"Deal."

"Well." Brodine looked up again.

Another dragon carrying one of Vexxion's men soared low, its claws nearly scraping on one of the towers as it passed over the main building. It soared down toward the valley. Perhaps they were on patrol.

It didn't matter. They were gone, and my life could get back to normal.

I didn't like the pang of disappointment I felt at the thought of him leaving.

We continued to the building housing the dining area and went inside, bellying up to the counter to select our food. They fed us well here. Healthy riders lived longer.

The woman working behind the glass counter lifted questioning eyebrows when it was my turn. I took in the options, my belly scowling and my mouth watering already.

She slid a tray off the top of the pile, stopping it in front of all the yummy goodness.

I pointed to the horig cakes. "I'll have—"

Vexxion politely nudged the woman to the side and locked his fingers on the sides of my tray, giving me what he probably thought was a smile but what came out as a grimace.

"Yes?" he asked.

I blinked. "I thought you left the fortress."

"You're wrong."

"She was already helping me." I pointed to the kitchen lady.

"You're holding up the line there, sis," Kinart said, his mouth twitching with humor. He and Reyla hustled around me and the woman, with a roll of her eyes, grabbed more trays and started getting their food.

"She's busy," Vexxion said pleasantly. "I'm happy to serve you." He deposited the empty tray onto the stack with the others and turned, lifting a new tray off the counter behind him, easing it across the panel to hand it to me. "Here you are. Enjoy."

I frowned at the food. "I want a horig cake." They coated the dough with horig crystals, which gave it a wonderful crunch when you bit into it.

He stared at the cakes sitting in the bin.

"They're good," I said. "I want at least one. Not this stuff." I lifted the tray and perched it on the panel, prepared to toss it at him if he kept doing... whatever it was he was doing.

"That *stuff* is... good for you. It's a safe meal."

Safe? "I don't doubt you're right, but I don't see a horig cake on that tray. Don't you know? Horig cakes balance out every meal."

He sucked in a breath and infused his exhale with a low snarl that made the kitchen woman shoot him a frown. Taking the tongs, he lifted a horig cake and glared at it hard enough to char it. His face smoothed, and he placed it on my plate. "Horig cake. Enjoy."

It seemed pointless to ask for a second, and I wasn't sure I'd want it if he scorched it with his eyes like he had the other. With a shrug, I took the tray and joined my friends at a table.

Vexxion, being as vexing as usual, sat at the end of our table with his own tray in front of him on the wooden surface. He didn't eat.

He watched me.

I tried to ignore him, feeding Drask tasty bits from my plate —though none of my precious horig cake.

Kinart glanced Vexxion's way and snickered. "Did you collect a bodyguard when we weren't looking?"

"More like a stalker," Brodine mumbled, shooting Vexxion a dark look.

"Neither," I barked, which made me cough again. Once I could speak, I lowered my voice. "He's not following me."

"I think he is." Reyla said softly, wiggling her eyebrows. "I thought he left, but . . . I guess it was just the other guys. Didn't he carry you back to your residence last night when you started to swoon?" Her humor fled as fast as it had risen, replaced with stark horror. "I mean, before . . ."

My world burned down around me.

"I don't swoon." I didn't want to think about the fire.

"Um . . ." Kinart held up his finger, his lips curling with only a touch of his usual humor.

"I drank four glasses of wine," I grumbled. "It's not the same thing at all."

"From where I was sitting, it sure looked the same."

"You were too busy driving your tongue down Reyla's throat."

"She likes it. I like it. You, however, had too much wine last night." He shook his finger in my face. "Don't do it again."

"Vexxion also rescued you last night when you would've burned." The pain in Reyla's eyes made me reach across the table and pat her arm. "And now he's . . . working in the kitchen for some odd reason we can't define."

"Probably because he's a better cook than you, sis," Kinart said.

I poked out at him with my fork, but he yanked his arm off the table before I could poke it. "And how does him taking up cooking relate to me?"

"Perhaps he helped the cook prepare something special for you." Reyla's smile chased away some of the shadows from her eyes. "He . . . likes you or something. Like Kinart likes me."

"I adore you," he said with such sweetness, my heart turned into a puddle.

As for Vexxion crushing on me? "No way."

"We'll see." She grabbed her fork and dug into her food.

I lifted my horig cake and bit into it. It tasted amazing.

We finished and went to the housing area to see where they'd assign us. If Vexxion skulked behind us, I didn't notice. Didn't care.

"I'm afraid I can't put you and Reyla together," the woman said, studying the log open on her desk. "But I can assign you in residences near each other."

"That's fine," Reyla said, clutching Kinart's hand. "I'll sleep anywhere."

"Thanks." I took the scrap of paper the woman handed me, though I'd already noted the number in my mind. Lovely. They'd put me with Delaine. The woman hated me and made sure I knew it.

We collected new clothing and took our things to our new rooms.

I dropped mine on my starched bed, grumbling about the stiff, scratchy blankets they issued to newbies, and opted to put my things away later.

Delaine sauntered out of her room and came to a halt when she saw me grumbling in the central seating area. "Why are you here?"

"I'm your new residence mate." I smirked.

She scowled. "No way."

"Aw, is that what you call a warm welcome?" Why I was putting the energy into irritating her when I could save it all for Vexxion was beyond me.

"Find another place to live."

"I can't. The other place burned to the ground."

"Well, you can't stay here." She crossed her arms on her ample chest and stomped her foot. Her one good feature, her long blonde curly hair, fluffed around her shoulders. "I'm going to the commander about this."

"Go right ahead. There's nowhere else for me to stay." I struggled to sound reasonable. This woman had irritated me almost from the moment I met her. She was one of the elite, her father was a lord or something like that. I think he worked with the king.

For some reason I hadn't bothered to explore, she hadn't wanted the marriage her parents arranged. No, the excitement and danger of being a rider held more appeal. You'd think no one would choose a career that would kill you. Yet, here she was, two years later, doing a decent job hacking up dregs.

"Why did I let them talk me into . . ."

I tilted my head, watching her face that remained snarly—nothing unusual for Delaine. "Talk you into what?" And who?

"Nothing," she snapped.

Drask squawked and dove toward her.

Shrieking, she reeled back. "Get that damned thing away from me. I can't believe I . . ." She shook her head. "It can't stay here. Make it stay outside. No, fuck it. Fuck your broken bird and fuck broken you."

I flinched.

She stomped past me and out the front door, her hair flouncing across her upper back.

Drask returned to my shoulder and pretty much preened.

"Thanks, but you need to stay away from her." I stroked his back. "I don't want to get stuck sleeping in the aerie."

He cawed.

I sighed.

Let her grumble to the commander. Maybe he'd find a new place to squish me into.

Then I wouldn't have to interact with Delaine even on a basic level.

10

TEMPEST

After changing out of Kinart's stuff and into clothing that actually fit, I left the residence with Drask in tow and went to the aerie. While he perched on the half-gate, I harnessed Seevar. Drask flew while I led Seevar to one of the three training areas, letting the dragon inside and removing his harness so he could fly around and expend some pent-up energy.

While Drask retook his perch on my shoulder, Seevar burst up into the air. I paused, leaning against the fence to watch him. His scales gleamed in the sunshine, and I'd never seen a prettier dragon.

"I've been assigned to work with you today," someone said, coming up behind me.

Turning, I had no problem scowling at Vexxion striding over briskly to join me.

"Why?" I asked, completely stunned by this latest development. "Actually, while we're at it, why do you exist? Why are you at the fortress? And why are you here, bothering me now?"

He scratched the back of his neck. "Perhaps I want to learn more about dragons."

Yeah, I doubted that. I flicked at the thin silver band of hair arching away from his temple. Damn, it was silky. And damn me for noticing something like that. No way would I tell him I found it hot, that it gave him . . . some bizarrely sexy appeal I didn't want to define. "You should be old enough by now to have settled into a career."

"I'm twenty-eight." He wrangled his fingers through the band as if he wanted to blend it in with the black. "I wasn't born with this."

"Some guys go gray when they start getting old." My lips twitched at my tease.

"Some guys earn silver like this when something . . . unsettling happens. Mine came early."

"How early?"

"When I was five."

My eyes widened, and my smile fled. "Five? Like, you were a little kid? What *unsettling* thing happened?"

"It's not uncommon for someone to take time to decide what they want to do with their life."

A slick change of subject. I went with it, though I would probe again later. "I bet you knew what was expected of you by the time you were . . . five." Alright then, I wasn't leaving this until later. Now would work quite nicely.

"I haven't decided on any particular job yet." He blinked. A tell? I'd test it to find out.

"You must be wealthy, then. You have no need to work."

"I survive." Another blink. This had to be a tell.

Oh, this was good. I bit back my urge to crow. "You come across as put together. Finished, I suppose."

"Trained like your dragon who's about to butt your cute ass?"

"My ass isn't cute."

"My observation is not open for debate."

I swatted behind me, tapping Seevar's snout, though not hard. He snorted and backed away, fleeing back up toward the top of the netting.

Vexxion's gaze locked on mine as if he was determined to discover everything I was willing to expose. "What makes you suspect I'm completely polished?"

"It's part of your makeup. Ingrained into you. As if someone carved you into what they needed because you otherwise wouldn't have fit."

When his jaw tightened, I discovered his second tell. Did I dare go for a third? "And now you're . . . lost."

He scowled, but I wasn't sure if he was responding to my taunt in general or if I'd guessed right.

"You suffered smoke inhalation last night," he said.

"That I did, but I'm over it now." My sudden cough negated that idea, as did my watering eyes.

"You should be resting, not training."

"You didn't answer my questions."

"I'm here under your commander's orders."

Ah, interesting. "Why not just state that to begin with?"

"Because it's not important."

"It's funny."

He waited multiple heartbeats before taking the bait. "What's funny?"

"That you're willing to do as the head of the fortress commands."

"You're wrong. He asked."

"Asked what in particular?"

"I agreed. Because I want to learn more about dragons."

Seevar landed behind me again, nudging my not-cute ass. "I'll get to you in a minute." Turning back to Vexxion, I lifted my eyebrows. "I'm hardly an expert. I'm just a simple trainer working in one of the many border fortresses."

"You're a woman carved by her own circumstances, molded into something that might not actually fit."

I kept my face neutral. No gift tells for Vexxion. "Like most here, I'm an orphan. But that doesn't mean I don't have a family or that I don't fit in." I tried so hard to fit in. How could he tell it was all pretend? This man saw me too well. He made me think, and I wasn't one for self-analysis. It hurt too much. Who needed pain like that? "What did you want to talk about?"

"Dragons."

Yeah, sure.

Leaving me, Vexxion walked around Seevar who was nibbling on some grass. He came right back over to me so fast, I stepped backward, bumping into the fence. Drask ruffled his wings and hopped sideways on the railing.

"Know this, fury," Vexxion said. "*I* control who I am today."

"Congratulations. So do I. As for dragon training, you're welcome to watch." Not really, but did I actually have any more say in this than last night when he carried me from the bar? "Remain by the fence and stay out of my way." I wasn't sure if I believed him or not about the commander, but there was no harm in him being here while I worked with Seevar.

"I understand you use an unusual training method with dragons." After studying my face long enough I began to suspect I hadn't gotten all the soot off my nose, Vexxion grabbed a brush and began to work on Seevar's tail, a delicate process at best.

Seevar was ticklish. Should I tell Vexxion? Nah, let him find out.

"I treat dragons as I'd wish to be treated myself," I said.

"You wish for someone to ride on your back?"

Jeez, was he sarcastic—and quick witted. I liked it. Then I was pissed off at myself for liking anything about him. My lips thinned. "You know what I mean."

"Gentleness has its place. I'm not sure it applies to dragons."

"See? You actually do have something to learn."

He snorted as if he didn't believe me. So why was he here? This was how I trained. Everyone knew that.

Though I doubted the commander knew I existed.

None of this explained why Vexxion was following me around all the time, conveniently being right where I needed him whether I realized it or not.

"I've been training in this manner forever," I said. I held back my squeal of joy when the sharp tip of Seevar's tail spiked down toward Vexxion. My dragon wouldn't hurt him, though he might poke a bit.

One tap on his thigh by Vexxion, and Seevar's tail flopped to the ground.

I grumbled, though I didn't want to see Vexxion hurt. Just... put in his place, something I was trying to do, though still floundering.

"If you're kind to them, they're loyal," I said.

"My dragon does what I ask. He's transportation, not a friend."

No one understood, sometimes not even me.

"Watch." I tossed my brush aside and grabbed a tool, striding over to Seevar's head. He sniffed my belly and nudged me, sending me a few steps backward. I grinned, something I only did with friends and a few dragons. "You know how they fight when you try to clean around their eyes."

"Bits of their scales work their way under the inner membrane. You have to restrain them to do something a thinking creature would know was for their own good."

"I've always treated this dragon gently."

"And yet you refer to him as a beast. No name?" His voice dripped with sarcasm. Why, oh, why was he behaving like this if he supposedly wanted to work with me?

"Naming is for whoever buys him." I stroked Seevar's face, not willing to admit to Vexxion that Seevar meant beautiful one in fae. I'd keep his name to myself, using it only when we were alone. Even my friends didn't know.

I didn't know why I'd chosen a fae name for Seevar. Nullens universally hated the fae and with good reason. Ages ago, they stole what little magic Nullens possessed, hoarding it for themselves.

I'd always wondered why the fae hadn't just chased down the Nullens and forced them to remain as servants. They had the power to force compliance.

"This dragon won't remain here?" Vexxion asked, vigorously brushing Seevar's left flank.

"He's too unruly." And I hated it only because that meant he'd be taken from me. "He'll soon do whatever I ask but there's no guarantee he'll behave for a different rider. The commander prefers we ride compliant dragons, not those who think for themselves."

"Yet you swear by your training technique." There was that sarcasm again, biting through what could've been a decent moment between us.

I patted Seevar's side. "Let's show this *old* man how it's done."

Vexxion's lips twitched, but he didn't call me out for the dig. I took strange pleasure in trying to get a rise out of him.

"Let me take care of your eyes, my beauty," I crooned.

Seevar placidly lowered his head. Taking the tool, I gently pried his right eye open and swept the infinitely soft tool across the inner part of the membrane, removing the bits of scale. I shook the tool to dislodge the grit then repeated the process with his other eye. He remained as calm as a baby and even sighed with pleasure when I finished.

"See?" I said smugly, my lips twitching at the spark of amazement in Vexxion's eyes.

"You . . ." He crimped his lips together. "Admirable skill. Perhaps there's something about using a gentle touch I hadn't considered."

"Everyone feels like you do, so I'm not surprised." I cleaned the tool and returned it to its cylinder, tossing that into the basket with everything else.

We continued grooming Seevar, me working on his claws while Vexxion continued along one side.

That's when I noticed . . . "You're missing the last digit of your right pinky finger."

His face tightened, and his eyes flickered, the blue darkening, though I couldn't tell what that might mean. He reached up to swipe his hand across the back of his neck before his hand dropped back to his side.

"What happened?" I asked softly.

"A childhood accident."

"How old were you?" Older or younger than five—I wanted to ask but didn't.

"It was long ago."

I could press, but I suspected he wouldn't tell me anything else.

"I bet it hurt. I'm sorry."

He gave me a curt nod and focused on Seevar's side.

"Tell me more about yourself," I said. "Where did you grow up?"

A long silence followed, only the scrape of tools on Seevar breaking through.

"Far from here," he finally said, like he didn't want to share anything but felt he must for some bizarre reason.

I suspected this man refused to lose control, which was why I kept trying to make him lose it. My face grew hot. "Are you from the middle of the continent or three mountain passes over from here?"

"Far away."

I huffed. "Any siblings?"

"More or less."

"I have Bro, Kinart, and Reyla. We're family. I share my secrets with them." Most of them. "I know I can always go to them when I need something beyond what I'd expect from a friend. That's the beauty of siblings."

"Some might make you reevaluate that opinion."

"Tell me all about Vexxion," I said casually, dropping Seevar's front right foot and moving to the back one. I used a lot of hands-on in my training. Part of my gentle technique involved lots of touch. Once they were used to me running my hands all over them, they were more willing to accept me sitting on their backs. Only after I'd accomplished that did I begin teaching them heel commands or strap on a saddle.

"Are you asking me to name my favorite color?"

"If you're willing to share such stimulating information."

His gaze locked on mine. "As green as the pabrilleen stone."

"I've never heard of a pabrilleen stone."

"It's mined by trolls in the caverns below a certain mountain range."

"Trolls." He had to be making this up.

"Yes, trolls." He grabbed another brush and started working on the dragon's back left thigh, rolling in slow circles to work the oil into Seevar's scales. This kept them supple, making it easier for the dragon to change direction quickly.

"What's your favorite food?" I asked.

"Horig cakes."

"That's disturbing."

He paused, one dark eyebrow lifting. "Why is it disturbing?"

"My eyes are green. I wanted a horig cake this morning. You reluctantly gave me one. I devoured it. I love them."

"Who says my tastes are even slightly related to you?"

"You didn't like the horig cake."

"Perhaps I did."

Alright. I was reading too much into this. He was a simple man visiting the fortress who'd decided to take some time while he was here to learn more about dragon training.

"Parents?" I asked.

"A mother and a father."

"Living or deceased?"

"This sounds like an interview. Are you planning to offer me the job, tiny storm?"

"Why do you keep twisting my fates-given name? There's nothing wrong with it. Tempest. Practice, and it'll roll right off your tongue."

His gaze dropped to my mouth where I'd dipped my tongue out to rub it across my upper lip. Sparks flickered in his eyes, reminding me of falling stars in the darkest night sky.

"Why did you originally come to the fortress?" I asked, dragging my tongue back inside my mouth.

"The commander asked a question, and I delivered the answer."

"Yes or no?"

"No, but then a possible yes with conditions."

"The commander needed something you couldn't grant him—"

"Not me."

"Whoever you work for."

He tilted his head before chipping out a nod, telling me I was close but not naming it exactly—and confirming he did have a job.

"Let me see. You needed something from the commander, so you . . ." I was guessing here, throwing out more bait to see if he'd nibble. "You told him you'd try to change someone's mind in exchange for something *you* need."

"You're quite perceptive for someone who's easily buffeted by the wind."

"We all have our strengths." I'd done more grooming on Seevar today than I had over the past week. It was time to settle on his back once more. Yet I remained where I was, currying the same area again just to have more time to quiz Vexxion. "Why are you stiff and snarly?"

"If you'd been molded from the time you were small, you'd also be snarly."

"Demanding too."

"It comes with the blood."

"You're full Nullen?" I wasn't sure why I asked. He wouldn't be here if he was anything else.

"Aren't we all?"

His vague replies were starting to get on my nerves. Actually, a lot about Vexxion got on my nerves. I tossed the brush into the bucket and returned to tap Seevar's leg, scrambling up onto his back after he dropped to the ground.

Like the fury Vexxion had named me, Seevar went feral. His ears flattened against his skull, and he peeled back his lips to gnash his fangs, shooting sparks at the rocky ground covering the open training area—sand-strewn for good reason.

Seevar erupted off the ground, his wings snapping out and his spine arching. His tail whipped up to smack me in the back, and he shifted from side to side to dislodge me.

I hung on, my bad leg quivering. Usually, I could maintain my seat for a solid period of time, but between the smoke I'd inhaled that was making me wheeze and my bum leg, this was more than my body could handle.

Seevar dove toward the ground, spinning, and when he jerked to soar back up to the top of the training area, I didn't go with him. Flung from his back, I landed hard in the sand. I stared at the sky, groaning.

With a huff, Seevar flew back down to settle beside me. His snout jutted out and he sniffed me, smoke from his nostrils coiling around my face.

That set me off and I started coughing. Tears streamed from my eyes, and my lungs felt like they were about to heave up more than just air. Eventually, my coughing waned, and I regained control of my wind.

Vexxion sauntered over to stand beside me, extending his hand. Under any other circumstances—let's face it, under *any* circumstances—I'd brush his hand aside and rise under my own effort. But he appeared concerned, a totally disconcerting expression for this man who was as rigid as the lightning I'd started calling his hair in my mind. I took his hand and let him pull me up onto my feet.

The world spun, but I didn't like the idea of using him as a crutch. I did brace myself with tight grips on his forearms. He'd pushed up his sleeves and it wasn't fair that he had such gorgeous arms, muscular with a dusting of just the right amount of hair. They went with his glorious everything else.

"I need to have sex," I muttered, detaching myself from his gloriousness.

"Is that an offer?" he asked dryly.

"I'm not that dizzy yet." And I was going to make sure I never got dizzy enough to drape myself all over this man.

Easing around him, I hobbled over to Seevar, mentally preparing myself for round two.

"You almost died last night," he said. "You need to stop for the day. At least take a break."

"Trainers don't take breaks. If you don't work with dragons regularly, they go feral."

"For fate's sake, then, bind him," he snapped. "Then he can't dislodge you."

I sent him a smirk over my shoulder. "Is that what you do with women?"

He stared at me, amusement brimming in his eyes. "I have no need to bind a woman. And they *never* try to dislodge me."

"Sad, Vexxion. Very sad. Maybe a girl enjoys a little binding every now and then."

"Are you speaking in general or stating your sexual preference?" His smoldering gaze dragged down my frame.

What was it with this man that made my insides going wild?

"You'll never find out." It wasn't much of a comeback, but I *was* tired. My lungs hurt. My leg hurt. I probably should go lie down. But I was too ornery. Too determined. Alright, I was also too stubborn to do something like that.

"You asked a lot of questions, but you haven't told me much about yourself," he said.

"Blue."

His eyebrows lifted. "Blue like my eyes?"

Yes. "No. Definitely not. Light blue, not a rich sapphire like yours."

"I see." His gaze bored into my mouth. Since that made them feel dry, I licked off the grit from my fall, spitting it aside. His gaze dropped lower. "You limp. What happened to your leg?"

"I'll never know you well enough to share something like that." I spun on my heel and hobbled along Seevar's side, wishing I could shed Vexxion as easily as I had the grit on my lips.

I ignored his huff of frustration. Where did he get off thinking he had any right to my secrets? With a sigh and a promise to my leg to massage it tonight, I tapped Seevar's side, signaling him to drop to the ground. He did so, and I scrambled up to settle on his bony spine.

He blasted toward the top of the netting.

I soon found myself lying on the sand once more.

11

VEXXION

I remained near Tempest over the next few days, shielding her while she trained with the others in hand-to-hand combat, worked with the golden dragon, and even when she slept in her residence at night.

I found no further evidence that anyone was trying to kill her. An odd feeling kept twitching down my spine, shouting beware. The ignite spell used told me someone wanted her dead. Who could I kill to protect her?

"Are you going to hover over me forever?" she asked four days later while she groomed the golden dragon.

"I'm not hovering."

"Sure you are."

"I'm not." I left her to lean against the fence, keeping an eye on everyone and everything around us. Growling whenever anyone came near, though she didn't seem to notice.

She watched me for a moment before shaking her head and

turning back to the dragon. "Aren't you a sweet little one," she crooned in his ear.

I gritted my teeth. From the moment I felt her, I knew what she'd become, what my role would be. As for the rest . . . That would have to come later.

Surprisingly, I liked her. She did not return my feelings. That must be why my insides snarled. I was irritated that when I finally made the effort, my dubious charms made no impact. The feeling had nothing to do with how she behaved with the dragon, treating it like it was a fluffy chall who'd nestle on her lap and purr.

Maybe the feeling was indigestion. I wasn't used to border food. I was consuming too many horig cakes.

Her crow ruffled his feathers, and she patted him as well, kissing his beak and nuzzling his wings with her slender nose.

I didn't like that either, but I pinched my lips together to keep from telling her she'd get sick if she kept putting her mouth on the bird.

That I wanted her mouth on *me*.

The dragon huffed softly from her touch, bumping her side with his snout, and she laughed, something she never did with me. The snarls tightened in my belly, working their way up to lash against my throat.

Finally, she told the beast to drop to the ground for mounting. "Go to the fence, Drask."

The bird obeyed her, flying over and landing on the gate beside me to watch.

Tempest climbed up the dragon's leg, her limp barely noticeable now, and settled in the saddle she'd started using two days ago. When the dragon rose to its feet and looked back, sniffing her shin, she sent me a triumphant look that made the snarls in my throat retreat.

At a nudge from her heel, the creature leaped from the ground, flapping his wings to capture the air and pick up speed. When he reached the top of the enormous cage, he leveled out —also at her command—and soared around the upper part of the structure like a well-groomed pet.

She guided him to dive down, turning him left and right, her bright laughter trilling through the air. Much of her hair had freed itself from her braid, and it streamed behind her in undulating waves. Her hair was an indigo sea teased by golden moonlight.

My dead heart cracked, and I didn't like it. I repaired the wall quickly, adding more mental bricks until it was secure and impenetrable once more. I did the same with the guards in my mind.

I never knew who might be watching.

Before the dragon could reach the ground and drag himself along one side to scrape her from his back, he leveled off— again at her command. He flapped his wings hard enough to propel himself above the sand, sending gusts of air in all directions. I shielded my eyes with my hand and couldn't hold back my smile when she asked the beast to land, and it did so immediately. She slipped from his spine.

Drask left his roost and landed on her shoulder, clinging. With him riding, she walked as quickly as her leg would take her to the dragon's head and wrapped her arms around his long snout. The bird cawed with joy. The dragon shot sparks against her leather-clad chest she brushed away with a laugh. Dropping to the ground, they extinguished.

Like I extinguished the burst of feelings inside me.

Leaving the fence, I strode toward her, clapping.

She startled and looked my way, and I had to admit, it irritated me that she'd forgotten I was there. But only for a heartbeat. I couldn't hold onto the feeling when she smiled and dipped forward in a bow crafted especially for me. "Thank you, kind sir."

I couldn't even host enough irritation to remind her never to call me sir.

"I'm done for the day," she said. "You're dismissed." Her words came out pert, as if she truly believed she was supervising anything I did here at the fortress.

"I choose when I'm dismissed," I noted dryly.

Her snort made the dragon glance our way. The crow cocked his head, his beady eyes studying me as intently as I always watched over her.

"I thought you might say that." Returning to the beast, Tempest gave the dragon another rubdown, cooing and telling him how wonderful he was, how much she adored him.

I remained right behind her, my arms crossed on my chest and with snarls scrambling up my throat once more.

She haltered the beast and led him from the training area, taking him to his aerie and making sure the outer gate remained secure. While the crow perched on the top of the half-door leading to the hall, she made sure the dragon had food and water and gave him one last pat. Turning, she nearly ran into me standing in the opening.

"Still my shadow, Vexxion?"

"Maybe I enjoy being with you."

"That's a lie."

"You can't know something like that," I bit out with taut strings of irritation plucking at my guts. "I *could* like you. Very much."

"That's creepy. Way too creepy." She gathered the crow off the gate and placed him gently on her shoulder before breezing past me, her limp pronounced. Seeing her in pain made me want to lift her and carry her everywhere. Demand she stop doing things that made her suffer.

And do all I could to make the discomfort fade.

Instead, I followed her across the compound and to her residence door.

"I'm not dining with you tonight," she said, her hand reaching for the knob. She didn't look my way. Thus, she didn't see the tightening of my mouth, or the way her pain's shadow cloaked me in gloom. "Go play with someone else. I need a break."

"You see this as a game."

Turning, she leaned against the panel. "Isn't it?"

"What makes you think I'm toying with you?" I stroked the hair off her face, smoothing it across her shoulder.

"Just a suspicion."

"So many do play with others. I can see why you'd think that. But this is no game."

She gazed at me for a long moment, suspicion clouding her eyes, before turning and entering her residence and closing the door in my face.

I leaned my back against the wall beside it and waited.

When the door opened again, I moved onto the path. She came out, her soaring crow heralding her arrival with a swipe of his wing across my cheek.

My heart came to a complete standstill.

My fury wore a simple skirt and a sleeveless top in a rich green that matched her eyes.

I couldn't breathe. Think. All I could do was stare.

"What?" she asked as she smoothed her hands down her top and pinched her skirt, fluffing it. "Do I have lint on my clothing or something?"

"No."

Her confused gaze met mine. "Then what is it?"

"You look . . . statuesque."

Her eyebrows lifted, and her lush lips twitched. "That's a new one for me. I'm short, remember? Otherwise, you wouldn't call me tiny anything." Her smile curled up before leveling out, though it quivered with humor. "I kind of like *statuesque* fury. *Statuesque* storm. You're welcome to use them instead." She eased around me and started toward the dining building, her crow flying around her in a crooked manner as uneven as everything inside me.

I bolted after her, catching up to walk beside her, leaning forward enough to see her face. "Statuesque can also mean stately."

"Stately, huh? They both make me sound like a statue. Is that how you describe someone you could *possibly* like?"

I moved in front of her, cutting off her path, shifting to each side when she tried to go around me.

She stopped and palmed her chin, tapping her finger on her cheek.

I swallowed the unexpected embarrassment torturing my throat. "You look gorgeous tonight, Tempest." Flames licked across my face. I hadn't felt this way about anyone in . . . I'd *never* felt this way about anyone.

Her breathing stuttered but her smile rose, sweeter than the horig cakes she adored. As soft as her skin. As stunning as this woman was every day of her life. "Thank you."

She strode around me, and I let her.

I remained a few paces behind even when she met up with her friends, linking arms with them. Reyla, Kinart, and Tempest all tipped their heads back and laughed. Brodine gave her a forlorn look. I now understood the feeling.

As they crossed the compound, I trudged behind them, leaving them with purpose when they joined the back of the line, waiting to be served their meals.

When I appeared, the woman in charge of the kitchen grumbled, but she made a grand show of ignoring me while I quickly prepared Tempest's meal with ingredients I kept in a cool box secured with a spell. I put everything on a magicked plate and strode over to the window in time to nod at Tempest.

With a half-smile, I handed the tray over the glass to her. "Elegant."

Her lips trembled, and her eyes shone brighter than the stars. No, stars paled when compared to her eyes.

Holding the tray, she followed her friends into the dining area and sat with them at a table.

After dishing up the rest of the food, I joined them at the far end.

"Refined," I murmured.

Her snort was muffled by her hand slapping over her mouth.

Kinart fed Reyla while she laughed and poked his belly. He kept chuckling, the motion making food drop from his fork. They lived for each other. A love like that was rare; I'd never seen anything like it. Where I came from, the only value a person held was in what they could be forced to relinquish. Affection was to be exploited. And even a hint of caring gave someone the means to make them behave.

Brodine watched them with envy, while my little fury ate, shooting me looks I couldn't define but I craved.

"Lovely," I whispered.

Her fork froze partway to her mouth before she delicately took the bite and chewed slowly.

I lifted a piece of bread and kept my gaze trained on it. "Flawless."

She swallowed her bite. It slid down her throat. I ached to place my fingers there, to run them across her smooth skin from her chin to the top of her breasts.

They finished and rose to take their trays up to the opening for cleaning.

I followed, remaining behind my fury. I eased up close enough to speak low by her ear. "Beautiful."

Her shoulders flicked up before straightening. She tilted her head toward Kinart and Reyla, who'd included her in their conversation, but I could tell she barely heard what they said.

All her senses were focused on me.

They parted at the head of the residence path, three of them aiming for the males' building, Tempest waving before striding toward her own.

"Exquisite," I said as she entered her residence for the night.

∽

THE NEXT MORNING, I arranged a safe meal for Tempest again, ate at her table, and followed her when she collected the golden dragon from the aerie. Her crow rode on her shoulder as always, his claws biting into the leather.

"I believe the golden dragon's polished enough for a sale," I pointed out as she led him into the training area.

"He was yesterday."

"He does everything you command now."

"*Yesterday.*"

After her endless grooming and crooning session, followed by the delivery of kisses to the beast's snout, I was ready to chew on the fence, confident I could rip chunks off and spit them out hard enough to make the world scatter.

"You're in a fine mood today," she said with a smirk. "Did you have a bad night's sleep?"

"It's nothing." Everything, though I'd never admit it. Again, I added more bricks to the wall around my heart and worked hard to shove out a scowl.

It did not come easy.

"Negativity can be quite draining. Didn't you know?" While Drask fluttered on her shoulder, she lifted the saddle onto the dragon's spine and secured it beneath his belly. "No wonder you're tired and cranky all the time." Rather than climb onto the beast's back, she gave him endless pats, kisses, and more grooming.

"I don't have negativity."

Her lips quirked up, but she said nothing.

Finally, she climbed the dragon and settled in the saddle, shooting me a smile that hit like a blade in the chest. My lips creaked when they lifted on the corners.

"Whoa," she said. "Is Vexxion actually giving me a smile? Sound the horns and fly a dragon sky parade. We need to celebrate this momentous occasion."

"I smile all the time."

"Not with me."

"Maybe I find it hard to give you a smile."

For a heartbeat, her grin faltered. "What is it with you?"

I could taste her words, bitter on my tongue. "What do you mean?"

"Never mind." She raked her gaze forward. "Go, Drask." Her words came out dull, but the bird obeyed her command, soaring over to land on the fence. Her chin trembled before she tightened her spine. Then she gave the dragon the signal to fly.

Like the day before, the creature obeyed her commands. It wasn't long before she was shrieking with joy and bellowing for everyone to come see. Her friends gathered at the fence, cheering for her while I slunk over and leaned against the metal. Hollow envy oozed into the voids within me.

She brought the dragon down to the ground, landing it

easily. After dismounting, she limped toward me—*me*—a grin splitting her face.

That smile...

My heart floundered, struggling to clamber up over the wall restraining it. Breathing no longer mattered. My lips curled up in an achingly painful way.

She was dawn's first light washing over a perennial nightfall.

Should I hold out my arms? Tempest enjoyed hugging her friends. My hands twitched at my sides.

She passed me and barreled into the others. The four of them rocked together, laughing, and for that one tiny moment...

Envy blasted through me on a frigid wind.

Jealousy was a new feeling for me, though I recognized the taint of it burning my tongue. Brodine lifted her and kissed her cheek before placing her back on her feet. Reyla and Kinart hopped around and hugged her the moment he released her.

Drask cawed and jerkily flew around her before landing on her shoulder.

Even the dragon watched her with what could only be described as an expression of absolute devotion.

Did my face mirror his?

Tempest looked over her shoulder at me, vaguely sharing her joy. But her smile fell, replaced with a frown and the tilt of her head.

Now *she* watched *me*.

I was showing too much. Feeling too much.

Shadows flickered through her eyes, and she dragged her attention back to her friends.

The horns mounted on the highest peaks of the fortress blared, though the tone was deeper. Ominously so.

"Raid," Kinart cried, his face widening with shock infused with excitement.

A man I'd seen around the compound jogged past the training areas. "Lucerna, Jarrn, Ebson, Careeb, you're up!" Continuing through the training area, he called out other names.

"The family. Has. Arrived," Kinart intoned. With a chuckle, he danced Reyla around before murmuring by her ear. "Stay close. Don't do anything dangerous."

"You too," she said, her gaze wild.

"Ho, baby, we're going on a raid." Kinart hopped over to Tempest. "You be careful. Promise, sis."

"I will if you do the same." She gave him a hug, breathing close to his ear. "I mean it. *Promise* me."

"I do."

"Bro?" Kinart leaped over to the other male, and even they hugged.

"Yup." Brodine patted Kinart's back. "Can't do anything else, now can I?"

Finally, Kinart took Reyla's hand, and they raced through the gate and toward the aerie with other riders streaming along beside him. Brodine held his hand out to Tempest, but she purposefully looked back at me.

Another horn blasted, so loud it snarled across my bones.

Grumbling, Brodine left her. He wrangled his way through the fence and bolted after the others.

Tempest hurried to the dragon.

"Gotta go, Seevar," she shouted as she unstrapped the saddle from the beast's back and tossed it onto the rack.

"Seevar?"

Her fingers stilled on the saddle. "I, um . . . Well, I named him that. I know he won't keep it once he's sold, but I like it. He does too."

"The word is fae."

"What of it?" She bristled. "It suits him."

"Seevar means beautiful one. You're right. It does suit him."

"Yeah. I'm going to miss him." Her hands shook as she gave the creature a quick pat and secured a harness around his snout. "I want to take him back to his stall in case . . ."

"The horn. Another dreg horde to chase back through the pass?"

"That low sound it made? It's . . . different."

"In what way?" I asked.

"A few of us are going on a raid. Me, my friends. Some others."

I strode beside her as she led the dragon through the gate. The term alone was enough to heat my insides to a boil. "Tell me what a raid entails."

"Sometimes, we don't rescue every Nullen after the dregs get them."

"*Them* meaning Nullen adults, children."

"Yeah." Snarling, she shook her head. "Once they're inside the caves, there's rarely anything we can do for them. Except, I suppose, put them out of their misery, but even then, that would mean following them into the caves."

"If they're too far gone, why a raid, then?"

"This is our chance to get some revenge."

We entered the aerie, and she led the golden beast to its pen. Opening the half-gate, she urged him inside, giving his side a pat as he passed. She tossed some treats in his bin and checked his water before securing the latch.

While the dragon watched her through the opening, she hurried down the hall to the small room where she'd left her weapons earlier, strapping them on.

Mine were already in place. I'd never remove them.

"What did you mean when you said I wasn't prepared?" she grated out through a hoarse throat as she secured a double sheath belt around her waist, hissing her long blades inside the snug leather guard. "I believe you saw how prepared I am when we defended the village." She added sheaths to her thighs, slickening them with thin blades. "I fought well."

"I wasn't referring to the dregs."

"The Lieges, then? No one knows much about them." She strapped smaller knives to her calves before securing a sheath to her back and plunging a sword as long as her arm into the leather pouch. "I'll admit I've only taken down two so far, and let me tell you, it was a challenge. Maybe I'll get another chance today." She shot me a smug smile.

"You don't know what you're dealing with." I wanted to tell her everything, but too much hinged on things I couldn't control.

I couldn't control much of anything outside of myself, and that thread had become dubious at best due to my unkept emotions for her. I walked along a wire stretched between two mountain peaks. One slip, and I'd plunge to my death.

I refused to take her with me.

"It's a raid, Vexxion," she said, striding as quickly as her leg could carry her toward the pen holding the ruby dragon, the sword shifting along her leg. "Someone's pinned down a dreg horde inside one of the caves and today, finally, we get the pleasure of eliminating each and every one of them. If we find live Nullens in cages, we free them. Some of them . . ." Pensive, she stared at the sand-strewn stone floor. "They're rarely who they were before, but at least they're alive, which is more than I can say about my parents."

"They were taken?"

"I assume so. Consumed like all the others." She picked up her pace, stomping over to open the half-gate while the ruby dragon snorted sparks onto the sand. Tempest paused, her hand on the metal structure. "This is where you and I say goodbye."

"I'm flying with you."

"You're interested in joining a raid? Surely that goes beyond your current . . . apprenticeship."

I scowled at the term. The time I needed to apprentice in anything had passed before I turned six. But she couldn't know that, and it was important that I maintain my thready ruse.

Her eyebrows lifted as her gaze slid down my frame, taking in my black leather pants, my tunic with rolled up sleeves. "You're not dressed for battling dregs, let alone Lieges."

I tapped the hilt of my blades secured at my waist, following the gesture with nudges to the sheathes strapped to my forearms, calves, and thighs. "I believe I'm well enough prepared for your raid."

"Hmm."

While she saddled her dragon, I strode to the stable mine was using while I remained at the fortress. Like always, I skipped the saddle, opened the outer door, and mounted Glim. At my command, he scrambled to the edge and plunged from the aerie. Once leveled, I eased him around.

Tempest's ruby dragon dashed from her stall, and they flew quickly past me, joining with others to form a flight.

I remained back, not part of their group.

While I'd savor eliminating dregs as much as them, that wasn't my purpose here today.

No, my only goal was to keep someone from murdering Tempest.

12

TEMPEST

I tried to ignore Vexxion, but wow, that man could ride. My butt had been in a dragon saddle from about the time I turned five. This was the norm for those raised in a border fortress. We had two purposes, to kill dregs and to train more dragons for flights or to sell to supplement the fortress's budget. Riders ate well, and we consumed a lot of resources. Someone had to pay for it, and the king wasn't eager to dole out the treasury's wealth.

"Let's kill some dregs," a guy shouted from a few dragons over.

My gaze was caught by Delaine, who was flying close enough to the guy, I worried the dragons would collide. Why hadn't she put her hair up? It might look wonderful draping artfully across her face when she sat in the bar, but we were about to fight dregs. Maybe Lieges. It would get in the way.

Her gaze met mine, and she scowled.

I saluted her anyway.

Despite her vocal complaints, the commander had not moved me to another residence. This woman had then set out to make my life miserable. She kept hiding my tooth powder, stating she moved it to make room for her things on the sink and she "must've placed it somewhere. Oh, where could it be?" All this was said with a smirk that raked across my hide like dragon claws.

When I left my favorite leather jacket draped on the sofa in our central living area, it somehow mysteriously collected new knife holes.

"You should take better care of your things," she said with a sly smile. "Yourself too, if this is how you *play*."

"I like my clothing holey," I quipped after tugging it on, poking my finger through one of the gaps. "Keeps me cooler during the summer."

She huffed, got up from her chair, and stalked into her room, slamming the door behind her.

I hoped she did well today—mostly. I mean, I didn't want to see her dead.

Injured?

Alright, no. I sighed, wishing I wasn't such a softy.

Maybe a dreg could knock her on her ass. I would grin while I rushed over and lobbed off its head, then smirk and say something witty about how she needed to be more careful.

She glanced past me, maybe checking out Vexxion, and she suddenly paled.

Well, we were all scared about what we'd soon do.

With a kick of her heels, she drove her dragon down to fly beside two other riders.

Brodine, mounted on my left, hooted, and I turned to look his way.

"I'm going to kill a bunch of Lieges," he crowed.

Others joined in, boasting about how they were going to take down ten, fifteen, or twenty dregs, when we'd each be grateful to kill a few and survive long enough to boast about our bravery after. Even with the wind snatching half of our words away, we could guess what the others said. It was common to crow and boost each other before battle.

Because, deep inside, we were scared. We'd be stupid not to be. Each time we survived a raid or beat back a horde was one more notch on a wall holding too few. Our luck might be solid with village battles, but more often than not, a few riders died during a raid.

A quick count showed twenty of us following the team leader, a decent flight made up of others I recognized from prior raids. They'd pull from the best. No newbies included since they were less apt to make it home after.

Were there enough of us today? We'd soon find out. If we were short, that just meant those of us included would have the pleasure of killing more than our usual share.

Vexxion flew his dragon behind mine, his face set in lines grim enough to frighten a corpse. What was it with him? He was not doing an apprenticeship with me. I knew this for a fact.

"We ride," I bellowed, shaking my fist in the air. There was nothing better than the wind buffeting my cheeks, my braid fluttering behind me, and that bitter sting in my eyes. Or the strong flap of Fawna's wings, the warmth of her body humming through my saddle.

The joy of this moment when we felt we could conquer the world.

Laughter erupted and others shouted the same thing, following it with *we kill* and *we win*.

For now. The sad part was there were so many Lieges and dregs that even if we went on daily raids, we'd never eliminate them all. Up here and with our blades ready to slash through them, we were invincible. Reality would soon smack us against the side of the head.

Reminding myself of what we faced—what might soon happen—sobered me in a way nothing else ever could, and while I smiled with my friends as they continued to use bravado to chase away their fear, we all knew.

With each raid, some of us may not make it home.

Finally, the team leader, Jessia, lifted her arm, and we slowed the pace of our dragons.

A respectable fear gobbled up our words, leaving only silence. The time for bragging was over. Now it was time to kill.

As we soared lower, only the flap of our beasts' wings gave us away, though we were high enough up even a Liege standing on the ground wouldn't hear us. He'd only be tipped off if we eclipsed the sun.

Jessia's dragon dove down, her beast's enormous wings smacking the air. We followed in formation, our faces sliced open by grim determination.

"Love you," Reyla told Kinart, keeping her voice low. Kinart angled his dragon to keep its wings from hitting Reyla's beast, and they locked fingers, though only for a moment before he peeled away. Dragon collisions mid-air were never pretty.

"Don't die," she growled his way. "Or I'll track you down in the underworld and kill you all over again."

"I will too," I said.

"Same," Brodine said.

Kinart saluted her, me, then Bro. "Same."

Like always, we four would challenge the world together.

My gaze cut to Vexxion, finding him watching—as always. I swore sometimes I could feel his gaze like fingertips trailing across my skin. I had to resist the urge to rub the feeling away.

Reyla gave Kinart one final nod and focused her gaze toward our destination, a tall cliff on the outer stretch of the Xandest Mountains. Our fortress was built on one of the tallest peaks in the long mountain range that partitioned the valley peppered with settlers and the wastelands where dregs thrived.

As we approached the ground, we slowed our dragons, urging them to coast without flapping their wings. We refused to give our presence away until we had our blades drawn, ready to plunge through dreg and Liege hearts.

Jessia drew her dragon up sharply and settled its hind legs on a broad slab of granite, the white crystals in the dusky gray catching the light and fracturing it in all directions. As her dragon's front feet delicately touched the ground, the rest of us landed our dragons nearby. No more joking or challenging the air. We'd save that for when this was over, when we were back at the bar and well into a cheap bottle of wine.

Vexxion's gaze glided down my leather-clad body, noting my weapons. From the way his lips tightened and the short suck of air he dragged into his lungs, he wanted to tell me to hold back, to let him handle this.

At least he held back the words.

I hurried past him, joining my friends gathering around Jessia.

"We go in," Jessia whispered, her intent gaze cutting across us all. "Kill as many as you can, especially Lieges if you can find them. Locate the cages. Free whoever might..."

Still be living. Who hadn't been drained of what little energy they contained.

"Then get out," she growled. "Meet back here and we fly."

The Lieges hid when we raided, leaving the dregs to fend for themselves. They melted into the network of caves and while some of us had ventured deeper during prior raids, it was rare to find even one.

I tapped my right pants pocket where the two bone coins I'd collected from Lieges awaited a third. If mine hadn't been left by accident inside my leathers being cleaned, they would've burned in the fire along with everything else. About the size of my thumbnail, they hung on rings from the Liege's wrist and each was embedded with a stone unique to their Liege.

Brodine grinned and tapped his three dangling on a ring from his waistband. He only pulled them out and let them hang when we battled, as if he thought the Lieges would see them and run in the opposite direction. Today was another day, another chance to add another bone coin to the two in my pocket. It wasn't a competition. A good Liege was a dead one, and one less meant fewer dregs churned out to steal Nullens from villages.

Reyla leaned against Kinart, and his arm was around the back of her waist. Each carried one bone coin somewhere on their person. Morbid, but most riders thought carrying them brought them good luck.

Vexxion was the only one not dressed in leathers, and while Jessia slanted him a long look, she didn't say a thing about him joining us.

While Jessia spoke quietly with one of the riders, I sidled closer to him.

"You should remain here," I hissed so softly, I doubted anyone but him could hear. "*You're* not prepared."

He didn't even twitch from my taunt, telling me I needed to up my game. "I've proven myself in ways you can't even imagine, *tantrum*."

"Your sword's decent. But you need to start wearing leathers if you want to play with riders." I flicked the tip of my long blade against his dark tunic that blended in with his black pants. The shirt was loose. His pants were snug. Too snug. I'd noted his ass earlier. *Noted*, I reminded myself. Not appreciated. "The color fits the occasion, but your tunic's too loose. It'll end up snagged on a dreg's claws and give it a way to drag you down to the ground where it'll rip your throat out."

He handed me his sword and stripped off his tunic, tossing it aside. "Better?"

Fuck, yeah. I'd have to be blind not to drool over the gorgeous play of muscles on his chest, the way his arms and shoulders bulged, and the slashed segments of his rippling abs. His scars only added to his stunning appeal.

He lifted my dropped jaw with a surprisingly gentle

fingertip and took back his sword. "Watch me, fury, and learn." He leaned close to whisper by my ear, his words trilling down my spine in a hot caress. "Remain behind me. Allow *me* to engage them."

I stepped away from him, dragging my gaze off his chest. "Not happening."

Jessia tapped my shoulder and tilted her head at Vexxion before continuing to move around the group, pairing us up.

I sighed but knew better than to argue. Her word was law.

"Stay together," she hissed. "Buddy system. Don't leave without the person you've been paired with."

Even if they were dead.

"Don't get yourself killed, partner," I huffed, wishing I'd been matched with anyone else.

"Do I hear caring in your voice, *fury*?"

"Never."

"Then you don't need to worry about my possible untimely demise."

Once she'd matched everyone, Jessia gave us the signal. We jogged toward the mouth of the cave in columns beside our matches.

We'd find the dregs inside and if the scout had been careful enough, the beasts would still be sleeping. During one raid, the scout must've tipped them off. When we rushed into the cave, they leaped from the shelves above while a solid mass of them poured toward us across the floor of the cave. If they were asleep, killing them would be relatively easy.

Then we could hunt Lieges.

We slipped into the cave, pausing to allow our eyes to adjust to the change of light. It might be daytime, but inside the cave system networking through this part of the mountain range, darkness ruled. The rank smell of sweat and raw meat scraped the back of my throat, and it was all I could do not to gag.

Someone ahead of us bellowed.

It was time.

I tightened my grip on the hilt of my sword and charged forward.

13

TEMPEST

*I*t was kill or have your heart gouged from your chest by dreg claws. I slashed through one after another, diving forward in a roll to come up behind some to sever their spines.

Close combat was never pretty. You did what you could with your sword because that kept you a solid arm's distance away from dreg claws, but more often than not, you fought from a distance.

I flung thin blades through eyeballs, impaling their brains, the best way to kill them. Once they were down, you could recover your knives.

Vexxion held his own, and I wasn't sure why that surprised me. I'd seen him in action during the dregs attack on the village the first day he arrived. He carved with infinite care, slicing through dreg throats with his sword while other times gouging the beasts through the eye, seeking their brains. I saw a dreg come close to hurting him only once when the dreg slunk up behind and slashed out with its claws. Vexxion reeled to the side and gutted the dreg with one touch of his blade.

Reyla and Kinart fought to my right, back-to-back as always to protect each other. Nothing would defeat that pair as long as they remained together.

I was battling a dreg, ripping and hacking while releasing feral grunts when its hand snapped out, slicing through my leather sleeve and raking a groove in my arm. Blood welled and the cut burned. Releasing a hoarse cry, I ignored my protesting leg and leaped at the dreg, knocking it backward with a solid kick. I drove a long blade into its right eye, barely avoiding the swipe of its claws. The beast toppled backward onto the cave floor, taking me with it. I lay on it after, panting.

"No kissing the dregs," Kinart said with a smirk, flicking his swords with both hands in a smooth dance that soon sent the dreg he battled to its grave. Once it was down, he stood over it, grinning, while I lumbered up off the dreg I'd killed.

"Where's Vexxion?" I peered around but didn't see him in the big open cavern, though the place was a mess of riders, swarming dregs, and boulders.

He shrugged. "I'm with Reyla." He tilted his head toward where my friend was finishing off a dreg. After she'd sliced its throat so deeply the head tipped off its shoulders, she spun and sashayed over to Kinart for a quick kiss.

"Watch and be amazed, sweetheart," she told him. "Watch and be amazed."

"You watch *me* and be amazed, cupcake," he said with a grin.

"Cupcake." She leaped into his arms, and they kissed but for only a second. We had work to do, and they knew it. She slid down his front. "Prove it."

"Oh, I will." He gave her a wink and darted forward with her hot on his heels.

Snapping at each other like pups at play, they raced toward the remaining group of dregs, quickly engaging them in battles that ended with the beasts' blood staining the floor and the front of their leathers.

Pausing to catch my breath, I scowled at my arm wound that was more of an irritation than anything else. It kept dripping blood, though, leaving a trail across the floor as I moved. I should've brought something to wrap it with. I'd be back at the fortress soon and could beg someone to tend to it then.

Soon, most of the dregs in the cave lay seeping gray blood onto the dirt floor.

"A cage," someone cried from my left. "There are survivors!"

Seeing some of the flight headed in that direction, I looked around, hoping a Liege would pop into view so I could send it back to its maker and add another bone coin to my pocket.

Irregular cave openings called to me from the back wall. Someone shouted Liege, and it was a free-for-all, many of us scrambling over carcasses to hunt dreg masters while other riders went to free the captives.

Diving into a cave, I paused to let my eyes adjust once more. Lieges and dregs could see well in the dark, which put them at an advantage. If I had to, I'd feel my way to them.

Light flared and flickered ahead, catching my eye.

Sensing a trap, I crept forward with the hilt of my sword tight in my hand. I was drawn to the light. It swayed and cavorted in the gusts of air, strangling through the endless cavern system.

I crouched forward as I moved through a long tunnel and emerged into a small cave. A candle, such as it was, flickered from a flat oval stone sitting in the center of the room. From here, passages continued ahead on the left and right, and hoarse cries rang out from riders battling straggler dregs or maybe even a Liege.

The candle was made up of a blob of wax about the size of my head with a wick stabbing up through the center. This wasn't a poured thing like some still used at the fortress. It looked like someone had taken a clump of slightly warm wax, wrapped it around a wick, and smashed it onto the rock. Still, the light moved in a seductive dance, tugging me closer.

I stopped beside the flat rock and crouched down, extending my hand toward the flame...

A shuffle to my right brought me to my senses, though too late. The flame crooked sideways, clawing toward the Liege stalking my way.

Straightening, I reeled backward, the foot of my bum leg snagging on something lying on the floor. Whatever I stepped on clattered.

The Liege's milky clawed hand snapped out, latching onto my wrist, and before I could pull away, he heaved my arm up his mouth. Clutching it like a tortuous lover, he licked my wound, grunting and moaning like he was in the throes of a powerful orgasm.

His bone coin dangled off his skeletal wrist, his flashing its tiny teal stone. It flickered as if it, too, was savoring my blood.

I barked out a cry and hauled backward, my boots scrambling across the uneven floor as I struggled to break free of his grasp.

He groaned and undulated, the torn hem of his cloak a sickening sway across his clawed feet. His tongue scraped across my wound as he gorged himself on my blood.

Horror tearing through my cry, I wrenched my arm from his grip. With a battle cry reaching up my throat, I stabbed my long blade toward him.

He slipped to the side much too easily, his robes rustling like dead leaves skittering through a crypt. His cackle echoed in the too small room.

"I don't remember when I've last tasted something this good," he rasped. "Please. Allow me to lick a bit more? I promise I won't eat too much. You have enough to spare a poor Liege like me, don't you?" The hood of his robe slipped back, revealing the face of a nightmare. When I killed his brethren during two other raids, I'd naturally looked. Who could resist when they made such an effort to remain covered?

Universally skeletal, they had lumpy, uneven skulls as if they'd been bludgeoned to death then resurrected. Over and over again.

This one appeared older, though I couldn't name why. Its whisps of gray hair were no different from the others I'd seen. Its bones contained the same cracks as if one kick would tear them apart.

His eyes . . . hollowed out with despair where the other

Lieges had been as steel gray colored as the soil covering the wasteland.

"Come to me, little one," he said, his voice like slick oil. He held out his skeletal hand and like with the candle, I couldn't resist stumbling toward him. "Yes, like that. So rich. So tender. So very tasty."

A thousand voices deep with me shrieked, and I wrenched my gaze away from his.

His snarl ripped out. "Come!"

"Fuck you." I slashed my blade up, driving it all the way through his chest. I wrenched it out and shoved it back in, burying it to the hilt once more.

The Liege toppled backward, my blade oozing free as he fell, and he landed on the floor with a dry rattle.

I straddled him and lifted my blade high overhead, determined to plunge it down hard enough to pin this wretched creature to the stone beneath.

"Don't you want to know the secret?" the words clattered around inside the creature's mouth like stones against teeth.

"I want nothing from you." Still, I couldn't force my body to drive my blade down. My need to end this twisted through my bones, but I couldn't make myself do it.

"We're not the only ones, and neither are you." His words slithered around me, scraping my skin to stab deep.

"You talk in riddles, corpse."

"Do you think we capture the Nullens only for ourselves?"

My breath hitched in and remained there. "You share the energy you drain with the dregs?" I hadn't heard that, but few knew much about the hordes that relentlessly attacked us.

"Dregs prefer brains."

Fuck, they ate our brains? That bought him and every dreg I could find an even faster death. I tightened my grip on my blade once more.

"Think harder, sweet one. We do as we're commanded."

"Someone's . . . You're saying someone is controlling you?" I was told they were it. Lieges. Dregs. There was no one else involved. The dregs captured the villagers, and the Lieges drained the Nullen's energy, using it to generate more dregs in a never-ending circle ruled by death.

"Not just controlling but . . . crafting, as if we're exquisite works of art."

More like horrors born from the churning mass of sludge found deep beneath the surface of the wasteland. "I thought Lieges made the dregs."

"So simple, don't you think?" His cackle was cut off by a gurgle in his throat. His blood poured from his wounds. Why wasn't he dead? "Who do you think makes us?"

"Tell me who's doing this to us," I bellowed.

"Look to the east for your answer," he hissed.

Nullen lands stretched from the wasteland to the veiled border, and beyond that—

"Seek and you shall find your future and your past."

"I know my future." Death during one of these raids. I didn't know my past but fuck them for dumping me. "You know nothing about me." Why did my hands shake? Why couldn't I end this?

"In that, tasty one, you're wrong." His bony lips twisted in a grimace, and his putrid gaze focused on the ceiling above. A quick glance showed me nothing was there.

Someone cried out in the cavern behind me, a wretched, tortured shriek. My friends needed me. I should go.

Enough of this crap, of this beast's twisted words.

I lifted my blade to finish this.

14

VEXXION

I slashed through one dreg after another, settling into a pace I could sustain for hours. Gouge. Cut. Slice through a throat. Move on to the next before the head smacked onto the blood-stained floor.

Fury. Where was she? A quick look around didn't show her in the cave. Damn cursed girl. Damn wretched woman.

She'd be my downfall if she had any say.

I had to find her.

A cry on the opposite side of the cavern wrenched my mind in that direction. I couldn't see well enough to tell who battled three dregs at once, their blades a blur of gray-speckled air. Damn rider clothing made them all look alike. Damn cavern made it too dark to see.

Gathering my strength, I used my power to move in that direction in what we called a flit. I fell to my knees when I landed. Rising, I staggered, cursing that a flit over such a short distance could now drain me.

I righted myself and started slashing, beheading one of the dregs and spinning on my heel to take out another. I turned in time to see a rider with their back to me, still battling the third. The dreg kicked, and the rider staggered backward, their arms flung upward. A leap, and the dreg landed on the rider's chest, biting through the person's throat as the two fell together in a morbid embrace too far away for me to make a difference.

I rushed toward them. One twist of my blade, and I'd beheaded the dreg. It collapsed on top of the rider, but from the bright red blood pooling around them, I was also too late to bring them back.

Someone screamed from across the cavern, the shriek ending in a soul-tortured whimper.

I gutted a dreg and spun to challenge another, breathing too fast from my flit and cussing the one who'd made it hard for me to do what used to come easy.

Another cry echoed in the enormous chamber.

Tempest?

A woman rushed past me, aiming for the downed rider. Not Tempest.

Damn my fury. Where was she?

Where?

Images shot through my mind. She was injured. Bleeding. And a Liege was draining her.

No!

Tightening my grip on my blades, I ran toward the openings

on the back wall and picked one, rushing down the passage beyond.

15

TEMPEST

I should've ended the Liege's wretched existence. But I paused again, my head cocked as I thought about what he'd said.

East... Our capital was on the opposite side of Nullen territory, far from the border.

His slick smile rose. "Not quite ready to kill me, then, my beauty? Lower your arm. Allow me to drink and regain my strength once more."

"Our king?" I snarled. "Is our king responsible for this?" I didn't think the king spent his time doing more than dining with dignitaries and indulging his only daughter. Well, and his new queen, her stepmother.

"No one is truly responsible for another," the Liege said. "Now are they?"

"Tell me!"

"You're not thinking hard enough, but then, such is the way

of Nullens. They're not clever enough to survive for much longer, though I will say they're quite appealing in their own way. Ripe, like the fruit your kind treasures." His glowing gaze remained locked on my arm. Blood from the stupid wound wormed across my skin and it dripped steadily, landing on the ground near his shoulder.

"Not the king then?" I asked, a sense of urgency filling me. I had to get out of this cave before . . . What?

"You're not looking far enough east," he croaked. His claws scrambled across the dirt by his arm, and he lifted a burgundy clump saturated with my blood, stuffing it into his mouth. Draining what little energy my fluid possessed. I could almost feel it leaking from me, coiling off my arm.

As he writhed and moaned, his bone coin tinkled against his wrist, creating a morbid melody that tore through my spine.

The only thing farther east was—

"The fae." Why was I surprised? Nullens fled faerie ages ago but not before the fae stole what little magic my people had, guzzling it down like gluttons. Now they were after what little energy we had left, the only thing keeping us alive.

"Now you're showing that you can rise above your brethren." Bits of dirt flicked off his lips as he spoke. He latched onto my leg. I should wrench away, but I was drawn into his glowing eyes and the need I saw there that only I could assuage.

Run.

The word echoed in my mind. Foreign—yet not.

Run!

Something fluttered past me. Drask landed on the Liege's

face and squawked, clawing and ripping while flailing his wings.

The fae were doing this to us, orchestrating the dregs to capture us, the Lieges to drain us, and the fae to sip from the cup presented to them by the Lieges.

"Fae," I bellowed.

The Liege smacked Drask aside, and my precious pet whipped across the room to hit the wall and fall to the ground.

"*Some* fae." The Liege's poisonous, treacherous, luring voice called me back to the endless pool of his eyes. "One very powerful fae lord in particular. Not all. Not yet."

"Who? Who is doing this?"

"Find out who cursed the Lydel, and you'll have your answer."

"That's a fairytale."

His head tilted. "Is it?"

"They say the king cursed the Lydels when their widowed high lady refused to go to his bed." No one could prove the rumor true because she'd disappeared before the court was consumed by a thorn infestation. Disappeared . . . or was she dead? "Are you saying Bledmire Court is responsible for everything?"

"Such a clever girl. Remember, one in particular."

"The king."

The Liege's bony mouth stretched wide in a slick smile.

"Why did you tell me all this. You're betraying your kind."

"Or perhaps I'm saving them."

"I don't understand."

"One day soon," he said. "You will." His sly smile grew.

"More blood, interesting Nullen? Just a little, please, and I promise you, we'll be closer than best friends." He reached up and dragged his claw down my arm, swiping away the blood that continued to flow. He coiled his hand up to his face and slithered his tongue along the claw, groaning as he licked off every drop.

Mesmerized, I watched each stroke of his oily tongue.

Drask struggled to his claws and picked his way across the rocky floor toward me.

The Liege swiped out smacking Drask again. His squawk of pain brought me back to this moment and this time and to everything I needed to do if I hoped to live.

"Fuck you." I drove my blade down, severing the liege's head from his shoulders. It toppled backward, rolling down the slope and across the floor before coming to rest against the wall.

Dark gray blood pulsed from the stump in a steady stream. He still wasn't dead. Would he ever just fucking finally die?

He lifted its arm and pointed . . .

. . . To where shrieks of pain echoed in the big cavern behind me.

His hoarse cackle echoed in the room as the arm dropped back to the floor.

Bellowing and blubbering, I sliced through his limbs. I hacked at his torso until it was nothing but a gray-stained mass of goo pulverized on the floor. I wildly grabbed his bone coin from the ground where it had fallen, holding it aloft while my body shook with spent adrenalin.

The Liege finally dead, I stumbled away. I staggered and dropped to my knees. I scooped up Drask and held him, kissing the top of his head and turning him this way and that to make sure he wasn't gravely injured.

He tugged free and flew up to land on my shoulder. While he cooed and brushed his head against my cheek, I rose and hitched my body toward where the screams still echoed in the cavern beyond. I limped up the passage, stuffing the bone coin into my pocket with the others.

When I reached the entrance, I stopped. My mouth opened in a scream that would never end, never release the agony gouging through my body.

My brain took in Reyla.

Sitting on the floor.

Holding something—*someone*—on her lap.

Ripped apart by the dregs, the person's bright red blood stained the floor around her.

Blood like the lifeforce still oozing down my arm to speckle the floor.

Only one part of the person's face remained, but it was enough. Just enough but *too much* to see who it was.

Kinart.

My wail leaped up my throat to echo in the big room.

No. *Please* no.

No!

His remaining glazed eye was fixed on the ceiling.

16

TEMPEST

I hobbled around dreg carcasses to reach Reyla and dropped to my knees beside her. I reached out before snatching my hand back. There was nothing I could offer. Nothing I could do.

Kinart...

It couldn't be true. I refused to believe it. He was my brother. How could I still be breathing if he wasn't?

This wasn't his body. I couldn't be him.

Reyla's tortured gaze drifted to mine. "He's . . . I think he's cold, Tempest."

Oh, shit, yeah. After tossing aside my blades, I yanked off my leather tunic and laid it across his torso. No, not *Kinart's* torso. Not my brother's. I . . . it wasn't possible.

Not possible.

Reyla stroked his forehead, smearing blood across it with each swipe. Tears sliced down her face, her nose, plopping on

Kinart, mixing with his blood.

So much blood.

Too much blood.

A void expanded inside me, filling with numbness entwined with searing pain. I was being torn apart by unyielding claws of agony.

"He's cold." Reyla lifted her head, her hands fretting with my shirt, tugging it up to his neck, then back down to cover what remained of his gutted torso.

No, not his torso.

This couldn't be Kinart.

"Someone get him a blanket," she croaked. "Kinart needs a blanket." Her voice dropped off to the bitter despair of nothing. "He's cold. Too damn cold."

Unable to look at him, I wrenched my gaze to the side. The world expanded, crowding in, roaring in my ears before backing off in heavy waves. Over and over until the sound of the screams trapped inside me would drive me insane.

Dreg bodies littered the cave. Delaine stood in the shadows of the back wall. Her eyes were locked onto me, but her face was etched with devastation. I couldn't drum up the energy to snarl at her, to tell her to look somewhere else. To look away from ... My jagged breathing wheezed in my throat. How could I be breathing when he ... *my brother*. I clawed my fingers down my face. Once more.

A dreg twitched—until a rider strode over and severed its head. Good. Kill them all. Kill every damn one of them. Kill the Lieges too.

And when we were done ... Someone else needed to pay.

I ripped myself from the floor, snatched up my blade and gouged it down into a dreg's body, stabbing over and over, turning it to a pulp.

Like Kinart.

When a hand dropped onto my shoulder, I shrieked and reeled around, dislodging Drask who'd tethered himself to me. He squawked and flew toward the cave entrance. He'd wait with Fawna or meet me back at the fortress.

I gaped at Vexxion. In most of our interactions, he'd shown almost no emotion, remaining stoic, his face as smoothly impassive as a statue. Now craters filled his face as if he shared my grief. He'd barely known Kinart, but maybe it had been enough.

"Someone get a healer," Reyla moaned; her hand furiously stroking his forehead. His cheek. Rubbing. Crooning. As if touching him would bring him back to life. "A healer! Someone." She kissed his forehead. "Someone. *Please help him.*"

She broke, her body consumed with sobs.

Brodine strode over and eased her out from under Kinart. She clung as his body slid off her lap, puddling on the floor. "Kinart. Kinart!"

"Let it go," Bro grumbled. "I'm here. I'm holding you."

Turning in Brodine's arms, Reyla wept, releasing deep, guttural cries that plunged into my chest and frayed what was left of my heart.

I pinched my eyes shut, and when I staggered, Vexxion's hand snapped out. He tugged me into his arms. I remained there, stiff yet sucking in the warmth he offered.

I couldn't cry, though I desperately needed to. So much.

Instead, I let rage forge my ground meat of a heart anew. My thirst for revenge was a bitter, snarling, gouging beast that would not stop until it had ripped the fae world asunder.

I only needed to put a few things in place and then I would do it.

Vexxion's gaze landed on my arm, and he sucked in a breath.

Jessia, walking by, reached into her pocket and pulled out a packet of simple medical supplies, giving it to Vexxion.

"Normally, I'd . . ." He didn't finish the thought. "Certain types of movement can be tiring. They drain me now when they never did before."

I had no idea what he meant, but it didn't matter.

"This will sting," he said softly as he blotted my wound.

Sting? I felt nothing except a burning anguish that would devour me if I didn't let it out. Avenging the brother of my heart was all that mattered. What was a cut when compared to . . . ?

"He's lying there," I croaked. "I . . . can't bear it."

Vexxion's gaze cut that way before returning to my arm.

"We know the risk when we go on a raid," I said. "But it's not supposed to happen to us."

"I agree." After cleansing my arm, he wrapped it with clean cloth and secured it all neat and tidy, as if that was all it took to fix everything in my life. He carefully repacked the supplies and placed them aside for Jessia to collect.

"I'm sorry." He drew me back into his arms, holding me with his chin resting on the top of my head.

I shouldn't lean into him, but I did.

I shouldn't allow my heart to crack wide open all over again, but *it* did.

I still bled.

As always, my biggest wounds were not on the surface.

∼

We only lost one rider in this raid.

Our solemn group stood in a circle around Kinart's body while Jessia and one of the other riders placed him in a large bag Jessia had brought in the pouch on her dragon. She must have more bags there, one for each of us. One for herself.

We fought. We died.

But we never left anyone behind.

"Fucking dregs," a rider said, coming over to rub my back.

Four of us took corners and carried him from the cave, moving around the gutted dreg carcasses. You'd think the Lieges would take advantage of our distraction to attack, but none ventured into the main cavern. Maybe they were too scared we'd decimate them all to get our revenge for Kinart's death. Or maybe they had slunk far into the lower passages to hide. They'd create new dregs to replace the ones we killed. New cages to replace the ones we'd destroyed.

And they'd come after us again. They'd never stop until we eliminated every single one of them.

Well . . . Unless one of us could crush the being not only creating but controlling the Lieges. It was all I could live for. All I needed.

Kinart, I'm going to stop this. Your death is going to be the last one. I wanted to shout the words, but I didn't need to. He heard.

And I'll watch out for Reyla.

That would be the only thing my brother would ask for.

After tying the bag on his dragon, who snorted and skittered sideways until a rider barked out a command, we mounted. Many doubled or tripled up with villagers they'd drop off on our way back to the fortress.

Drask fluttered down to land on my shoulder and pecked my neck. I didn't have the energy to scold him. It was all I could do to mount Fawna and give her the command to fly.

After dropping off the villagers, we flew in formation back to the fortress, the bag draped across Kinart's empty mount an endless scream. The echoes of it melted down my spine. Clawed at my insides.

Wrenched through me all over again.

Reyla rode in Brodine's arms. He kept shooting me looks so full of pain that my throat tightened into a chokehold. My breathing rasped, and my fingers fidgeted on my saddle.

Vexxion remained silent, keeping his mount near mine, though a tad behind, as if even in this, he still felt the need to remain in a position where he could guard me.

If only he'd felt the need to guard Kinart.

Bile kept rising into my mouth, and I choked it back down.

I didn't blame Vexxion. How could I?

I blamed the fates. I blamed the Lieges for creating the dregs and sending them after us. And I blamed the fae king for directing it all. Wasn't stealing Nullen magic enough? Relentless, the king wouldn't stop until he'd drained what little energy we had left.

When we landed, I stood solemnly beside Vexxion while they took Kinart's body bag across the compound, toward the healer. There was no hope of reviving him, of course. The healers kept the bodies in a back room until a pyre could be built.

That was the last place he'd lie.

Brodine carried Reyla, walking slowly behind them. She'd stopped crying. If she was lucky, she'd stopped feeling. I couldn't seem to shut that tortured part of myself off.

"I need to take care of Fawna." I turned back to enter the aerie.

"I'll do it." Vexxion strode beside me, watching my face. Did he expect to see anything but overwhelming grief?

"I can do it," I snapped. I was boiling over, scorching everything around me. If he didn't back down, I was going to blast him to the opposite end of the compound.

"You don't need to do this," he said softly, gently enough to give me pause. His intent gaze met mine. "For once, would you let someone help you?" He didn't bark. He didn't come across as snide.

Yet his words stung like a thousand bees.

"I accept help." The defensiveness in my voice closed off my throat. "Sometimes."

"Never from me."

I swallowed and my pride went down hard. "We'll do it together." I eased around him and limped toward the aerie with Drask bobbing on my shoulder.

With a sigh, he followed. "It wouldn't hurt you to let someone take care of you every now and then."

"Someone like you?" I kept walking until I realized he'd stopped. Turning back, I lifted an eyebrow. "I'll say it again. *Someone like you?*"

"Yes."

"Why do you want to help me?" My words came out tiny; even I could barely hear them.

"Because I can't *not* help you."

I rolled my eyes and entered the aerie with renewed vigor. Anger could only fuel me for so long. I needed to control it, not let it control me. Easy to say, hard to do.

He said nothing as we rubbed Fawna down and fed her, giving her water. After, we took care of the others, even Kinart's dragon.

The commander would assign the beast to another. A new rider would join our flight.

And we'd battle as one when the dregs next attacked.

Finally, we moved to the stall holding Vexxion's mount and did the same, the dragon huffing gently against his side.

Vexxion may not have named the beast who carried him from one destination to another, but he'd been kind to the creature. It showed in the way the dragon looked at him, how he shifted over to make room for Vexxion to work his way down the creature's flank, and how it lifted its legs for Vexxion to inspect his claws.

We left the aerie.

"Where are you going now?" he asked, sticking to my side.

"I need to shower. Change." I cocked my head to look up at him. "You're not following me there."

"Wouldn't want to," he said with a snort.

"What, you're not offering me sex to help me forget?"

He stopped, a glare twisting his face. "Would sex make you forget about the death of your friend?"

Absolutely not. "Maybe. For a moment. If you're good at it."

He stalked right up to me. I took a stumbling step backward. I would've fallen if his hand hadn't snapped out to hold me steady. "I'm good. *Very* good. The best you'll ever have."

"Such conceit." Sarcasm oozed from my words. "So common in a man." I shrugged off his hand. "Since I'm not having sex with you, your reputation will remain solid." I pivoted on my heel and aimed for my residence.

The infernal man caught up and walked with me. "Don't do anything reckless."

"As if you care."

"Caring has nothing to do with it."

Interesting. The tic had erupted on his brow.

"Don't fall for me," I barked. "You won't enjoy the outcome."

"I could say the same for you, little tornado."

"Do you think I'll find these nicknames endearing? Is that how you prove your sexual prowess?" I was taunting him, and with each snarled word, a bit of my fury diffused. I sensed the real storm was coming, and if I kept poking the dark cloud, it would erupt and scorch me.

Come for me. I dare you.

I'd meet his rage with my arms wide open. I'd tip my head back to feel his rain smack against my face. I'd let his lightning blast the ground I stood upon.

He stopped when we reached the door to my residence. I

wanted to poke him again, ask him why he used stupid twists of my name to mock me, but I didn't.

I opened the door and stomped inside. Drask left my shoulder, veering in a crooked way over to his roost, where he landed. He watched us, his sharp dark eyes darting between Vexxion and me.

Vexxion actually dared to follow me inside.

"This is my place," I snapped. "You don't belong here."

"I won't remain for long." He strode to my room and poked his head inside, sniffing. "Damn, you're a mess, aren't you?"

"In so many ways. Want to try to clean me up?"

His lips twisted, and he walked to the small bathing area between my bedroom and Delaine's, once more peering inside.

"If you find my tooth powder, let me know. I had to use my roommate's this morning," I lifted my voice. "Because someone keeps hiding mine."

"I heard that," she snapped from her room, her voice sounding muffled. Maybe she was stuffing her face into her pillow. I was tempted to stride to her room and press down on her head, stuffing her even farther. "Don't touch my things."

"Ditto."

Her door banged shut, closing us out.

Vexxion glared at my room for a long moment before walking past me and out the front door, closing it behind him.

"Yeah, nice talking with you too," I shouted at the door.

As if someone had popped me with a blade, I collapsed. On dead feet, I walked to my room, where I stripped everything off and tossed it into the basket. Staff would collect it for washing, and I didn't envy them that job. Although, it sure beat mine.

I dispensed death. They just tidied up the remains.

Naked, I left my room and was walking toward the bathing area when our front door opened.

Expecting Brodine or Reyla or Kinart—fuck, no longer Kinart—I paused, smacking my hands over my breasts.

Vexxion froze. His eyes traveled down my frame, leaving a trail of fire wherever his gaze touched.

"What are you doing?" I shrieked.

He backed up until his shoulder hit the side of the door. "I was going to . . ." Sputtering, his thought gave way. As if he lost it. Lost all the control he exuded.

His eyes remained locked on my body. I did not read lust in his eyes. It had to be disgust. Dreg blood had soaked through my leathers to stain my skin in gray corpse blotches. Bruises took up every other part of my body. And my fucking scars . . . They warped the length of my left thigh.

"I was going to remind you to see a healer for your arm," he said thickly.

"Stop looking at me," I snarled.

He dragged his gaze away, jerking it to the floor by his feet.

"I'll see the healer. Go. Don't come back."

With a nod, he turned and left once more.

I huffed and entered the bathing area. Men. You'd think he'd knock or say something before storming inside someone else's residence.

Drask flew in and landed on the sink. He looked in the mirror above and preened. Cute. I kissed the top of his head.

I shrugged off my irritation, though touches of it lingered, and focused on how soothing it felt to bathe. The shower felt wonderful. So did my hands washing off dreg blood. I was careful with my arm, almost hating to remove the bandage Vexxion had so lovingly applied.

My derision rang out in the tiny, steamy chamber in a low snort. *Lovingly?* As if.

Dry, I wrapped the cloth around my body to wear to my room. No strutting about when Vexxion might walk in and gape.

Fucking man. He had no right to look.

No right to touch.

17

TEMPEST

*E*nergized after my shower and armed in my leathers once more, it was time to put my plan into place. This was the only way I could do something for Kinart—for all the Nullens who'd already been wrongfully abused by the fae.

With Drask riding my shoulder, I left my residence and strode toward the main building and the commander's office. No need to see the healer. My arm was fine. Slightly red around the wound, but I'd rigged a wrap to cover it, and it would be sealed over by morning. I'd always healed quickly, and this time would be like any other.

Welcome to my body, latest scar. Allow me to introduce you to the others.

I had to wait to see the commander. Busy guy and all that. But I stood when the door opened and gasped when Reyla stumbled out.

That's when it hit me all over again. I staggered, falling

against the wall as my brother's death overwhelmed me once more. My eyes stung, and I shoved away from the stone surface and palmed off my tears.

Be there for Reyla. Kinart's stern voice hissed in my ear.

Drask fluttered his wings and settled.

Reyla took one look at me and started sobbing, her arms lifting as she rushed to me, nearly knocking me over.

"Kinart," she whimpered over and over. "I still can't believe it. I can't, and I won't."

"I'm sorry." Though everyone said them, words like that were crap. They meant nothing when everything inside you had been scraped and scraped until there was nothing left but an echo within hollow walls.

Crying out Kinart's name, she collapsed. I grabbed her, easing her into the chair I'd just vacated. Staring down at her only strengthened my resolve.

I'm doing it, brother. I'm going to make him pay.

"You wanted to speak with me?" The commander stood in his open doorway. He flicked his hand my way and turned. "Don't dally. I have other things to see to today."

"Wait here," I told her. "I've ... got a plan."

She sucked in a breath and the rage in her eyes when she looked up at me made me stagger. "I have a plan too. Don't worry."

With that, she rose and on much steadier feet, left the commander's office. I'd catch up with her as soon as I could because whatever she planned in this state of mind needed to be vetted. Protecting her was as important as avenging my brother.

Inside the commander's office, I sat. Fidgeted, really, something I rarely did. A blade had been dragged across my nerves, leaving only frayed fragments behind.

Drask, sensing how nervous I was, squawked.

"If that thing won't remain silent, it has to leave," the commander said.

I patted Drask and said nothing.

"Name?" the commander barked, returning to sort through papers on his desk.

"Tempest Lucerna."

"What can I do for you today?"

"Make eye contact with me, for one thing."

His finger paused on the paper lying on his desk. "Excuse me?"

"I'm here. Sitting in the chair. I need to speak to you, and you should look at me while I do it."

With a sigh, he lifted his gaze to meet mine. "Speak, then."

"I want to go to the Claiming."

He blinked for a moment. "*Tempest Lucerna*, you say? And you want to go to the Claiming?"

"Yes."

"That's . . ." Fear flashed through his eyes that darted to the closed door behind me.

A glance behind showed me it remained closed.

"From what I remember, you were slated to stay here," he said. "You specifically came here months ago and asked not to be placed on the list, didn't you?"

"I've changed my mind."

"Why?"

"I need to do something."

"I'd think a rider like you, especially after the unfortunate incident earlier today, would wish to remain here to kill dregs."

Oh, I did, but I could decimate their population by killing their king instead, thank you very much.

"I said I need to do something," I ground out.

"In the fae realm? What sort of thing would a rider need to do there? You know they have their own trainers."

I didn't miss the sneer in his voice. "I need to do something." I'd snarl it five times. Ten if I had to until he finally listened.

"I have no problem . . . adding *your* name to the list." He opened his top desk drawer and pulled out a simple piece of paper, laying it on the blotter in front of him.

I sat forward, curious to read the names. Would they really take three of us from the fortress? There were plenty of orphans to replace us, thanks to the dregs and Lieges, but it took time to raise them, train them well enough so we wouldn't lose all of them during their first battle.

He laid his big hand over the names, blocking them from my view. "No, I haven't sent it in already. It . . . was delayed." Again, he glanced at the door.

And again, I found no one there.

"I'm in?" I asked, eager to get out of here. It was past time I had a mug of wine. It was the only thing that could deaden the stark raving anger boiling across my insides.

"You're in." He gave me a jovial smile, totally inappropriate after "the incident earlier today," but whatever.

Actually, as long as I was here . . .

"What's the fae king's name?" That was the only other detail I needed now.

"Ivenrail Levestan, of course. You don't pay attention during your classes, do you? While we don't cover much fae history here, we do teach the basics." He leaned back in his chair and steepled his fingers in front of his burly chest, warming up to the subject despite getting in his dig first. "Only one court has the determination to rule them all and that's Bledmire. The others live to serve, and if they don't like it, well, they keep their mouths shut. The king's quite formidable. So I've heard. I haven't met him myself, although I'd thought soon—" He coughed and his jovial mood fled, replaced with a scowl.

"He cursed the Lydels?"

"The curse is a myth," he scoffed, returning the list to his drawer.

"They say it's covered in thorns. That everyone living there disappeared." My hands tightened on the arms of the chair to the point I seriously thought I'd crush them.

"Another rumor. *If* a curse was placed on the Lydel Court, the king could very well be involved. He'd profit most from their demise. Did you know? His court used to be second only to Lydel."

The Liege hadn't spoken out of the goodness of his heart. He'd purposefully shared specific information with me. Why hand me such a formidable weapon?

I hoped to one day find out.

"Does the fae king interact with the Lieges?"

His eyes widened. Maybe. It was hard to tell by the way he angled his face. "Why would he do something like that?"

To control them, but I couldn't outright name that.

"Because they're on this continent. If they make it past us, I imagine they'll keep going, all the way across the fae realm."

"I'm sure he's aware of this."

He was.

The commander's head tilted, and he studied my face. "Why do you want to know all this?"

"When I'm claimed, I want to go to the most powerful court," I told the commander. "You just said it's Bledmire."

"It won't matter which court you wind up in since you'll only work as a servant."

A servant or . . .? A few suggested something more sinister happened to the Nullens selected. No one really knew since none had ever returned after the Claiming.

"Bledmire Court is dark and much too wicked for a pretty girl like you," the commander said. "You'll survive longer with the Riftflames. They're . . . sweeter, if such a thing exists within the faerie realm. Theirs is the only court that hasn't been fully absorbed into Bledmire, though I'm sure that's the king's goal."

"How does a Nullen make sure a fae from one particular court chooses them?" That might be the way around this.

"You speak again of Bledmire? I'm telling you you'd be wiser to dream of another."

I'd do whatever I damned well pleased.

I smiled. He saw me as a pretty, simple girl seeking to glean whatever power might rub off the fae who chose her at the Claiming. Let him keep believing this.

I'd be plotting. Infiltrating. Killing.

"As for being chosen, you have no say," he added. "That's up to the whim of the fae lords who attend the Claiming."

There had to be a way, and I'd find it. Nullens attending the Claiming would leave in a few days but would be housed on the border before the event. Maybe I could learn more once I'd arrived.

"Is there anything else I can do for you?" he asked, already returning to the papers on his desk.

"I want to take Seevar with me." Drask was a given.

The commander's eyebrows lifted. "Who is Seevar?"

"The gold dragon I've been working with," I said.

He frowned. "You speak of the unruly one? The one that refuses to be trained?"

"I'm training him. Riding him." More or less. "I want him to go with me."

"I'm afraid we've got a buyer for him already."

"So quickly? I wanted . . ." I slumped in my chair.

"If you'd like, I could speak to the person interested in purchasing him. See if he'll consider a different dragon."

"Why would you do that?"

"It's rare for anyone to volunteer for the Claiming."

No one had ever volunteered, not to my knowledge.

He huffed. "Consider it a reward."

It didn't matter as long as I could take Seevar with me.

"They have their own dragons in faerie," he said. "They may see no use in one of ours. Do you truly think he'll carry a rider all the way across the continent? Without bucking you off, I mean. I've seen him. Watched you work with him through the front windows. It doesn't appear to me that he's coming along well enough for anyone to want him."

"Yet you were going to sell him. To whom?"

"The payment has not yet been received," he said smoothly. "I'll tell him the dragon is no longer available. Consider him a gift."

Why was I pushing this?

"If he doesn't behave, we can tether him," I said. "I'm sure you have dragons in mind to transport those traveling to the Claiming."

"We always do. As for a tether . . ." He sighed. "I suppose it could be arranged. You do know that once you're claimed by one of the fae that you'll have very little time to work with an unruly dragon."

"I'm aware of that."

His gaze shot back to his papers, his fingers sliding along a line of numbers.

"If that will be all?" he asked, not looking up. "I'll note that you're taking the gold dragon with you."

"I don't need anything else. Thank you. Sir." I added the last as I stood.

He said nothing as I left his office.

18

VEXXION

Seek...
  Here.
Yes.

Tempest sat at a table with a few riders on the opposite side of the bar, the crow watching everyone in the room while bobbing on her shoulder.

What I didn't expect was for her to sense me standing in my created disguise near the door. She looked up; her gaze locking on me as if I stood out in the open, on the cliff, completely exposed. Instead of scowling, she waved for me to join her and her friend.

I let my threads drop away, be absorbed.

Reyla was missing, but I wasn't surprised that she wasn't up for an evening like this. Or perhaps she'd already left, as well into her cups as my little fury appeared to be.

"Are you going in or out? Because you're blocking the way," a man said from behind me.

I shot him a scowl but moved to the side.

When Tempest waved again, I made my way through the crowded room toward the table she sat at with Brodine. He couldn't stop staring at her like he'd enjoy swallowing her whole. From what I'd seen, she didn't look ready to suck on anything he owned, let alone swallow.

This could be why she'd waved for me to join them. She wanted a buffer. She didn't particularly want *me*.

But then, no one else did either.

Stopped beside the table, I peered down at them both. The bird tipped his head back and studied me through one of his midnight blue eyes before hopping off her shoulder to land on the damp wooden surface. The bird poked his beak into Brodine's cup.

"Hey. Don't do that, Drask," the male cried, snatching up his mug and holding it close to his chest. "Tell your damn crow to get his own wine."

"Get your own wine, Drask," she said in a silky voice. The wine had . . . mellowed her, and if I was wise, I'd pivot and leave immediately.

Instead, I remained where I was.

"Sit," she said brightly, flicking a wine bottle in my direction before lowering it back onto the table. "Have a drink." When I continued to scowl, she huffed. "Unless our wine isn't good enough for your illustrious palate."

"What makes you think my palate is illustrious?" I asked.

"Just a feeling." She returned my scowl with one of her own that only made her look... precious. "Why did you come over here if you don't plan on joining us? You're looming, something you do quite well, but something that I find particularly irritating."

"I'm taller than you. I'll always loom when I'm beside you."

She grunted.

"And what makes you think I don't plan on sitting?" I asked.

"The fact that you're still standing there. Looming."

"He doesn't want to sit with us," Brodine slurred, telling me who'd drained most of the wine. "Let him go find a friend to sit with." His guttural laugh rang out. "Oh, yes, that's right. His friends left about a week ago. There's no one left here who wants to drink with him."

My little storm elbowed her friend. "*I'm* offering him a seat and a drink."

"No idea why," he said.

Just to irk him—not her—I dragged out a chair and settled in it.

"Let me get you . . ." Tempest was up and moving across the room before I could speak.

The bird tracked her with his gaze before taking flight, darting through the mass of people walking around the inside of the bar. It landed on her shoulder once more.

I turned back.

Brodine puffed his chest, tightening his grip on the edge of the table and glaring at me. "Don't think you're getting her out of her clothes."

"I never suggested I was planning anything of the sort."

Though the thought *had* crossed my mind. More times than I liked.

"Then you're not like at least half the guys at the fortress."

They weren't blind, after all.

I'd *seen* her without her clothing, and the image was branded into my mind. Curves I ached to sink my fingers into. Large breasts she kept hidden beneath her tunic. Long, shapely legs hardened with muscles.

A network of thick scars across the front of her left thigh. Seeing them gave me pause. I wasn't disgusted by them. Not at all. The weight of the ones I carried on my insides clung to me like a pall, equally as thick as those on the surface of my chest and neck.

Stunned to silence, all I could think of was how much pain she must've been in when it happened. I'd barely resisted storming across the room to pull her into my arms. Hold her. Tell her everything would be alright.

That would be a lie.

"Tempest is . . ." Brodine shook his head and sighed. "Special. I wish she'd see me."

"I'm sure she does." And that was the problem.

He removed a ring from his pocket where three Liege bone coins dangled and laid it on the table, fingering each of the coins one by one in morbid fascination. "Tempest has had it rough. We all have, I suppose. But she's one of the few who's been here from the time she was really little." He lifted his mug and drank deeply, swiping the back of his hand across his mouth as he lowered the cup to the table. "I came when I was older, which isn't as bad. At least someone cared about me before I got here." He stroked each coin with his thumb before starting all over again with the first.

"I'm sorry. Did dregs capture your parents?"

He nodded. "Same with her. They keep taking and taking and we can't replace ourselves anywhere near as fast as they can. I'd like to think we'll one day kill them all, but I'm beginning to believe it'll never come true. I probably should apply for a chit. I could travel to the middle of the continent, far from the dregs and Lieges. Build a small farm. Find a wife and have a bunch of kids. Grow crops and try to forget I was ever a rider."

"I wish you well if you do."

He nodded slowly with his gaze caught on Tempest.

I didn't want to sit here while he languished about his feelings for my fury. But before I could rise, she returned, placing a mug on the table in front of me, plus adding a second bottle beside the first.

The bird hopped off her shoulder again, landing near Brodine's mug. He lifted it and tucked it close to his chest. When the bird hopped closer to his bone coins lying on the table, Brodine scooped them up and stuffed them back into his pocket.

"I asked them for wine fit for someone stuffy," she said brightly. To irritate me.

It was going to be fun showing her that her words held no power.

I smiled, a true one. Like so few of the others I'd given her before. I just... let it out.

She sucked in a breath and dragged her gaze from my face.

My smile sharpened.

Taking her seat, she avoided looking my way, uncorking the bottle and filling my mug. For a heartbeat, I was almost disappointed that she'd given up so easily.

But then my tiny hurricane roared onto shore.

"To Kinart," she said, raising her mug.

"Kinart," I rasped. "No one should die that young."

"Happens all the time around here." She drank and looked down at the wine sloshing inside her mug. "Take a look. Do you see anyone other than the commander here who's over thirty? The dregs keep coming and coming and killing us."

"There must be a way to wipe them all out," the male said.

"I wish there was, Bro." Tempest shuddered. "It's not like the king will do anything about it."

"He's busy," Brodine said, jumping to their king's defense. "He dispenses justice. Monitors the border with the fae to ensure they respect the treaty."

"He sends us nothing," Tempest said bitterly. Her voice lowered to a whisper. "Nothing. He keeps it all for himself."

"Do you expect him to live like us?" Brodine asked. "He has power because he wields it. A king isn't respected if he's surrounded by squalor."

"No squalor for this king," she said, and I wondered why she was focused on this. And why now. "He and his pretty daughter remain behind their pretty high walls, attending parties. Savoring fine food and good wine." She stared into her mug. "Better than the crap they serve here."

"Can you blame him? If I was king, I'd live that way too."

"Now he's married, spending more coins on his wedding to his bride who's barely older than his daughter. We need that money." She tapped the hilt of the blade at her side. "We're always short on weapons. Supplies. Feed for the dragons."

"We get by just fine," he said. "You know that. I don't begrudge our sovereign from taking his due."

She sighed. "I suppose not. I wish..."

"What?" I asked.

Her head cocked to the side, and she peered up at me. "I wish we had what we needed to keep us from dying."

I couldn't argue with that.

She sighed again and looked down at her arm. She'd covered the wound, though not well. I assumed she did the bandaging herself.

"You didn't go to the healer," I chided, though gently. She'd been through a lot today already. No need for me to pile more on her shoulders.

"Did a dreg do that?" Brodine asked.

"No, a Liege." Her gaze met mine and if I hadn't already faced the worst things life could offer, I would've been shaken to my core.

"When did you face a Liege?" I bit out. And how had I lost track of her inside the cavern? She'd come stumbling out of a passage and passed me, not seeming to realize I was there. I'd turned and followed her back to the main cavern.

"He was in a cave behind the main one," she said, her brow pensive. "It was weird."

"What was weird?" Brodine asked, leaning toward her.

She deliberately shifted her chair closer to mine, though I wasn't sure she realized she did it.

Our thighs brushed. I should move my chair away.

I didn't.

"I saw flickering light and followed it," she said.

I frowned, not sure what she meant.

"When I entered the small cave, there was a head-sized clumpy candle burning on a large flat stone in the center. The light wavered in the air. I couldn't look away until..."

Brodine leaned closer, his eyes wide.

"The Liege left it for you," I said. "A lure."

She shrugged. "It sounds like you know more about Lieges than me, which means you need to share."

I remained silent.

She scowled. "Right, yes. He must've left it. For me or some other rider, I guess. Lucky me found it." Her swallow went down hard. "And the Liege found *me*." Her fingertip traced the line of her wound through the bandage.

She'd discover tomorrow that it had completely healed. I couldn't do much for her, but I could give her that.

"You killed him," Brodine said. "And added another bone coin to the two you already claimed."

"Yeah, I guess." Her wild gaze met mine. Why was she spooked? This wasn't about the bone coin. I could come up with many reasons *why*, but I wanted to hear hers. "It grabbed my arm." The words burst from her throat loud enough a few riders at nearby tables looked our way before returning to their conversations and mugs.

Brodine sucked in a breath. "Did you kill it *then*?"

She jerked out a nod. "Killed it right away. Cut off its head to make sure it wouldn't rise again." When her gaze met mine, I knew she wasn't telling us everything.

"What else happened?" I asked softly.

Frowning, Brodine looked back and forth between us.

"I hacked it up. Pulverized it."

"You know what I mean."

She dragged her gaze to the table, but I lifted her jaw with my finger, making her meet my eyes.

"What. Happened?"

"Nothing!'

"Leave her alone." Brodine stood up so fast, his chair toppled sideways, smacking into a male at a nearby table. The other guy growled and started to rise until his attention fell on me. He crashed back into his seat and turned away.

She wrenched away from me and lifted her mug, gobbling down her wine before smacking her empty cup onto the table. "You want to know what happened today? A fucking dreg murdered Kinart. What's happening *now* is that it's time to drink enough wine to make me forget."

My lips twisted. "Getting drunk won't improve the situation."

"Are you offering a different cure?" She leaned close to me.

The bird tilted its head, eyeing me just as intently.

I should be disgusted by the smell of wine on her breath, but I could only drink in her sweet scent and the way her hair lay fluffed around her shoulders and spearing halfway down her back. A few strands brushed her cheek, and it was all I could do not to grab onto them. Run those strands across my lips. She'd worn her hair in a braid from the moment I arrived here.

She should always wear it down like this, thick and long and available for my touch.

I slid my fingers through it. Wrapped it around my hand until I reached the nape of her neck. I held her head in place like I'd done with my fingers on her jaw.

"Nothing," I said bitterly. "Nothing will ever make things better." I spoke of so much more than the loss of her friend or of the tenuous situation all the riders faced this close to the border. I spoke of things I hoped she'd never have to understand.

Yet if my plan worked, she would.

Oh, yes, she would.

And she'd hate me for it.

19

TEMPEST

"Getting rather intimate with my hair, aren't you?" I said, tapping his arm. "If I didn't know better, I'd think you enjoy touching it." Since he'd conveniently rolled up the sleeves of his tunic, exposing his tender skin, I'd jab him with a nail if he didn't release me.

His fingers sprung wide, and he jerked his hand away, staring at it with a frown before dropping it and smacking his back against his chair. His full lips twitching, he watched me with those gorgeous sapphire eyes.

"What if I did?" Death lurked in his seductive voice. The tone alone made molten flames course through my veins.

We were treading in dangerous territory, and I wasn't sure if I should leave right now or wait to see what, if anything, came from this sudden change in direction.

"Fuck this," Brodine said, still standing beside the table.

Startled by his outburst, I looked up at him with one

eyebrow lifting. "Yeah, fuck this, right?" I chuckled, but my smile fled when his didn't join in.

For one second, he glared at me with so much anger, it froze the wind in my lungs. His gaze raked over to Vexxion before returning to me. "Fuck," he barked.

Pivoting, he stormed across the bar, shoving riders out of the way to reach the door. When he yanked it inward, it ricocheted against the wall, and he stormed through the opening.

I blinked, unsure what had happened but worried something had irrevocably changed between me and my friend. My breathing came out jerky, as if I'd run for days.

"I'm sorry about Bro," I said. What should I do now?

I knew, but it was much easier to let him go than track him down and acknowledge why he was so pissed off at me now when he never had been before.

He'd liked it when I snarled at Vexxion.

He'd been dismayed when I dropped my wall for a moment to let Vexxion inside.

"It's not for you to apologize," Vexxion said, staring down into his cup.

Drask hopped over to Bro's mug and dipped his beak in. I swiped it away before he had too much.

"Stop," I said, though gently. "You don't need that." I handed it to a passing server. "You ever see a bird get drunk enough to smack into walls?" I asked Vexxion.

"I can't say that I have."

"Some find it funny. Not me." Frowning, I stroked Drask's spine. "He's already my crooked little friend. I don't want to see him get hurt."

Drask gave me a look of disgust. He squawked, flapped his wings, and took flight, soaring across the bar and out the door a woman had just opened.

"He'll find his way home." I felt oddly bereft, as if all my friends had abandoned me.

"I'm sure he will."

"He'll be there by morning, begging for treats." At least I could count on my crow.

Maybe it was the wine, though I'd only had the one mug. Or maybe I was feeling so broken that I couldn't scramble around fast enough to pick up the pieces. But the words burst out of me. "When did I start to care?"

Vexxion's thoughtful gaze lifted to my face. I suspected my eyes were wild. Feral. Whatever had been brewing inside me was bubbling to the surface, and I couldn't hold it back.

"I've lived here most of my life," I said.

"You're an orphan." A statement, not a question.

"My parents were taken like so many others. Someone must've found me wailing somewhere because they brought me here. *Dumped* me here."

"I'm sorry."

"As you said, it's not your fault. All of this is an assumption on my part because no one fucking knows." My voice cratered. "No one fucking knows. Not my real name, not who I really am. Just dumped and left to be raised by whoever might be around inside the fortress. I built a wall around myself. But it collapsed."

His lips compressed, making any hint of plumpness disappear.

"I'm not the first to arrive here without any history," I said. "They put me in a ward with the other children, though from what I've heard, I have the distinction of being one of the youngest dropped here in years. And because I refused to tell them what it was, they gave me a name. Tempest. I was four."

He nodded. I was grateful he didn't offer platitudes or speak. If he did, the pieces of me blasting outward would keep going, not snap back like they always did eventually to remake me, harden me. I was never the same after. Never complete. Never fully healed.

"While there are staff who feed us, especially toddlers like me, we pretty much raise ourselves. I . . . didn't get along well with my peers."

"No," he sighed.

"Would you?"

He shrugged.

"I didn't have any true friends until Bro arrived. He was older than me but basically a child too, yet he watched out for me. He was the big brother I needed. Kinart and Reyla were dropped here not long after that, and the four of us . . . we bonded. We took the nothing we had left and built a family." Staring down at the bit of wine in my mug, such a dark red it could be blood, I gulped. "Please. Tell me how to stop caring?"

"When it's been sliced off your hide . . ." Shaking his head, his face contorted. He lowered his voice to the point I had to lean closer to hear him. "When you realize that allowing emotions to take hold only results in more pain, you . . ."

Such bleakness in his eyes. I wanted to stroke his face, to tell him it would be alright. That one day, he'd . . . What? Fall in love and everything would be perfect after that?

We both knew that wasn't true. Not in my profession, anyway. If I loved someone . . . well, I'd lose them too.

"I need to figure out how to shut it off," I said. "I care too much. Love too much. It's a flaw. A stupid, cursed flaw."

"Some say true love is enough to move mountains."

"They didn't meet me. I can't even move a clod of dirt, let alone keep my best friends alive."

"You weren't with him when he died."

"No, I was playing with a Liege deep within the cavern."

"You haven't told me what the Liege did."

"And I'm not going to," I said. "Back to telling me how to stop caring. You seem like a hardened guy. Care to share how you shut off your emotions?"

"By consuming them rather than letting them consume you."

I tilted my head. "And how do you do that?"

"Practice."

"I wish I could do it that easily."

"I never said it was easy."

"True." I sipped what was left of Brodine's wine, pinching my eyes shut, but that only made things worse. All I could see was Kinart's remaining eye turned blankly toward the cavern ceiling.

All I could hear was Reyla whimpering his name, begging him to come back to her when she knew he'd already left.

"My family was murdered." I snarled the words loudly enough that a guy sitting nearby looked my way. He quickly returned to his drink. Kinart wasn't the first, and he wouldn't be the last of us to die. It was never going to end . . .

Until I stopped it.

"I'm sorry I'm sobbing out my life story," I said, my voice stilted. Heat roared up into my face. "I'm filling your evening with crap you'd probably rather not be a part of."

"If nothing else, I can listen." He sounded . . . kind. Even understanding. I wasn't sure what to make of it because this was a vastly different Vexxion than the one I'd seen thus far.

"Your turn to share." I took another sip of wine, swallowing down my endless grief along with it. Sady, it didn't work. Pain had turned into a solid mass in my throat, choking me. "I spilled my history. Now it's your turn. Distract me."

"I'd have to drink a lot more than this," He lifted the half-empty bottle, "before I would have the strength to do something like that."

"You mean you don't want me to suck down your soul?"

"That, tiniest fury, is something you never want to do."

And there was that blink of his eyes. I wasn't sure what to make of his tell in this situation, so I shrugged it aside.

"Don't call me fury."

"How about tantrum, then, *temper*?"

"I'll keep fury."

"You should go back to your residence," he said. "Sleep. You'll feel better in the morning."

"Do you really think sleep will cure this?"

"Sleep gives you a few moments to forget."

"Then you wake in the morning and overwhelming grief drowns you once more."

He raised his mug, and we tapped ours together, sipping after.

"It's not that late, is it?" I peered around, realizing the place was nearly empty. It had cleared out while I was dumping my past into Vexxion's dubious hands. "Or maybe it is." Rising, a wave of dizziness smacked into me. When had I last eaten? This morning or maybe last night. I couldn't remember.

"I'll walk you back." He said it so grimly, as if he truly was my bodyguard, and now he had to, once again, make sure I made it home safely.

The thought sent torturous bleakness scraping across my soul. I compressed the feeling, tossed it aside. Tried to, that is.

I made it outside before my damn leg gave way. I would've fallen if Vexxion hadn't been close enough to catch me. Sweep me up. Hold me against his chest as if I mattered.

"Which way to your new residence?" he asked, tucking me against his chest.

"It's with the others." I pointed toward the low glow of the residential buildings, and he started walking.

"You're all sharp angles. There's no softness to you," I added as he strode across the compound, leaving the last bit of my boisterousness behind at the bar.

"I can't help the way I'm shaped."

"I like your muscles." Too much. The way they played beneath his smooth skin. It was all I could do not to touch them now that they were close. "I meant you in general."

"And yet, here I am, softly carrying you once more because you cannot walk."

"It's an occupational hazard." *I* was a hazard. He'd better beware.

"What happened to your leg?"

"You saw my scars of course. Asked about them too." I sighed. "Do you want the cute story or the truth?"

"Always the truth, Tempest. Never lie to me." He continued toward my residence.

"Your statement sounds like a warning."

"Take it how you will."

"And there you go again. Sharp." Cutting me like a blade. "I don't know."

"You don't know how you were injured? Your scars . . ."

"They're hideous, right? I can barely look at them myself, and I've lived with them for as long as I can remember. I arrived here with them. It would be nice to say dregs did it, that one raked its claws down my thigh, over and over. That I screamed as I severed his head from his shoulders. That's the heroic story."

"You said you were four when you were brought here."

"I know some people remember that far back. I don't. Not anything from before I arrived." Whenever I tried to drag up even one memory, I hit a black wall.

He started down the long row of residences, aiming for mine. If I was lucky, Delaine would be asleep or sleeping someplace else.

I'd never been that lucky in my life.

"Were your wounds fresh when you were brought here?" he asked, easily placing one foot in front of the other, behaving as if he carried nothing. Although, as he too-often pointed out, I *was* tiny.

"They say so. Still bleeding, even. That time's also dark."

"Dark?"

"I don't remember much of my early years here. The pain, naturally. But nothing else. Someone sutured me up, and honestly, they should find a new profession because they did a crappy job. I've got horrible scars . . . as you saw."

"Yes." He ground his teeth together. "I'm sorry. For all of it."

I shrugged. "It wasn't you."

"No. It wasn't *me*. I wish I'd been here . . . I would've protected you."

For a sharp bodied man, he was otherwise impressive. Almost heroic.

"If you keep carrying me around and talking sweet like this, I'll start thinking you care." I said it in a flippant way, but I watched his face.

Damn me for watching his face. Damn me for being greedy for whatever expression he might give me.

"Don't *care* for me," he said.

"You don't get to control something like that."

He stopped at the head of the path leading only to my residence and glared down at me. "Do not. *Ever.*"

"Whoa." I puffed out the word, and the heat of embarrassment blasted across my chest and up into my face once more. "You're rather firm about that, aren't you? Didn't you tell me I'd be yours not long after we met?"

"You will be."

"Sometimes, caring comes with that."

"I've done things. I'll do more. I'm not someone anyone should care about."

And that was sad. "Don't you wonder, every now and then, what it might be like to love someone? To give everything you have inside to them alone?"

"No." Yet tiny stars flickered in his deep blue eyes, and he blinked. I wasn't sure how to interpret the blink right now.

He paused at the head of the path leading only to my residence and stared down at me, probing me with his gaze enough I dragged mine away. "Weren't you just asking me how to stop caring?"

"Because it hurts when you lose them."

"And there's your answer."

Not really. "It's not easy to shut off emotions. If it was, I would've done it already." As for caring for Vexxion? I sensed, deep inside where I still held a hint of softness, that I could.

He stopped at the front door and wrangled with the knob. To be helpful, I leaned over, brushed his hand to the side, and opened it myself. He kicked the panel wide and strode inside.

I waved to the room on the right, grateful Delaine wasn't around to gape while Vexxion held me.

He carried me into my bedroom, taking in the sparse furnishings with a twist of his lips. "You had other blankets before."

"I did. Good ones. I saved up to buy them. They burned along with everything else." I gazed up at him. "Are you leaving the fortress soon?"

"Trying to get rid of me already?"

"I have plans that don't include you."

He'd started to lean forward to lay me on my bed—definitely romantic, right there—but he paused with me dangling in his arms. My hands remained locked around his neck, and it was all I could do not to notice how soft his hair felt on my bare forearm. How much I wanted to rake my fingers through the thick strands. Tug on them.

"What plans?" he bit out.

"Nothing you need to be concerned about," I said pleasantly. "Are you going to hold me here or are you going to put me to bed?"

"Put you to bed," he growled, lowering me onto the surface in a sweeter way than his growl implied he'd like to.

I kept my arms locked around his neck. I was clingy tonight. It was nothing else.

"Want to stay?" I wanted to bite back the words, but they were already out.

"I don't," he said.

And there was that blink. I'd riled him up and now . . .

I was desperate to un-rile him.

"Stay."

His gaze dropped to my mouth, and I read hunger there. It stole every breath of air from my lungs.

I was tipsy, but that was no excuse. I'd only had one mug of wine. While it would be wonderful to keep guzzling it until I forgot who Kinart was, there wasn't enough alcohol in the world that could steal his memory from me. I'd learned that ages ago.

While it hurt, the best way to handle the situation was to face it head-on. I wouldn't survive as a rider if I didn't.

However, I wasn't so drunk that I didn't know what I was doing.

I tugged his head down while lifting my own.

And I kissed him.

I expected him to jerk back and snarl. For that mask to drop across his face and block out everything worth seeing.

Instead, he wrapped his body around mine, dropping down heavily on top of me. He caged me with his arms and his torso and the heat of his mouth.

My heart pounded with desire unlike anything I'd felt before. As if, all these years, I'd lived only for this one single moment. This heartbeat in time when . . . all of me could be fused back together.

Hunger invaded me as his tongue sliced across my lips, demanding entrance. I surrendered to it, to him, moaning as I let him inside.

He went feral, as if the heavy restraints he kept around his heart broke and let him fly free. His mouth was insistent, demanding on mine, dragging out every response I was capable of giving.

I wanted to give him all I had. I craved this man like no other. And that fucking scared me. Still, I couldn't push him away, couldn't *scold* him away. I needed this now more than anything else.

I'd been with other guys. It took years to realize that getting drunk didn't help, and a few more to admit that I couldn't fuck my emotions back into the locked box where I tried to keep them. Nothing and no one compared to him.

Being trapped between his rock-hard body and the bed

should make me frantic to escape, but all I could do was moan and sink my fingers into his hair. It was silky, the only softness this man made up of granite edges possessed.

I should end this. Send him away.

But I couldn't.

No, all I could do was drown in his kiss and buck against his hand on my breast. He squeezed until he found the nipple, rolling it while I gasped into his mouth. His fingers dove into my hair, and he wrapped some of it tightly in his fist again, tipping my head back to deepen his kiss.

I roamed my hands across his chest, whimpering and yanking at the fabric between us. It needed to be gone. I *had* to touch him.

His head lifted, and his smoldering gaze stabbed down into mine, seeking... I didn't know what he expected to find, but his eyes softened.

This was wild and unexpected. I'd told myself I'd stop feeling, yet, here I was, doing it all over again.

Caring.

For a man I wasn't even sure I *liked*. And here I'd only recently vowed I'd never develop feelings for him.

"Damn," I moaned, wedging my hands between us to rub my face. Block my gaze from his. "Damn!"

"Yeah." He dropped away from me to lay beside me on the bed, wedging his vast body between me and the wall. My bed was a narrow thing. We might sleep with each other, but admin had no interest in giving us bigger beds to make it easier.

"That didn't happen," he bit out. "It never happened."

And yet it had.

"Denying it won't make it go away," I said.

"No. Do. Not. *Ever*. Love me either."

"I believe you made that clear already," I gritted out. Like always, I couldn't seem to stop myself from caring. But actually *love* Vexxion? I wasn't sure I could. I sensed loving him would mean giving up everything inside me. Allowing him to swallow me whole.

And I was never going to give that kind of power to anyone.

"Don't worry about me," I said. "I'm in full control of my emotions."

And that was a complete lie.

Rolling, he faced me, studying my face before nodding. I wasn't sure what conclusion he came to, but his face softened for a second time.

Then he tugged me into his arms and held me.

And curse me to the fates and beyond, but I let him.

20

TEMPEST

When I woke the next morning, Vexxion was gone.

I scratched an itch on my right wrist and snuggled deeper into the super-soft covers.

Super-soft covers?

Opening my eyes, I pawed at my blankets. I was draped in flooferdar from my chin to my toes.

I wasn't quite sure what to make of him somehow finding and bringing me my favorite blankets. Laid them over me while I was sleeping. I'd bought the others and used them; none of my friends even noticed.

Vexxion somehow knew I mourned the loss of them in the fire and replaced them.

Drask cawed. Perched on my windowsill, he fluttered his wings. His head tilted while he watched me. When he realized I was awake, he flew over to land on my chest, dropping something from his beak.

I picked up the tiny shell, turning it this way and that. "Where did you get this? It's a long way to the ocean."

He cocked his head this way and that before flying back to the window.

I laid the shell on the side table and flopped back on the bed.

Vexxion. How could I feel bereft that he'd left before I woke when he'd bought me soft blankets?

We'd shared the bed. He'd offered me comfort, the warmth of his body. I'd be a weak, pitiful thing if I cried because he hadn't woken me to tell me goodbye.

"Not doing that." Pushing the fluffy blankets back, I swung around, dropping my legs over the side of the bed. My head pounded, but it didn't come from the wine.

Why had I shared so many of my secrets with Vexxion last night? I'd basically bared my soul to him as if he was my best friend.

Or my boyfriend.

No. Absolutely, *no.*

"He caught you when your guard was down." I slid off the bed and padded to the bathroom. "That was all that happened."

While I took care of my teeth, I avoided looking in the mirror. I didn't want to see the vulnerability lurking in my eyes. "You shared more than you would if you were sober, that's all. He's probably forgotten most of what you said. You won't do it again."

But man, did I ever crave to feel his fingertips on my cheek, his lips on mine once more.

Even when I was sober.

After bathing and dressing in my leathers, and with Drask on my shoulder, I walked out to the central area and slid my blades into the sheaths at my waist and on my thighs. The latter had extra straps that kept them from slapping around as I walked.

Delaine was lounging on the sofa, munching on something that rained crumbs down the front of her nightgown.

"There you are," she said, not looking my way. "You've *finally* emerged."

"It's not that late." I'd slept better last night than . . . Well, I couldn't remember the last time I'd slept that deeply, let alone through the night. "I'm getting breakfast. Want some?" It was only polite to ask if she wanted to go with me, though I doubted she'd ever deign to eat with me and my friends.

"Already got it." She held up half of a fruit tart. "This was the last."

Figured. Another favorite of mine.

Now that I'd acted polite and all that shit, I strode to the door. I was reaching for the knob when she spoke, though I didn't turn.

"I'm surprised you'd sleep with one of them." The pure malice in her voice rivaled dragon claws raking down my spine.

"I don't know what you're talking about."

Actually, I suddenly *knew*.

Why hadn't I seen it? Inside, I floundered, my world shattering around me once more.

"Now that's rich. How could you miss something like that?" Her shrill laugh rang out.

"Talk, Delaine. Stop gloating."

She chuckled again and spoke around a bite of the tart. "Vexxion's a high lord of Weldsbane Court. He's fae."

21

TEMPEST

"How do you know this?" He was a diplomat. A friend of the commander's. A visiting dignitary.

Not fae.

Yet they looked just like us, behaved like us unless they were interested in using their magic, something strictly forbidden.

"I've met him before," Delaine said with a smirk.

"How?"

"My father knows him."

How had I not seen this? The tiny clues tumbled through my mind, adding up.

The way he'd made Brodine back off in the bar.

The odd silver bands I swore I'd seen snaking around him when he saved me from the fire.

The almost pristine way he battled.

I'd thought the latter was because he worked with our king, perhaps. He had a lot of training.

Never because he had the body of one of the highly-gifted fae.

Fucking fae lord. To think I'd started to trust him. *Like* him.

Delaine cackled. "Maybe you *didn't* know. Sad isn't it? You're not very observant, are you? Maybe last night, it didn't matter. They say the fae can lull Nullens like us, so he might've done something like that to you."

Her laughter dragged across me like pumice on scorched skin.

I didn't need to stand here while she continued to taunt me.

Whirling, I left the residence, Drask whisking out through the front door to fly above me as I stomped down the path.

Anger tore through me. I was so mad I could rip chunks from the foundation of the building with my bare hands. Rather than slam through our living area or smack Delaine, things frowned upon at the fortress, I decided to save my *fury* for one particular fae.

He was leaning against the wall when I emerged and bumped off to follow me as I strode ahead of him on the path.

"When were you going to tell me?" I snapped.

"Tell you what?" Oh, he sounded perfectly snide. As if he had no clue what I meant.

He'd *used* me, though I had no idea why.

My simmering rage boiled over.

In a flash, I spun on my heel while pulling a blade. In a second flash, I'd pinned his arm down by his side and pressed the tip of my very sharp blade against his throat. I leaned into his hard chest while shoving my knife up enough to nick his delicate fae flesh.

A drop of blood slithered from the prick, tainting my bright silver knife.

Just as fast, I found myself lying on the ground with Vexxion caging me in place with his body forged from steel, the blade now gouging against *my* throat.

I pinched the tip of the blade and dragged it sideways. He, unlike me, did not draw blood. "Did you need to use fae magic to do that?"

His face . . . changed, the irritation quickly changing to dismay before he snapped his control back into place and tightened his features into a mask of nothing. He jerked off me and stood over me, now caging me with his boots grinding into my ribs instead of his rocky arms wedging my shoulders.

"What makes you think I'm fae?" he bit out.

"Weldsbane. Evidently, it's common knowledge." Not to my friends and me, but did everyone else know?

The tic burst into fury on his temple.

"Congratulations. You fooled me, though you won't do it again." I scrambled to my feet, my thigh barking at me to take it slowly, and held out my hand for my blade.

He offered it to me hilt first, and I swiped his blood off on my thigh before returning it to the sheath.

Pivoting, I started toward the dining area.

The damn fae bastard continued to follow, to stalk me like always.

"I can't believe I kissed you," I huffed.

"Never fear, my tiny storm, it won't happen again."

I ignored the part about him not kissing me again. "I'm. Not. Your. Anything."

"Not yet."

I spun and stomped right up into his face. He didn't back down. I suspected this man would never give ground, not even if it meant the cost of his life. "What's that supposed to mean?"

One of his black slash-of-an-eyebrows lifted. "You can take it any way you please."

"I'm not taking anything from you."

He stepped backward and crossed his arms on his chest, giving me that sardonic look that used to make my rage whip right through me. Now it did wild things to my insides. Scrambled them, and I didn't like that he had even this much control over my emotions.

"I don't have time for this." Whirling around, I continued across the compound and entered the dining area. When he appeared on the other side of the glass where the food was kept with that snide expression locked on his face, I wanted to growl.

Here I was trying to find my way into the fae kingdom to murder his king. *He* was fae.

And I needed him.

Fuck, fuck, fuck. The realization gouged through my bones and made my belly pinch tight.

"Give me three horig cakes, please," I told the woman working behind the counter.

Her lips twisted, and she edged backward to allow Vexxion to take her place. Using tongs, he delicately lifted one cake after another, glaring at them before placing them on my plate.

So much for telling me he enjoyed them.

He gave me a slick smile as he handed the tray over the glass.

I stomped away from him and out into the dining room, aiming for Brodine and Reyla sitting together near the bank of windows. After setting my tray on the table, I settled in the seat across from them.

Her eyes red and her face splotchy, Reyla gave me a pitiful look. She shoved eggs and slices of rusher around on her plate with her fork, but it didn't look like she'd taken even one bite. I wanted to tell her I was going to handle this, that no one hurt our family without paying the ultimate price. But there were so many moving parts in this game to glue into place before I could share something like that. Getting her hopes up would only make it worse if I couldn't make things happen.

Or if I ended up dead. The odds were solid that I wouldn't get far with my plan.

Someone clanked a tray onto the table beside me, but I didn't look his way. Damn fae.

Brodine took one look at Vexxion, shot me a glare, and left, abandoning his half-eaten meal and leaving the tray behind. Reyla didn't look up but kept driving her rusher from one side of her plate to the other and sighing.

My throat closed off tight, and I lowered the horig cake I'd just bitten into onto my plate.

Vexxion picked it up and popped the entire thing into his mouth.

"Hey," I snapped. "That's mine."

"Delicious." His gaze was trained on my mouth. What was it with him? First stating that he'd never kiss me again, now locking his eyes on my lips like he wanted to bow me over the table and claim my mouth once more. He'd taste like horig. Sweet when this man was anything but.

As for the cakes, it was clear he couldn't decide, just like with me, no doubt.

With a snarl of disgust, I rose and stacked my tray on top of Brodine's. "Done?" I asked Reyla. She nodded, sucked in a breath and shot it out, making her bangs flip up before settling on her forehead again.

"I'm going to the Claiming," she announced, not looking up from the table. Her hand continued to shift above the table as if she still held her fork and the rusher still needed moving.

"So am I," I said.

Her soul-gutted gaze met mine. "Why?"

"Reasons."

Vexxion didn't appear surprised, though why would he? He couldn't know that I was slated to stay here but had asked the commander to send me instead.

She nodded thoughtfully.

"Why do *you* want to go?" I asked, curious.

"I need a complete change. If I stay here . . ." She glanced around. "He's everywhere, you know? I keep hearing him speaking to me. When I close my eyes, he's kissing the side of my neck, stroking my shoulder. Teasing my hair. I can't ride a dragon without remembering the time we snuck out on mine, soaring through the sky together. They like doing that, you know, flying when we're not trying to kill dregs all the time." Her fingers twitched on the table. "I hate dregs. I want to kill them all, then revive them so I can kill them again. Torture them like they're torturing me. But they just keep multiplying. Murdering us. Murdering *Kinart*."

She wore a mask of pure, exquisite devastation. My face must look the same. He was my brother. Fucking dregs.

Kinart.

"I'll make them pay," I swore softly.

Vexxion shot an odd look my way, though he said nothing.

"Me too," she said in an almost mechanical voice, as if she'd suddenly found a way to separate her emotions from her mind. Could she teach me how to do it? "All of them. I won't stop until we wipe every single one of them off the continent." With that, she rose and left us, drifting across the room like a husk of the bright person I used to know.

When she opened the door, Drask flew in, soaring over to land on my shoulder.

"Where have you been, buddy?" I asked, stroking his feathers.

He flapped his wings and cawed.

"Your friend is going to get herself killed," Vexxion said. "A fae lord will claim her and eat her alive."

"I guess when it comes down to the fae, you'd be the one to know."

It wasn't going to happen if I had anything to say about it. I'd find a way to keep her safe or die while trying.

"I notice you don't seem worried about anyone doing that to me," I said.

"You're stronger than her." His penetrating gaze met mine. "You didn't answer my question."

"Which one in particular?"

He gazed down at the rest of his meal. "How you found out what I am."

"Someone told me. You should've been that someone."

"Nullens hate us. Why reveal details you don't need to know?"

The fae stole our magic. They ruined everything. Now we were stuck with the residue they'd left behind and they were clamoring for that as well.

"You took the choice from me," I said.

He swung about to face me, his elbow hitting his tray and sending it flying off the table. It clattered when it hit the floor, but he didn't appear to notice. Others did, but it wasn't that odd for someone to drop a tray. All but a few went back to their meals and conversation.

Drask only stared at him, a new one for my pet who startled so easily.

Rising to his feet, Vexxion advanced on me fast. I backed up, but he gripped my upper arms and held me in place.

"Do you really believe you have choices in anything?" Vexxion asked.

"Everyone does." Not truly, but I wouldn't hand this man another piece of my soul.

"Ah, yes, I suppose you could marry your soft boyfriend. He'll take you far from here if you ask, and he'll build you a house. Care for you for the rest of your days. Protect you if the dregs attack."

"What's wrong with that?" I ignored the boyfriend comment. By the sharp glint in his eyes, Vexxion had said it to make me flame, something I refused to do at his command.

"You'd be wasted on such a life."

I shrugged. "As you said, he'd care for me, protect me, though I'll point out I'm good at doing that all on my own."

"Yes," he drawled. "You did so well just now outside your residence."

"You surprised me."

"Liar. You believe you're invincible, and I know why." He shook me, though relatively gently. "It's practically bred into the Nullens growing up on the border. If you didn't think you had a chance of surviving to see the next day, you wouldn't put up a fight. You'd let the dregs swarm over you, take you. Then drain you."

"Moving far from here means I'd be away from the border, away from all that."

He scowled. "He'll never satisfy you."

"Ah, and now we're talking about my sexuality."

"Such as it is."

"When you were kissing me last night, you had no problem enjoying it. I swear I heard you groan."

"I felt bad for you."

Maybe he *had* stabbed me with my own blade on the path. I felt it sinking into my lungs and twisting.

I had nothing more to say to him, a first for me. Because his comment hurt. I hated that it did, but I wasn't one who was good at compressing my emotions. I might drown them with wine sometimes, but in the morning, I admitted to them.

Wrenching away from him, I meticulously stacked the plates and lifted them, easing around him. Making sure I didn't touch him. If I did, well . . . I wasn't sure what would happen next. For all I knew, a simple brush of my body against his might be all he'd need to control me. Is that what he'd done last night?

Why couldn't I forget about our kiss?

With a growl, I stomped across the room and ditched the trays, Drask fluttering his wings but remaining perched on my shoulder.

I left the dining area with my infernal shadow haunting me.

"Why won't you leave me alone?" I snarled.

"Believe me. Sometimes, I'd like to."

"Then just . . . do it." I spun on him, Drask's claws digging in to hold his position, and struck Vexxion's chest with my finger. "Turn around, walk in the opposite direction, and forget you ever met me. While you're at it, take your fae magic with you so I'll forget you ever kissed me, touched me." Held me all through the night when I was at my lowest and in desperate need.

Gave me fucking blankets like what we'd shared actually meant *something*.

He braced my arms again as I glared into his face. "I want to. So much. But I *can't*." With that, he jerked away from me and stalked past me, aiming for the aerie.

Since I had to go there myself, I followed him. Inside, he walked to Seevar's stall and released the latch holding the upper part of the gate closed. Seevar nudged it while Vexxion was tugging it around to secure on the outside wall. He poked his head out and whoofed when he saw me, sparks drifting down from his nostrils to speckle the sand-strewn floor like unruly stars.

"Nice to see you this morning too," I said, feeling alive for the first time in ages. The distance between yesterday and today could be a million lifetimes.

I didn't like that Vexxion had admitted he might feel the same as me. I should snarl at him—again. Demand he leave me alone once more. But I couldn't. Each time I tried to voice the words, something giddy inside me choked them out.

I rubbed Seevar's face and kissed his snout. He blasted my head with sparks, and I smacked at them before they lit my hair aflame. My laugh burst out, surprising me as much as Seevar. His head jerked up, and he stepped backward.

He'd come into his fire soon. If I didn't finish teaching him restraint, I'd need to start wearing armor.

I harnessed him and led him out of the aerie, across the compound, and into the training area I used the most. On either side of us, other trainers worked in similar net-covered structures with dragons.

Vexxion joined us inside the open sandy area.

"I didn't mean it," he said softly. "I shouldn't have said that. I wanted to be with you last night."

I ignored him, gently urging Drask onto the top of the fence. He wouldn't stay there for long. My winged pet preferred to ride on me most of the time. But it would keep him out of the way for now.

Then I proceeded to groom Seevar's scales with a coarse brush.

Vexxion started working on the dragon's other side.

We groomed the dragon in what some might call harmony. I called it an uneasy truce. If I didn't need him, I'd find a way to permanently get rid of him. Not murder him—

outright. But I'd find a way to make sure he stopped following me.

"You were jealous." Yeah, that would do it.

He snorted and kept rubbing Seevar's scales, making them gleam in the sunlight. "Who, may I ask, was I supposed to be jealous of?"

If I didn't see the tic in his temple, I'd have doubts. "Brodine."

"The last person I'd see as competition is your fluffy friend."

"He's strong. A good fighter. A decent guy."

"So many admirable qualities. I can see why you're considering marrying him."

Taunting me, eh?

"Yes, it's definitely a possibility." There was no way I'd ever marry Brodine, but Vexxion would be the last to know. My emotions belonged to me first and only second to those I chose to share them with.

That would never be this prick of a fae man.

I moved to Seevar's flank and started working on his larger scales. Dragons would lay anywhere, even on their own shit, and their scales needed constant attention. "I need you to do something to me." I kept my eyes on my task, though I watched Vexxion out of the corner of my eye.

"If you need favors, perhaps you should ask your fiancé?"

"He's not fae."

"I noticed."

"How can you tell?"

He shrugged. "What do you need?"

"The Claiming's coming up."

"Yes."

"As I told Reyla at breakfast, I'm going."

"You shouldn't. You're safer here," he said, all his attention focused on Seevar's scales.

"No one's safe here. No one is safe anywhere inside the Nullen kingdom."

"Such an interesting observation." His eyes flashed to mine, and his air of indifference was belayed by sapphire sharpness. "I assume you feel this way after speaking with the Liege."

"I never said I spoke to it."

"But you did." His hand started moving, but it remained in one place, not shifting to other scales that needed attention.

"I'm going to the Claiming. That's not up for debate."

He jerked out a nod.

"How can I make sure I'm claimed by a fae who can get me to Bledmire Court?"

His hand paused on Seevar's shoulder. "Why Bledmire Court in particular?"

"I don't want another court to pick me."

"That's not an answer."

"Once I'm inside Bledmire, I'm going to kill someone."

"Even more interesting." One of his eyebrows lifted. "And who might that be?"

I might be foolish to trust him, but I was desperate. There wasn't anyone else I could ask for help. So I braced myself and spit it out. "Ivenrail Levestan, the high lord of Bledmire Court, and the king of the fae."

22

VEXXION

How ironic.

My laughter rang out, dryer than the empty husks on last summer's grass.

"I can do it." She said it so fiercely, so ardently. If she only knew.

"You'll be dead within a heartbeat of entering the castle," I said.

"Which is why I need to be claimed by someone who can get me inside."

"Whoever claims you will *own* you. What makes you think that person will take you to Bledmire and let you do something like that?"

Her head tilted. "*Own* me in what way?"

"*Every* way."

Only the subtle shake of her fingers on the brush gave her away. "I own myself."

"Not once you're collared."

"What? I haven't heard about that."

"Do you never listen?"

"What's that supposed to mean?"

She was sweet. Innocent. And she'd be swept up and dragged so far into this, she'd never find her way back. Once they'd drained her innocence from her, there'd be nothing left to return to.

"Nullens agreed to the Claiming. One would think you'd make sure you understood what was involved before leaping into this."

"So tell me."

"During the Claiming," I said, smoothing my hand across the back of my neck, "the fae who chooses you will place a collar around your throat. It locks with magic. Tamper with it, and it'll tighten."

"How tight are we talking about?"

"Until the sides meet in the middle."

A shiver rippled across the exposed skin of her arms. "I guess I'll leave the collar alone. Why a collar?"

"The collar ensures cooperation. Access."

Her color fading, she swallowed hard. "I'll get around it."

"There is no getting around it. Why do you think they collar Nullens?"

She shrugged. "You said to ensure cooperation. Access, whatever that is. I assume you want to make sure we follow your commands. I can behave in a passive manner. Whoever claims me will relax their guard and give me more freedom. Then I can take care of the problem."

My laugh rang out. "There will be no relaxing their guard or allowing you to roam Bledmire castle unfettered. You'll be collared and there will be nothing left in your future but obedience."

"Why would anyone do this?"

"For a taste of our power."

"Not me."

"Everyone falls eventually."

"Not. Me."

"You wouldn't be the first to say that," I drawled.

She huffed. "That's why I need you to help me. I need to find someone who can get me inside, maybe without the collar."

"Only the claimed can cross through the veil and all those claimed receive a collar."

"I might be impulsive, but I'm also determined. I'm not giving up."

"Why do you want to kill the king?"

She leaned against Seevar and lowered her voice. "He made the Lieges, and he's responsible for everything. *He's* the one draining us of the tiny bit of energy we may have left. He's sucking out our souls."

"*May* have left?"

"That's what I heard. It's stupid. We're called Nullen because we have no magic. You guys stole it from us."

Why had the Liege suggested she might have power? She'd killed it, so there'd be no discovering the answer now.

"You'd be better off marrying your sweet boy and moving as far from the border as possible," I said. "Actually, take a ship to another continent and keep going until you come across people who've never heard of the fae."

"He killed Kinart," she growled.

"A dreg killed your friend. I, in turn, removed the dreg's head."

"I can't let him keep doing this to us. He killed my parents!"

If there was ever a time to show nothing on my face, it was now. "Is that what you believe?"

"It's what I know."

"You told me you were dumped here, that you don't know anything about your background."

"I was dumped here along with a bunch of other kids, all older than me, after dregs invaded a village. Dreg invasion, dead Nullens, kids dumped. Sounds conclusive to me."

"This doesn't prove Ivenrail drained your parents."

Her attention drifted to my temple. "He killed them. He killed Kinart. And I'm going to end his measly existence."

"I admire your determination if nothing else."

"Then you'll help me choose the right fae at the Claiming?"

"Why in the world would I do something like that?" I had to hand it to her, my tiny fury had fire. It licked across her soul. If I wasn't careful, it would lick across mine, marking me forever.

"Because you owe me."

I snorted, strangely amused by her vehemence, by how fierce she was. As if she truly could storm through Bledmire Court and get within killing distance of the fae king. He wouldn't need to go near her to burn her out of existence. "I don't owe you anything."

"You didn't tell me you were one of the wicked fae."

My smile curled up. "Why do you suppose Nullens call us wicked?"

"You lull us, make us do things we never would otherwise."

"Such as?"

"Kiss them."

I couldn't keep my gaze off her mouth or my mind off the feel of her pressing her body against mine. The way her nipple hardened beneath my hand still haunted me, as did the moans working up her throat in response to my touch.

"The need you felt for me last night was purely your own," I growled. "*You* kissed *me*."

"Not sure why I bothered," she said with a snort. "It wasn't much of a kiss."

A flash of light on the top of the main compound building caught my eye, but when it wasn't repeated, I returned my attention to this too sweet woman who was going to get herself killed.

"You crave me, fury."

She rolled her eyes. "Worried about your reputation? I won't tell a soul it's merely a rumor."

"Keep taunting me, and I'll prove it's no rumor." I walked to the dragon's tail and inspected the tip. Sometimes, tiny creatures got into the beast's stalls and caused damage.

Destroy.

Another flash of light on the roof stole my air. A roar filled my ears, and my gaze snapped to Tempest's crow. Its gaze met mine, sharpened with pure terror.

I flitted to Tempest, grabbing her around the waist, and flung us onto the sand. With my arms around her, I rolled us beneath the dragon's belly, bringing her to a stop with her trapped beneath my body, the dragon between us and the roof.

Drask shrieked and dove off the fence, thrashing toward us as if he could protect her all on its own.

The dragon snarled and leaped, his wings extending, only to flop back onto the sand and snap his head back and forth, sparks erupting from his nostrils.

The air gasped out of my fury's lungs in violent jerks. "What are you doing?" She smacked my shoulder. "Get off me."

I laid my fingertip on her plush lips and shook my head. Her eyes widening, she nodded. Crawling off her, I tugged her up, keeping low and making sure she was behind me and the dragon.

The dragon growled and scrambled to reach his left flank.

"By the fates," Tempest cried, hobbling around me to reach toward the beast.

She was limping worse than usual. For one moment, I *loathed* myself. Somehow, I'd brought this to her, though it would've found her even if I'd never been involved. I tried to tell myself I could ignore what happened to them, but . . .

That was when I didn't know who she was.

Drask landed on her shoulder and shrieked, his wings flapping.

"I'm alright," she told the bird absently, her hands fisting at her sides as she gazed at the dragon.

An arrow quivered, embedded in Seevar's left flank. An arrow meant for *my fury*.

Rage uncoiled inside me, a beast spreading its wings and thundering across the sky.

I flitted, landing squarely on the roof.

A man rose from the clay surface by my feet and barked out a cry, scrambling away from me. His crossbow slipped from his hands and clattered on the tiles, hitching down them to plunge toward the ground.

I grabbed him by the neck and lifted him. "Who?"

His feet flailing in the air, he gurgled.

I released him enough so he could breathe.

"Who?" I snarled, pressing my face into his.

Choking, he continued to gasp, unable to suck in air for reasons other than me.

Disgust flooded me, and I lowered him onto his back on the roof, pinning him in place with my boot. "If you tell me who tried to kill Tempest, I'll make this easier for you."

He was dying already, the spell whoever sent him had planted. It was triggered when he failed—no, when I caught him. Whoever had done this made sure he'd never make it off the roof after releasing that bolt. I could smell the taint of the magic in the air.

His death would be a painful one.

Then his lips started moving.

I leaned close enough to hear the hissed name.

With a nod, I ended him and flitted back to Tempest.

23

TEMPEST

My heart hammered against my ribcage. My leg kept spasming from the tumble across the ground. Vexxion had saved my life—again. Before I could ask him what was going on, he disappeared. Like poof. Here, then gone.

Brodine rushed into the training area, leaving the gate wide open, his gaze locked on the arrow. "Fuck, what happened?" He peered around, but I'd already looked. No one was training with a crossbow in the vicinity.

Someone had tried to kill me. Again.

Vexxion magically appeared on the other side of Seevar, his intent gaze landing solidly on me and remaining there. His body wavered, but he stiffened his spine and secured his feet to the ground.

I'd figure out what he'd done later.

Cooing and with my hand extended toward him, I

approached Seevar, my limp more pronounced than ever. At this rate, I wasn't going to be able to walk within a week.

Or I'd be dead. Nice little thought right there.

"Let me look, sweet one," I said softly. "I only want to help." I glanced Brodine's way, finding him glaring at Vexxion. "Go get the animal healer," I barked. He could take his jealousy with him.

Brodine gave me a long look before stalking across the training area. At least he closed the gate when he left. The last thing I needed was for Seevar to escape and take off with an arrow sticking out of his flank.

"Poor sweetie," I said, stroking his thick hide.

He'd lifted his back leg off the ground, and the arrow shook along with his body. Everyone thought dragons were ferocious creatures, but other than the random shooting of flames, they were gentler than a fluffy chall.

"Help's coming." I stroked his face. "He needs to remain still," I told Vexxion. "Movement might sink the arrow deeper."

"He'll be alright."

How could he know? Still, I trusted him. Fancy that, me trusting one of the fae when I'd happily kill them all for how one was running rampant through our lives.

The animal healer raced across the training area, a leather bag in his hand. He took one look at the arrow and nodded, easing closer at a slower pace.

"I need to remove that bolt." He dropped his bag on the sand and opened the top. "Someone will need to hold him." When his gaze fell on me, his lips tightened. "You're too small. He'll hurt you, and then I'll be dealing with two patients."

"I'm not going anywhere." I continued to stroke Seevar's cheeks. He wasn't mortally wounded, but my guts kept twisting and my air kept scissoring inside my throat. "He's hurt, and he needs me."

"I'll help her." Vexxion strode over to stand with me, his arms bracing the dragon's neck.

Seevar's eyes rolled around wildly, but I stared into them, forcing him to look only at me.

"I'm with you, sweet one," I said. "With you. Always."

The beast calmed. He stared at me, his eyes almost glazing.

"Do it," I hissed at the healer.

Frowning, he looked from Seevar to me. "I, what . . .?" He shook his head and tugged equipment out of his bag, moving over to stand beside the dragon's flank. "Deep," he hissed. "Half the shaft's buried. I'll put him on something to prevent infection, but he won't be training or flying for a while."

"Just help him." Whatever band I'd somehow stretched between me and Seevar's mind was fraying, tiny strands snapping, the main line thinning. I couldn't think of any other way to describe it.

The healer jerked the arrow from Seevar's flank. My dragon groaned but remained still, his eyes locked on mine.

"Yes," Vexxion said. I assumed he was speaking to the healer until I glanced his way and noted his gaze fixed on me.

"What?"

"Nothing."

I shrugged him off and returned my attention to Seevar who still stared.

Drask flapped his wings and cawed before settling on my

shoulder once more. He tiptoed closer and pressed his head against my cheek, offering comfort.

"Alright," the healer said with a sigh. He finished securing a bandage over Seevar's wound. "I don't expect that to remain in place for long. When he moves, his scales will shift. It'll loosen and fall off. But for now, it'll keep the ointment in place and give it a chance to sink into the wound. I'll check on him in his aerie later, apply more ointment to the wound." He frowned at me, studying my face. "What did you do?"

"Do?" I asked, still stroking Seevar's cheeks. "Such a good dragon."

"I've never seen even the tamest beasts hold still at a time like this."

I shrugged. "I treat all creatures with kindness. Maybe that makes them trust me."

"Maybe." His frown remaining, the healer packed up his things and left, taking his bag with him.

"Let's get you to your aerie where you can rest," I told Seevar. I grabbed his harness and gently secured it. My heart kept leaping, slamming against the inside of my ribcage. It hurt, but nothing was going to heal me now.

Everything seemed to be falling apart. How could I grab the pieces and hold them together?

Someone had tried to kill me again, and I needed to track them down and eliminate them before they succeeded.

Vexxion knew something. He'd . . . disappeared, and I wasn't sure how. Or where he went for that matter. Damn fae magic.

We led Seevar out of the training area and started across the compound at a slow pace. He huffed as he moved, and each time he winced, I did too.

Vexxion paid more attention to our surroundings than to Seevar.

"Why are you really here?" I asked as we slowly made our way across the open area in front of the main building.

"I told you I needed to speak with the commander."

"A conversation takes moments, not a week or more. You've spoken more with me than him. You never leave my side."

"Maybe I'm enamored with your stimulating conversational skills."

I couldn't even drum up a smile. Kinart was dead, though that couldn't be related to whatever was threatening me. No dreg was smart enough to plan something like this. They followed commands only. The Lieges? They were more than capable of trying to harm me, but there was no motive I could discern. I was one of many riders. One of many trainers. Not someone special.

The king? He didn't even know I existed.

"You don't even like me," I stated.

"What makes you think that?"

"Don't patronize me."

He paused. I did the same. Seevar also stopped, savoring the rest.

"I didn't come here to protect you," he said.

I could read the truth in his words. "Yet you are."

He chipped out a nod.

"It's not because you like me."

"I don't." He blinked.

Ah, he blinked.

I wasn't sure what to think about that. Or what to do about the way my heart stumbled at the realization.

"You contradict yourself, Vexxion," I said.

He said nothing.

"I don't want this," I said. "Whatever I'm dealing with now."

"Yet it found you," he snarled.

"Now there's the fae I've come to know and . . ." Oh, no. I'd never love him.

He started walking again. "We shouldn't talk here."

"Where *can* we talk?"

"Nowhere."

I sighed. "Would you give me a straight answer? Why are you protecting me?"

"Because I have to."

I didn't hear desperation in his voice. Didn't *want* to hear it, that is. "My world is fragmenting." I'd never been one to wallow in self-pity, but I was sorely tempted to do so now.

"You're not alone."

But I was. Always. Even now, speaking with him, that desolate feeling lingered. "Don't go all mushy on me."

"Never," he said with a wry laugh. "Have no fear of that."

We reached the entrance to the aerie. Drask left my shoulder and flew up to land on the roof.

I slowly led Seevar inside. Before, I'd liked that his pen was near the end, less dragons around to disturb him. He benefited from low stimulation. But as he huffed and moved with an awkward gait to the end, I wished his pen was near the front.

"Why would someone want to kill me?" I asked.

"That's a good question."

I held open the gate while Seevar hobbled inside his pen. My leg ached in sympathy. Would I ever have a time when it didn't hurt, when it didn't keep me from doing everything I needed to do? I'd mostly accepted that I was defective, but every now and then, I wanted to be able to move as easily as everyone else.

I was definitely a hindrance here at the fortress.

After making sure he had food and water and that the sand he'd lay on was clean, I secured the top gate to reduce stimulation and leaned against the door, facing Vexxion in the hall. "I think you decided to protect me before someone tried to burn me alive."

"Maybe I've hung around because I've started to feel mushy."

My breath catching, I blinked at him, catching his sly smile. "That's not true." I felt foolish. Childish. Woefully inexperienced when faced with his obvious sophistication.

He shrugged and moved over to lean against the gate beside me. He smelled too good, like spice and leather. Heat and lust.

"You follow me everywhere."

"Not always."

"Other than your new kitchen position, though I only see you working when I want food. You're no more interested in working in the kitchen than me."

"I like to cook."

I turned to face him, bracing my shoulder against the gate and taking the weight off my bad leg. "Really?"

He flashed a smile that made my heart tumble. I feared it would never right itself again. "Really."

I wanted to growl, to find some reason to hold myself back from him, but he was making it incredibly difficult. He was too gorgeous, too . . . No, sweet wasn't the right word, but it would do for now. "You've been all over me from the moment you got here—to only speak with the commander, you said. You didn't leave after."

"I like it here."

"We're on the edge of the border. Dregs attack almost on a daily basis. It's cloudy more than the sun shines and it gets freeze-your-ass cold in the winter. No one likes it here."

"You do."

Did I? "I've lived here most of my life. It's . . . home, I guess." Damn, I sounded pitiful saying that.

"You guess?"

"I don't have anything else." And damn me for croaking that statement. I didn't like feeling, not anything. Not after this shit of a life I'd lived, the way my stupid leg held me back, and Kinart's death.

Kinart.

I pinched my eyes closed but that only made it worse. I could see him lying in that cavern, ripped apart. I could still hear Reyla's wails.

"Maybe you need to stop analyzing everything all the time." He sounded close, like I could step forward and suck in his warmth and the dubious comfort he provided.

"I want to stop aching all the time." The words were wrenched out of me. "I feel pain here," I tapped my thigh that hurt something fierce, "here," and my head, "and especially here." This time, I laid my palm over my heart. "How do you make it stop?"

"I'm not sure you can," he rasped. "Believe me, I've tried."

Opening my eyes, my gaze fell to the network of scars snaking up from his shirt collar. A fierce need to defend this man roared through me. I wanted to ask, *Who the fuck hurt you,* but I didn't, biting my lips to hold back the words. If I had a name, I'd have to add them to my kill list.

His gaze fell on my mouth and stayed there. I'd kissed enough guys to know that Vexxion's were special. And that terrified me almost as much as the thought of losing another friend in battle.

I'd never thought I'd feel anything for one of the fae, yet I *craved* this man like no other. He was beautiful with his unruly dark hair outlining that wicked strip of silver. A blaze of lightning, it was. His scars coiling around his throat only added to his appeal.

And his mouth . . . His lips were slightly puffy, and they'd felt pillowy against mine—until his kiss turned demanding. Then it was like drinking from fire, breathing it down, fusing parts of me to him in a way I'd never imagined possible.

If he agreed to what I'd soon ask, because I could see I had no other choice, would it change the dynamic between us? I suspected it would, and I wasn't sure if I should welcome that change with open arms or turn and bolt in the opposite direction. I'd be safer if I fled, but I suspected I'd miss out on something utterly perfect. Something that could change me completely.

His breathing whispered around me, and if I listened closely, I could almost hear the secrets he held back. When had I gone from disliking him to knowing that if he brushed past me now and left the aerie, I'd lose everything?

His fingers smoothed back the loose strands of hair that had slipped from my braid, bundling them against the rest as if that would keep them secure. That done, his fingertips traced across the quivering nape of my neck. His eyes never left mine, and flickers of light like tiny stars flashed through them. He was as vast and mysterious as the night sky.

I should back away. Tell him to keep his hands to himself.

Instead, I leaned closer.

"You're full of energy," he sighed. "It shoots out of you like sunbeams at dawn. Why can't I walk away from you like every other?"

Jealousy scraped across my skin, leaving me exposed and raw. "It's never good to mention one woman to another."

"No one can compare to you."

The words thrilled through me, making my body come alive for the very first time. I'd barely existed before I met him.

"And yet you warned me not to fall in love with you," I pointed out.

"I did." His other hand came up to trace up and down my arm, making tingles turn into flames that threatened to consume me alive.

"Did you change your mind?"

"I can't." The anguish in his words gave me pause.

I was too far gone in this moment—in him—to back away

now. I stepped closer to him, eliminating the distance, pressing myself against his hard, unyielding frame.

His fingers coiled around my braid, and he tugged on it, tipping my face up, making my eyes lock on his. I never wanted to look away.

This attraction between us was going to either eat me alive or save me. Need coiled low in my belly, a greedy warmth I couldn't deny. I was playing a dangerous game that might shove me off a very steep cliff. Yet I couldn't make myself leave him.

"Saying stuff like that might make me *like* you, Vex," I said.

"Don't like me either."

"What if it's too late?"

"Then we're both doomed."

He jerked me against his rock-hard frame, and his mouth crashed down on mine with a need that nearly drove me to my knees.

How could I deny *this*—deny this man anything?

His hands loosened on my upper arms, stroking around to my back, gliding up and down until one worked its way into my hair once more. With a groan, he tipped my head, angling my mouth so he could literally devour me.

His tongue parted my lips and slid inside. I expected his need to fuse with mine, to become ravenous, demanding. But he gentled his touch, still drinking from my lips while giving back tenfold.

Heat spiraled through me, tightening and loosening, crashing through my body in waves that made me moan from his simple touch. How was I going to go on? How was I going to breathe if he stopped kissing me?

I was greedy, climbing him, wrapping my arms around his neck and clinging while jerking my legs up to latch onto his hips.

We tumbled down to the sand; me straddling him while he held me tight. He deepened our kiss, groaning as he rolled us until I lay beneath him, his hips pinning mine to the sandy floor.

I went feral, wild and consumed by a fever only this man could tame. I cupped his head with my palm and dragged him down on top of me, needing his hardness, his touch.

His fingers roamed up and down my side before sliding beneath the thin top I wore beneath my leather tunic.

An insatiable need bellowed through me. Wiggling, I urged him up but only long enough to wrench at the fastenings of my leather shirt keeping my skin away from his touch. I wrenched it off and ripped the thin top over my head.

His smoldering gaze flicked from my eyes to my breasts and his face . . . softened. "Fury. My fury," he growled before his hot mouth captured my nipple and sucked.

Tracing his hand across my belly, he slid it between my legs, cupping me through the leather.

He rolled my nipple between his teeth and tongue, the slight pinch exquisite.

Fuck, fuck, fuck. I bowed my spine, driving my breast into his mouth, unable to hold back the moans erupting from my throat. My hitched cries echoed in the aerie, and the dragons behind the gates shifted and hissed.

I should stop him, wrench myself out from beneath him, but I couldn't. I was lost in him, lost in this moment. Anyone could walk in on us, and that only heightened the pleasure I found from his touch.

His palm raked up and down my side before he started stroking my left thigh, making circles. Slowly driving that hand closer to my core again. When he slid his palm between my legs, my guttural groan rang out.

Looking up at me, he continued to stroke the hard bud of my nipple with his tongue. His hand paused between my legs, and I read it in his eyes. He wouldn't take this further unless I told him it was alright.

And that crushed me more than anything. With anyone else and by this time, he'd be wrenching his pants and mine aside and taking what he needed, whether I was ready or not. I hadn't been forced, but sometimes, it would've been nice for the guy to ask before claiming what I had to offer.

"Yes." I stroked his hair, my touch sweet and endearing. That scared me more than anything. When I battled with dregs, I could thrust aside my fear to focus on the battle. With Vexxion, I felt exposed, incredibly vulnerable. He could strip off my armor with one glance and seek out the quivering me hiding beneath.

I didn't like feeling this way, but I was too far gone in his gaze and his touch. It would sever my soul from my body if I refused him.

He undid my pants with a gentleness I'd never expected. This male was all hard edges and gritty demands. He wasn't kind or sweet. He took what he wanted with sharp precision.

Except now, with me.

With a soft smile, he parted my pants and eased them

down. When I lay naked beneath him with only the leather between me and the sand, he took a long moment just to look. "You're beautiful. Perfect."

My hand snaked down between us, my fingers spreading wide as if I could cover the scars consuming most of my left thigh. "Not my leg."

"Everything," he breathed. He nudged my hand to the side and replaced it with his own, softly stroking before moving his fingertips lightly across the network of ridges. He knew just where to press and where to lighten his touch.

When I was a quivering wreck, dazed if I had to name it, he eased my thighs apart and crawled between them. He continued to rub my legs, drawing out my gasping bites of pleasure. How could such a simple thing bring me this much joy?

My body melted beneath him, becoming utterly compliant. I surrendered, willing him to do with me whatever he pleased.

And oh, he pleased.

With a curl of his sensual mouth, he lifted my legs onto his shoulders and growled. "I've been aching to taste you forever."

"You haven't known me forever."

"Oh, but I have."

Before I could question him or even frown, he dove between my legs and licked from my entrance to my clit.

My sharp gasp jerked out of me, needy and demanding.

When he slid a finger inside me, I arched my spine and hitched out a cry.

"Like that," he mumbled around my saturated flesh. "Be a good girl for me and show me how beautifully you come."

"Like, this second? Talk about a quick buffet."

He growled at my tease and the look in his eyes told me I was going to pay. Then he focused on my clit, sucking on it. Needling it with his teeth in a way that made me press my thighs against his head. I couldn't take it, but I never wanted it to end.

His finger pumped into me, pulling out before plunging back inside. He added more, and I gasped at the exquisite stretch. His mouth was all over my clit, his tongue dragging across it while I whimpered and moaned.

I writhed beneath him, so far into this I didn't care if I ever found a way back.

His finger took over for his tongue that glided down to dip inside me, alternating with his fingers. I crested and ebbed backward. I was a storm at sea, roaring toward the shore, only to retreat to gather the strength to blast through anything in its path once more.

And when I crashed, I sensed this man would devastate me in a way no one else ever had.

He devoured every bit of me, driving his tongue inside before gliding it up to drag across my clit. His other hand slid up to find my nipple, and when he rolled it, my shriek rang out. I began cascading, my body tightening before easing, climbing so high, I didn't think I could stand it.

"Come," he crooned.

And just like that, I did, giving into his call while giving in to the dangerous pleasure vibrating through every fiber of my body.

He pumped faster, harder, pushing me for another. I couldn't resist.

His fingers finally slowed inside me, stroking while he brought me back down. And when I finally collapsed beneath him, he shifted back onto his haunches.

He watched me as he slowly licked all that was left of me off his fingers.

24

TEMPEST

*H*is gentleness continued when he helped me dress and as he lifted me and carried me all the way to my residence. Drask cawed when we appeared outside and rather than seeking my shoulder, he swooped above us, soaring back and forth like a tipsy hawk looking for prey in the deep grass.

Vexxion left me outside the door with only a soft stroke of his knuckles down my cheek.

Afraid if I opened my mouth to ask questions, I'd instead make demands or that I'd ask him to stay, I bit down on my lips. I didn't like needing him this much, didn't like feeling consumed by someone. I could barely tell where I ended, and he began.

I let him turn and walk away. I didn't call out to him. I didn't beg.

I wasn't going to love him.

I *wasn't.*

~

THE NEXT MORNING, when I left my residence dressed in my usual leathers and with my hair neatly braided, the thick strand twisting down my spine, Vexxion was waiting. He bumped off the outer wall and stepped into pace beside me as I headed toward the dining area.

Drask cawed and made short, crooked swooping passes in front of us like a swallow seeking flies.

I still wasn't sure how to look at Vexxion or what to say. What we'd done . . . What he'd done . . . I couldn't figure out how to deal with it.

"Still following me?" I said pleasantly.

"Still toying with a tantrum, temper?"

Sighing, I stopped in the middle of the compound. People streamed around us, some going to eat, others heading toward the aerie. "Before my friends join me, is there something you need to say?"

His eyebrows slashed upward. "What would I have to say?" Leaning near my ear, he lowered his voice to a raspy drawl. "That I'd rather eat you for breakfast than anything inside the dining area?"

I reeled away from him, not because his words or tone shocked me, but because my body was ready to melt all over again, as if I still lay on the aerie floor with his head between my legs.

"I've decided I do like you," he declared.

Lovely. Just lovely. "Decided, huh?"

"I like you," he growled.

While his statement trilled through me, he was fae, and I should never fully trust him. Use him, yes, but trust took time and had to be built, not just handed over because a man was hot, and he ate me out so well.

"Wanting and liking are completely different things," he said, striding around me, aiming for the dining area. "Coming?"

I already had. And I wanted to do it again. Fuck, fuck, fuck.

"You're saying you're fine with me craving your body, but I need to keep heavier emotions out of the equation." I hurried forward to catch up to him.

We entered the dining area, and I joined the line.

He eased backward, clearly heading for the kitchen once more. "That's about right."

"Why are you doing all this?" I flicked my hand toward the kitchen.

"Someone has tried to kill you three times now," he said softly.

My breath jerked into my lungs. "Three? The fire could've been caused by almost anything."

"It wasn't."

I tapped a second finger. "The crossbow bolt was the second attempt, though that could've been random. People practice with crossbows here all the time. Sometimes we attack the dregs from a distance. We cut down their numbers first, then go in with swords slashing to clean up the rest."

"Do your archers practice from the top of the main building's roof?"

Not there. My appetite swallowed my belly. I struggled to breathe through a choked-off throat. "You said three," I croaked.

He strode right up to me, and I stepped backward. He leaned close—his scent and the warmth of his body nearly driving me to my knees—once again. "Someone was tampering with your food."

With that, he pivoted and left, nudging the door open and entering the kitchen.

Tampering, like trying to poison me?

Brodine entered the big open room, his gaze locking on me. He swaggered toward me with the ghost of Reyla drifting behind him, her mindless gaze focused on nothing.

"Still haven't gotten rid of your new friend?" he asked with an edge in his voice I didn't like.

"We're not actually friends." Though I had no idea *what* we were instead.

"That's good." He urged me forward, and we joined the back of the line.

"Hey, Reyla," I said. Her eyes were milky with vagueness, and she didn't hug me like always. She also didn't ask me about Vexxion or if I was going to work with the golden dragon this morning.

A wraith had consumed her body, as if she'd eaten nothing in weeks and hadn't slept in years. Her reddish-blonde hair hung in straggly bands around her pretty face. I'd always envied how gorgeous she was. My best friend was fading, and I couldn't do a thing about it.

"How are you?" I asked, rubbing her arm.

She shrugged, her eyes shimmering. "I don't feel anything, and I think that's a great way to live."

But she wasn't living.

"After breakfast, I'll go with you to your residence and help you get cleaned up," I said.

"Why bother?"

Ahead of us, Brodine took his tray of food and stepped to the side, waiting for us to be served.

"I want to talk to you." I needed to find out the real reason she was volunteering for the Claiming. She'd never said anything about being interested in something like that. None of us had. Getting away from here wasn't a good enough excuse.

Was she hoping for someone to claim her then kill her? My friend wasn't one who'd do such a thing to herself, but she wasn't above driving someone else to do it for her. Except . . . Look at her. She was killing herself before my eyes.

"Alright," she said, staring forward blankly.

Vexxion handed me my tray while the lady behind the counter took care of Reyla, and my friends and I shambled over to an empty table, sitting. Vexxion soon joined us with his own meal.

Brodine growled.

I ate, feeding Drask tidbits of my horig cake he gobbled up, leaving crumbs on my shoulder.

Vexxion said nothing, just ate as well.

I couldn't stop thinking about what he'd said about my food. Being fae, he could use magic to discover if something had been poisoned, which explained him glaring at my horig cakes. Knowing someone here wanted me dead was enough to make me nudge everything around on my plate without taking a bite.

Vexxion leaned close and snatched up one of my horig cakes, stuffing the entire thing into his mouth and reminding me that as sharp as his angles were, he wasn't much older than me. What had happened to mold him into the intent, determined man I saw now? And who gave him those scars?

The twist in my chest meant nothing. I wasn't feeling sympathy toward him. Fates, he'd snarl if he thought I was. I just...

Despite telling myself I wouldn't do it; I was close to falling for him.

The door opened and his friends walked in, striding over to stand on his side. One leaned close and spoke in too low a voice for me to hear.

"I thought they left," Brodine said, glancing that way, voicing the thought as if he'd plucked it from my mind.

"So did I. It appears they've come back." To take Vexxion with them? I should welcome that, right? I watched as they spoke to each other, only one of them looking my way.

Brodine smacked my arm, though not hard enough to make me wince. "If you gape at Vexxion long enough, he might ask you to the ball."

"We don't hold a ball."

"My point stands."

"I'm not staring at him."

"You are. Take him to your bed," he snapped. "Get him out of your system. Then you can focus on more important things."

Important things meaning him.

Reyla sat on the opposite side of the table, her gaze shifting between us. She hadn't touched her food. When I left, I'd wrap the cakes on her plate and make her eat them.

"I don't want him," I said. A complete lie. Since last night, it was all I could think about. Maybe I *should* take him to my bed and get him out of my system. He might be total crap between the sheets and then I could put him from my mind and focus on killing the fae king who'd not only murdered Kinart but who was doing all he could to destroy the Nullen realm. He must hope to claim this territory too.

Brodine leaned near, and I prepared myself to smack him if he did something stupid like put his arm around me or tease his fingertips up and down my face. Gestures I used to welcome when they weren't manifested to drive my emotions in the wrong direction.

Instead of touching me, he tugged something from beneath my plate and dangled it in front of my face.

A clear green stone the size of my thumbnail hung from the thin golden chain, catching the sunlight and shattering it into shards of every color of emerald imaginable.

"From you?" I croaked, my gaze seeking Vexxion's.

He studied the stone, his gaze moving to lock on mine.

"That's pabrilleen, isn't it?" Reyla asked, coming out of her stupor long enough to frown at the twirling stone.

"It matches your eyes," Brodine said softly. "Perfectly."

"Is it from you?" I growled.

Bro shrugged and gave me a lopsided smile.

I snatched it from the air, tugging it out of his grip, and stuffed it into my pocket.

Standing, I took a cloth and placed Reyla's horig cakes on top of it, wrapping them snug. I stacked our trays and walked around to her side. "Let's go."

Her lower lip jutted forward. "I decided I don't want to bathe."

"I told you I also need to talk."

"I don't want to do that either."

I didn't want to make a scene, but I had to shake my friend out of this. Kinart would be horrified to think she was giving up. He'd want her to live, to find a way to be happy if she could.

My emotions were being driven by a purpose when I sensed she had none.

I grabbed her arm to tug her up, but she wrenched away. She did stand, however, leaving her chair on the other side and stalking toward the exit.

"Get the trays, would you?" I asked Brodine. I hurried after Reyla, Drask bobbing on my shoulder.

Outside, Reyla reeled around to face me.

Drask took one look at her, squawked, and flew to land on the top of the squat building.

"Stop following me," Reyla snarled. "Stop trying to help me."

"I can't do anything else. You know that."

Vexxion came through the door and leaned against the wall. I had no idea where his friends were now. Perhaps they'd taken over his duties in the kitchen while he followed me.

I wanted to tell him to go away, but he wouldn't.

Why take on the role of my bodyguard? It irritated me, but it also made me question everything he did. I was nobody, certainly not someone a fae lord might find worth saving.

"Will you do this for me?" I asked Reyla, taking her hand, something we used to do back when life was rosy. Kinart would laugh and tell us we could be a threesome, though I knew he was only teasing.

I missed him. His laughter. The way he gave such amazing hugs. And how he always told me I had value.

The world was a gloomy place without him.

"Alright," Reyla huffed.

Pleased she didn't tug away, I urged her toward her residence and took her inside, shutting the door in Vexxion's face. Inside, I sat her in a chair and put the wrapped horig cakes on her lap. "Eat at least one."

"They taste like sand."

"They do to me too. I hate this. Hate that we lost him."

She snarled, glaring up at me. "We didn't *lose* him. He was fucking slaughtered."

I jerked out a nod. "He loved you more than anything."

Her shoulders slumped, the energy from her outburst whooshing out of her. "He was all I had to live for." She fingered the edge of the cloth holding the horig cakes. "I'm only going through the motions. I used to think that was a stupid thing to say, but it's true. Now I get it."

"So do I."

She unwrapped the horig cakes and lifted one, biting and chewing, speaking around it. "I can't sleep. I don't want to eat. I don't want to do anything, though I know I have to." Her fierce gaze met mine. "There's only one thing I want to do."

"What's that?"

"Kill dregs."

"Both of us. All of them."

"Yes." Finishing the first cake, she ate the other.

My heart lightened. I couldn't bring Kinart back, but I could do my best to protect Reyla.

After she'd eaten, I dragged her to the bathing room and made her strip and shower. I handed her clothing to don after she'd dried, and while she remained listless, she did as I asked. Back out in the living area, we sat on the sofa. Tears trickled down her damp cheeks. I wanted to weep too, but how could I? Someone had to remain strong, and I'd always been the one who had that extra bit of something inside me. Maybe because I kept everyone at a distance, even my friends.

"Tell me why you're going to the Claiming," I said. "The real reason."

She stared straight ahead, still crying. "Brodine told me to do it."

What the . . .? "Why would he do something like that?"

She shrugged. "It doesn't matter. I probably would've thought of it myself. A few of us have to go, so why not me? I don't care what happens to me now. Might as well let some random fae collar me and turn me into their servant. At least I'll have a purpose fulfilling his or her commands."

"No one should do something like this on a whim."

Her head cocked, and she actually looked at me with curiosity. "Why are *you* doing it then?"

Revenge. "Probably for the same reason."

I had no choice in this now and not because I'd made my

wishes clear to the commander. If Reyla was going, so was I. Now I had to make sure we ended up together. Feeling responsible for my friend wasn't a burden; I welcomed the chance to do *something*.

Her arm went around my shoulders. "I miss him. I'm going to love him forever. But I'm glad I've still got you and Bro."

"We've got Bro until we leave." I'd miss him too. A lot. But what I'd miss most was the guy I grew up with, not the man he'd turned into when his proprietary gaze landed on me.

"Didn't he tell you? He's going too. It'll be the three of us."

"What?"

"Yeah, he volunteered just like us." Reyla snorted. "This is a first."

"What do you mean?"

"Three volunteers. The commander must be thrilled. Usually, they have to drag those selected to dragons and pretty much tie them down to get them to the Claiming."

"Why is Brodine doing this?" Actually, I didn't need to ask. "He heard I was going, didn't he?" I purposefully hadn't told him but someone had. Who?

"Yeah, I guess so. Isn't it great?" She didn't smile. She didn't even look at me. Her voice lacked inflection. "Maybe we'll get claimed by fae in the same court and can stay together."

"Maybe." I was going to owe someone a ton of favors.

Eventually, I stood. "I need to go see the golden dragon." Should I go to the commander again and beg him to send the three of us to Bledmire Court? Maybe Reyla and Brodine should go somewhere else. I wouldn't want to drag them into my scheme. If I failed . . . I didn't want to think of what the king might do if he thought they were involved.

"Don't let that dragon burn you," she said as I opened the door.

"Dragons love me. None of them want to burn me."

"I suppose." Whatever animation she'd drummed up was gone. She sniffed, and tears continued to trickle from her eyes. At least she'd eaten. At least she'd bathed. Small steps, a few at a time.

"I'll find you for lunch," I said.

She didn't say a thing.

Vexxion waited outside with Drask on the ground beside him. New friends? I didn't ask. Drask soared up and landed on my shoulder.

Vexxion followed me to the aerie. The animal healer was there, examining Seevar. He stepped out of the pen and nodded to me, frowning when his gaze landed on Vexxion.

"I can't believe it," the healer said.

Was something horribly wrong with Seevar? I should've come here first thing rather than squabble with Vexxion on my way to breakfast.

"Nothing's wrong," the healer said, patting my shoulder. "I was told you were taking this dragon with you to the Claiming, and I'd planned to suggest that you have him sent later, give him more time to heal before flying. But he's made a miraculous recovery."

This, I had to see. I moved past him, entering the stall, and Seevar huffed and shot sparks my way.

"Nice to see you this morning too." I stroked along his side to reach the flank that had been wounded, where I gently probed the area that was not only scabbed over but didn't appear as deep as it had the day before.

"As you can see, he's doing very well. I plan to tell the commander I've released the dragon from my care. You're welcome to either ride him or tether him to a different mount while you travel to the Claiming."

How was this possible?

The slight smile on Vexxion's face smoothed when he caught my eye. If he kept doing nice things, I wasn't going to be able to resist him.

"I'll look at him one more time early tomorrow, but I'd say you're clear to fly." The healer left.

"What did you do?" I asked Vexxion softly. I ran my fingertip along the wound on my arm the dreg gave me in the cave. I'd always healed fast, but never this fast. Vexxion's touch as well?

"I don't know what you mean."

"Alright. Sure." I gave Seevar a bunch of pats and returned to the hall, securing his gate.

I'd give Seevar another day to fully recover, because we were leaving for the Claiming tomorrow morning, and he would need to fly.

"Thank you for helping him." My voice came out gruff.

We walked toward the exit.

"It sounds like you had a hard time saying thanks," he said. "Do you need more practice?"

"Don't push it."

He laughed; a full, robust sound that made me freeze in

place. It was all I could do not to gape at him because, damn, he was even prettier when he was happy.

I led a different dragon out to the training area, but today's work was anticlimactic. The light blue dragon loved being ridden. He adored being groomed. And he lifted his feet for claw oil before I could give them a tap.

"I'll sign off on this one when I return him to the aerie," I said when I'd landed him for the fifth time. He'd perfectly executed my commands. In combat, our dragons needed to do exactly what we told them. If they didn't, we could die.

Upon returning him to his stall in the aerie, we rubbed him down and gave him food and water.

Outside, I leaned against the closed gate.

When Vexxion eased into place beside me, I shifted to my left. I wasn't going down that path again. He was right, it would be a huge mistake to love him, and my feelings weren't only driven by what happened to Kinart.

Loving Vexxion could destroy me, which meant I had to keep my heart in line.

"I need you to do something new for me." The words burst from my throat, husky and raw.

His gaze fell on my mouth. Truly, he needed to help me out here and not do things like that. The heat in his eyes made my insides flip over and my heart thud faster than it should. "What do you need?"

"Can any fae lord take me to Bledmire Court?"

"Yes."

The smolder fled his eyes, replaced with the sharpness I'd seen the first day he arrived. He was all business now with any thought of pleasure shoved to the side. What would it be like to be able to turn my emotions on and off like that?

"Claim me."

The catch of his breath told me I'd surprised him. A feat for me. At least he'd dragged his attention off my mouth. "Are you actually suggesting that—"

"Collar me at the Claiming and take me to Bledmire Court."

"Why would I want to do that?" Death had edged into his voice.

"I don't trust anyone else. It's pointless to be claimed by someone who can't get me inside. You could do that for me."

"And what if I don't want to take you there?"

"I'll make a deal with someone else."

He growled. "No one will make a deal with you but me, Tempest. You need to back away from this plan. You won't live more than moments after you walk through the front door. And if he discovers what you hope to do, your death won't come quickly."

"I have to try."

"You shouldn't trust me, not even in this."

I huffed. "Don't worry. I don't trust you *that* much." Stepping toward him, I lowered my voice. We were alone, but that didn't mean someone outside might not overhear us. "I need help on the inside. That person could be you."

"You don't want this. Go build a pretty life and forget you ever spoke with the Liege."

"I can't. Don't you see? I can't. My need for revenge . . . Not just revenge, but my need to end this permanently, is going to scorch through me if I don't let it out."

"Then go kill a bunch of dregs. I'll cover your back. Get it all out with your blade and throw away this asinine plan that will never succeed."

"I can kill him."

"Don't you see? You *can't* do this. Not as you are." His voice dropped to a dark whisper. "You'd need a lifetime of training, and even then, it wouldn't be enough. An Awakening and then more training."

"What's an Awakening?"

"You don't need the definition unless you're claimed."

"I guess I'll find out soon, then, because I'm going to the Claiming, and I'm going to beg whoever claims me to take me to Bledmire."

"They'll kill you."

"For asking to go to the most impressive court?" I batted my eyelashes and simpered. "Please, gorgeous fae lord. I've been nothing all my life. But if I can serve in Bledmire Court, I'll feel as if my life's complete. In fact, I'll make it very much worth your while."

He latched onto my upper arms, though his grip was surprisingly gentle, a direct contradiction to his face. He fumed. "Do not offer yourself to anyone but me."

I shrugged away from him, backing up a few steps and lowering my voice to a normal tone. "You turned me down."

Swearing, he slammed his fingers through his hair hard enough to rip it out.

"There are too many secrets surrounding this process," I said. "Frankly, I'd be stupid if I wasn't scared about how this might turn out. I'm a lowly Nullen with no past and no future, but if I don't try, I'll never forgive myself."

I would not be the failure so many called me behind my back.

"Claim me," I said. "Just do it. Bring me to Bledmire Court and dump me if that makes you feel better. You can forget you ever knew me."

"Why do you think that would make me feel better? Why do you think I want to forget you?" He strode right up to me and grabbed my arms again. "You really want me to claim you?"

"I do." For good or for bad, I was all in.

His gaze locked on mine. "Once I claim you, there's no turning back. I'll *own* you, Tempest."

I lifted my chin. "It doesn't have to be permanent."

"Collaring is for forever."

Fear flashed through me. "There's no way out?"

"Only through death. Some lords . . ."

"What?"

"If they get tired of the Nullen they've claimed, they eliminate them. They can only own one at a time."

"We should know this before we're sent to the Claiming."

"In the treaty, it states we don't need to tell you anything about it. Nullens agreed, and that's that. Once collared, you're under fae control. You won't like this. You'll rebel. You're too cocky, too impulsive and damn you, but your wildness is going to get you killed." Shaking his head, he swallowed.

The anguish in his voice stunned me.

"You said the collar ensures cooperation, but it also gives *access*," I whispered. "What does that mean?"

"Access to whatever you have to offer."

"You mean sex."

He shrugged. "For some, though not all the fae."

That wasn't reassuring, but the time for taking the easy road had long since passed. I'd forged a new course when I left the Liege's cave. Seeing Kinart dead only tightened my resolve to do what was right.

"I can't think of another way to get to him, can you?" I spoke in a reasonable tone because Vexxion was quite eager to protect me. I still needed to find out why, but that conversation was for later. "He's controlling all this, sending dregs and Lieges after us. They're going to overrun every fortress soon and there will be nothing to stop them from swarming across the continent after that. They'll drain and kill every man, woman, and child, giving that energy to him. I can only imagine what he's doing with it. Soon, there will be none of us left."

"If nothing else, that'll stop the annual Claiming," he said dryly.

"I'm not letting this go."

"You're foolish. You don't realize the risk you're taking."

"I risk my life every time I go on a raid or defend a village. What's the difference?"

He said nothing. Probably because there was nothing left to say.

"Claim me. We'll find a way to get the collar off after this is over without killing me. If you can get me to Bledmire Court, I'll owe you ... whatever."

His head tilted. "A favor?"

Never give favors to the fae. They'll twist it. Use you. Then toss you aside. I couldn't remember where I'd heard that, but remembering sent stark, raving terror slicing across my soul.

I wasn't giving up. I couldn't.

Fates, I hated to say the words, but I did. "Please, Vexxion."

His long sigh bled out, and he jerked his hands off my arms, backing away with them lifted. "Alright. I'll do it."

25

VEXXION

Once Tempest was asleep with a ward surrounding her room, I made my move. Since I wanted to conserve power, I made a short flit from the hall outside the commander's office, cloaked in the threads I'd learned to call and then master before I turned six. *No one* could see through my threads of lightning, as I joyfully named them once I'd embraced them. If anyone glanced in my direction, all they saw was the image of what was behind me. My threads projected it.

I clenched my hands into fists at my sides, my nails biting into my palms. Opened them. Snapped them closed once more.

Then I released my threads, and they plunged down to weave around my legs. Coiling. Eager. Waiting.

"As you know, I'm leaving the fortress soon to escort the three Nullens to the Claiming," I told the commander who sat at his desk, unaware I'd arrived.

He fumbled the papers on his desk and stood fast enough to

nearly topple his chair backward. "I . . . I'm terribly sorry. *Sir!* I didn't see you enter."

Because I didn't want him to see me enter.

"You're leaving the fortress, you say?" he blustered. "It's been . . . delightful having you here."

"Delightful."

"You told me you were staying for an indefinite time, but you never mentioned exactly why you remained."

"I didn't."

His face drained of color. "And, of course, I don't need to know. How . . . foolish of me to mention it. It's only . . . I've been . . . curious."

"Something you should guard against."

He collapsed back in his chair. "You're right." His swallow took a long time to go down. "Once you've returned, you'll do what you promised?"

It hadn't been a promise, but an offer. "I told you I would."

"Oh, oh," he sputtered, his face now florid. "Yes, you did. I deeply apologize for mentioning it."

"However . . ."

His eyes bulged, but he kept his mouth shut. See? He *could* learn and rather quickly.

Not quickly enough.

I advanced toward him, placing my palms on his desk with my threads of lightning hissing around my feet, reflecting the wooden floorboards below.

"I've reconsidered," I said.

"Um, what in particular?" His eyes darted to the door to the outer room and the hall.

"I won't speak with him," I said.

His air jerked back and forth, and his hands twitched on his thighs. "Why not?"

At my command, my threads swarmed, flowing around and under the desk in a shocking silver wave.

He cried out when they reached him, when they snaked around his legs, torso, and neck, sinking their teeth into him—though only lightly for now.

"Who?" I asked quite pleasantly. I straightened, watching shadows bolt through his eyes.

"I don't... What are you talking about?" he shrieked.

"The man who shot a crossbow at Tempest named you, but you're not acting alone. *Who* wants to kill her?" Only a taste of the anger churning inside me since the bolt impaled Seevar in the flank came through in my voice.

My fury had come too close to dying.

"I... I..." He raked his fingers across his throat, trying to wedge them between my threads and his neck.

I tightened them and stalked around his desk to lean close to his ear. "Who?"

Gone was my façade. My beast had taken his rightful place, and he *raged*.

"Tell me," I growled low. My restraint hung on a wisp.

His face darkened. He scrambled his fingers across my threads, clawing at them, but they'd already sunk too deeply to be dislodged by anyone but me.

"I... can't," he hissed. "You... understand."

"Do you truly believe this person is worse than me?" Impatience writhed beneath my skin, and it was all I could do to rein back the power slashing its way through me.

He'd *hurt* her.

"You're ... no one," he snarled. "Just a fae messenger."

"I don't believe I formally introduced myself when I arrived," I whispered into his ear. "Some call me the beast." I spoke so low, even someone using magic in the next room would not be able to overhear. But he could.

He flailed in his chair, his face darkening to match the rich fessalile wood his lovely desk had been crafted from. "No!"

I gripped his shoulders, pinning him in place. "I only need a name. You can whisper it. No one will hear but me."

Unable to draw wind to speak, he could only nod.

I loosened the threads and gave him a smile that made the lightning crackle.

His eyes blazed with terror, but he gave me the information I needed.

"Very good." I turned away from him, striding around the desk.

He thrashed in his chair, his feet thumping on the floor in a rhythmic fashion. He'd tried to kill Tempest. He'd been so close that my soul still trembled.

Now that I knew who'd given him the command, nothing else mattered here.

As he gurgled for the last time, I flitted from his office.

I left my threads behind to feed.

26

TEMPEST

The next morning, there was an uproar at the main compound building, shouts and cries of shock.

By then, I'd already mounted Seevar with my paltry belongings stuffed into a bag and lashed to his side. After giving Fawna lots of kisses and treats and telling her I'd love her forever, I'd flown Seevar to the top of the aerie, landing on the roof to wait with my friends.

I was taking a chance flying Seevar across the continent to the eastern border where the Claiming would take place, but I hated to tether him and tug him behind. This would be an excellent time to continue his training. His wound was completely healed, and by the way he'd danced in his pen when I entered, butting me playfully in the side, he needed to expend some energy. What better way than flying?

Drask clung to my shoulder. He'd remain there for most of the journey, though he'd probably peel off periodically to fly on his own. We'd travel for three days and camp three nights, arriving at the ceremonial area partway into the fourth day. Our general traveling supplies had been bound to an unmounted dragon who'd travel with us.

"What's going on over there?" Brodine asked from nearby, mounted on the dragon he'd been assigned for the journey. He stared toward the central area of the compound.

"I have no idea." I squinted in that direction, seeing people rushing from the main building, others hurrying inside. "It's not a raid or an attack or we'd know it." I looked toward the horns mounted on the top of the building, as if viewing them would make them bellow.

If they did, we'd only be able to wish the riders well. We needed to leave today if we wanted to reach the eastern border on time.

Reyla slumped on her dragon on the other side of Bro, staring at nothing. She hadn't said a word when I packed her belongings, such as they were after the fire, then led her to the aerie and helped her mount.

Vexxion's friends waited a short distance away, shifting too often on the backs of their dragons.

Were they fae as well?

I didn't like the way one of them watched Reyla. Farnoll. Yes, that was his name. I remembered Vexxion mentioning it the first time they came to the fortress. I caught his eye and gave him a glare. She was much too vulnerable to repel a lure.

We'd all had minimal training in blocking magical intrusions into our minds. It was part of our regular education here, a holdover from the days when Nullens interacted with the fae on a regular basis.

Now I understood why they trained us. They'd kept up the classes because they suspected the wicked fae wouldn't respect the treaty.

As for Vexxion, I hadn't seen him yet, though I wasn't concerned. He wouldn't change his mind. We had an agreement, and he wasn't going to let me out of his sight until I was collared.

My skin quivered at the thought. The first chance I got, I was going to ask him more about the process and exactly what he'd do with me once he *owned* me. There would be time once we arrived at the area where they held the ceremony. I remembered hearing the Claiming didn't take place until the day after everyone got there.

Vexxion's dragon flew out of its aerie, and he banked it around, landing it lightly on the roof near his friends. "I'm leading the group."

Brodine's eyebrows lifted, and his gaze shot my way. "Why you?"

"Maybe he came here to collect us," I said. My gaze caught Vexxion's, and I gave him a subtle nod, urging to use that excuse for remaining at the fortress.

"Maybe," was all he said.

Reyla ignored the conversation and continued to stare at her hands writhing on her lap.

"What's happening at the compound?" I asked, peering back that way but seeing nothing new.

Vexxion's gaze lingered on me, his eyes drifting down my front as if assessing me. "No idea."

"Should we wait to make sure everything's alright?" Brodine asked. He edged his dragon between mine and Vexxion's. "They may need us."

"It's too late," I said. "They'll have to learn to get by without us. We . . ." My gaze met Vexxion's. "The fae own us now."

Brodine huffed. "No one's going to own me."

There was a time when I'd take his hand and calmly explain—and he'd listen. But that time had passed.

"We'll have to wait and see," I said.

Our family had changed, and it wasn't all due to Kinart's death. We'd started to dissolve a few years ago when Reyla and Kinart more intimately hooked up. Brodine must've decided we'd make an equally devoted couple. I felt sad for him. Angered about the whole situation, actually. He'd never be more to me than a friend, and I knew he'd rage once he'd finally received the message.

"Go." Vexxion urged his dragon to dive off the roof, and we followed.

Seevar responded perfectly to my commands, and that perked me up so much, I sent him spiraling downward for the fun of it. Drask cawed and hunkered close to my neck, tucking his head beneath my braid. He squawked in protest and pecked me.

I reached up to hold him on my shoulder, and I was unable to restrain my shrill laugh. This snarly dragon had been worth the patience I'd extended.

Finally, I leveled him out, and we soared back up to join the others flying over the compound. People still rushed here and there, and I imagined I'd one day find out what happened. For now, my focus was forward, toward the vast continent we still had to cross and the Claiming that would follow.

We flew all day and before it got dark, brought our mounts down to the ground in a large meadow along the edge of a dark forest. A river gushed through the woods a short distance away, and we led our mounts there to drink. Since it continued across Nullen territory, all the way to the place where they'd hold the Claiming, we'd used the river as a guide while we flew.

I splashed my face and neck, savoring the trickle of cool water beneath my sweaty leathers. I'd brought a few changes of clothing, though I wouldn't be allowed to wear my leathers to the Claiming. The fae were picky about what we wore during the event, and they'd provide what we needed. I could only imagine what that might be.

After we'd unpacked our supplies from the dragons, erected tents, and collected wood for a fire, we groomed our mounts and tethered them to graze. While they enjoyed meat, they were just as happy to munch on grass.

I gave Seevar extra pats before joining my friends sitting near the fire. Vexxion and the other two males sat opposite us, Farnoll occasionally tossing wood onto the blaze when it started to die down.

The forest swallowed the sun, leaving only streaks of blood orange painting the sky. Cool air drifted from the dense vegetation and wrapped around us in a cloaking mist, a damp pall that made me feel restless.

Vexxion handed out bars commonly eaten when someone

traveled, a mix of fruit, nuts, and bits of grain all smooshed together. Some were spicy and salty while others were sweet, and everyone but Reyla took a few of each.

Sitting beside me, she laid the one bar she'd taken on her thigh and stared at it.

"You should eat," I said. "We flew all day. You must be hungry."

She shrugged.

My gaze caught Vexxion's, but he directed it to his friends, who both watched Reyla. Zayde looked away. Farnoll did not.

Vexxion grunted and returned to whittling. Earlier, he'd collected a branch and stripped off the bark. Now it looked like he was slowly transforming it into a crouched dragon, though it was hard to tell with the flames roping and twisting between us.

After finishing my meal and washing it down with water from my canteen, I leaned close to Reyla, keeping my voice low. "Eat. Please."

"I don't want to," she said sullenly. Her fingers twitched on her lap before snapping to her waist.

"Just a few bites? Come on, do it for me if not for yourself."

Brodine watched, his lips thinner than paper. I liked the sympathy shining on his face. I didn't like how his gaze raked down my front.

"I. Don't. Want. To. Eat," she snarled.

"You didn't eat breakfast."

"I did!"

"I sat across from you," I said. "You moved things around on your plate, but you haven't eaten enough to keep Drask alive."

Shifting on the ground to face me, she glared. The bar slid off her thigh and landed on the ground. "I told you I ate."

I picked the bar up and brushed it off, holding it out to her. "Eat half of it. Kinart wouldn't want you to starve to death."

Drask fluttered his wings and squawked.

"You don't know what Kinart would say."

"I do.

"You don't!"

With a snarl stuttering up her throat, Reyla pulled the forearm-long blade from the sheath at her waist.

She wrenched it up toward my chest.

27

TEMPEST

The world roared through my brain, and everything . . . slowed.

I deflected Reyla's blade with a flick of my hand and latched onto her wrist, compressing it to the point her fragile bones shifted beneath her skin.

"What the fuck, Reyla?" I gasped as the world centered itself once more.

Drask took flight, sweeping across the meadow and darting into the woods on the other side.

Reyla blinked down at the knife. "I . . . I . . . I don't know why I did that." A guttural wail wrenched up her throat, echoing in the mist-drenched meadow and making the dragons lift their heads and skitter sideways. She wrenched free from my grip and flung the blade to the ground where the tip impaled itself and thrummed.

Her gaze jerked up to mine. For a moment, I swore this was

not the friend I'd grown up with. She whimpered before leaping to her feet and racing around the fire to weave among the dragons.

"What the fuck?" Brodine asked, staring after her.

With a shrug that shouted a casualness I didn't feel, I pulled the blade from the ground, cleaned the dirt off on my pants, and laid it on the ground near the fire.

Vexxion's eyes shimmered with anger. He looked from me, to Brodine, and to his friends before he tossed what he was whittling toward the fire.

I scrambled to my feet and snatched it from the air before the flames could coil around it. Rocking back to the ground on my ass, I cupped what he'd made like it was the soul of my dead parents.

It was a dragon, a perfectly shaped replica of Seevar. Why did he want to destroy something this amazing?

The heavy heat of his gaze thrilled across my frame, but I didn't look up.

We finished eating, though my belly protested the food.

Reyla came back but slunk inside her tent, securing the fastenings and shutting us out.

Vexxion rose and stretched his arms over his head. His shirt hitched up, revealing his abs, and honestly, I stared. I couldn't help it. He'd been sculpted from granite by a master, and I couldn't look away.

Brodine huffed and rose, only to walk over to his tent and slink inside. His snarl rang out as he settled inside.

"Walk with me," Vexxion told Farnoll.

His friend rose, and they strode across the mist-covered

meadow together, taking a path winding through the woods. Zayde stared after them for a long time before he turned back, his gaze meeting mine. It fell fast, locking onto the flames. With a grunt, he rose and fed it, making it blaze. Sparks coiled and slithered toward the sky.

I grabbed the knife and went over to Reyla's tent, scratching the flap. "It's me. Let me in." My tone made it clear that no was not an acceptable answer.

She released the ties and the flap sagged to the right, revealing her flopping back on top of her blankets.

Since the tent only reached my thighs in height, I ducked down and crawled inside, dropping beside her on the bedding. It was tight, but we'd often shared a bed when we were little when thunder woke us or one of us got into trouble and feared what the administrators might do. We'd comforted each other like sisters back then.

Now I felt as if I lay beside a stranger.

I held the knife toward her.

"I don't . . ." Her gulp rang out in the flickering darkness painted with shadows from the fire. "I can't take it."

"Alright." No need to push it when the idea of arming her again in such a tight space made my spine quiver. We'd trained together forever, and she was almost as good as me in battle. Inside a tight space? Yeah, I was happy enough not to risk it.

I sat up and stared at her, but she kept her eyes hidden with her arm draped across her face. "Come wash up with me at the river."

"I can't."

"You're going to stink tomorrow. We sweated all day in our

leathers." The sun at this time of year was infernally hot, especially when we were exposed, flying across the sky.

"I don't want to wash. Don't you see? I don't care if I eat. If I stink. If I even suck in my next breath of air."

"He wouldn't want this for you."

"Do not tell *me* what Kinart would want."

Swallowing hard, I pinched my eyes closed but flashed them open fast. I wasn't sure I trusted Reyla any longer, and that thought sliced through my veins, leaving them wide open.

"I'm sorry," I said. "I loved him too."

She sagged; her anger spent. "I know that, but it was different between us. He was the reason I got up each morning. My reason to train harder for each raid." Her voice croaked. "The only reason I could smile. Without him, all I have is . . . well, nothing."

"That's not true. You have me and Bro." Until the Claiming, that is.

I wanted to tell her this would get better, though how could it? Pure, unadulterated rage and a thirst for revenge had muffled my feelings. Only when I stood over the body of the fae lord who'd murdered Kinart would I give my anguish free rein. She didn't have that to cling to.

"I love you, Reyla," I whispered. "I mean it."

Her face awash with tears, she nodded. "I love you too."

"If you won't fight for him, fight for me."

Bolting upright, she snarled in my face. "Don't lay that on me. Don't make me fight unless I want to."

"Don't give in to this. Don't steal another piece of my soul."

"I'll . . ." She dropped back and closed her eyes. When she

opened them, they swam with agony. "I'll try. I can't give you anything but that."

"Good. Take this." I nudged the hilt of the blade her way again. "Find a reason to live."

"Does one exist?"

Revenge. Sweet, soul-washing revenge.

"I hope so," was all I would say. If I told her why I was going to the Claiming and about the deal I'd made with one of the wicked fae, she wouldn't try to dissuade me. No, she'd want in on the plan.

I was willing to sacrifice myself, but I couldn't bear to watch her die.

"If you find a reason, let me know?" she said.

"I will." Again, I held out her blade. "Put this in your sheath."

Her gaze slithered to the blade, and a shiver wracked her too-thin frame. "You keep it."

"What will you use to defend yourself?"

"See, I don't know *why* I did it." Her gaze shot from me to the tent opening. "I was pissed at you for pushing me to eat, but I'd never . . ." Her eyes snapped shut and her face twisted with anguish. "*I'd never.* Yet I did." A huff erupted from her throat. "Good thing you were always better than me at knife fights in close quarters."

A sound snagged in my mind, and I glanced over my shoulder, seeing Vexxion emerging from the woods. Zayde still crouched by the fire, but I didn't see Farnoll. He must be around somewhere, perhaps checking on the dragons.

"It's alright," I told Reyla. "I know you didn't mean any harm."

I wasn't completely sure I believed that.

"I didn't," she swore, her hand clutching my forearm.

"I'm sure it won't happen again," I added.

I'd be on guard at all times.

"It won't," she swore with a reverence reserved for when people prayed to the fates. Let's hope they heard her.

"Go," she said. "I'm going to sleep. I'll see you in the morning."

"When you'll wash and eat."

"I'll *try*."

A step up from where she was now. She nestled into her blankets and closed her eyes.

Leaving her, I grabbed my bag of things and went to the river to brush my teeth. Then I stretched out my spine and went through the exercises a healer had shown me ages ago, insisting they'd help my leg. While I wasn't sure the ritual made much difference, I didn't dare stop to find out.

Pacing the movements to the rippling trickle of the river, I let my body relax. Moonlight played with the current, outlining each swirl as the river skipped around rocks. It didn't look deep in this section, but a subtle roar drew me to the right. I walked along the shore, following a game trail until the river curved away from where we'd made camp.

Low falls cascaded over big rocks, landing in a pool before the river continued flowing to the east. I carefully made my way down to the spread of water and peered around, using all my senses to determine if I was alone.

Drask joined me, flying in low across the river, his tiny claws twitching when they touched the water. He landed on my shoulder and ruffled his feathers.

I stroked his silky body. "Where have you been? I missed you."

He pecked at my cheek, though gently.

"Leave some skin, will ya?"

He tipped his head back and cawed.

I'd almost kill to bathe and dress in clean clothing. I could rinse out my leathers and hang them to dry. If they were still wet in the morning, I'd hook them to Seevar and let the buffeting air finish them off. I had a clean second set I could wear tomorrow.

With Drask rocking on my shoulder, I rifled through my bag, pulling out one of the thin tunics I wore to bed, plus a drying cloth. I draped both over a thorny bush low on the shore. Then, after peering around and listening, hearing nothing but a few birds calling out in the distance and small creatures rustling through leaves on the opposite shore, I started removing my clothing.

As I tugged down my pants, Drask fluttered off my shoulder, landing on the ground. He picked his way to the water and poked his beak in to drink.

My leather tunic soon joined my pants on the ground along with the thin sleeveless top and underpants I wore beneath to protect my skin from rubbing. Naked, I delicately tiptoed down the mossy bank, stopping beside the crow.

He peered up at me and returned to drinking.

I stepped into the water and gasped.

"It's frigid, Drask," I hissed.

He dove forward, plunging into the low water near the shore. When he rose to the surface, he fluttered and swirled about, splashing to clean his feathers.

The thought of going to bed sweaty was enough to make me edge farther into the pool. I kept going, cringing and sucking in gulps of air as the water licked across my thighs, my butt, and my torso. Finally, with the river flowing across my breasts in a gentle caress, I pushed off with my feet and sunk beneath the surface.

I broke through the top and grinned. The water felt utterly amazing. Cool. Refreshing. And incredibly freeing. There was no river near the fortress, though we'd traveled to one periodically since I was young. That was where I learned not to drown.

I made my way back to the shore and grabbed my soap, splashing backward into the water, letting it engulf me and suck me down. Popping my head up, I untangled my braid, biting down on the strand of leather I used to secure it. I lathered my hair and rinsed it. Again. Then I washed my body, not stopping until my skin squeaked and felt wonderfully clean.

After tossing the soap up onto the shore, soaring it over Drask, who squawked and flapped his wings, I floated in the pool.

Finally, with my skin puckered and quivering from the chill, I left the water. I was tugging my drying cloth off the bush when a sound in the woods above me brought me to a bone-shattering freeze.

My breath caught and my eyes widened as I strained to see what—if anything—might be there.

Vexxion eased closer, though he remained partly hidden in the dense vegetation. What looked like inky, undulating bands of silver—something impossible to fathom—coiled around his body. I couldn't come up with any other way to describe it.

If I'd blinked, I would've missed seeing him. Seeing them. And maybe I was only imagining this. Things like that didn't exist in the world I came from.

They might in his.

My arms loosened, and I started dragging the cloth across my skin, wicking up each droplet from the river. I didn't speak, and neither did he.

He watched, his sapphire eyes smoldering, as I tugged on my tunic and stuffed my feet into my boots. As I combed and braided my wet hair. As I washed my leathers and shook off the excess water.

As I started up the bank, he turned and walked toward the camp.

I followed with Drask soaring through the woods beside me.

Back at the camp, everyone else had gone to bed. Vexxion rounded the fire and hunkered down beside it.

His heavy gaze followed me as I collected the carved dragon. As I hung my leather clothing on a low branch. Even while I walked to my tent, kicked off my boots, and dropped to my knees to crawl inside. I secured the flap and flopped back onto my flooferdar blankets.

My body flamed like the blaze outside.

I couldn't sleep.

My skin kept rippling with raw, tortuous need—a need I knew only Vexxion could satisfy.

∼

I DID SLEEP, though my dreams were haunted by silvery bands of lightning, Reyla feral and slashing out with her blade, and Drask cawing. In my dreams, I could understand what Drask said.

Be very afraid.

I woke when the sun pierced the canvas overhead, gouging my eyes, and quickly packed my bedding, stuffing it into my bag. Outside, I dismantled my tent. My leather clothing was dry, and I tucked it into my bag as well.

Reyla and Brodine emerged from their tents, both murmuring a greeting before trudging into the woods in opposite directions.

Vexxion was already up, assuming he'd left his vigilant watch by the fire. He helped me pack my tent in its canvas sack before he slung my bags over his shoulder, taking them to the dragon who'd transport them to our next stopping point tonight.

Brodine and Reyla returned and meandered to the river. I was grateful Reyla held her bag of things. Maybe she'd wash, comb her hair, and put on clean clothing.

The only way to move forward was to drag your body even if it kicked and screamed.

They came back—Reyla looking much more like her old self—and we loaded the last of our belongings on the dragons.

I stroked Seevar's nose and told him how pleased I was with how he was behaving. "Make sure you listen to me today, little guy."

He bunted my belly with his nose and deluged me with a nice shower of sparks I had to stomp on to keep them from setting the meadow ablaze. I groomed him, savoring the normalcy of the moment when I stood on the cusp of something terrifyingly new. He moaned and shivered while I worked on his shoulders, pushing hard to loosen up his muscles. Unused to flying all day, he must be as sore as me. At least I had exercises I could do to work out the stiffness.

After I finished, he sighed while I stroked his face, giving him forehead kisses. He truly was a sweet creature, and I was grateful I'd given him a chance.

While I saddled him and climbed up his leg, Vexxion kicked dirt over the smoldering ruins of the fire. He pivoted and walked over to where we waited on our dragons.

I peered around.

Brodine. Reyla. Zayde, me, and Vexxion.

"Where's Farnoll?" I asked as Vexxion leaped up onto the spine of his mount standing not far from mine.

Zayde said nothing, his attention focused on the woods to our left.

Gold flickered through Vexxion's deep blue eyes when he cast them my way. "Farnoll won't be joining us."

"Why not?"

"He's indisposed."

28

VEXXION

We flew through the day, only stopping to eat lunch, drink from the river, and take care of our needs. As the sun melted into the horizon, we landed in another meadow. I'd purposefully kept us away from villages and settlements. The fewer people who saw us, the better. Some were fairly good at identifying the fae, and I didn't want to deal with potential anger.

We gathered wood and built a fire, sitting around it while we ate, though Reyla only picked at her meal.

"Don't waste it," I barked as I passed her.

She jumped and shot me a shocked look before lifting her hand to study the food clutched there. With a heavy sigh, she bit into it, chewing slowly. She was making herself eat because she was worried about what I might do if she refused. Fear could push someone to fight for survival much better than pain.

Another lesson etched into my soul when I was almost too young to remember. Along with her screams.

Tempest helped me erect the tents.

"Five of us still," she said, her gaze scanning the clearing. "Is Farnoll still indisposed?"

"Yes."

Her eyes remained locked on mine for a very long time, but something as simple, as gloriously seductive actually, as that, wouldn't make even one of my muscles twitch. Finally, she dragged her gaze away. "Alright."

"Would you take a stroll with me," I asked.

Brodine frowned our way.

Tempest's lips twitched upward before she smoothed them. "Of course."

"I'll go with you two." Brodine started to rise. My low growl made him smack his ass back on the ground. Reyla startled again, peering at him with a vacant frown before she took another bite of her bar.

Brodine's pleading gaze tracked Tempest as we walked across the meadow.

I led her toward the river, blocking out the image of her bathing the night before. I hadn't intended to spy on her, only protect her. But nothing, absolutely *nothing*, could've made me look away when she started to remove her clothing.

She made me crave her in a way I'd never wanted anyone else before. A tearing, piercing desire scorched through me whenever she looked at me. My soul-drenching need kept me awake at night.

All my newly discovered colors paled when compared to

the exquisite, torturous vulnerability this woman dragged from deep inside me.

"Where *is* Farnoll?" she asked as I wedged a branch out of the way to keep it from scratching her as she walked beside me on the animal track etching through the forest toward the river.

"He won't be rejoining us."

"You . . . What happened to him?"

"What makes you think anything happened to him?"

She studied my face. "Did he go on ahead?"

"Perhaps."

"That's vague."

"What would you like me to say?"

"Tell me the truth."

We stopped at the top of the bank, scanning the river. Wide in this section, it was also deeper. She wouldn't need to seek an isolated pool tonight if she wanted to bathe.

"Since answers often create more questions," I said. "I'll defer at this time."

Her lips thinned. "And that's cryptic."

"It's honest."

"Hmm." She sucked in a breath and released it. "Why did you offer me an evening walk? I assume you didn't bring me here to compare my beauty to the moon."

"There's no moon tonight. Not even a star, which I believe would make a better comparison to your beauty."

"Why a star?"

"Despite their ethereal beauty, they're flawed."

Her hand went to her thigh. "Yes, that's me. Flawed."

I didn't like that my simple words cut her, that they could

pierce the fierce armor she surrounded herself with. "Your every scar, your every flaw, is a brilliant burst of a star fighting the sun's light at dawn. You're real, raw, and imperfectly perfect."

Her fingers twitched on her thigh before her hand shot to her neck, clenching in front of her throat. "How can someone be imperfectly perfect? It's a contradiction."

"So are you. I didn't bring you here to compare your beauty to the stars and the moon, both of which you eclipse. You're not prepared."

"There you go again. I don't know what you mean, and when I asked, you didn't tell me."

"I'm Claiming you in two days."

"But you didn't plan on Claiming me until I begged you to do so. You told me I wasn't prepared before I set myself on this course toward destruction."

"Would you have me stand by and do nothing while someone attempts to kill you?" Sarcasm dripped from my words. "You won't be able to skip into Bledmire Castle and slash the king's throat."

"I never assumed this would be easy." Her voice came out small.

I wanted to lift her, hold her, buffet her with praise. Lay her in the soft moss along the shore and stroke her body until she could do nothing else but succumb. Until she moaned my name. Then I'd show her how much I craved every perfectly imperfect part of her body. But we didn't have time.

Not now. Not ever for us.

"As you are right now," I said. "He'll see through you the

moment you arrive and slash you to bits with a flick of his finger. Unless you've created an impenetrable barrier that he can't see through, this entire mission of yours is hopeless."

"If I'm not prepared." Her chin lifted. "Then prepare me."

"We'll start your training now."

Her hand went to the blade at her side.

"Your guards, not your defensive moves, though we'll work on those eventually as well."

"You're bigger than me. Stronger. More muscular. Taller. More magicker."

"That is not a word."

Her lips curled, a sock in my stomach that stole my air. "Sure it is. My point is, I'm never going to be as good as you at anything."

I flashed her a quick smile. "Don't forget I'm also incredibly wise."

Grinning, she smacked my arm. "And conceited." Her smile made my heart explode, blasting against my ribcage.

I froze, stunned all over again by the color of her eyes and the lushness of her black hair shot through with strands of pure gold. How her pink cheeks glowed in the dim light. How the pale peach of the thin shirt she wore underneath her leathers peeked at her collar. That color was the only scrap another might call feminine.

Yet she was the most beautiful woman I'd ever seen.

I wanted to pull her close and use my teeth to tug that bit of shirt away from the crest of her breasts, then place my mouth in that very location.

"We'll work on your mind's guard tonight and from now

on," I growled, encasing myself in the stoic cloak I'd worn for most of my life, the thing that protected me the best.

There was no defending myself against this woman. But the thought of anyone harming her, wounding her, coming even close enough to touch her, sent hot rage roaring through me. The only way she stood a chance was if she was ready.

"A guard?" she said with a nod. "They taught us about them at the fortress."

"Nowhere near enough."

One of her eyebrows lifted. "Are you saying you've been roaming around inside my mind?"

"You shout your thoughts. There's been no need for me to *roam*."

"I don't disagree. I am vocal. Opinionated."

"Don't forget obstinate."

"Never," she vowed with a smirk. "Plus, endearing."

So much. Too much.

Her smirk smoothed quickly. "Alright, then, hot, wicked fae, show me everything."

Oh, how I longed to give into her request.

"Guard up," I snapped to drag my thoughts away from all the precious things I ached to do with her body. I attacked her mind to give her a taste of my power, a fraction of me.

She gasped and reeled backward.

My hand snapped out to keep her from tumbling down the embankment.

Wrenching away from me, she lifted her hands, backing along the trail snaking beside the river.

I stalked her, barraging her mind, needling her with my own.

"Stop!" she said with a wince. "Please."

Put up your guard. Reinforce it. Don't flounder around. Use it!

"It's up," she shrieked.

"It's paltry," I said in disgust. "You'll need a lot of work if you hope to live long enough to get close to the Bledmire king. At this point, I doubt you'll do more than scratch his skin."

She deflated beside a spindly tree. "You'll be with me while I'm there."

Always. Picture a forest.

She cocked her head. "Trees?"

"Trees."

"Alright."

"No, make them thicker, so thick no one can pass through them. So tightly woven together and tall enough to stretch up over your mind that they meet up in the middle and tangle in one glorious mass coating the top."

She jerked out a nod and eased around me, stalking back to where we'd started.

I attacked her again, meeting fragile resistance. *Better.*

I kept at her, poking and prodding at her mind while she scrambled to hold onto her forest. Overhead, clouds skittered across the night sky, masking and revealing the stars until the bands thinned and the orbs blazed.

Like her. The shimmer of her power was unlike anything I'd seen before. I could feel it in a hot wave across my skin.

One day soon, she'd let loose, and the entire world would know.

"Again," I snapped. I'd end this soon, but the more I worked with her, the better chance she had of surviving.

Stark cold fear kept ripping through my guts. There wasn't enough time, but it would have to be enough.

"Picture the forest," I said with as much patience as I could dredge to the surface.

She nodded; her gaze focused inward.

I battered it with fire and watched it burn. "It's not thick enough."

"I'm trying."

"Not enough." I slashed through her trees with a white-hot blade.

She staggered. "Not fair. You're fae. You have an advantage."

"You have the ability to raise a worthy guard. You just need practice."

When she grunted to show she was ready, I attacked her with wind, buffeting and battering at her guard. I didn't stop until sweat coiled down her temples, and she collapsed against a tree.

"I'm done," she cried, clutching her head. "No more. Please."

"Is that what you'll tell Ivenrail when he discovers why you're inside his castle?"

"No." She was a sullen little thing, and I adored her. Through it all, she was ever the glorious, bitingly exquisite woman I was...

"Keep practicing," I snarled. "I want your guard up at all times. I'll randomly attack it while we fly tomorrow."

"It's hard."

"It is."

"We learned about guards, but I've never used one outside the classroom, and the last lecture was years ago."

"Such a mistake. Do you think I'm the only fae in the Nullen realm who would be eager to paw through your mind?"

Her sharp gaze met mine. "You're implying fae are breaking the treaty all the time."

"I'm stating it."

"What about the rule that if you cross the border, you're not allowed to use more than rudimentary magic? I think sorting through my mind counts for more than that."

"Rules are only good if they're enforced."

Her growl ripped out. "Our king..."

"Is more interested in his mistresses than his people."

"His people other than his daughter, Brenna, you mean. I saw her once when a contingent of us flew to the city. She rode in a pretty little open carriage through the street, dressed in a flouncy gown I wouldn't wear even if my life depended on it. She smiled and waved, and frankly, she seemed almost too sweet and innocent for castle life."

"I've met her as well, though only once, and she's as you describe. Kind and too naïve."

"Maybe she takes after the dead queen."

"My visit took place a few years ago. I didn't meet the queen at that time."

"She's been gone for ten years now. The king remarried. But all this doesn't matter. We have to fix this, somehow. Try at least."

"We'll *succeed*," I said. "Trying isn't enough for me."

The strain in her gaze told me I'd barraged her enough for one night. We'd continue working on her guard tomorrow.

"This will be easier for you after the Awakening," I said.

"Another thing you didn't explain." Starlight picked up her frown. Tapping her chin, she studied my eyes, watching me as intently as I did her. "Control. Awakening. Access. I assume they come in that order."

Very smart. "The Awakening will unlock your magic."

29

TEMPEST

"I don't have magic. You know that. Just wisps of energy I'm expending to plant that forest around my mind." I held out my arms as if the truth is blazing on my skin.

"The fae king wouldn't bother with the straggling bits of energy Nullens still possess."

Which meant . . . It couldn't be true. "He's going after our *energy*, what's left of our souls. We don't have magic. We don't have power." My words came out weak because, damn them all, but it made complete sense. "That's what we were told."

"This proves once again that your upbringing has left you unprepared."

"We truly have magic?" I couldn't believe it. Didn't want to believe it.

"Most Nullens do. It's been suppressed."

"Mine as well?"

He nodded.

"How can you tell? Maybe I don't have any."

"Your skill with dragons."

"That doesn't prove anything. I treat them with kindness," I said. "That's why they listen, why they do what I ask."

"Yet you haven't worked at all with Seevar while we've traveled."

"I work with him all day long while we fly."

"No bucking. No attempts to dislodge you. Not one."

"He's smart. He learned quickly." Doubts crowded into my mind. "It has nothing to do with magic."

"You deflected Reyla's attack."

"And what's up with that? I'm a decent fighter, but even I was stunned by how quickly I could..."

His tight smile rose. "Finish the thought."

"I felt like the world...slowed."

"It didn't slow. You were able to respond faster. Each person's magic works differently, and each has a special skill, something they're better at than many others. After you've been Awakened, we'll work to find out what your skill is."

I still couldn't fathom this. And I was pissed off. Who else knew about this? "How long have you known?"

His gaze fell to the ground, and he sucked in a breath, releasing it. "For as long as I have memory."

"Can you sense anything about my magic?"

He watched me for a heartbeat before blinking. "No." His blink could be a natural reflex. Or was he hiding something? Fear skipped through my veins.

He wouldn't be one of the wicked fae if he didn't keep secrets.

"Since we've finished for the night, I'm going to bathe." Planning to grab my things and return to the river, I started up the path weaving through the woods, but stopped and turned back to face Vexxion. "Are you going to be a pervert and watch me?"

His slick smile rose, but his eyes remained sharp. "If I was a pervert, I'd make my way through the woods and come up behind you. I'd join you in the water, and I'd . . ."

Heat seared across my skin, and my heartrate spiraled. I huffed and started walking again, not looking back. "Maybe I like my men perverted."

His breath caught.

Grinning, I kept walking, now with a nice spring to my step. My brain might be fried, but my body still functioned fairly normally. At least our training hadn't made my leg ache any more than usual. Riding all day was enough. If we'd trained with weapons, I'd be hobbling.

"There you are," Brodine said when I appeared at the edge of the meadow. He sat opposite the fire from Zayde.

"Where's Reyla?" I didn't see her near the fire or with the dragons.

"She went to sleep."

I took in her unlit tent. She used to love reading at night. I'd packed her things and hadn't thought about tossing in a book. She hadn't mentioned it either. My friend was slipping away, and I wasn't sure how to keep her with me.

Sitting by the fire, I tugged the necklace out of my pocket.

I'd only looked at it a few times since Brodine pulled it from beneath my plate in the dining area. I held it up to capture the flames. Emerald beams arched off facets as it spun.

Brodine appeared transfixed by it. It was hard not to get snagged by it myself.

Vexxion came up behind me. I felt him rather than heard him, because I'd met no one who could move as stealthily as this man through the woods.

"Would you like me to secure it around your neck?" he asked, and I nodded. He stooped down, taking the necklace and undoing the clasp, dropping it around my neck. It dangled on top of my leather tunic, beauty splashed across the coarse garb of a soldier. Once he'd fastened it, he lifted it to catch the firelight again. "It fits, don't you think?"

Did he mean the length? He must, because he tucked it beneath my shirt to rest against my skin where it would be safer.

He left me, walking around the fire, where he nodded to Zayde. The two males stepped away from the fire and spoke too quietly for me to hear.

"Can we talk?" Brodine asked, rising. He came around the fire and grabbed my arm, tugging me up from the ground to stand with him. His voice lowered. "We're arriving at the ceremonial area tomorrow, and there are some details," glancing toward the other men, he whispered, "things that you need to know.'

I'd be a fool to believe Vexxion would tell me everything I needed to know. He seemed to reveal only what he had to, the information he felt I truly needed. Was he holding back something vital? I'd be a fool to completely trust him. We were uneasy allies, and that was good enough for me. He'd serve his purpose and then I'd step away from him, assuming I could find a way to do so after he'd wrapped a collar around my neck.

He wouldn't try to keep control of me after, would he?

"So talk. Tell me what's so important."

"Not here."

"Why not?"

"Come with me!" He latched onto my arm hard enough I winced.

A silver band snapped through the fire, splitting the flames and poking Brodine's arm. He reeled backward, clutching the place that smoldered.

"Fuck," he snapped.

Vexxion and Zayde had turned away from us and appeared oblivious to whatever had happened.

He growled, scowling down at me. "Are you telling me you don't have time to speak with me? Not even a few minutes?" His gaze traveled beyond me, and the warmth scorching my face told me Vexxion was looking our way once more. "Or are you too busy fucking the fae lord?"

"He's not a lord." At least, I didn't think he was.

"He's a bastard, but from what I've heard, he inherited a title. An estate."

Oh, really? Maybe I *did* want to make time to hear whatever Brodine had to tell me but not here. Not in front of the others.

"Let's talk tomorrow." I kept my tone light. This was Bro, my other brother. The last thing I wanted to do was say something that would permanently drive him away. I kept hoping that what we'd had could be salvaged. "Before we leave."

His mouth twisted and his snarl ripped out. "Yeah, I get it. You've chosen."

"My choice was made long before Vexxion came to the fortress. You know this."

His hand jerked up, and he slammed his palm toward my face.

I deflected the blow, another stunning, unexpected move by one of my friends. It wasn't cold, but chills wracked down my spine.

Vexxion snarled, and a wave of something hot and sulfurous washed over us. The slender whipcords of silver threads I'd seen coiling around his legs last night erupted from him, gouging toward Brodine, snapping around his wrist, bringing his hand to a halt before he touched me. Other strands whipped around his throat.

My heart pounded against my ribcage.

Brodine's eyes widened, and he stumbled away from me. He'd realized how close he was to . . . death. I knew this in my soul. He'd been warned. The threads wouldn't release him next time. Vexxion would kill him.

"I . . . I'm sorry. I didn't mean to do that." Brodine pivoted and rushed to his tent, nearly ripping the flap off when he opened it. He dropped down and plunged inside, snapping the flap closed behind him.

I swallowed hard to force down the fear still tightening inside me. My eyes closed, and I took a deep breath. Another. I remained motionless with the heat of the fire roasting my right side as cold shock spread across my left.

I grabbed my things from my tent. As I strode past Vexxion, I made his gaze meet mine. His eyes smoldered with something I couldn't name. It reached inside and stroked me. Adored me. Part of me luxuriated in the feeling.

The rest of me was terrified of his power.

I was limping by the time I reached the river. I shoved aside my unease about what I'd seen and growled. I wanted to kick something. Brodine would be nice. What was up with my friends acting like they...

Wanted to kill me.

It couldn't be true, but the rage he and Reyla showed me meant something. I just wasn't sure what it could be. Stress about the upcoming Claiming? I'd like to think that was all this was, and it could be the case with Reyla. Brodine's anger was plain old jealousy. No matter how many times I told him I wasn't interested, he refused to listen. He seemed to think if he kept at it, I'd eventually give in. I never would have, not even if Vexxion hadn't come into my life.

I dropped onto the bank in the soft grass and gingerly stretched out my leg. Starting with a light touch, I rubbed it, trying to work out the kinks. It spasmed, the ache reminding me all over again that I'd never be whole.

"Let me." Vexxion plunged to his knees in front of me, his intent gaze seeking mine. I found only sympathy there, though perhaps still a spark of the anger I'd seen at the campsite.

He gently removed my hands from my leg, placing each one

carefully at my side. "If you were wearing less, I could massage deeper."

"I'll take my clothes off when I go for a swim."

"You still plan to swim?" He studiously stared at my leg, not meeting my gaze.

"I'm not letting anyone keep me from doing something that brings me joy."

"Now there's the woman I've come to respect and admire."

"Is that all you feel?"

He sent me a crooked smile that made everything inside me ignite.

"I will take things off," I croaked. Rising, I slipped off my pants. My leather top didn't drop lower than the tops of my hips, but I wore underwear. It wasn't like he hadn't seen me —*tasted me*—before.

When I sat, his lips curved up before smoothing. He eased between my legs and started rubbing my thigh, deepening his touch, the pressure enough to work out the kinks in the twisted muscles while chasing the spasms away.

"You could do this for a living," I purred, leaning back on my palms. He made me want to curl up in his arms. Bask in everything that made up Vexxion. Fall completely, irrevocably in love with him.

What would I give to have him look at me with more than simple affection? My emotions were in such a turmoil, I didn't trust myself.

Yet I couldn't make myself look away from him.

While he stroked my leg, I watched his face that expressed only concern. "Tell me if I hurt you," he whispered.

I nodded, my throat clogging off. My obsession with this man was going to bring about my downfall. I knew it. Yet I couldn't find the will to drag myself away from his orbit, from his touch, from the way he made everything inside me come alive.

Because I couldn't bear for him to see whatever feelings I might expose in my eyes, I closed them and gave myself over to his touch.

"You need to massage your leg regularly or it'll start locking up," he said.

"It already has. Not during battle, thankfully, but once when I was working with a dragon. Many times during hand-to-hand training in the gym."

"You weren't hurt," he growled.

I shook my head. "My friends wouldn't do anything like that."

"Not even Brodine?"

"I'm not going to talk about him." Or think about him. "As for the dragon I was working with, this is where my kindness comes into play. My leg just . . . stopped working. I tumbled off the beast, smacking onto the sand beside him. He shifted around and dropped his nose down to sniff me as if he was worried I might be dead. When I lay there with my thigh on fire, he huffed with disgust. He let me climb back onto his back once I'd recovered."

"We're going to include regular massage in your training."

My smile trickled upward. "Do you have someone in mind to perform this delightful service?"

"*No one* but me is allowed to touch you in any way."

"I thought you'd say that. You're doing a good job; consider yourself hired."

His low laugh rang out, and I melted.

I opened my eyes to find him watching my face. He was everything beautiful and everything forbidden.

He continued to alternate the pressure on my thigh between firm and light. I moaned, my breath hissing out.

"You do this well," I said.

"I do *everything* well."

I snorted. "Except act humble."

"Would you enjoy being with me if I was humble?"

"Probably not."

"And there, you have your answer. You like me just the way I am." The edge in his voice told me he was testing me in this.

"I believe so," I said. There was no way I'd admit that he'd worked his way through my emotional barriers and was rampaging through my determination to resist him.

One of his chiseled eyebrows shot up. "*Believe?*"

"Alright, I *do* like you as you are. What else do you want me to admit?"

"Expose yourself to me, tiny fury," he purred. "I won't cause you harm."

That remained to be seen.

Trust. Give it lightly, and you risked the person ripping you apart.

"You'll have to do more than massage my leg if you want me to do something like that," I said.

"Then I've got a lot of work ahead of me." His fingers

paused on my leg, but he didn't look up. "I've found a solution for your friend."

"Which friend?"

"Reyla."

My breath jerked in, and it was a struggle to force it back out. "What part of *her* life are you going to take care of?"

"The Claiming. Zayde will do it."

He seemed like a decent enough guy.

"He's fae," I pointed out, and I didn't trust any of them.

Vexxion nodded. "He won't hurt her. I promise."

My eyes stung. There were a lot of things this man could do that might impress me, but he'd found the perfect way to edge beneath my guards, by helping someone I loved. It was rarely about me or my own needs, but it was always about theirs.

"Thank you." Closing my eyes, I pressed out the tears.

He reached up and caught them with his thumbs. Lifting his hands, he slid them into his mouth.

I gasped. "Some people might find that disturbing."

"Do you?"

"No. It's . . ." Incredibly arousing. I nudged him to the side and stood. "My leg feels better. Thanks. I want to swim now." Drench my body in icy water. Wash away this overwhelming desire to consume every bit of him until I couldn't remember where he ended, and I started. Convince myself it wasn't too late, that I had even a shred of control over what happened between us.

I was floundering, drowning, and there was no lifeline in sight.

"Do you want me to leave?" He still knelt at my feet, and even in this position, he overwhelmed me.

"You could look away."

Rising, he slid a few strands of hair that had escaped my braid over my shoulder, meshing them with the rest and holding it tight as if that would keep the wind from snagging them once more. "I'd rather watch."

He was a single star, bursting into view on a dark horizon. My heart pounded, crushed against my ribcage. A feeling of destiny exploded inside me.

I eased around him, and he turned, still watching me as I approached the water. I didn't need to look; I could feel his gaze on my spine, a sweet, yet twisted caress.

Hunger unlike anything I'd felt before clawed through me, wrenching my world in a direction I'd never anticipated. Never believed was possible for a person like me. He was ripping me apart, then remaking me anew. And I'd let him do it, over and over, until there was so little left of the real me, I wouldn't recognize myself.

My inhibitions peeled away along with my clothing. A bar of soap in hand, I splashed into the water, sucking in the cool freshness, coating my skin with it, as if that would calm my explosive desire for this man.

I'd never craved anyone the way I did this wicked fae, and I didn't like it. The tang of vulnerability clogged my throat. I paused with the water swirling around my breasts, closing my eyes and pulling in one breath of air after another. With each exhale, I mentally pushed him away. Like the forest he'd told me to envision to protect my mind from invasion, I needed something equally strong to guard my heart.

So, I built a fortress, starting with huge blocks of stone and thick mortar, laying one on top of the other until it was so tall, nothing and no one would ever be able to scale it, not even this unbelievably tempting yet incredibly sly fae man. I pictured the wall covered in thorns thick enough that no one could ever gouge their way through. Then I added a veil of shifting colors that would project an image of nothing.

"What are you doing?" he asked from the shore.

Protecting myself from you. "Nothing."

He snorted. "It doesn't feel like nothing."

Maybe I *did* have a touch of magic buried deep inside me.

There was something incredibly decadent about bathing while a man watched, standing guard. My skin tingled with hyper-awareness, and a languidness stole through me like I'd drunk an entire bottle of wine.

I washed my hair, rubbing it with soap until bubbles clouded the water around me. I gathered the long strands up, coiling them on top of my head to make a crown. Then I lathered the soap and ran my fingertips down my neck to the tops of my breasts. Those got equal attention. With sudsy hands, I "cleansed" my breasts, gliding my hands down across my belly. Up and down, each stroke surging my fingertips closer to my core.

His soft hiss rang out, and I looked up to find stark, raving hunger blazing in his eyes. His cock strained against his leather pants, and it was all I could do not to leave the water, undo the fastenings of his pants and tug them down. I'd bend before him. Touch him. Take all he had to give and return it with my tongue.

He was casting a spell on me. I knew it. Yet my walls remained intact around my heart. I'd kept my mind guard in place.

Plunging down, I rinsed before bobbing back up to the surface.

Vexxion no longer stood on the shore.

Fear skated across my skin, biting through the surface. I spun, looking for movement within the dense, dark woods surrounding me.

He grabbed onto my leg and tugged me down into his watery embrace.

30

TEMPEST

Vexxion entwined his body around mine. He was as naked as me, and the notion trilled through me in a way nothing else ever had. We bobbed above the water, and I twisted around to latch onto his shoulders, laughing. His fingertips teased across my lower back, tugging me against his chest.

Not long ago, he'd had his head buried between my legs, his tongue driving me wild, but his body had remained a mystery.

The weight of his cock pressed against my abs, thick and long and arousing, making goosebumps prickle across my skin.

With his slicked-back black hair woven through with that thin band of silver and water droplets clinging to his long lashes, he looked like a selkie come to life.

"Let me guess," I whispered. "You were sweaty from giving my leg a massage and needed a bath."

"Something like that." His grin rose, and for one second, he looked sweet and innocent. Carefree. As if he could only shed the dark, grim mask he wore when we were alone. That only now could he be the man he held back from everyone else.

The space between us felt charged, like he was the lightning to my storm. One touch, and we'd ignite. We'd level the ground around us.

If I were wise, I'd leave the water. Rush to my tent and duck inside. Hide from the endless longing in his eyes that mirrored the emotions tightening in thick bands around my heart.

His gaze drifted downward, and a proprietary gleam smoldered in his eyes.

His hand glided up my back and when it reached my shoulder, his touch lightened to the point it almost tickled. His knuckles slowly teased across my collarbone to my neck before sliding down to smooth across the peak of my breast. They stopped only to lift the pabrilleen stone away from my wet skin.

"I'd never seen anything this green before. The world this full of vibrant colors. Not until I met you." His throat worked with his swallow. "You're beautiful. I was stunned when I saw you. The stone's the perfect match, don't you think?"

"For what?" It sounded like I was playing dumb, but I needed to hear him speak the words.

His gaze shot up to lock on mine. "You know."

"*You* put it on my tray." Brodine wasn't capable of selecting something as exquisite as this for me.

"I don't believe there's anything I wouldn't give you, Tempest." The reverence in his tone sparked through me, lighting me aflame.

His eyes smoldered with endless hunger. They tore me wide open, stomped across my walls, and ravaged everything inside.

I wrapped my legs around his waist and rocked against him. I wasn't quite ready to give him everything, but I couldn't resist his pull. I suspected I'd never be able to resist his lure. He was fae. Was all this made-up? A magical trick to make me behave the way he wished? It couldn't be.

Curse me forever if it was because there was no turning back now.

The knowledge that I existed only for him stabbed through me. The Tempest I was before paled, leaving a raw, exposed woman behind. He could cleave through me if he chose, and I wouldn't be able to stop him.

Alone and floating with the current, with the stars cutting through the darkness above, it felt like we were the only two people in the world.

I sensed that everything I was and everything I might ever be was wrapped up in this man's hands. As if he was my destiny.

Or my complete and utter downfall.

I stroked his face with my fingertips, watching his eyes as I traced across the network of scars beginning at his sharp jawline and twisting and curling around to the back of his neck and to his chest. When I first met him, I thought they stopped at his tunic collar, but he'd removed his shirt during the raid, exposing himself to me.

The torture of his scars continued, splashing outward across his torso, only stopping when they reached his right hip.

"What happened to you?" I croaked, pummeled by shock and drowning in sorrow for the pain he must've gone through.

"Some I know are, shall we say, unkind."

"It wasn't an accident?"

"Nothing done to me has been an accident."

What kind of life had he lived that put him in the path of those who'd torture him like this?

"The scars sink deep." I leaned forward and kissed the network on his neck.

A shudder ripped through him, and his fingertips bit into my hips.

"*Tempest*," he grated out, his voice hoarse with emotions I couldn't define. "How can something so simple mean this much?"

His words thrummed through me, emboldening me. I stroked his shoulders slick from the river and brought my fingertips in to map the scars on his chest. They were as much a part of him as the silver streak in his hair and his burning sapphire eyes.

Moving my hands down his slick back, I cupped his ass, squeezing. So tight and strong.

His smile brought out the boyish side he hid at all times, and I got a taste of how he might look if people hadn't tried their hardest to ruin him.

I glided my fingertips across his lower belly and wrapped them around his thick staff, moving them up the length and stroking my thumb across the tip. He was big. My fingers barely met at the top when I held him.

This wasn't enough.

I sucked in a deep breath and ducked down beneath the surface, quickly drawing as much of his cock as I could into my mouth.

He bucked, letting loose his tight restraints and giving himself over to me, if only for this moment.

Who needed air when I could taste everything? I swirled my tongue across the head of his cock, sucking on it with greed. I would stake anything that Vexxion had never once dropped his iron guard and let someone inside.

Until me.

The power of that humbled me as much as it thrilled me.

Milking his cock with my mouth, I slid my fingers down his back and around his hip, roaming and stroking across to his rigid abs. There wasn't any part of him I adored more than the other, but his muscles . . . I'd never get enough of touching them.

Tempest.

His voice echoed in my mind as I sucked harder, determined to give him this one solitary moment if I couldn't give him another.

Tempest!

I was drowning in his taste, the feel of his cock getting stiffer. Frantic to feel it all. Throttled and desperate for air, I remained between his legs, giving him pleasure. Until his fingers latched onto my arms and he dragged me to the surface. I sucked air into my lungs and whimpered. I wrapped my hand around his cock while holding him in place with a palm on his spine.

Emotion suffused his face, cratered with a need only *I* could satisfy.

I could tell he knew this. It was burned into his soul as deeply as it was embedded within me.

He thrust my thighs apart with his knee.

My grip tightened on his cock, stroking from the root to the tip of his shaft.

He plunged his fingers between my legs, dragging them through my folds that even in the water had slicked with desire. Moaning, I arched my spine, spreading my legs wider, wrapping myself around him.

While bracing my body in place, he thrust his fingers deep within me. When he pulled them out, he drew them across my clit.

I cried out, lost in this moment. In this man.

Coiling his fingers inside me, he stroked my inner walls while I thrashed against him.

I didn't lose touch with the pleasure I was still determined to give him. I moved my hand along his cock harder. Faster. He groaned and let everything go, giving me what he'd never give another.

"You're beautiful," he growled. He bit down on my shoulder hard enough to leave a mark but not break the skin. It stung, and I relished knowing I'd carry his brand tomorrow and into the Claiming.

As I moved my hand faster, so did he. We writhed in the water, and it was a wonder we didn't drown. We were both lost in this moment. This pleasure. This growing bond between us.

"You're incredibly responsive," he snarled in my ear. "Look how well you take my fingers. You'll take my cock even better."

He could drive it inside me now, and I'd ignite.

"My need to touch you consumes my every waking moment," he groaned. "When I sleep, you're there, teasing your fingers across my body. Driving me to the edge like you're doing right now." While he continued rocking his hand up inside me and dragging it back out, rubbing my clit with each pass, his other hand rose to tilt my jaw, making my gaze lock with his. "You're mine, Tempest. Agree."

"I am."

"I need to hear you say it."

"I'm yours."

"Yes. Yes, you are."

"And you're mine," I said. "It goes both ways, Vexxion. Always."

He jerked out a nod and closed his eyes, slamming his cock into my hand while plunging his fingers inside me.

I came suddenly, the feeling splitting my bones into a billion pieces.

Vexxion did the same, barking out a cry of bliss while he shuddered in my arms.

31

VEXXION

I carried her to the shore and gently dried her body. Pure, soul-crushing possession scorched through my veins.

She was mine. *All mine.*

Forever.

Soon, I'd place my collar around her throat. I'd claim her. Did she truly know what that meant in the fae world?

She wasn't prepared. The knowledge of that ripped through me like jagged wire. Honestly, she'd never be prepared enough for what she must face. All I could do was teach her all I could, then stand beside her. Hold her if she lets me. Give her everything inside me, then offer it to her once more. I'd lay my pulverized heart in her tiny hands if she let me.

She was limp in my arms, and that smile . . . She kept shooting it my way, and a pride unlike anything I'd known before expanded within my chest, cracking my ribs. Her light stroke on my arm knit me back together once more.

Once we were dressed, I gathered our things and swept her up in my arms.

"I can walk," she whispered, still grinning at me in a sappy way that made my lungs ache.

She definitely wasn't prepared and yet... she was perfect as she was. Devastatingly perfect. I'd do all I could to make sure she knew it.

Zayde looked our way when we appeared at the head of the path, before darting his eyes down to the fire. He added wood and sparks flung themselves into the sky. Stupid things. Didn't they know they'd never rival the stars?

They'd burn out as quickly as me.

I carried Tempest over to her tent and kicked the flap to the side. Then I dropped to my knees and crawled inside with her still in my arms. I laid her on her bed, and she clung, her fingers meshed tightly at the back of my neck.

"Stay," she said in a sleepy voice that rippled across my soul.

I wanted to. So much.

But I shouldn't.

Couldn't.

"Sleep, tiny fury," I said as she yawned. "You need your energy to become the storm."

As I went to leave her, to remove myself from her tent, she cupped my face, forcing me to look into her eyes just as I'd done while in the water.

"Don't forget this, Vexxion," she said. "Don't forget me."

"I won't. I can't. You're... *everything*."

With that, I made myself leave, though I'd shred my way through the entire world if it meant I could lay with her tonight.

Drask flew inside and landed near her side. He watched me, his head cocked, his gaze of night locked on mine.

Securing her tent flap, I turned to face Zayde, reading the disapproval in his eyes. He didn't speak, and I didn't join him at the fire. Turning, I stalked toward the path leading away from the river. Inside the network of trees and with my bones humming with magic, I bolted.

I didn't stop until I was near collapse. Only then did I drop to my knees. Cupping my face in my palms, I let loose a bellow along with my threads. They snaked away from me, snapping against trees. Downing them with one blow. Severing bushes and coiling outward farther before flinging themselves back inside me.

Every creature in the vicinity froze in stark, raving terror.

32

TEMPEST

My body still hummed when I woke. I stretched, luxuriating in the feeling, smiling as I remembered what we'd done in the water. Today, we'd reach the ceremonial area and tomorrow, he'd claim me. How long before we arrived at Bledmire Court, and I could put my plan in motion?

I was about to unleash chaos on the fae world, devastate them completely, and all I could do was grin.

Drask fluttered his wings, standing on the tips of his claws. He pecked my arm, and I stroked his feathers while he crooned.

"What do you say, little guy?" I asked. "What's going to happen between Vexxion and I once the Claiming is over?"

Training, training, training, since I *wasn't prepared*.

Magic.

"Why didn't anyone tell me about the Awakening?" I asked. "Maybe they thought I didn't need to know. I was never destined for the Claiming."

No one wanted you to know.

Such an interesting notion.

I watched sunlight play with the canvas roof overhead and dreamed of dragging Vexxion back to the water. I'd allow my thoughts to go there for now. As soon as I emerged from the tent, I would reinforce not only the guard protecting my mind but the one shielding my heart.

Vexxion had been right when he said I should never love him. Doing so would only lead to a broken heart.

My upcoming conversation with Brodine loomed, and I sighed. My pulse ground out a heavy thump. I dressed inside my tent, a torturous thing right there when donning leather garments, and emerged to find the others packing their things and stowing them on the dragons.

Drask flew out and landed on my shoulder, riding along with me.

Reyla was speaking quietly with Zayde, and I hoped he was telling her he'd claim her tomorrow, that she didn't have anything to fear. Knowing someone wouldn't harm her reassured me. It allowed me to center my focus on the enormous task I'd given myself: killing Ivenrail Levestan.

If I survived, was there a chance Vexxion and I could be together? I hated how my need for him made me weak. He said his desire for me consumed him, and it went both ways.

I went to the river, stopping on the way to take care of my needs behind a bush. While Drask soared over the water, flicking his toes across the surface and catching bugs for breakfast, I brushed my teeth and rinsed the gritty powder from my mouth.

Brodine came up behind me, tapping on my spine. "There you are."

I straightened and turned, tucking my brush and container of powder into my bag. "Here I am."

"Are you ready to talk now?" His ever-present scowl tightened.

"Sure. Talk." Should we sit on the bank? That's what we would've done in the past. Now, I opted to stand in place, looking him in the eye.

He glanced around and spoke in a normal tone. Odd that he didn't lower his voice when I could see Vexxion standing inside the tree line. He must think whatever he had to say couldn't be overheard by the other man.

"At the Claiming, they're going to collar us," he said.

Vexxion's sharp eyebrows lifted.

"I've heard that."

"And you didn't tell me?" Brodine asked.

"I should have. I'm sorry." He and Reyla meant everything to me. *Why* hadn't I shared this with them?

"You're always too busy with that bastard."

"Don't call him that," I snapped.

"It's what he is. *Who* he is."

Never to me.

"He'll own you once he collars you," Brodine snapped. "What do you think about that? You've always been too independent, too resistant to anything and everyone around you."

"I knew that as well." I ignored all his crap about me resisting.

"He's going to break you." A thread of desperation came through in his voice. "Break you in ways you can't imagine."

Vexxion could break me even without the collar.

"I'll protect myself."

"No one can protect themselves from the fae."

"Then why are you going to the Claiming? You could've remained at the fortress. From the sounds of it, you'd be safer fighting dregs than being claimed."

"You know why."

"You went to the commander before I did; you couldn't know what I planned to do."

"I guessed. If you were going, I wanted to go too."

"Jeez, Bro." I started to pace back and forth on the shore in front of him. "Please don't tell me you think you can protect me."

"I love you, Tempest." He slammed his fingers through his hair, snarling it, and making it stand on end in places.

"As a friend." Please don't go there.

He grabbed me as I passed and latched onto my shoulders, gripping tight enough I winced. "I love you more than anyone. Anything." His mouth crashed down on mine.

I writhed and wrenched myself away.

Silver bands of magic snapped around Brodine and flung him into the water. His body was sucked down.

I raced to the shore and waited for his head to appear above the surface. Silvery beams coiled and snarled deep below the surface.

Brodine didn't come up. Not even after I'd counted to twenty.

"Leave him alone," I cried, stomping into the water fully dressed, thrashing my arms around, seeking my friend.

He bobbed up, gasping, and snapped his head in all directions. His gaze locked onto me, and he swam toward the shore.

"Did you do that?" he snarled as he stomped past me.

"I'm Nullen. I can't do magic."

"That's not what I've heard."

My heart froze. I spun on my heel. "*What* have you heard?"

"I guess you're about to find out."

"Don't be like that." I felt like everything was falling apart. I'd built a small yet secure life at the fortress, and it had been caught by the wind and swept away. I could tell myself I was stepping away from them because of Bro's interest in me, but was that the only reason why?

Kinart's death had changed things. It had broken something I'd trusted in, something I'd thought nothing could shatter.

"We're still friends," I said, though it sounded weak. "Please." I wasn't even sure what I was begging for. There was no going back. I'd learned that all through my childhood, though I guess I'd started to forget.

"Friends," he said bitterly. "Yeah." He stomped up the bank and onto the trail, passing Vexxion without looking his way.

"Did you enjoy that?" I snarled once Brodine had disappeared from view. My frustration with everything kept roaring up to the surface.

Vexxion literally shuddered. His eyes snapped closed before he opened them, his intent gaze pinning me in place. "You see me."

"Brodine didn't fly through the air on his own and nearly drown himself."

"Then you *believed* I was somewhere nearby. You didn't see me here."

With a huff, I strode past him, heading toward the campsite. "You've been standing right here. I saw you long before Brodine touched me."

In utter silence, he followed me back to the others.

Ah, yes. He was brooding once more. If only I didn't find this part of him equally appealing.

Brodine was snarling around the campsite, loading things onto the dragons. I wanted to tell him to go back to the fortress and make the commander send someone else. He'd never listen. He was too stubborn, too infuriating.

And as determined as me.

I hated the thought of hurting him. I'd told him we'd never be together, and I wanted to kick him until he bellowed that he understood. Could our friendship survive this rift?

"I don't need saving," I snapped as I passed him with a tight roll of bound blankets in my arms.

He stopped and sent me an odd look, one that made me pause. "That's just it. You *do* need saving. I wish I was the one you'd come to for protection."

I shook my head, suddenly spooked.

His gaze traveled beyond me. "This isn't only about the Claiming."

I didn't need to turn to see who stood nearby; I could feel the caress of Vexxion's eyes on my spine.

"He won't purposefully hurt me." I knew this in my heart. Despite his secrets, I saw all of him.

I refused to back away.

"Promise me you'll be careful," Bro said.

"Yes, be careful," Reyla intoned as she passed us with a bag holding her things. "Of everything."

"What's with you two? I don't need guardians."

Brodine shook his head. "You're wrong, Tempest. We're friends first. Families watch out for each other."

"They do."

His eyes darkened to cold spears plunging into my heart. "I'll . . ." So many emotions swirled in his big brown eyes. They wrenched me in every direction. "I'll let the rest go. I promise. I don't like it, but I love you no matter what. That's never changing."

My throat was tight; I couldn't drag in a breath. My life was shattering, getting tossed in every direction. I'd never find all the pieces. "I love you too, Bro. That won't change either."

He gave me a long look before sighing and returning to pack up the rest of the campsite.

I finished loading my things on the pack dragon and looked around, wanting to make sure I hadn't missed anything.

A bolt of pain seared through my brain.

You're not even trying. Vexxion appeared beside me, his face taut with a scowl.

"Ah, there you are." I slapped my guards in place. My tangled emotions had made me forget.

"You said you saw me while you were speaking with Brodine." His gaze snapped from one end of the meadow to the other as if he was categorizing any potential threats. He must see Brodine in there somewhere.

"You were there, listening to us."

"I was making sure he didn't harm you."

"Brodine can be a pain in the ass, but he'd never hurt me."

"He was going to hit you last night."

"He wouldn't have followed through."

"He didn't because I stopped him." He huffed.

"You don't need to hover over me all the time," I said. "You only showed up at the fortress a few weeks ago. I grew up there and learned to defend myself there. Brodine's just . . . He's like a brother to me."

"He doesn't see you as a sister."

"He's starting to come around. He'll get there." If I battered it into his skull enough, he'd finally see.

Vexxion's voice lowered to a sharp, guttural tone. "How did you see me inside the forest?"

"Because you were there, just like the night before. I told you that."

He gripped my shoulders and watched my eyes. "How. Did. You. See. Me?"

I grumbled. "What's the big mystery? If you want to secretly watch me, though I'm not sure why, since you seem comfortable joining me whenever you please, you should climb a tree or something. Hide in the canopy. Crouch behind some bushes."

"You saw me," he said in awe.

"Yeah. My sight's fairly good." I turned to walk away.

"Since you've so nicely issued an invitation, expect me to be with you all the time."

With that, my skin ignited.

I stacked another layer of stone around my heart and reinforced the jolt wire at the top. When I felt in control of my body's response to his nearness, I faced him.

"When do we leave?" Hopefully, I was the only one who could hear the shaking in my voice.

"You're ready?"

"For the Claiming? I'm not sure about that, but to fly toward the ceremonial area? Sure."

He studied my face. My eyes. Even my body. "Are you alright?" The tenderness in his voice would be my undoing.

My heart hurt, but I wasn't going to bring that up. I felt like a cavern had opened up between me and Brodine, but I wouldn't mention that either. I'd benefit with a good cry. Not doing that.

Eventually, he nodded. "Keep your guards up," was all he said as he strode over to his dragon and leaped onto its spine.

We flew for a few hours, eating in our saddles as we traveled, and I marveled again at how wonderfully Seevar responded to my commands. Was this magic? I'd never felt lacking in any way other than with my leg, but I did now. As if some part of me kept whispering. If I could listen hard enough, I might understand.

Vexxion flew his dragon close to Seevar, who nipped at the other beast before a nudge of my heel made him settle.

You're not paying attention. Vexxion attacked, barraging my guard. It collapsed, a pile of sticks and rubble beneath his stomping feet.

"You're using tricks you didn't teach me last night," I snapped.

"Do you think others will only lightly tease your guard? They'll plunge inside you. They'll shred whatever you can offer. And then they'll ravage through your mind."

"I know this. I'm practicing. I'll get there. I'll keep practicing until I can handle anything you throw my way."

"You'll never be able to handle everything I throw your way."

"Watch me. I'm not giving up. I'm not giving in." If anything, I was more determined than ever to master this skill. "One day soon, you won't be able to get inside." Not inside my mind, and never inside my heart.

Brodine and Reyla flew in the lead, chatting, a welcome sign for Reyla. Maybe she'd thought about my words. Zayde has taken the rear, though he'd only dropped back to that spot when Vexxion flew up beside me.

"You could forget all this," he said. "Live a normal life."

"I can't believe you're bringing this up again."

"You won't get past his guards and if you can't do that, you won't make the slightest impact."

"Then teach me. I want to know everything."

"It won't be easy, and we don't have a lot of time."

"He'll still be waiting even if it takes me six months or a year to get me to the point where you reluctantly agree I might, actually," I deepened my voice, "be prepared."

"We don't have a year or even six months."

"Why not?"

"Because he's going to marry the Nullen king's daughter."

"Brenna? Why does that make a difference?" With luck, she didn't love him, because I planned to make her a widow.

"He believes she's the long-lost heir of the cursed kingdom."

"The Lydel Court?"

"What do you know about the Lydel?"

"Not much. It was supposedly cursed a long time ago. Some believe the king cast the spell, but no one knows for sure if he did or why. Well, other than the high lady refused to go to his bed. The only other thing I've heard is that every Lydel is dead."

"They say the heir was sent away before the court was cursed, that her mother did it to protect her."

"Now you're suggesting Brenna's not the king's true daughter but a Lydel?"

"His adopted daughter. She was found wandering in the castle gardens when she was a toddler. The queen adored her, and back then, he indulged his queen."

"You're speaking of the old queen. The one who died ten years ago. I thought Brenna was hers." Why hadn't I heard the story of Brenna wandering in a garden and being adopted? "The king remarried not long after the first queen died."

"The new queen hasn't conceived an heir to the throne, and since the king has killed off all the relatives who might stand a chance of challenging him for the throne, he's calling Brenna his heir."

"And he's giving her to the fae king, the one who's draining people of their power."

"And soon her." His words dragged across my exposed skin like a jagged blade. "Despite the incredible power the Lydel heir is supposed to have, she won't last long."

"Why does he think she's the long-lost daughter of the Lydel Court?"

"She bears their mark, a scrolling L."

"Maybe it's just a birthmark."

"The fae king doesn't think so. He's been after her since he found out. If she's the heir, her power will be immense. Lydel Court ruled them for ages until they were cursed. Bledmire was second to them in everything and the king hated it."

"Who will rule after I kill Ivenrail?"

"His eldest, I assume, though only one of his sons counts."

"Why do you say that?"

"Because that person is the decent one."

A relative term when it came to the fae.

"Has he molded the eldest after himself?"

"In every way he can."

I'd have to be wary of the Bledmire lords. Everyone within the court, actually.

"Maybe the decent one will help me kill his father," I said.

"He cares for his father for some unexplainable reason. He won't aid you in your cause."

I didn't like hurting others, but this was about more than one fae son's love for his father.

"Our king won't allow Ivenrail to drain his daughter. Something like this will drag his mind away from his mistresses." I huffed out a breath. "We have to kill him before he hurts her."

"They're getting married in two months. He'll collar her immediately after the wedding. He'll start taking what he wants that night. Once he begins draining her, she won't last more than a week."

33

TEMPEST

"Two months?" I gulped. "You're going to collar me, awaken my magic, and teach me everything I need to know to carry out an assassination of the fae king in only two fucking months?"

My voice lifted enough Bro shot a sharp look over his shoulder. I thought he'd drop back to ask what was wrong, but his gaze cut to Vexxion, and his lips twisted. He turned back to Reyla, who then looked my way with a frown. Yeah, go ahead and talk. Gang up on me. What I'd soon face topped anything they could come up with.

Drask leaned into my neck to break the wind and pecked my cheek. I stroked his spine to soothe him.

"You have a month, perhaps a few weeks more than that," Vexxion said. "We'll need to get you inside the court and set the plan in motion before the wedding, and that won't happen overnight. This is why I'll state this again. Give this up. Go back to the fortress. Or go to some village in the middle of the continent where you'll be relatively safe. Live a boring life. Have a few kids. Forget about Awakenings or revenge."

"It gnaws on me." How could I explain? "The moment the Liege told me who was killing all those people and who I soon learned was responsible for Kinart's death, something inside me snapped." Just thinking about it made my heart pound, loud and demanding. Every breath seared my lungs with white-hot fury as the image of what that wretched fae king had done flickered in my mind. "I see Kinart lying in Reyla's arms whenever I close my eyes. I have nightmares of him staring at the cavern roof, of the light in him, everything that made him the brother I loved, winking out as if the Bledmire fae king had reached inside Kinart's chest and ripped out his heart."

"I understand the thirst for revenge, the driving need you feel."

"Do you? I'm hollowed out. There's not much left inside me except rage. I'm full of this dark, thick sludge called hatred. It flows through my veins instead of blood. It gnaws on me—constant and unrelenting. It's a beast born from the bowels of despair and it's steadily chewing through whatever peace I found at the fortress. Don't you see? I can't give up now. I *have* to do this. And I'm close."

"You're nowhere near close."

"I'll get where I need to be. So we have about six weeks. We'll do it. I'll work all the time to make this happen. I'll push hard and at the end, you'll announce that maybe, just maybe, I stand a chance. And then, you know what?"

He jerked his head.

"I'll kill him."

"And what will be left of Tempest when you're done?"

I shrugged. "At this point, I don't care."

"*I* care."

"Do you? I mean, really, truly, do you?"

His gaze fell to the stone I wore around my neck. The thought of removing it shook me to my core. That should tell me everything I needed to know about my feelings for this wicked fae. "If you have to ask that, then you're not ready for my answer."

Go ahead. Reject me like my family had. Vexxion had irritated me from the moment I met him, but I'd allowed him to get close, and in turn, I'd softened. Perhaps my only allegiance should be to my driving need for revenge.

I rubbed Drask's back, grateful I at least had him.

Vexxion's lips thinned. "Don't turn this into an obsession."

"I need something to hold onto. Does that make it an obsession? Perhaps. But without it pushing me, I don't know if I can do what I have to."

"Killing him won't bring back your brother or any of the people he drained."

"I know that, but damn, it'll taste sweet to hand Reyla his head."

"Don't let it change you." Why did such stark despair come through in his voice?

"It already has. I'm not the person I was before Kinart was murdered. That Tempest is gone. She's been replaced by one who's stronger, though she has more scars on her soul than before. She's also the only one who has the guts to do this."

He stared forward for a long while, his jaw tighter than stone, before his body loosened. "Alright."

"Alright." I nudge Seevar to fly toward Bro and Reyla. Before I reached them, they stopped talking. Bro dove his dragon down and slowed it until he flew beside Zayde.

Vexxion clawed at my mind, trying to get past my guard. I repelled him quite easily. Was he trying, or was I actually getting good at this?

"You're being mean to Brodine," Reyla said.

While I mentally threw Vexxion over the cliff on the edge of my forest, I tried to focus on my friend. "I'm glad to hear a little spirit in your voice."

Her lips thinned. "We're family. Don't mess this up."

"Brodine messed it up. He wants more than a sister, and I can't give that to him."

"Can you blame him? I think he's been in love with you almost since the moment you two met."

"I was a child."

She shrugged. "Children have crushes."

"He needs to let it go. I'll never be his."

Reyla's hand snapped out, and she latched onto my arm. "Don't throw away something beautiful."

"I don't love him! Please, don't you push me too."

"I'd give anything to be with Kinart again. *Anything*." Her voice cracked with despair. "Just one second in his arms. To feel his mouth on mine, his hand stroking my face."

"It was different for you two. You were . . ." Soulmates. Fated mates like some of the fae. He was someone she'd loved above all others, to the point she'd willingly die to be with him once more. I couldn't imagine feeling that way for anyone.

I shot a glance back at Vexxion. He could probably hear what we were saying, but it wasn't anything new. He knew how I felt about Bro.

"Talk with him," Reyla said softly. "Give him a chance."

"I don't want him. I'll never want him. Don't you understand?"

Her hand whipped up, away from my arm, and with a growl, she urged her dragon to fly down. She kept going until there was enough space between us, I doubted even shouting would make her hear me.

Thanks, Bro. Now Reyla was angry with me too.

Brodine's attention remained locked on me. I didn't like the bitterness I saw on his face.

I faced forward again. My eyes stung, but I swallowed the sorrow, using it to harden my heart.

Suddenly, I couldn't wait for the Claiming. And I prayed whoever chose Brodine took him far from Bledmire Court.

When Vexxion attacked my mind once again, I let my trees take care of him. Branches whipped his needling claws, and thorns raked across the skin of his mind. I sent a storm rolling his way for good measure.

Very good.

I shot him a smile and gave Drask a quick hug. He squawked and took flight, soaring beside Seevar, but I could tell he wasn't upset.

Maybe there was hope for me yet.

I saw the ceremonial area before we reached it, an enormous meadow encircled with flowering trees. It looked pretty from up here, a stark contrast to what I knew would soon happen to all the Nullens sent to be Claimed.

"It looks normal," I told Reyla who'd joined me as we got closer. Thankfully, she hadn't mentioned Brodine again.

Vexxion flew behind us with Zayde in the front. Brodine's dragon soared not far behind Zayde, and he thankfully had stopped glaring at me.

"I've heard a few scary things about what's going to happen." Reyla's voice quivered. "I'm worried."

"I think things will be alright. But you can say no. Turn back now. You could return to the fortress or go somewhere completely different. There are plenty of villages that would welcome you."

"Live alone?" Closing her eyes, she shook her head. "I don't want to do either of those things. I want something new. It won't be wonderful." Her gaze met mine. "I'm floating into nowhere, but at least the fae kingdom will be a change of setting."

I didn't expect her to find someone new to love, but I hoped she found peace. And I hoped mine would come after I'd killed the person responsible for murdering Kinart, plus so many others.

"You don't *need* to do this," I said.

"It'll be over soon, and they'll take us to the fae realm. What do you think it's like there?"

"I assume it's like here." But I didn't know. More secrets they'd kept from us. The split happened so long ago, no one could remember. If there were documents that might share that information, they weren't passed out at the border fortresses. "Even our king hasn't been there."

She nibbled on her lower lip. "I'm clinging to this."

"Why?" I had my reasons, but wanting a change didn't match up with the friend I'd known for most of my life.

"Before he died," her swallow went down hard. "Kinart . . . He whispered something to me."

"What did he say?"

"That I needed to expose the secrets of the fae."

My heart came to a shuddering halt. "What secrets?"

She shrugged. "I guess I'll find out and then I'll tell the world."

"The collars control us. You may not be allowed to tell anyone anything."

"I'll find a way. I'm doing it for him. I don't have anything worth doing for myself. It's given me a purpose, you know?" Her gaze drifted to mine, and she forced a smile. "Well, other than trying to fix you up."

"Don't bother with that. Take care of you, Reyla. That's what Kinart would want."

"I know." She stared at the ground and pointed. "Look. Someone's waiting."

A woman wearing a long, pale blue gown stood in the center of the meadow, her head tilted back, and her arms lifted as if she was embracing the air.

Brodine flew in to travel beside us, taking a place on Reyla's other side. The curt nod he gave me suggested he might've come to the right decision. Perhaps we could find a way back to our family again.

Because tomorrow? We'd be torn apart.

"Where do you think we'll sleep?" Reyla squinted at the meadow.

Bro shrugged. "On the ground? It doesn't matter." He paused. "We three could share a room if they've got one."

"I'll sleep with Reyla," I said.

His lips thinned, and he jerked his head to stare forward, his jaw tighter than a noose after someone placed it around my neck and pushed me off the cliff.

"We should do something tonight," Reyla said, her brow scrunching. "Just the three of us. It might be our last chance."

"Do you think there's a bar here?" Bro asked. "One that serves decent wine?"

She snorted. "They must drink something. Why not wine?"

We flew lower, coasting our dragons toward the meadow. Zayde came up on my left side while Vexxion flew next to Brodine, the two of them escorting us. Or making sure we didn't change our minds and flee in the opposite direction. But, no, he'd told me over and over I could back out of this, that I could walk away.

Who would take my place if I did? I doubted the fae lords eager to claim a Nullen would be happy to see any of us leave.

Drask tightened his claws on my shoulder. Sensing he was nervous; I stroked his back. He leaned into my neck and pecked my cheek gently.

We banked our dragons over the woman who gave us a welcoming smile. Nice that they'd sent someone to greet us.

When we landed, she strode over to stand beside Vexxion's dragon, waiting until he'd leaped off.

She cupped his jaw with her palms.

Rising onto her toes, she kissed him.

34

VEXXION

I pried Selitta's hands off my face and leaned away from her to break her kiss.

She pouted. "This is how you greet me, Vex? It's been too long." She nestled against my chest, blinking up at me coyly. "I missed you. I couldn't wait to see you. You said you'd bring me something the next time we met up."

"I forgot."

Her foot landed hard on my instep. "Is that any way to treat me? And here you are, hoping to sneak into my bed tonight."

"No."

"So you say now." Her fingertip skipped down the fastenings of my tunic. "I'll be waiting. Don't make me wait too long."

"No."

Her smile dropped, and anger brewed in her eyes. "*No one rejects me.*"

"You'll replace me quickly enough."

Her magic lashed out, making the trees in the forest sway and a blast of wind stab across the meadow. With her fists clenched at her sides, she snarled. Truly, however, she had nothing on Tempest's fury. Her gaze locked on mine, and she tilted her head. "Ah, so it's like that, is it?"

My heart shuddered. I couldn't let her see.

"Like what?" My threads snapped to attention at my command and shot through my body, coiling around my mind while I stilled my expression.

She continued to study my eyes, the only place not under thread control. Her brow tightened. She grabbed my hand and flipped it back and forth, studying my wrist. "I don't see any marks but . . ." Her fingernail struck my chest hard enough to bite. "Tell me."

"Tell you what?"

"Which one is it?" She peered toward the others dismounting from their dragons. "Yes, yes, of course. It's obvious. So much power. I can taste it, and it's quite appealing." With a giddy laugh, she started probing Tempest.

I unleashed my threads on her.

Her spine jolted, and she gasped, staggering backward. For the first time since I met her twelve years ago, she gaped at me with true fear.

"No tasting. No touching."

"Does she know who—"

I tightened the threads around her neck, cutting off her words. Her air. Her very life force if she was foolish enough to keep speaking.

Gurgling, she jerked out a nod.

I pulled my threads back, and they reluctantly left her.

She wiggled her neck and glared. "Don't ever do that to me again or..."

"You'll what?"

"You don't want to test me, *Vexxion*."

I didn't fear her. There was nothing she could do to me that someone else hadn't already done other than kill me. She was flighty, and while her soul wasn't dark enough to commit murder yet, that time would soon come. I'd never trusted her. I wasn't even sure why I gave into her that one time. "Behave, and this won't be a problem."

"You're taking a grave risk. Does your—"

"Life is about risk." I barely remembered what it was like not to have someone else trying to control me. Steal what they could from me. Kill me.

"I'll make sure your . . . guests are settled, and then we should talk." She started striding toward the others.

I tugged her back with my threads, though in a gentler manner, such as it was. "I'll see to this myself."

She drew herself up stiffly. "I'm the host here, not you."

"I'll do it."

"Very well." Pivoting, she stalked toward the path leading into the woods.

I stared after her, knowing I'd added another enemy to the very long list.

"A friend?" Tempest asked as she joined me, her voice colder than the peaks of the highest mountain range in the fae kingdom.

"Not any longer."

"I see."

But she didn't. She couldn't. I walked along that wire once more, only I was no longer alone. She stood precariously behind me, her arms extended at her sides and her face full of terror. She didn't realize she was there yet, but she soon would.

Knowing I was not quite alone in this should hearten me. Instead, it only made the palpable dread coiling inside me tighten to the point I'd soon snap.

"Collect your things," I announced to the group in general. "I'll take you to where you'll stay tonight. Staff will take care of your dragons, this I promise."

"If you want to spend time with her, do it," my tiny ball of fury hissed, like a feral, spitting chall in dire need of taming. If only I had a lifetime to do it.

"Why would I want to do something like that?" I drawled.

"She kissed you."

Oh, Tempest was deliciously miffed. The taste of her jealousy couldn't be any sweeter.

"You'll note I did *not* kiss her back."

"It sure looked that way to me."

"Then you weren't watching closely enough."

Her shoulders sagged before resolve spiked through her eyes. "You can be with whoever you please."

A true smile curved my lips, and I leaned close enough to her ear I could nibble on it if I chose. "What if there's only one person I ache to be with?"

"You're playing with me. I bet you have . . . fae women everywhere, waiting to do your bidding."

I kissed the shell of her ear. "She'll never compare to you, mighty storm." No one ever would.

She huffed, but I could almost smell her softening. Her smile rose once more, though it contained a hint of conniving. "Do remember that."

I loved that spark, that touch of fury blazing through her eyes. She pleased me so much. Her fire. Her determination. The taste of her on my tongue.

My low laugh rang out. "I won't forget."

Drask soared low across the meadow and drew up, landing lightly on her shoulder. He squawked and flapped his wings. When Tempest stroked his back, he settled, his dark gaze scanning the area for threats.

I grabbed her things, plus my own, and urged them to follow me into the woods, taking the same path as Selitta. But when we reached the split, I led them right. She would go left to the estate reserved for the fae traveling here for the Claiming. I'd be expected to make an appearance, and I'd do so, though I'd yank myself out of whatever gathering they'd planned as soon as I could.

I'd barely be welcomed as it is.

We left the woods, walking across a much smaller open area full of long, wavering strands of grass speckled with tiny blue flowers, meeting up with other Nullens. They were playing a game but stopped when they saw us. Their ball hit the ground with a splat, but none of them ran to it. Silently, they watched as we crossed the meadow and approached the cottages reserved for those selected for the Claiming.

"Tempest," I said. "You and Reyla will share." I nudged my

chin to the last building on the left. The mark on the door showed no one else had been assigned to use it. I removed the mark with magic.

"It's pretty," Reyla said softly. "Flowers and everything."

They grew in the window boxes and in the narrow beds below, stretching all the way around the building.

"Brodine, you're in the cottage to the right of theirs. Remain there tonight."

He snorted. "Maybe I want to go out. It's my last night of freedom, right? Tomorrow, one of you will snap something around my throat and make me behave."

I'd be glad to see the end of this asshole. May he be chosen by someone who'd take him far from Tempest.

"Rest if you want, but be out here in an hour for collection," I said.

Zayde grunted, his gaze on Reyla. I trusted him, but only so far. His loyalty lay with another. But then, everyone's loyalty lay with someone other than me.

Except my tiny fury. For a short time, she'd begun to trust me. Selitta had sliced through our fragile beginning as if she'd wielded the Blade of Alessa. Another lost object from the fae past.

Selitta had only hastened things along.

After tomorrow, the odds of Tempest trusting me again would be over.

35

TEMPEST

It took Reyla and me about two seconds to unpack. We'd each brought a spare set of leathers, numerous weapons because we were badasses, plus a few toiletries. I'd brought a cloak, though I had no idea if I'd ever wear it.

Tomorrow, we were supposed to dress in the clothing they'd bring us. I assumed they'd provide something ruffly for the women. Stoic and somber for the men.

Would anyone complain if I showed up in leathers and bristled with weapons? Probably. The fae might be forbidden to use magic in the Nullen realm, but we stood on the border, the cusp between their world and ours. Here, they could probably do whatever they pleased. There was no need to draw anger my way.

Reyla sagged onto the bed. "Zayde told me he's going to claim me tomorrow."

"Yes."

"You knew, and you didn't tell me?"

I didn't like the accusation in her voice, but she was right. I was holding things back when I should be sharing everything with my family. "I'm sorry. It's been a tough time."

"You think I don't know that?" Her lips thinned. "I see the way you look at Vexxion. He's dangerous. If I were you, I'd run in the opposite direction."

"He's Claiming me tomorrow."

"I suspected something like that was in the works. Are you sure you want to belong to someone like him for the rest of your life?"

I sat on the narrow bed opposite hers, my boots planted on the braided rug stretching between them. "I have plans." That I wasn't going to share with her. She was right; I was keeping secrets. But if I told her what I was going to do . . . Well, it would put her in danger. She might try to help, and she was too fragile. She wasn't strong enough to handle any of this.

"You and Brodine should tell them you've changed your mind," I said, starting down this torturous path once more. "Say you want to leave. Go to a village in the middle of the continent. Hide from the dregs." And the Lieges. And the high fae lord who was eager to drain them.

"What if I don't want to collect Brodine and sashay off to the middle of the continent with him to hide?" she snarled.

"I want you safe."

"Like you'll be safe?"

I sighed. "I promised Kinart I'd watch out for you."

"Then break the promise. You have no say in what I do,

Tempest. I get it. You think I'm weak and broken, that I need someone to stand in front of me like a shield." Her chin lifted and her steely gaze met mine. "I've been slashed wide open, and I'm still bleeding, but I've sutured the wound."

"If you went back to the fortress, you could kill a bunch of dregs."

"The fates know I felt that way right after, but revenge is more your thing than mine. Stop trying to talk me out of this. I'm looking forward to the Awakening. That's about the only good thing about this."

"You *want* to use magic?" Growing up, I'd never heard of a Nullen craving power, let alone my friend.

She looked around and lowered her voice. "I've already been experimenting. Watch." Lifting her finger, she focused on it. Light burst from the tip and impacted with the ceiling . . . that smoldered.

"Where did you learn to do that?"

"I found a book in the fortress library and while a lot of it was a bunch of stories about the fae and essentially junk, the author handwrote a few spells on the inside of the front cover."

"Where's this book?"

She shrugged. "It burned with all the rest of our stuff."

"A shame."

"Right. I'd only played with this one spell. So, while you think I'm going to die an early death after being claimed, I'm looking forward to everything I might be able to learn." She gave me a lopsided smile, the first true one since Kinart died. It gave me hope that she'd be alright, that I might not have to watch out for her as intently as I'd planned. That I could trust

Zayde to hide her where she'd be safe while I took care of business.

"Why didn't anyone tell us we still have power?"

"Because then we'd try to use it. I think all of us have a bit of fae magic in us, and they don't want us to know."

"I wouldn't put anything past the fae or our king." I'd never felt there was anything inside me waiting to burst free. But what did I know? This Awakening might reveal a new potential. I'd need all the armor I could get if I was going to kill the fae king. "Teach me that spell."

"Okay." She gave me a sunny smile and explained the simple wording she'd spoken in her mind to make light that could burn if she left it in place long enough. "I can't hold it long, though. All I can do is create a puff of smoke. Maybe you can do better."

I held up my finger and hummed the spell across my soul like she told me, but nothing happened.

I glared at my finger and tried again. Still nothing.

"How long did it take you?" I asked.

"I was able to generate a tiny light the first time I tried. Smoke the second time, though I haven't progressed since. I believe it's a simple spell. I'm not exactly a strong person." She nudged her chin my way. "Maybe keep practicing and it'll happen for you."

Or maybe I didn't have even a speck of magic trapped inside me.

For the first time, dread coated my mind in a smoldering pall. Could I actually kill a high fae lord who possessed endless magic with only my blades?

Brodine opened the door and stuffed his head inside. "Can I come in?"

"Sure." Reyla shot me a look of warning, but she should be directing it at him. I didn't like that she'd taken his side in this.

He dropped onto the foot of my bed and hitched one leg up, facing me. "Want to know what I just heard about the Claiming?"

Reyla nodded.

I watched him, impassive. I was as open to hearing secrets about this mysterious process as anyone else, but Brodine's reveals always came at a price I wasn't willing to pay.

"It happens tomorrow morning," he said.

"We already knew that," Reyla said.

"What you probably don't know is that the fae king plans to attend this one."

"Really?" Reyla breathed, her wide-eyed gaze meeting mine. "Why?"

"Maybe he wants to claim one of the Nullens." Brodine's attention remained on me. "Or maybe he just wants to watch."

"Where did you hear this?" My belly churned. Why was the fae king coming to the Claiming? I needed to find Vexxion and make sure he knew. He might give me some insight.

Maybe, while he was here, I could . . . I shut off the thought. Vexxion was right when he said I wasn't prepared.

"That fae woman who was here when we arrived told me about it. She came knocking on my door and . . ." His smile grew slick.

"Jeez, Bro." Reyla reached over and swatted his arm. "Can't

you keep it in your pants for even one day? Here I am, supporting you, and you're fucking someone you just met."

"Who said I fucked her?" His smiled dropped as fast as it had risen. "I'm not that easy. Well, maybe for one person."

I slid off the bed. "I think it's time to go."

"It hasn't been an hour yet, has it?" Reyla asked, looking around as if there might be a clock sitting nearby.

"You two can keep speculating about the fae king. I'll wait outside." I eased past Brodine, grateful when he didn't try to block my way.

"I'm coming," Reyla said, grabbing her shoes off the floor where she'd kicked them. "Wait up."

I pressed my forehead against the inside of the wooden door, sucking in the coolness, wishing I could melt away and reappear after this was over.

"I'm sorry." Bro laid his hand on my shoulder. "I'm trying. It's tough."

I didn't turn. Didn't speak.

"I know I should give up," he whispered. "You keep telling me there's no hope but . . ."

"You're persistent," Reyla said. "I understand. If Kinart had fought against us being together, I would've kept working on him. It's like that when you're in love."

"Would you two just stop?" I growled. "I'm part of this, and I said no. I'm not interested, Brodine. I never will be. Pursuing me forever won't make a difference."

"And that's where you're wrong," he said. "I've got patience, though. No worries about that."

Whipping around, I lifted my finger. I cast the spell, and it worked. Not only that, but I also shot fire straight at Brodine's nose.

He cried out, reeling backward, his hands lifting to cup his face.

"What are you doing?" Reyla bellowed, shoving her way between us. "What the fuck are you doing?" Her glare hit me like a hammer in the head.

But it was the look of pure hatred Brodine shot me that hurt the most.

36

TEMPEST

I'd wanted to make Brodine stop, and I'd found a way.

I hated how my life was falling apart, and I couldn't find a way to cling to the way it was before.

I rushed out of the cottage, ran across the tiny porch, and leaped over the three front steps. Hitting the ground hard, I ran into the woods on the trail we'd taken with Vexxion. When it split, I went in the other direction. While I could go be with Seevar, that was the first place my friends would look for me.

Assuming they decided to follow. They might be back in the cottage nodding at each other and stating good riddance.

Drask squawked from the woods to my right, but he didn't come close. Hunting, most likely.

The trail split once more, and I turned right again, stomping down a rough path jumbled with broken branches and rocks.

After running along the trail for fifteen minutes or so,

pushing my leg harder than I should, I slowed to a brisk walk. I continued on the trail weaving through deeper and deeper woods where sunlight barely penetrated. The sun would set soon. Would the moon shine tonight?

I stopped and looked around, finding myself alone, thankfully. Spying a stump, I walked over to it and sat. I lifted my legs to prop my heels on the jagged wood and wrapped my arms around my legs, dropping my chin onto my knees.

Drask landed on a branch of a tree above me, but he didn't come close. That was alright; I needed this time alone to think.

No matter how I looked at the conversation back in the cottage, I couldn't find enough reason for hurting my friend. I'd apologize when I saw him and hope he'd listen. I wasn't only going to tell him I was sorry for my anger that he'd brought with his words. I was going to lay everything out for him and convince him we'd only ever be friends.

I was so focused on practicing what I'd say that I didn't hear someone approaching on the path.

"If it isn't the interesting Nullen," she said.

The woman who'd kissed Vexxion strode over to me, still wearing the long blue gown with gold embroidery across the top. Her feet were bare. Totally impractical, but since she appeared to the ceremonial greeter and not much of anything else, maybe she didn't need to wear fancy shoes. Odd choice for a walk in the woods, but I didn't care enough to ask why.

While I'd relaxed my guard when I left the cottage, I reinforced it, making sure the forest was thicker than the one surrounding me.

With her long skirt swishing around her ankles, she picked

her way around sticks and clumps of downed vegetation, stopping in front of me. Her lips thinned as she stared. "I'm Selitta." She thrust her hand in front of my face.

I took one of her fingers and wiggled it.

"Interesting, as I said." One corner of her mouth curled up, but her smile didn't dispel the sharpness in her smoky gray eyes.

"Tempest." I wasn't up for a conversation and certainly not with a woman who made it plain she wanted Vexxion. Chall fights had never been my thing. In the past, if another woman wanted a guy I was interested in, I'd lift my hands and walk away. No guy was worth antagonizing another woman.

"I couldn't help noting *Vex's* interest in you," she said.

Here we go. She was going to warn me away. Tell me she and *Vex* went way back, that there was no way I could understand him the way she did.

"*Vex* and I are merely friends," I said. Finger fucking friends, but she didn't need to know that.

"He looks at you like he'd like to swallow you whole."

"What's the point of this?" Not liking the fact that I had to look up to meet her eye, I slid off the stump and rounded it to put it between us. She was fae. She could use magic. She could lull.

I wasn't interested in being twisted into performing for a fae whim tonight.

"You're pretty. I'll say that for you." She leaned across the stump to flick my braid lying on my chest. "In a rough and tumble sort of way."

Done with this conversation, I stalked around her, aiming for the path.

She latched onto my arm, and I literally froze. I couldn't move even a finger. I couldn't blink. "Don't think you'll hold his attention for long. He loses interest quickly, and I'm afraid your poor little Nullen heart will be damaged when he tosses you aside."

I might not be able to speak, but I could glare.

Cupping my face, she studied my features, particularly my eyes. "You *are* pretty. Too lovely for a Nullen. Do you have fae blood? I almost believe I can see it in your eyes." She sneered. "It won't be enough to hold him."

A caw rang out and Drask slashed down from the tree above, gouging across her face with his claws. She flung herself backward, crying out, clutching her cheek while blood leaked around her fingers. "That thing clawed me!"

His wings slapped the air as he slashed toward her again. She shrieked while he cawed. Suddenly freed from her spell, I bolted for the trail with Drask swooping in to land on my shoulder, jostling as he clung to the leather.

She did ... something, because she went from behind me to standing on the trail.

I smacked into her.

I flung myself to the side before she could touch me again and lifted my finger, creating the light.

"What do you hope to do with something like that, puny Nullen who may or may not have a touch of fae magic lurking in her veins?"

My finger light fizzled.

"Stay away from me." I was proud that my voice held no fear. It thrived in my mind, however, scrambling to take hold. Pulling a blade from the sheath at my waist, I snarled, slashing out at her.

She rolled her eyes. With a flick of her finger, my long blade went flying, embedding itself in a tree. "To think he sees something in an insignificant Nullen like you."

Run.

Drask flew at her again, a flurry of squawks and battling wings. He clawed her face as I bolted past her.

Her hand snapped out, grabbing my arm, bringing me to a shuddering halt.

While my pulse slammed in my throat, I froze once more. I couldn't move my legs. My chest. My arms. Soon, all that worked was my brain, spiraling as panic took hold.

She flung Drask away with one hand, keeping a tight grip on my arm with the other. The world roared through my mind, but I couldn't move.

Couldn't breathe.

My heart slowed. And slowed. And slowed...

As blackness skirted across my vision, thin bolts of silver lightning coiled around her throat, jerking her off her feet and flinging her away from me. She cried out.

I shuddered and sucked in air. Clutching my hand to my throat, I dropped to my knees and toppled onto my chest.

My face bit the ground, and I knew nothing...

I woke to Drask standing on my chest and the canopy rustling overhead. Darkness had fallen, but the moon had appeared, its soft white glow bathing the world around me.

Drask playfully pecked my cheek. I wanted to hug him.

"You're amazing," I said. "You attacked her and . . ." I frowned. "Where is the nasty fae bitch?" I sat up, clutching my head, hoping it would stop pounding. Drask clawed his way up the front of my leather tunic to perch on my shoulder. I didn't see Selitta, but she must be here somewhere. Lurking. Waiting for the next opportunity to finish what she'd started. Someone had been trying to kill me for weeks.

Had it been her?

Her or someone working with her. Damn wicked fae. I couldn't trust any of them except Vexxion.

Scrambling to my feet, I latched onto a bush when the world started spinning. Something pierced my flesh, and I hissed, snatching my hand away from the thorn that stabbed me. My leg protested the movement, spasming, sending pain jolting through my brain. I wasn't sure my leg would support me for long. I had to get to the cottage before she came after me again.

Shooting wild looks around me and with my mind whispering that each shadow stalked me, I hobbled onto the path, hitching my way through the woods as fast as I could make my leg move.

It took too long. Stark cold fear clawed down my spine, and I cursed myself for not only running, but entering the woods this close to the veil. It felt like hours before I reached the edge of the meadow holding the cabins. Lights inside my cottage drew me like a male dragon to a female in heat, but I didn't dare leave the dubious shelter of the woods.

What if she waited somewhere nearby? She'd see me and attack.

My throat closed off with fear. I sought any movement that might give her away before I stumbled out into the meadow, hunched over to avoid detection.

"Wait."

Vexxion came up behind me and I spun, nearly toppling backward when my leg gave way. He swept me up in his arms, and I coiled my body around his.

I sensed Drask leaving, but all I could see was Vexxion and feel his arms enfolding me. He carried me back into the shelter of the woods, out of the prying moonlight.

"Selitta..." My words jerked out of me. My teeth chattered, and my heart had gone wild. I could barely speak through the panic lashing my soul.

"I've got you. You're safe." He closed his eyes, though only for a heartbeat before opening them. White light arced through them, a match for the streak slicing through his hair.

His thick bands of silver wrapped around us, encasing us in bolts of lightning.

"You... She..." I pressed my forehead against his chest and breathed in his scent.

"No one will hear us now." He lowered me to my feet and stroked my face, my shoulders, before crushing me against his hard frame. His hands roamed my back, driving reassurance into my bones. "You're alright? No wounds?"

Horror kept gurgling up inside me in thick, bilious waves, threatening to drown me. "Selitta's in the woods, she's—"

"Selitta is no longer a threat." He held my face, making my eyes lock onto his. "I promise you this."

I jerked out a nod and scrambled to piece myself back together again. "You were there."

"I'm *always* here for you."

I could only feel relief at that statement. "What did you do to her?"

"Made sure she will never hurt you again."

He'd killed her; I knew this. And I was glad.

"What . . .?" He lifted my hand, gently turning it over, and hissed when he saw my wound courtesy of the thorn bush.

"It's nothing."

"It's everything." He smoothed his finger over it and the sting disappeared. When he released me, the wound had sealed over. "If only I could heal this." He laid his palm over my heart. My ribs warmed as if he could infuse them with the lightning threads still swirling around us.

"I don't mind another scar." Rising onto my toes, I kissed his scars exposed by his tunic, ran my tongue across the wounds he still carried. If only I could make them disappear. Not because they bothered me, but because they didn't. They showed me he'd lived. He'd healed and was stronger because of it now.

I sucked in a breath, needing to tell him what I'd heard. "The fae king's coming to the Claiming."

"I know."

"I don't . . . You're right. I'm not ready to do this yet." Not tonight. Not for a long time. I suspected six weeks would not be enough time to prepare me, though we didn't have longer than that.

It wasn't just about the power I might possess, my skill with blades, or whatever conniving plan we'd come up with. Selitta had given me a taste of what the fae king would do if he discovered I intended to kill him. If he caught me, his punishment would be a thousand times worse than hers.

"You *will* be ready." He continued to stare into my eyes, his flickering with flames. His magic.

When mine was unleashed, would it come even close to the power this man possessed?

"I want you to trust me." His words lashed against the barrier he'd created to protect me from the world. "Promise me? Trust me no matter what."

"I do." From the moment I'd met him, he'd done everything in his power to keep me safe. I was very close to handing him my heart, and I knew he'd protect that with equal fervor.

His mouth crashed down on mine, and he staked his claim. While I moaned and pressed myself against him, opening my mouth to deepen our kiss, his hands roamed my spine. He lifted me and stumbled to press me against the tree behind me, kneeing my legs apart to step between them.

I wrapped myself around him, clinging while a fever took hold.

His mouth was hot and demanding, taking everything I could offer and insisting on more.

I gave all I had to him, moaning while stroking his face, his scars, his chest exposed at the top of his tunic.

How did he know that I needed to lose myself in him and his touch, to feel his hands on my body, his mouth hard on mine, and his cock . . . Fuck, yeah, his cock pressing hard between my legs?

He caged me between the tree and his big body, making me feel secure while making me come undone. I could only cling, kiss him with the lust and adoration roaring through me and rock against his stiff cock.

One of his hands gripped my ass, holding me up while squeezing and releasing. He used it to shove my hips forward while he ground against that sweet spot between my legs.

I was saturated, dripping for him alone, and no one was ever going to take me to this soaring height again. I welcomed that fact; saturated myself in it, actually. He was mine. I was his. And one day soon, I was going to claim him, and the entire world would see we belonged together.

His other hand touched me with infinite care. He glided his knuckles across my jaw to my ear, then slid his fingers into my hair. He teased his fingertips down my braid before holding it, using it to angle my head for his kiss.

His tongue stroked mine, his expert touch making me melt.

I ripped at his tunic, needing to feel his skin beneath my palms, and I was rewarded when the fastenings tore, baring him to me.

When he lifted his head and his gaze locked on mine, I ripped my leather shirt up over my head, throwing it aside, followed by the thin top I wore beneath.

He watched his fingers as they trailed down my chest. As they cupped my exposed breast. As he gently pinched my nipple and rolled it.

My moan ripped up my throat and echoed around me.

"Fury," he growled. "*My* fury. Always."

So far gone and my clit a throbbing wreck, I could only nod. Only succumb to this man in a way I'd done with no other.

I stroked my hand along his scars and cupped his jaw, making him meet my gaze this time. "And you're mine, Vexxion. *Mine.*"

He paused for an infinite second before jerking out a nod.

Before I could speak further, his mouth caught mine again, though gentler this time, his tongue stroking mine while his fingers continued to drive me insane at my breasts. My nipples were pebbles, wanton needy things only his touch would ever satisfy.

Lifting his head, he locked his gaze on mine while he continued to slide his cock against me, only scraps of leather keeping us apart.

It was just him and me, alone in the woods, our gazes delving deep while we rocked together. I clung to his arms, my moans roaring from me, while he growled.

I wrapped the ends of his hair around my fingers and held tight, keeping his eyes on mine while we moved harder, faster together.

He'd told me to never love him. Did he still feel the same? I didn't ask. Couldn't ask. He'd agreed he was mine, but I sensed there were secrets trapped inside this man he'd always refuse to share.

Still, I couldn't back away, couldn't demand he release me. I was lost in the utter madness of him, the pure intensity of my feelings driving me against him.

With a growl, he jerked his hips forward harder, channeling

his thick cock in a way that rocked against my core before stroking my clit.

With a hoarse cry, I gave way, sliding into him, through him, before snapping back into myself. His guttural shout followed, and he moved faster, rubbing harder. The bands of silver coiling around us, hiding us, flared brightly in rippling waves.

I crashed again, shuddering in his embrace, kissing his chest and his scars.

That's when the walls surrounding my heart began to crumble.

37

VEXXION

"I'll take you to your cottage," I said. It was as good of an excuse as any to hold her. If only I could keep her in my arms forever.

Not yet.

Maybe never.

"Tell me one thing," she said.

I nodded and helped her tug on her shirt and leather tunic, dragging my gaze from her pert nipples before I lowered her to the forest floor and staked my claim on them. I would suck on them forever. Pleasure her for hours.

"Why are you helping me? I mean, I doubt my powers of persuasion are that strong. You have a lot to lose if I fail, and the odds are good that I will."

"Not once I've trained you."

"We have about six weeks. I doubt even you can make me strong enough to kill someone as powerful as him."

"It's enough time." Barely.

"But why? If I fail, you'll pay the same price as me."

She was correct. Yet my life was worth nothing.

I wanted to share everything with her, but one misstep, and I'd tumble off that wire I kept imagining in my mind. She was safer if she remained oblivious to everything going on behind her.

"I guess you don't have to tell me," she finally said.

If I didn't share one secret, she'd never trust me. I needed that more than anything. It was the only part of all this that was keeping me sane.

"I want him dead as much as you," I said. I'd never lie to her. I'd hold things back if that meant I could protect her, but this, I could share. "He sliced my mother to pieces in front of me and forced me to watch. He used magic to keep my head in position, magic to pry my eyelids open, and magic to seal my mouth shut when I wouldn't stop screaming."

"That's horrible! I'm so sorry." Her hands fisted at her sides. "It makes me even more eager to kill him."

My mouth twisted up on one side, revealing my appreciation of her vehemence.

"He did this to you too, didn't he?" Her eyes shimmering with tears, she traced her fingertip across my scars.

"Yes." And so much more.

She jerked in a tiny breath. "Now, it makes sense." The grim smile she gave me through her tears was almost as conniving as the endless need churning through my soul. "I'm sorry."

I swept her up in my arms and loosened my threads only enough to allow free movement. They glided around us as I carried her across the starkly open meadow etched with moonlight bright enough to make the dew on the grass sparkle.

Only when we stood outside the cottage door did I lower her to her feet. I held her face, aching to find some way to avoid what must be done. But I'd been through it a billion times and there was only one course that had even a fraction of a chance of success.

"Goodnight," she whispered, giving me a shy smile.

I cupped the feeling that smile generated inside my heart and secured it with magic.

After I backed down the steps, still cloaked in my threads, I remained where I was, watching.

She opened the door and slipped inside.

I stared at the door while the lock snicked closed, and it was only when I heard low voices inside that I turned and walked into the woods, taking the trail toward the fae estate.

I climbed the broad stone front steps and strode across the open deck spanning the entire front of the enormous building. But when I reached to open the two-story front door, Zayde stepped out of the shadows on my right.

"Do you really think you can keep her?" he asked.

"I'm going inside."

"Not yet." He jerked his head toward the lawn.

Because I wasn't opposed to sitting with him, I followed him around the open decking and down to the path. Our feet remained silent as we walked. He didn't speak again until we sat inside a gazebo on the back lawn and my threads had encased the structure.

"You won't be *allowed* to keep her." Zayde leaned back against the wooden surround.

"I have some say in this," I said.

"Do you? I mean, really? I get it. You want to fuck her. I would too. She's gorgeous, she has a lot of fire, and she's—"

My threads compressed, and the gazebo structure groaned and started bucking.

Zayde looked up, one eyebrow lifting. "Alright, so you like her as well."

It was much more than that. While I trusted him to a point, I'd never share everything. That would put both of us in too much danger.

"Take what she offers," he said in a more reasonable tone, his fingers tapping on the wooden rail encircling the eight-sided, open-air building. "Fuck her and let her go."

"There's more to this than just a simple fuck." That was all I was willing to say.

"How so?"

I said nothing.

He sighed. "*You* claim Reyla tomorrow. I'll take Tempest."

The roof overhead snapped beneath the squeeze of my threads. Wooded fragments the size of my thumb spiked down on us, a few embedding their sharp tips in the decking.

"Why?" Zayde asked, plucking a shard out of his exposed forearm. A tap of his finger near the wound sealed it over as if it had never been there.

"Why did I pierce your arm?" I asked blandly.

His lips thinned. "You know what I mean. Jealousy pierced my arm."

I sucked in a breath, but there was no denying it. I'd kill for her. Do anything to please her.

And I'd put a dangerous game into play when I placed that collar around her neck.

"*I* will claim Tempest tomorrow," I said.

"You know if I said I wanted her, she'd be mine."

Ripping the gazebo apart and stabbing him through the heart with one of the posts wouldn't win me any favors. Many would seek revenge, and I had enough fae out to murder me as it was.

Killing him would also eliminate the only person who even vaguely liked me inside the fae realm. But I couldn't stop my threads from pulsing, from squeezing the structure to the point it would implode.

"Tame yourself." Zayde lifted one leg to cross it over the other. "Or I'll do it for you."

"I dare you to try."

"It's me, Vexxion. Cool off. Now."

Because he was one of the few people I cared about, I did as he asked. *Not* because he'd made a threat.

"You heard the fae king's here," he said.

"And I heard he may leave before the Claiming."

Zayde shrugged. "It's hard to say with him. He can't claim anyone himself. He already collared Varissa."

"You know he won't allow her to stand in his way."

"You're suggesting he'd kill her?"

"He can't claim another until she's dead. I don't know what he'll do, but why not? If she's served her purpose and is no longer useful to him, he'll break the bond and take another."

Never Tempest. I'd sacrifice myself to keep that from happening. "Is Varissa with him?"

"Not that I've heard, but he could be keeping her inside his suite." His gaze shot to the upper floor of the estate. Only the fae king had access to that level.

He rarely let Varissa out, not wanting her far in case he had the urge to access all she had to offer. She'd been powerful once. Was she any longer?

"I recommend you stay away from him while he's here," Zayde said, rising.

This was why Zayde had cornered me, challenged me, though he'd also taken the moment to warn me to take care with Tempest.

I got up as well. "I plan to avoid him as much as I can."

He turned and leaned against the wooden door, facing me. "You're determined to claim her tomorrow. Collar her."

"Yes."

"Then what?"

"My goals are unchanged."

"Don't you think your involvement with her might have an impact on those goals?"

It would, which was *why* I was Claiming her. That and because I couldn't bear to do anything else.

She was my one weakness. My one desire. My one obsession.

I wasn't letting her go.

If anyone other than Zayde found out what she meant to me, they'd use her to destroy me.

38

TEMPEST

*A*s I stepped inside the cottage, Drask swooped in along with me and landed on my shoulder. I closed the door, making sure it was locked. My body hummed from what Vexxion and I had done in the woods. It had been perfect. Sublime. I wasn't sure I'd be able to slam my barriers high enough to keep that man out.

But I was still a touch wound up after what happened with Selitta.

Reyla lay on her bed, reading a book. She peered around it, frowning. "I was worried. Where have you been?"

"I'm sorry. I ran through the woods."

"In the dark?"

"It's quiet there."

I'd also tangled with a fae bitch, but there was no need to get into that now. He made sure she'd never hurt me again.

It would come out soon enough. Not his role or mine, but

tonight or tomorrow, at the Claiming, someone was bound to ask where she was.

"How did your leg like the run?" Reyla asked, turning the page in her book. Ignoring me.

I couldn't blame her. How could I make amends for hurting Bro and slamming out of here? "It hated it, as usual."

"You missed dinner." Her lips remained a slash on her face, but she nudged her chin toward the table between our beds. "I brought you back a plate."

I accepted her offer of a truce. "Thanks."

Drask flew off my shoulder and landed on the bedpost, eyeing my meal. I sat on the side and put the plate onto my lap, looking it over before offering him a nice sized chunk of meat.

It had gone cold, but I was famished and ate every bite, sharing it with my crow.

"I'm sorry," I whispered.

She nodded. "We're all stressed."

"Yeah. What are you reading?" I dropped the empty plate onto the small table between the beds and tugged my pack up off the floor, placing it in on the bed beside me.

"Something I found in the estate's library. You should see that place. It's amazing."

"The library?" Digging through the bag, I tugged out the wooden dragon Vexxion had carved, admiring the details in the face. It looked just like Seevar. Why had he tried to toss it into the fire? Didn't he know how much I'd treasure it, not only because it looked like my golden dragon but because Vexxion had made it?

If the commander hadn't changed his mind about selling Seevar, this would be all I'd have to remind me of him.

"It's an amazing library," Reyla said. "There are three floors and thousands of books."

That's when it hit me, and I knew who'd tried to buy him. My eyes stung, and I blinked fast, staring at the ceiling, not wanting Reyla to notice my tears.

"I was talking about the fae estate, though." She laid her book pages down on her chest and stared toward the single window in the cabin placed to the right of the door. "These cottages are cute, but the estate? It's stunning."

Vexxion was going to buy Seevar to make sure he went to a good home, that no one would hurt him. That he'd be treated kindly. Was there anything that man wouldn't do for me?

"That's where the fae lords stay prior to the Claiming," Reyla said. "The building's six stories high and made up exclusively of suites, plus sitting rooms on each level where the fae can lounge. We weren't allowed to go anywhere except to the dining room, and they'd assigned guards as if they thought we'd steal something." She snorted. "I peeked inside one of the rooms as we passed and got a rap on my back for my effort."

"They allowed you inside the library, though?"

Her smile curved up on one side and her eyes sparkled. "Well, you know me."

"Let me guess. You said you had to go to the bathroom, but you snuck in."

"Yes," she breathed. "I didn't stay long, just made my way through a few stacks. I grabbed this book because it looked interesting and stuffed it down inside my tunic. No one suspected a thing."

"They might if they find it here after we leave."

"I'll take it with me." She stroked the spine with scrolling letters saying, *Ember's Shadow*.

Maybe it was a novel featuring dashing Nullen males and ladies in distress? She adored them.

"Was it worth it?" I asked.

She shrugged. "I haven't figured that out yet. At dinner, they said that some of the fae had already arrived. They were upstairs. I guess there's a ballroom there, and they were hosting a big event." She pursed her lips. "We weren't invited to that either."

"How many are coming to the Claiming?" I laid the dragon figurine on my pillow and scooted back to lean against the wall with my legs thrust out in front of me.

"No one mentioned fae numbers, but there are thirty-two Nullens available for Claiming." Sitting up, she closed the book and tucked it under her pillow. Her intent gaze fell on my face. "Bro and I were worried about you. You took off and didn't come back."

Lifting my pendant, I stroked my fingertip across the smooth stone. "I needed time to think." And battle a bitch. Although Vexxion and Drask did all the fighting.

I leaned over to rub his back and silently promised him more treats in the morning.

"Did you come to any conclusions?" she asked.

"Not really."

"I did."

I nodded, unsure where this was going but hoping she wouldn't drag Brodine's feelings for me into it.

"I owe you an apology." She swung her legs around to sit on the side of the bed. "I shouldn't have pushed you about Bro. I was feeling bad for him. He's adored you forever. After Kinart was murdered . . ." When she opened her eyes, they shimmered with tears. "I guess I just wanted to see *someone* happy, even if it could never be me."

"Thanks for saying that."

"I won't push you on him any longer. I'll stop telling you to give him a chance."

Even better. "It won't matter soon. We'll be claimed, and the odds are good he'll leave for a different fae court."

"There are only three. Four if you count the cursed one, but since all of them seem to have been turned to stone there, I doubt they'll send anyone to the Claiming."

"I thought they were dead. They were turned to stone?" My mind flashed to Selitta freezing me in the forest. I couldn't breathe. My heart was slowly turning to ice. Only my mind continued to whirl. If she'd succeeded in whatever she intended to do to me, would I have remained standing in the forest, aware of everything going on around me but unable to move? My heart had started to slow—

"That's what Brodine told me."

"I wouldn't think Brodine would care much about the Lydel Court."

"He's as curious about the fae as I am," she said. Her voice dropped to a hoarse whisper. "We saw the fae king."

My fingers bit into my thigh and I stifled a yelp. "You did?"

My limbs quaked, and I masked it by dropping my pendant and rubbing my bad leg, implying to Reyla—who watched me—that the limb was sore from my run. Which it was. No lie there, though I was using it as a distraction.

"He stepped into the dining room briefly," she said. "He greeted us and spoke to each and every one of us. He's nice. I'm not sure why he has a reputation for being nasty."

To think I might've had the chance to stab him while he strolled around the dining room. Instead, I was battling for my life in the woods.

"What does he look like?" I'd never seen him.

Her lips curled up. "He's gorgeous, but I guess he would be since he's fae. Aren't they all beautiful? They made us leave as soon as dinner was over and come back here. I wanted to sneak up the stairs and get a peek at the ballroom, but they were quite firm about that."

The last thing I cared about was a fae party. "Did you learn anything else about the Claiming?"

"Not much. I'm sure we'll find out more tomorrow." She frowned. "Anyway, the rumor spread during dinner—when the fae king wasn't around, I'll add—is that the Claiming hurts. That it's pretty much torture."

Why wouldn't Vexxion tell me that?

"I don't understand how it could be that bad, though," she said. "I think this is just gossip. The whole thing is a big unknown. It's natural to assume the worst."

I couldn't keep my soul from quivering.

39

TEMPEST

We went to bed, and I slept better than expected, waking when dawn peeked through the window and prodded my eyes.

Someone knocked on the door. "Come eat. You'll prepare yourselves after breakfast."

Reyla swung her legs around, dropping them onto the floor, and stretched, facing me where I sat on the edge of my bed. "This is it, I guess. Food, no more leathers. No more riding dragons."

"I'm taking the golden dragon with me. The commander said I could."

"If Vexxion lets you. While I don't expect to be tortured today, I'm not sure I'll have a lot of say about my future once this is over."

"Are we stupid to do this?" I had a driving reason, but she didn't. "I still think you could—"

"Please." Leaning forward, she took my hands and squeezed them. "The time to back out has passed. I'm doing it, and I'd rather you stood beside me, supporting me, than trying to force me away."

"I worry about you. I promised—"

"Kinart's ghost you'd watch out for me." She blinked up at the ceiling. "And I made a promise to him too. Remember?"

She had some fae secrets to expose. Had he learned something about the king?

Reyla choked back a sob. "I feel like he's right there, almost behind me. If I turn, he'll give me that crooked smile I loved so much. He'll stroke my face like he used to, and everything will be perfect again. But I turn and he's not there. I want this." An almost feral vehemence came through in her words. "I need to do this. I don't think I'll feel him the same once I'm inside faerie. This is a new start. I have my memories, and I'm taking them with me, but I can't . . . I just can't stay where he haunts me. Do you understand?"

My eyes stinging, I nodded.

"I know you want to protect me," she said. "But you know what? I can do that for myself. You take care of Tempest. I suspect you've got a full agenda already."

"What makes you think that?"

"You and Vexxion whispering all the time."

"Maybe I like him, and I can't stay away."

"Oh, you like him, for sure. You should watch out or he'll hurt you."

It might already be too late for that.

"He's one of the wicked fae," she said. "Remember how the

commander used to call them that, like they were the villains of our world out to get us? Instead, it's the dregs and the Lieges."

"Maybe they're all connected." That was as far as I was going to take this.

"It wouldn't surprise me. The dregs are born from magic and despair, and while I know some of us have suppressed power, not one of us has what it takes to create beasts like them."

But the fae did. And they—one particular fae lord—not only created them but also controlled them.

"Let's go eat." She slipped off the bed. "They'll tell us what to expect after that."

We washed in the tiny bathroom and dressed in our second set of leathers. I'd left my blades in the woods. Why hadn't I retrieved them? Oh, yeah, I'd barely had the energy to cling to Vexxion while he carried me through the dark. I'd jumped at each snap of a stick or howl in the distance. At least I still had my short knives.

They'd set up tables outside the cottages. So much for seeing the estate Reyla had gushed about. We sat, Brodine across from us and not meeting my eyes, and everyone ate, grabbing rolls stuffed with meat and cheese from baskets placed in the center, washing them down with water. A simple, yet filling, meal.

None of the fae were around. An old Nullen man refilled our water and the baskets of rolls, standing off to the side while everyone chatted about nothing and filled their bellies.

Nervous, I picked at my roll. Where was Vexxion? I didn't

want to go to the Claiming without seeing him first. Touching him.

So foolish on my part. Where had my independence gone? I didn't like relying on him. All he had to do was show up and do his part. Well, there was that little thing called the Awakening that would follow. And training. Lots of that. Oh, and he had to get me inside Bledmire Court and make sure I got close enough to the fae king to kill him.

Was I stupid to come here? So much could go wrong. I wasn't up for this. I didn't have what—

"Hey."

I looked up from where I was mangling a roll, crumbs and bits of meat raining down on my plate, to find Brodine looking at me with the crooked smile I remember from before things got complicated between us.

"It's going to be alright," he said. "I've heard it doesn't take much time. Before you know it, we'll be claimed and on our way to the court of our new lord. We'll have the chance to learn magic. We'll . . . have meaning."

"About last night." At least his nose looked fine. "I shouldn't have hurt you. I'm sorry."

"I shouldn't have pushed it. I'm sorry too."

I wanted to hug him. So much. But things were different between us, and I had no idea how to bridge the gap. However, I was grateful to have my old friend back, not the pushy man who'd made me uncomfortable since he propositioned me when I got tipsy on my eighteenth birthday.

"You're right. It's going to be alright." Somehow.I placed what was left of my roll on my plate and brushed my hands together to get rid of the crumbs. I drained my water and stood, finding many of the others finishing up as well. "Thanks, Bro. I appreciate it."

Rising, he leaned across the table and squeezed my shoulder. "Anytime."

"If you're finished," the old man said, striding over to stand at the head of the table. "Leave your plates. Return to your cottages. Clothing waits for you there. Cleanse yourselves, please. Dress. Comb your hair, of course. I encourage you to make sure you appear tidy. Leave your belongings inside the cottage and come outside. I'll lead you to the Claiming after that."

"That's it?" Reyla hissed by my ear. "No explanations other than get dressed and come back here?"

I suspected the time for explanations was over.

"One other thing," the man said, pausing. "Do not bring weapons to the Claiming."

Truly? I was a rider. I didn't go anywhere unless I was armed, not even to sleep.

"Let's go." Dread coiled tight inside me. I didn't like anything about this, but nothing would make me back out now.

We returned to the cottage, finding gowns lying on our beds, Reyla's in pink with a flouncy neckline, which made her purse her lips and scowl, mine in a green that matched my eyes and my pabrilleen stone. I cupped it and made a wish that this would turn out alright, that it would be over soon and that nothing would go wrong from here.

"Pretty." Reyla flicked her hand toward the set of shell combs nestled on the bed beside the gown. "Why do you get baubles when I don't?" Her smirk told me she didn't care about such things but that she did enjoy teasing. I welcomed the humor in her voice, the returning sparkle in her eyes.

"I'm special." I shot her a grin, and we both burst into high-strung laughter.

We took turns in the bathroom and got dressed, arranging each other's hair, though she insisted I keep hers simple and coil it up in a knot on the back of her head.

"You, my beauty," she said, pointing to the solitary chair in the room, "need a more artful arrangement."

"My regular braid's good enough for me."

"Not for today."

"Why today in particular?"

"As you said, you're special." She patted the solitary chair in the room.

"So are you."

A pensive look took over her face. "I always thought I was."

I sat in the chair. "You always will be to me."

"Thank you." She held up the combs, twisting them this way and that to let the tiny green jewels catch the light. "I think these are the same stone as your pendant. I've never seen anything this intricately carved before." She held them out to me. "Do you think they're fae?"

I shrugged. "We're on the border, so they could be."

"They'll look amazing in your hair." She proceeded to sweep my hair up, leaving artful coils around my face. I had to admit, it looked gorgeous when she'd finished.

"Are you ready to go?" she asked, coming around the chair to smooth one stray strand of hair behind my ear.

"Just one second." In the bathroom, I hitched up my skirt.

I defied the old man. Probably defied the entire fae kingdom by doing it, but I strapped a knife to my left thigh.

An unarmed rider was a dead one.

When we stepped outside, we found the others leaving their cottages too, the men wearing formal pants and tunics with fancy stitching across the shoulders and around their collars, the women dressed in long gowns like ours.

Some of the women were riders. Why not let *us* wear pants like the men? Such was the curse of being female. Funny how no one cared about our sex when we were killing dregs.

Drask soared over to land on my shoulder, digging his claws into the fabric of my gown to get a solid grip. He bobbed around as I walked over to join the others.

Once we'd gathered in a cluster near the old man, he cleared his throat. None of us had been talking much, nervousness stealing our voices, but that brought us to attention.

"If you'll follow me." He pivoted and strode into the woods, taking a trail I hadn't noticed the day before. I was pretty observant about things like this. Had it been here then, or had it magically appeared when the man needed it?

We walked single file behind him. Reyla strode along the path ahead of me, and Bro took up the rear of our diminished family unit. After about ten minutes, light bloomed ahead, and we exited the thick woods, walking out into a meadow bathed in sunlight and beauty. On any other day, we'd all be admiring the fist-sized pink flowers swaying in the deep grass. The sun bursting through the clear blue sky overhead. And the trill of birds singing merrily in the woods.

Instead, this felt like the perfect setting for a gruesome crime.

There was no one here except for the old guy and us Nullens.

Reyla took my hand and extended her other toward Brodine. We three bunched together for what might be the very last time.

"Love you," she whispered.

I squeezed her hand and my pinched gaze swept across Bro as well as her. "Love you guys."

Brodine choked on whatever he might've been planning to say and nodded.

"Form a circle," the old man growled. "We don't have time for dallying. Do not hold hands."

We released each other, and with the rest of the group, formed a ring around the man, though the three of us remained side by side. Brodine looked about the oldest of the group at twenty-seven, but I assumed the fae weren't interested in claiming someone later in their life.

"Close your eyes," the gray-haired man said.

"Why?" Brodine asked. "I like seeing what's coming at me."

"Do as I ask, or you will pay the price."

"What price?" a guy with shockingly red hair standing a few Nullens over on my left asked. He grinned at the woman fidgeting on his other side. "I don't see anyone here to collect a fee."

He blinked, his smile fading, replaced with a pinch of his thick lips. Gasping, he smacked his palm on his chest. He keeled forward, landing hard on the ground, crushing grass and a few big pink flowers.

Drask sucked in a breath only to release it with a shrill squawk. He remained on my shoulder, watching as the woman cried out, scrambling over to drop to her knees beside the fallen guy.

"Ford. Ford!" She rolled him onto his back.

He gazed at the sky, his eyes milky white, and his face stretched in a tortured grimace.

The woman wailed and collapsed on top of his chest. "Ford. Ford!"

"Stand," the old man said. "Take your place again in the circle or..."

Her face completely devoid of color, she leaped to her feet. But rather than step back to where she'd been before, she fisted her skirt up and raced toward the woods. In a blink of the old man's eyes, she lay face-down on the grass like Ford.

The rest of us kept our mouths shut and our eyes trained on the old guy's face after that.

"Does anyone else have questions?" he asked with a low laugh that clawed its way down my spine. "I thought not." Fire flashed through his eyes.

Not Nullen, then.

The wicked fae had been aptly named.

"Let's start again, shall we?" he said lightly. "Close your eyes."

I did, swallowing back the bile retching up my throat. I was grateful I'd eaten almost nothing. Someone else wasn't as lucky; their guttural hurls echoed in the pretty meadow. I didn't open my eyes to see if they lived long enough to finish emptying their belly.

Reyla's teeth chattered. If I wasn't clenching my jaw hard enough to make it ache, mine would rattle too.

Drask ruffled his wings, as unsettled as me, though he'd stopped squawking after the second person was killed.

What had we gotten ourselves into?

Something snapped from the ground with a hiss and whipped around my body, lashing my arms to my sides and strapping my legs together at my thighs.

Drask shrieked and took flight, hurling himself away from me.

Before I could gulp in a breath, the world collapsed beneath me.

I plunged down.

40

TEMPEST

I landed hard, my spine jarring as my butt smacked onto the broad seat of a stone chair. Around me, other Nullens here for the Claiming did the same, some crying out in pain when they hit.

Reyla yelped when she landed sideways on the chair to my left, her head smacking the backrest, and Brodine bellowed when he splatted on the stone floor in front of his chair.

The restraints coiling around my body hissed and smoked, disintegrating before my eyes. Before I could leap from the chair, deep purple vines erupted from the stone by my feet. Some snapped around my legs, spreading them wide enough to pin them to the legs of the chair, while others coiled up like furious snakes to pin my wrists to the armrests.

The vines lifted Reyla and Brodine and jerked them through the air before smacking them onto the seats in a sitting position. They gasped as other vines secured them in place like me.

Breathing fast, I snapped my head this way and that, taking in a rocky cave just big enough to hold thirty or so stone chairs placed in a circle. A round mosaic about the size of Fawna took up the center, crafted in an ornate pattern I didn't recognize, but for some reason struck fear through me.

Panicked cries boiled over from the Nullens around me.

If I could break free, there were two ways out, through arched stone openings on either side of the room leading to shadowy tunnels beyond.

Snarling, I yanked on the bonds, but no matter how hard I wrenched my arms up and my legs forward, I couldn't snap the vines. I twisted my hand, twisting it, but I couldn't reach my skirt to bunch it up and pull my knife. Because, fates, I was getting out of here if I could.

Leaden footsteps echoed from the opening on my right, and silence descended as if everyone's windpipe had been compressed. My head snapped up; my gaze trained in that direction.

Sobbing, Reyla sent me a tear-stained look, her eyes shocked dark blue with terror. Brodine grunted and gnashed his teeth, his muscles bulging as he tried to pry his body out of the chair. His attention remained on the dark passage where a tiny light suddenly bloomed. It dipped and swayed, dancing in sickening moves as it came closer. Like a malicious sprite swirling across a blood-drenched meadow, it burst from the tunnel. It soared over to hover above the mosaic in the center of the room and stopped moving.

The tension level dropped and a few Nullens around me relaxed, their gazes fixed on the light. Even Brodine and Reyla couldn't seem to look away. Some of the women sighed as they stared at the light. It *was* pretty with its pale blue sparkles coiling around a bright pink center, but I'd never trust anything presented by the wicked fae, let alone something involved in the secretive Claiming.

I swallowed hard, my saliva scraping down my throat that was as dry as the wasteland beyond the valley.

The light exploded, showering us with sparks that burned where they touched. I bit my lower lip until it bled to keep from crying out. Others wailed, their shrill voices echoing in the low-ceilinged room.

When the blast winked out, a circle of fae lords and ladies stood on the mosaic circle. The men wore ornately embroidered velvet tunics and dark trousers, and the women were dressed in elaborate gowns with puffy sleeves and skirts spread out like the bells on the pink flowers above. Vexxion and Zayde stood on the edge of the group.

I lost count at forty fae. There had to be twice the number of Nullens here to be claimed. None of them held anything in their hands. Where were the collars?

My bones turned to frost, though I couldn't name why.

Vexxion's gaze locked on mine, and a sudden calm fell over me, as if he'd found a way to wrap himself around me and hold me snug in his embrace. Like nothing and no one would ever tear us apart.

A lull? If so, my pounding heart welcomed his magic.

A tall fae woman standing on the edge of the group

grunted. As one, they peeled away from the others, oozing off the circular mosaic to stride up to the Nullens pinned to stone chairs.

They latched onto faces, jerking the heads of friends and strangers and stared into eyes before scoffing and moving on to someone new. One fae lord flipped a Nullen's hand over hard enough to make the snap of breaking bones ring out in the room. The guy's cry of pain cut off swiftly, and he slumped in the chair.

They *inspected* Nullens like meat hanging from hooks for sale at the butchers.

Reyla's sobs ended in a gurgling swallow, and she shot me a look so full of dismay, it made my limbs quake. Brodine stared forward stoically, but his fingers shook on the arms of his chair, his nails creating a tap-tap-tap-tap sound that drilled through my skull. His gaze shot to his hands, and he gasped in a breath before stilling them.

Vexxion stalked straight over to me, the other fae parting, reeling back as if one touch, one look from him, would burn them alive.

My gaze dropped to his hands. Would the collar appear there? They remained empty like every other fae hand in the room.

He came to a halt in front of me, his gaze locked on mine. The stars I used to see swirling there were gone, replaced by shadows that flicked in one direction, then another as if the ghosts of fae past had merged with his mind.

His hand snapped forward, and he pressed the pad of his thumb against the center of my forehead.

Something coiled beneath—no, *into*—my skin.

"Don't say anything." His voice whispered low enough for my ears alone.

Vines flung themselves up from the ground by my feet and snapped around my head, hurtling it back against the high back of the stone chair hard enough to rattle my brain. I bit my tongue again, tasting the blood of my horror, but I held in my gasp.

Tips of the vines undulated away from my head, rippling toward Vexxion. The lavender spikes on the ends gently glided across his forehead, though they left no mark.

With a snap, the tips spun and plunged toward my throat, scratching as they encircled my neck.

They tightened.

And tightened. Until I was sure they'd meet in the middle and my head would be severed and roll down my chest to land with a wet smack at Vexxion's feet.

Zayde stood in front of Reyla, who kept releasing shrill cries, her body jerking as if seizing.

Brodine stared forward still, his jaw twitching and his nails tap-tap-tap-tapping on the arms of his chair. No one approached him. No one claimed him. No one directed a vine collar to wrap around his neck.

While I wheezed and the bleakness of this horrifying fae world crashed through my mind, Vexxion stepped closer. Closer. He delicately lifted my chin, making me stare into his eyes.

I floundered in the deep sapphire depths where lightning flickered, and a vault of secrets still waited.

"I claim you, Tempest Lucerna," he rasped. "You. Are. *Mine*."

The vines loosened around my neck, yet they didn't snap free. If my hands weren't bound, I'd claw at them. Wrench them away. I struggled, the restraints biting into my skin.

"Vexxion!" someone bellowed from the tunnel on my right, the man's voice coiling and snapping with rage.

His head twisted in that direction, and when his gaze locked on mine again, true fear blazed there for the very first time.

"Who did the bastard piss off this time?" one of the fae muttered.

Someone more dangerous than these wicked fae was coming. Footsteps echoed, hollow and bone jarring, and they were approaching the cave from the tunnel.

Vexxion attacked the vines pinning me to the chair, clawing at them while stark desperation overran his face. The strands of lightning he'd used to protect me so many times lashed at the vines on my legs, but they didn't release. What kind of plant could resist this man's magic?

"Knife," I wheezed, keeping my voice low, though it hardly mattered when everyone around me was screaming and writhing in their chairs as they were claimed. "Strapped to my left thigh."

"Smart." For one second, his smile coiled up, both decadent and sweet.

"I'm disobedient."

"As you should be," he purred. His eyes shot to the tunnel. "I wish I had time to be gentle, tiny fury." He yanked up my skirt and ripped the knife from its sheath before gouging at the vines. They severed, twisting against the stone chair, hissing and snapping through the air like poisonous serpents.

Once I was free, Vexxion hauled me off the chair and with me in his arms, bolted toward the left tunnel.

Brodine bellowed my name, and a glance back showed he still hadn't been claimed.

Zayde still stood in front of Reyla. Strangled shrieks erupted from her throat in a rhythmic manner, and tears razored down her cheeks.

Vexxion lowered me to my feet. He shoved me into the tunnel and handed me the knife. "Run. Hide." He spun and stalked back into the room.

I hurtled up the tunnel, stumbling and tripping on things littering the ground because I couldn't see where I was going. When I smacked into a stone wall on my right, jarring my shoulder, I slowed to a walk, stretching out my hand to avoid breaking a leg or impaling myself on something.

Behind me, guttural groans echoed in the cave of horrors. Among those cries, I swore I heard Vexxion.

Coming to a stop, I flexed my hand on the hilt of my blade. Leaving him to whatever was coming felt wrong. Yet he'd told me to run.

I couldn't. I whirled around and scrambled back down the slope, not stopping until I reached the end of the tunnel. With my back pinned to the cold stone wall and my body masked by the cool, welcoming darkness, I carefully peered into the room.

Almost all the fae and nearly all the Nullens had disappeared.

Brodine was the only Nullen left in the room.

A fae lord with black hair and brutal scars networking his face stood in front of my friend, staring in amusement while deep purple vines coiled and twisted around Bro's throat. When my friend gasped, the fae lord laughed. How could anyone find joy in someone else's pain?

Brodine thrashed and twitched in the chair, his hoarse groans pinching up his throat. His hands snapped free, and he raked his neck, gouging his skin. Blood funneled down his fingers, splattering his formerly pristine tunic and the gray stone floor around him.

The fae lord lifted his arms. When he dropped them, Brodine stilled other than his hands flopping on his thighs. He stared forward, and the blankness there sucked every bit of air from my lungs.

With a snap of the fae lord's fingers, the two of them disappeared, leaving the room empty...

... Except for Vexxion lying in the center of the mosaic tile.

41

VEXXION

"Wake up," someone snarled in my ear. "Please, wake up. I can't help you if you don't wake up!"

They latched onto my wrist and tried to drag me, my body skidding only a short distance across a cold, hard floor.

Snapping my eyes open, I found my tiny fury so aptly named standing above me, glaring at me.

Seeing me awake, she dropped to her knees beside me again.

"Don't kneel," I said hoarsely, trying to remember what happened.

Someone... beyond angry.

Attacking me.

Nothing else.

"You can either lie on the floor until you rot or help me get you onto your feet," Tempest snapped.

"There's my tiny fury rising to the surface." I stroked her face, as always, stunned by how beautiful she was, how her inner strength shone in her green eyes.

"Fuck that crap, Vexxion. We've got to get you out of here before . . ." Her head snapped up, and she squinted toward a dark tunnel on my right.

"The Claiming." If my brand on her forehead didn't convince me, the scarlet slash across her throat would do it. Collars always sunk deep, fusing the surface skin behind them.

A taste of her power shot through me, sweet on the tip of my tongue.

"I don't know what that fae lord did to you, but he claimed Brodine. Everyone else is gone."

"Those claimed are taken to the fae realm for Awakening and training."

She frowned. "We need to talk about that soon, but for now, can you get your sweet ass moving?"

"Sweet ass?"

"It looks good. I'd be lying if I denied it."

I sat up and rubbed my head that throbbed as if a thousand beasts had smashed their way through it. Just one, however. "Only *good*?"

"Stop fishing for compliments and start moving."

With her help—something that mortified me—I rose to my feet.

"Which tunnel should we take?" Her wild gaze snapped around the room.

"The one that'll get us out of here."

"Stop fooling around. You know what I mean."

"You were supposed to run. Hide." The glare I gave her would've made a room full of fae drop to their knees.

Her fucking neck... Seeing the mark and knowing I gave it to her sobered me in a way nothing else ever could. I slid my fingertip across the mark, adding a spell to help her heal quickly. "The pain will fade."

"What about the feeling that something's crawling beneath my skin? Will that fade as well?" Pure, unadulterated rage churned through her voice. "You could've told me about the vines. This wretched collar. What was going to happen here."

"I agree. You have every right to be angry," I said.

Wait until she discovered *everything* I'd done.

Then her fury would know no bounds.

She'd be glorious. Spiteful. And completely amazing.

If only that anger wasn't going to be directed at me.

42

TEMPEST

"Which tunnel?" I asked him. I wasn't pissed at him. The sight of him lying on the tile without knowing if he was alive or dead had burned through my anger about the Claiming. Nothing could gut me more than seeing him crumpled and vulnerable. I couldn't breathe. I couldn't think.

I'd hurtled myself to him, not caring if anyone saw me, if anyone tried to grab me, if anyone blasted me to the very fates with their wicked magic. All I could think of was him.

My collar tightened. The twist of vines beneath my skin made a gag jerk up my throat. They were digging.

Tasting.

Writhing with unfettered joy.

I clung to the knowledge that killing me would eliminate their host. For now, that meant I could breathe.

When he lifted his finger, pointing toward the tunnel I'd

bolted through, I laid his arm over my shoulder and urged him toward the dark opening.

He grunted and tugged his arm away from me. "I'm not helpless."

He staggered.

I grabbed onto his arm, keeping him from toppling over, snarling. "I decide about that."

His infernally sexy lips twitched upward. "I like it when you snap at me. I can taste your storm. Your snide tartness. It's a dish that thrills through me every time."

I reeled back, though I kept my hand on his arm, holding him in place. "Are you drunk?"

"More like hungover. Bad magic. My stupid head won't stop pounding."

"Use your magical touch to take away the pain."

His grin grew wider, heated in that way that made my knees buckle. "Magical touch?"

"You know what I mean. You healed Seevar and my arm after the dreg raid because there was no way it could seal over that fast on its own. You said you would've helped Kinart if you could."

His smile fell. "My magical touch, as you call it, won't work on me."

"I'm sorry." I draped his arm over my shoulders again, and this time, he let me help him cross the room and enter the tunnel. "Who attacked you?"

"Someone with more power than me."

"Who was it?"

"A very dangerous person."

"Who else do I need to kill?" I snarled.

"I adore your persistence."

"Enough to share his name?"

He crooked his head my way. "No."

I grumbled, but there was no forcing Vexxion. "Where should I take you? I assume the cottage I stayed in last night is no longer an option. The same with the fae estate for you."

We slowly moved up the tunnel.

"We need to leave this area as soon as possible," he said.

"Before your *friend* comes back?"

"Something like that."

"You don't have the energy to walk much farther than the end of this tunnel."

His voice curled around me. *Caressed me.* "You'd be surprised at the energy I'd have with the right incentive."

"Don't make this sexual."

"Who says I am?"

"Me. I say you are."

"I believe when it comes to you, tiny fury," he drawled, "there's no way to separate the sexual from everything else."

I rolled my eyes. "You couldn't kiss me or satisfy me at the moment."

In a flash, I was pressed against the stone tunnel wall, and his mouth was crashing down on mine. Devouring me while I moaned and wrapped myself around him. Proving that he *could* make me melt whenever he pleased.

I should fight him. Push him away. But his tongue . . . His tongue demanded entrance to my mouth, and I surrendered. I could raise no resistance to this cursed fae lord.

He lifted his head. "You were saying?"

"It wasn't *that* good."

"I'm *always* good," he purred.

"That has yet to be proven."

"Because I can't..."

I'd give anything to hear him finish his thought. Now wasn't the time.

I uncoiled myself from around him. With my feet planted solidly on the ground, I took his hand.

He linked our fingers, and it was such a silly, simple thing for him to do, yet it made joy dance through me. We'd get out of here, and we'd hide until we figured out what we should do next.

"Will whoever hurt you come after us?" I asked.

"Unfortunately, yes."

"I'm not the only one being hunted, then."

"Someone or another has hunted me since the day I was born. Before then, actually."

I couldn't fathom such a thing. Sure, I was dumped at the fortress, and the dregs were anything but a joy to battle, but I had my friends. A job. A sense of security even if the foundation it rested on was shaky.

"They left you on the mosaic floor." Hurt. Motionless. My stupid eyes stung when I should be shoring up my will to remain strong. He didn't need my pity. And he'd already made it plain he didn't want my love.

Not that I loved him. Despite the crumbling walls around my heart, I refused to let myself love him.

"You said the person after us claimed someone. That'll keep

them occupied for a while," Vexxion said.

"What comes next?" I lightly touched my neck, and the vines twisted, poking as if telling me to leave them alone. "I hate this thing."

"I'm sorry, but it's for the best."

"That's up for debate."

"You'll see."

Since it was the only way I could enter the fae realm, he was probably right.

"We'd better hustle." I tugged on his hand, and he strode along beside me, proving that the fae did heal faster than any Nullen. They were practically immortal.

I was not.

I needed to remember that before I let myself drown in his kiss again. Succumb to his endless charms. Or hand my heart over to him with complete abandon.

We reached the top of the tunnel and paused at the opening. The sun had fled the sky, leaving a moonless expanse behind. How long were we inside the cave?

The forest stretched around us, and something shrieked not far away.

My heart shuddered. I pressed my back against the side of the hill, studying the woods.

When something smacked into my left shoulder, I bit back a shriek.

"Drask." My knees wobbled, and I barely remained upright. While he fluffed his wings and settled in, I stroked his back. "Maybe give me a warning before you latch onto my shoulder next time?"

He pecked my cheek.

"Where should we go?" I asked Vexxion.

"The veil isn't far." He kept his voice low. "Give me a moment, and I'll be fully recovered. I can take us to a safe spot."

"Does it hurt to pass through the veil?"

"Not me."

"Great. How about pitiful Nullens?"

"You're anything but pitiful." When I drilled him with my gaze, he shrugged. "The collar will help. It's fae."

"No," I breathed with a touch of sarcasm.

"Without it, you'd be marked. Hunted. And you wouldn't want to live after they caught you."

Now, wasn't that delightful? My skin quivered, and I hefted my skirt up to my thighs to make it easier to move.

His smoldering gaze tracked the movement. "And here you said I wasn't that good."

"Don't get too excited." I pulled the knife and gripped it tightly, savoring the feel of it in my hand.

"You took a grave chance bringing that with you."

"Why couldn't you free me from the chair? Isn't your magic powerful enough?"

"I'm more powerful than you know."

"Yet my simple—forbidden—knife saved both of our asses." I huffed. "How's that recovery going?"

He grunted. "Even with my magic suppressed, I'm more formidable than you can imagine."

"Then why are we standing here, baiting the cave entrance?"

"I don't sense anything near that will cause harm."

Except whatever shrieked in the woods. "Yet."

"At all," he bit out.

"Can we get my things?" I felt almost defenseless with only a tiny knife in my hand.

"That would be a colossal mistake."

I pinched my stupid dress. "I miss my leathers already."

"And I miss how they hug your cute ass."

"Oversharing a lot tonight, aren't you?"

He stilled. "Does it bother you?"

I sighed. "I wish it would."

His smile curled up again, devastating and gorgeous enough to make my heart stop. Sadly, he saw the effect he had on me because his smile grew wider. "Do I disturb you, *Tempest*?"

I'd gotten so used to him calling me storm and fury that my true name sounded odd on his tongue. "No."

"Just no? No quip or snarl about how you're strong enough to resist me?"

I turned to face him. "Why would I say that when we both know it's not true?"

Heat flashed in his eyes, and his hand lifted toward my face.

A sound to my right snagged my attention. Lifting my knife, I flung myself between Vexxion and a shadowy creature exploding across the meadow.

A dragon-sized beast with a scaled hide and finger-length fangs rushed toward us, slashing its horns through the air.

43

TEMPEST

The stupid, wicked fae lord latched onto me and flung me behind him as if he had the strength to defend us both. He braced his legs and faced the creature from a nightmare hurtling toward us with only his bare hands lifted. Did he truly think he had what it took to defeat something like that?

Silver bands coiled off his fingers, snapping toward the beast. The bolts hit, and the creature shuddered. But it shook its horns and renewed its red-eyed glare, galloping toward us on its clawed feet.

"New plan." I placed my fingertips inside my mouth in just the right way and blew. Grabbing Vexxion's arm, I dragged him close to the steep hill and peered up. "If you boost me onto the top, are you recovered enough to follow?"

He wrapped his arms around me, drawing me sweetly against his chest.

"Not the time, Vexxion," I snarled.

A blink, and we stood on top of the hill, grass snapping against our knees in the wind.

"How did you do that?" This was how he'd moved to the top of the main fortress building and how the fae bitch, Selitta, moved to stand in front of me on the path.

"One of my magic tricks you abhor."

"Teach me."

He kissed the tip of my nose. "I plan to, and so many other things."

The beast reached the base of the hill and paused, clawing at the ground and snorting. It tipped its head back and locked its gaze on us before it rushed toward the shallow slope of the hill on our left.

A cry rang out overhead and Seevar swooped down toward us.

"Reinforcements have arrived," I said with a grin.

Seevar snarled and sucked in a deep breath. He blasted flames at the beast.

While the grass caught fire and smoke billowed into the air, the beast shook its head. It kept coming, the ground thundering from its movement.

"Seevar has fire." Even when I was about to die, I could marvel that my youngling dragon could blast already.

"Admire him later." Vexxion latched onto my hand and led us on a collision course with Seevar's incoming flight. "Let's see how your dragon handles two." He gathered me in his arms and leaped as Seevar dropped low enough to skim his clawed feet across the tips of the tall grass.

The horned beast bellowed.

Seevar sent more fire over his shoulder.

And we landed on the dragon's spine hard enough to make my teeth snap together.

Seevar flapped his wings. The grass billowed in the stiff wind, and the fire erupted into a roaring inferno. With his neck outstretched and his tail spiking behind, Seevar surged above the beast.

The creature sprung up, raking out with its claws but missing. As it dropped back to the blazing grass, Seevar took us higher, flying above the forest and toward the fae realm.

"Who's the one with the power now?" I crowed. "Name it, Vexxion. Name it."

Drask, miraculously on my shoulder still, released a birdy snicker.

"*I* flitted us to the top of the hill," Vexxion whispered across my ear.

I bit my fingers into his arms wrapped around my waist from where he sat behind me. "Name it."

"You, fury." His lips quivered across the skin at the base of my neck. "*You* have all the power."

It was all I could do not to turn in his lap and coil my body around his, drag his mouth down to meet mine. "So, flitting." Damn my voice for croaking with need. "Add flitting to your list of things to teach me."

"I'll show you what to do, but only a few have the ability."

"What about awakened Nullens?"

"That remains to be seen."

"I guess we'll find out over the next few weeks."

He dropped his chin to the top of my head and nodded.

"Where should I tell Seevar to take us now?" I asked.

"I'll control your beast."

As handily as he controlled me. "Should we go back for yours?"

"He'll sense I'm gone and follow."

"For a dragon you didn't bother to name, he's incredibly loyal."

"Glim."

I blinked. "His name is Glim?"

"I just told you, didn't I?"

"You're softer than you appear." On the inside, perhaps. His exterior was pure fae steel. It would be better if I continued to believe he was as wicked as the rest of them and not... different.

"Don't get used to it," he said.

"There you are again."

"Excuse me?" How could he jump from kissing the back of my neck to sounding snide?

"You've proved my point."

His laugh burst out.

I stilled, shocked by how happy he sounded. "How, um..." I cleared my throat. "How far do we have to travel before we reach wherever we're going?"

"It's a few hours flight to my mother's estate."

"Where are Reyla and Brodine?"

"With those who claimed them."

I'd known it would happen, but I felt like a part of me had been severed and dragged away.

Nodding, I scooted around to face him, which meant I had to wrap my legs around his waist and press my body against his. Of course, I had no choice in this.

He stared down at me, his sharp eyebrows lifted, his arms tightening to bands across my spine.

"I'm trying to get comfortable," I said. "You're hard."

His lips twitched. "Not as hard as I can be."

"Why all this sexy talk?" I actually wanted to know. Since the cave, he'd felt approachable. Almost lovable, a thought that made cold terror bolt through me. If he sneered and kept me at arm's length, it was much easier to resist him.

If this man ever turned on his charm, I'd succumb within seconds.

"Maybe I've wanted to speak to you like this from the start," he said.

"Back when you hung around watching me?"

"When I saw something in you no one else had."

Air got caught in my lungs. "You hated me then, though I'm not sure why."

"I've never hated you, fury. What makes you think that?"

"You kept snapping at me."

"No more than you did me. Why do you think you snapped at me?"

I knew very well why, though I refused to name it. "Because you were a jerk. You were incredibly irritating. I couldn't do anything *but* snap at you."

"And now I've collared you."

"That was terrifying." I dragged my gaze from his. "You

should've found a way to tell me what the vines would do. Write it down if you couldn't speak the words."

"You're right."

My breath hitched. "If you keep agreeing with me all the time, I'm going to think you're a sweet guy."

"I give praise where it's due."

"And you don't think the way I fought the dregs that first day was worthy of praise?"

"Everything you've done, Tempest, has been worthy. You're incredibly strong. Not strong enough for what's coming, but you will be."

"There you go again, boosting me up only to drag me back down."

"You were raised in a Nullen fortress. Why would I expect you to be strong enough for what you'll soon face?"

Because I'd taken on Lieges and won. "Thank you for Seevar."

He stilled. "You found out."

"The commander didn't outright state *you* were buying him. He said someone was. But when I said I wanted to take him with me, the commander said he was a gift. I knew it couldn't be from him because that man gives away nothing." I looked up at him. "You gut me when you do things like that."

"That's something I never want to do." His kindness, his thoughtfulness stunned me. "I'm glad you're pleased with my gift."

"I was worried about him. I didn't want anyone to hurt him."

"And that's why I did it."

We flew for a while, saying nothing further. My thoughts churned, however, taking me back to what I still faced.

"When will you awaken my magic?" Now that I knew it was possible, I was greedy to taste whatever power trapped within me. "And how much magic are we talking about?"

"Nullens have varying degrees of magic. Usually, the Awakening unlocks one special skill. A few other tricks can be taught, but please don't expect to be flitting any time soon. If you're able to flit, it won't be for a very long time."

"Since I never knew I had magical abilities, I can live with that, assuming you think whatever I learn will be enough to get me close enough to kill the fae king."

"You won't be able to kill him with magic, or not the magic I can teach you in only a few short weeks."

"Will I kill him with a blade, then?"

"Not that either."

I tilted my head. "Then how *will* I kill him?"

"That's a very good question."

"One that you need to answer." I needled his chest with my nails, though not hard enough to pinch. He wore a simple blue tunic tonight, not the black leather shirt I'd gotten used to seeing—and admiring—him wearing back at the fortress. The other fae wore fancier garb. Vexxion would look amazing in almost anything, but I liked it when he dressed in simple clothing. He didn't need to wear regal stuff to stand out.

"He won't be easy to kill," he said.

"Why haven't you done it already?"

"I've tried but . . . He put a spell on me that makes it impossible for me to end his measly existence."

That was why he needed me. Would I have what it took to do this? That has yet to be seen, but the fire that had ignited my goal still burned within me. I could taste the torturous bliss of it on my tongue.

"Now you can control me through the collar," I said.

"I can."

"And I assume access includes you drawing from whatever measly power I can produce."

He nodded.

"Can I tap *your* magic through this horrifying thing?" I trailed my fingertip across the welt encircling my neck. My skin had sealed over, but if I thought clawing at it and ripping it open again would allow me to yank out the vines, I'd be tempted to do it.

"No one has before." His intent gaze met mine. "Rumors say it's possible, however."

Interesting. "I have so much to learn. Are we stupid to try this so soon? As much as I want to help Brenna, perhaps we should delay traveling to Bledmire Court until I'm more prepared."

"Once he's drained Lydel Court's power, he'll be indestructible."

"Then a few weeks of training it is."

"Yes."

We didn't say anything else as we traveled.

The farther we flew into the fae realm, the more I felt the

magic of this place, though I couldn't quite articulate exactly what I was feeling. Something whispered across my skin. No, I could feel the heat of a flame deep within me, as if white hot fire had ignited.

Strangely enough, I felt alive.

44

VEXXION

Hours later, as Seevar skimmed above the forest, I guided him lower. The estate my mother had left me had been built in an open meadow. Its slate roofline gleamed in the moonlight, and the stone walls that had given me shelter for only a few short years of my life appeared to glisten as if the building knew its lord had finally come home.

I'd secretly flitted here a few times, though not for many years. Had it been forgotten?

Tempest slept in my arms. She trusted me to teach her the skills she needed to kill the fae king, but not only that. She appeared to believe I'd be able to keep her safe from harm.

Strangely enough, it was her soft sighs as she slept and the way her hands clung to my tunic that broke me. Me, who'd survived the fae king's rage, who'd watched him cut my mother to pieces, who'd gone hoarse from screaming and hadn't spoken for over a year after it happened.

I'd never crave anyone as much as I did my fury.

I'd never be able to claim her as my own, and not only because she was too good for me, too precious, but because she'd hate me once she'd unlocked all my secrets.

I longed to hold her like this always.

Because I was much too weak, my inner fortress crumbling, I didn't wake her. Not when I landed Seevar lightly in front of the estate and urged him toward the aerie where he'd find food and water left by magic. Not when I carried her inside the three-story stone structure.

And not when I laid her in my bed.

Her crow flew into the room behind us, landing lightly on the bed's footboard, watching me a moment before tucking his beak and resting on the wood.

I eased Tempest out of the gown and tossed it aside. When I saw her wearing it, it was all I could do to focus on protecting her as much as I could during the Claiming. But she'd stunned me once more with her beauty. I'd picked the dress for her, making sure the fabric perfectly matched her eyes and it was as soft as the flooferdar she adored. I sent pretty combs for her to wear in her hair.

The gown itself was nothing until she filled it.

The combs were merely carved bits of shell until they adorned her hair.

She murmured my name and sighed as I tugged the soft blanket over her. What I wouldn't give to hold her all night, to sleep with her, to wake beside her knowing she wouldn't gaze at me with hatred.

I'd been on this course too long to veer off it now.

She was beauty itself, not only physically but in her very soul. She was pure while I was what she'd so aptly named me—wicked. Nullens called us that, the wicked fae, and no one deserved the name more than me.

She shifted on the bed—*my* bed—and my gaze was drawn to her once more.

How could such a small, seemingly weak person contain this much strength and take so much joy from the simple things of life? She could battle the dregs with a skill that would astonish many. Tame creatures with only her touch. Tame me with one glance from her pabrilleen eyes. And savor everything the world around us had to offer.

Seeing her still wearing the stone I'd strung myself and gifted her crushed me. Would she still wear it when she found out, or would she rip it from her throat and fling it away?

From the moment I met her, I hadn't been able to drag my gaze away from her. I'd imprinted the shape of her face, of her body, of her goodness deep within me. Striking it across my soul with my threads of lightning. An aching need for her pounded through my bones, twisting in my throat tight enough to choke me.

The knowledge that only this woman would ever make me feel complete pierced me, leaving me a bleeding wreck. I lifted my hands, watching as they trembled, as they exposed me completely.

I needed to leave before I did something forbidden, like release my fragile constraints and allowed myself to love her.

"Sleep, my fury," I said softly, still unable to look away. In rest, she was lovely. Awake, she was perfection. I couldn't wait to see what she'd become. "In the morning, we'll awaken your power and begin your training."

I dared to dream for one solitary heartbeat, only long enough to lean over and kiss her.

Her lips softened beneath mine, and she murmured in her sleep. She reached out, grasping the front of my tunic. Hissing when I tried to tug away.

Life had twisted me beyond recognition. I was too scarred and unworthy for one such as her.

Yet I found myself giving in.

"Just once."

I stripped quickly. Lifting the blanket, I slipped into bed with her, gathering her into my arms. Holding her like I'd ached to do since the moment I first sucked in a true breath, from the moment I saw the vibrant colors she'd given me.

My need for her consumed me, and I was her willing slave.

I kissed her again and held her, staring through the window, watching. Guarding her with every fiber of my being.

Did we stand a chance of success?

I could lock my home down with wards so thick, no one would ever find a way through.

Except him. Nothing would stop him now that he knew. The beast he'd sent had been a warning, though a paltry one at best.

We had too little time, too little left of anything to cling to.

Once he'd found his way through, he'd end me.

And then he'd kill her.

45

TEMPEST

I dreamed I slept with Vexxion. That he stroked my back, that he kissed my lips sweetly. Warm and content, I allowed myself to slip into a dream that I knew would shatter when I woke.

As expected, I roused to a cold bed with no dent in the pillow beside mine. This bed had to be Vexxion's, because his scent lingered on everything from the bedding to the pillow that had cradled my head, to the spicy essence in the room itself.

I wasn't wearing much, but that didn't concern me. He'd seen everything I had to offer, and for some reason, he hadn't turned away. He'd touched my scars, and he'd held me in his arms while I formed new ones. If that didn't scare him away, I wasn't sure what would.

He opened the door and swept inside holding a tray.

Drask soared across the room and landed on the headboard

above me, which was far better than my shoulder while I wore almost nothing.

I stroked his back as Vexxion walked through the sunbeams slaking through the broad expanse of windows on my left. He stopped beside the bed, and his gaze traveled from my face to where I'd pushed back the covers, though only the tops of my breasts were exposed.

I didn't miss the darkening of his eyes. How they smoldered. Heat coiled deep within me and slid lower.

He might tell me not to love him. He might push me away more often than I liked.

But he wanted me. I suspected he craved me as much as I did him.

Would it be wrong to steal something for myself from this quest for revenge? Only danger and devastation lay in that direction, so yes, it would be wrong. But when he set the tray of steaming food on the side table, fluffed the pillows behind me as I sat up, and kissed my forehead, I wavered.

When I saw the carved dragon sitting beside the cup of tea on the tray, I completely gave way.

"You... I left it behind." And I'd mourned its loss already.

"You appeared to enjoy it, so I retrieved it for you this morning along with yours and Reyla's things."

Our bags now sat on the floor beside a tall armoire.

"You flew a dragon all the way to the Claiming area to get them?"

"While my flitting abilities are somewhat lacking now, I can travel short distances."

Then he'd flitted, rested, then flitted once more, continuing until he could fetch something he'd been willing to throw away only because I found it precious.

He was either very good at this or I'd completely misjudged him. This fae lord couldn't be as wicked as the rest.

"Did you sleep well?" he murmured, dropping the tray onto my lap.

A bud vase perched on the side of the tray holding a solitary rose—black with silver sparkles dusting the tips.

"You . . ." I gaped up at him, remembering the same rose back in Brodine and Kinart's residence.

His lips curled up in one corner. "Me?"

I flicked the edge of the rose. The petals were silky, the silver sharper, though not sharp enough to cut my finger.

"This isn't the first black and silver rose I've seen," I said carefully.

"I'm sure you've seen others." Like he was my servant, he lifted the cloth napkin off the tray and spread it on my lap. Unlike a servant, he ran his knuckles across the tops of my breasts exposed by the blankets. Shivers tracked across my skin, raising goosebumps.

"Cold?" he asked pleasantly.

"You know I'm not cold."

"I know nothing of the sort." He crossed the room to the fireplace and crouched down to light the wood. Soon, it blazed, the flames crackling and snapping, coiling in golden ribbons to swirl up the chimney.

"Did you bring me here to seduce me?" I sounded like an ancient virgin. "If so, you're doing a great job."

"I brought you here to awaken you," he drawled. "Although, I'm also quite willing to teach you my wicked ways."

Oh, this man was good. Very good. "When will you awaken me?" To cover the shake of my fingers, I lifted the fork and dug it into the fluffy eggs.

Turning, he stood with his back to the flames. His gaze traveled down my body once more. Damn my heart for flipping over. "As soon as you're ready."

"That's vague."

"Accurate."

"This morning?"

"Yes."

"Should I eat or keep my belly empty?" I had no interest in throwing up.

He stalked toward me, stopping at the foot of the bed. "You'll find the Awakening easier than the Claiming."

I ran my fingertip along the collar binding me to him. The vines stirred and tightened. They hurt. Even asleep, I could still vaguely feel them. "It won't take much to make the Awakening easier."

"There are no vines involved in this. I promise you."

"Only magic."

"Always magic, but that's the whole point. It takes magic to awaken your hidden potential."

"What would happen if it was never awakened?" I lowered my hand to my side.

"I suspect you'd die."

I sucked in a breath. "Unreleased magic would kill me?"

"Something like that." His attention fell to my feet.

I picked up my fork again and took a bite, chewing and swallowing carefully. The vines relaxed and stopped poking my throat.

"I've drawn a bath for you in the adjoining chamber."

"That's kind of you."

"I *am* kind," he said with a sly smile.

"You're also conceited." Too nervous about the Awakening to eat, I slide the tray onto the bed beside me.

"You've just discovered this now?"

"I'm mentioning it now."

His gaze landed on the tray. "You need to eat more. I prepared it especially for you."

"I'm not hungry."

His frown deepened.

To placate him, I picked up a slice of bread and took a bite. "Satisfied?" I asked while chewing.

"I like watching you eat the food I made. Love seeing you lying in my bed even more."

"That's disturbing."

"Yes, that's me. Disturbing." He came over to stand at the side of the bed and took the bud vase from the tray, carefully placing the bloom on the bedside table before lifting the tray. "Finish the bread. Take a bath. Dress in the clothing I left for you."

"Are they yours as well?"

He smirked. "If I thought my clothing would fit you, then you'd be wearing it."

"Some guys get excited when they see a woman strutting

around wearing only his shirt," I called after him as he walked toward the door. "Do you?"

"Try it and find out." He left, and the panel clicked closed behind him.

"Stalker fae," I grumbled. "Wicked fae. *Devastating* fae."

I finished the bread and slipped from beneath the silky sheets, striding toward the adjoining chamber with Drask swooping along behind me.

Vexxion had closed the curtains inside the bathing chamber. And he'd covered every available surface with lit candles.

They flickered and danced, chasing shadows across the inside wall.

And on the lip of the enormous tub brimming with steaming water, he'd placed another vase—holding a solitary black rose tipped in silver.

46

TEMPEST

*A*fter bathing, I dried my body and walked over to the chair holding the outfit I'd wear to the Awakening.

Drask plunged into the water and splashed about, bathing while I held up the clothing Vexxion had left me.

The rose and candles had been . . . not exactly disturbing. No, they were lovely. They showed me how thoughtful he was. I'd expected to find something equally odd about the clothing he'd selected. Instead, I found plain black pants that would hug my curves plus a simple, unadorned gray tunic that would hang low enough on my hips to hide those curves.

I dressed and sat in the chair to don the shoes, watching while Drask finished bathing.

"Looking good there, little guy," I said, rising and using my drying cloth to blot the water from his feathers.

Perched on the side of the tub, he flapped them. Then he flew at a cockeyed angle into the bedroom with me following.

Vexxion stood in front of the fireplace. His eyes strolled down my body, and the gleam of approval there made them blaze almost as high as the flames behind him.

"It's not the gown I wore last night," I said.

"You looked gorgeous in the one I sent."

"Were you responsible for the combs as well?" I'd lost them somewhere between the tunnel and arriving here, and the loss made sadness bloom inside me.

"I wouldn't let you wear anything from another man."

"That sounds controlling. Stalkerish."

"It's only controlling or stalkerish if you don't like it." He strode over to stand in front of me, lifting a strand of my damp hair. "I so rarely see it down like this. It's beautiful."

"I usually braid it to keep it off my face. I don't need hair getting in my way when I'm fighting dregs."

"Will you wear it down like this for me sometimes?"

"Perhaps. If you ask nicely."

His eyes glowed with humor. "I can be very nice. Will you be a good girl in exchange?"

My body thrilled from his seductive tone. This man was dangerous. He'd burn me if I wasn't careful.

"Should I pull my hair back for the Awakening?" I asked.

"Please don't."

I was almost tempted to braid it while he watched just to show him I did what I pleased. But I didn't. As I followed him out of his bedroom with Drask flying at my side, I wondered why.

By the time he'd led me down two flights of stairs to the first level and into a big library full of books and with a big wooden desk perched in the back, I still didn't have an answer.

He pointed to a straight-back chair placed in the middle of the room. "Sit."

A shudder ripped through me, but I did my best to suppress it. "I'd like to be armed when you do this."

With the lift of one sharp eyebrow, he strode to the wall holding pictures of stern-faced men along with two mounted, ornate crystal swords crafted from deep blue glass. A color that perfectly matched his eyes.

He lifted one of them off the mount and returned to stand close enough to me I caught his spicy scent.

"You bathed too," I said.

"Would you rather I didn't?"

"If I said yes, how long would you go, how stinky would you allow yourself to get, before you did what you wanted instead of what I requested?"

"Test it, tiny fury, and you'll find out how far I'll go to please you."

"I prefer that you don't stink."

"I'll keep that in mind." He held out the sword, hilt first, and gave me a short bow. "For you."

"It's pretty." I hefted it, slashing it lightly through the air opposite where he stood. "Will it shatter the first time I lob off a dreg's head?"

"I promise you it won't."

"It's gorgeous, but my hands are too hard and worn to be holding something this lovely."

"Nothing compares to you, Tempest," he growled. "Nothing. Remember that."

"Alright." To say his words didn't make my heart flutter would be lying. "You're very good at this."

"At what in particular?"

"Impressing me. If that's your intention."

"I'm glad it's working."

I forced my mind back to the situation at hand. "It's a beautiful sword. Perfectly weighted. And you've assured me it won't shatter the first time I use it. But could I have something . . . I don't know. Less ostentatious? Something grittier, like me?"

"This blade is well-suited for you, but I understand your concern." He replaced it on the mount and crossed over to the desk, sitting in the big leather chair behind it and sliding open the top right drawer. He returned to my side holding a blade in the style I used to fight dregs. Long enough to add to my reach, yet well weighted and manageable enough to wear at my side without gouging my thigh if I moved quickly.

"This belonged to my mother's father," he said reverently. He stroked his fingertip up the silver blade to the hilt, where a fuchsia stone glowed in the sunlight filtering in through the curtains to my left.

Before I touched it, I ran my fingertip down his right pinky finger to the tip that was missing. Would he share what happened? I suspected there was more to this than a simple accident. This man held back parts of himself, and while I had no right to everything, I was greedy.

I wanted it all.

He withdrew, placing the blade in his left hand, offering it to me. "Please. Take it."

"I don't want to borrow a family heirloom."

He nudged it toward me. "It's yours. My grandfather would be honored."

"You say the sweetest things, Vexxion." I didn't like how my voice rose in pitch and fluttered, but everything he did made me swoon.

I'd never swooned for any man before.

He watched me, saying nothing, the blade lying across his palms. "Take the blade." His gruff voice tickled down my spine.

"Thank you." I lifted it, brandishing it through the air as he strode back to the desk. "It's also a gorgeous weapon."

"It suits its new owner, then."

He returned with a leather sheath to strap around my waist. When I slid the blade into the holder, I sighed.

Vexxion smiled. "Feeling better?"

"Infinitely."

"I promise you won't need to fight dregs while you're here."

"They haven't traveled this far from the border?"

"There are some in faerie, but none dare come near my home."

I squinted around. "It's a lovely home."

"From what I remember, my mother loved it here." His grim tone sunk through me. He'd watched her die. Listened to her tortured screams. It was a wonder there was anything decent left in this man after an experience like that.

"Thank you for what you've done for me," I said.

"Don't thank me. You're serving my purpose as well as your own."

"I never thought I'd make a bargain with one of the fae."

"The *wicked* fae."

I nodded. "I imagine the term is well suited."

"Very much so."

"For you?"

His smile deepened, turning almost feral. "Wear my shirt and nothing else, and you'll see how truly wicked I can be."

My skin prickled. This man was still holding things back; there was no denying it. I needed to keep reminding myself of that fact.

"Will you sit now?" he asked.

"Time for the Awakening?"

"It would be a mistake to wait too long."

"I understand the clock is ticking. We only have weeks, but what difference will an hour or two make?"

"Everything, fury. *Everything*."

I glanced at the chair but didn't sit. "Why not do this inside a cave?"

"Would you prefer we did it in a cave?"

As I shook my head, I contemplated the double meaning in his question. Since we'd left the fortress, he'd lowered his guard. Not on his mind—I'd poked at that more times than I should—but he'd relaxed and let me catch a glimpse of the real Vexxion.

I liked him. Too much.

"A wooden chair, not one made of unforgiving stone." I perched on the edge.

He nudged my thighs apart and stepped between them, then lifted my body to slide me back on the surface. "I could make this unpleasant for you if you'd like."

"I'm sure you could." Swallowing hard, I looked up at him, making sure my voice came out bravely. "Bring on the vines."

I sounded fine, but inside, I shook. The memory of the Claiming kept slithering through my mind, dragging dismay along with it.

"This won't take long. Drop your guards."

"Are they that good already? I keep practicing, but I'm sure you can riffle through my mind whenever you please."

"You're surprisingly good with them."

"Just *good*?" I quipped, tossing his words back at him.

"Excellent, in fact."

His words pleased me, but I gave him a hesitant smile. Maybe this wouldn't be too bad. It would be over quickly and then we'd—

His hands snapped out, and he latched onto my jaw.

I only had time to suck in a strangled breath.

Then his thumbs dropped onto my eyelids.

Sliding them closed.

Leaving me in darkness haunted by screams.

47

VEXXION

Tempest's mind tasted... *delicious*. I shouldn't drench myself in its splendor.

But I did.

So much power. So much potential. And so little time to prepare her for what was coming. I was doing all I could to hold it back, to give her the time she needed to adjust, but this game was a wall of water roaring toward us both.

It would soon engulf us.

Drown us if I let it.

Drask cried out, and I shushed him.

Her guards were down, but numerous restraints remained on her magic. I'd never seen anything like this before, and the fates knew I'd seen plenty.

I sorted through everything, even the areas she thought she kept hidden.

She was mine. I drenched myself in that knowledge for as long as I dared.

Tiny parts of her mind had been burned, and while I made my way through, I healed them. Whoever had done this to her had used a rough touch.

When I discovered who it was, my *touch* on them would be rougher.

Finally, I broke through the surface of a shield held in place by the very air she'd breathed from the moment she was born, and dove down, down. I sunk as far as I dared. Power like hers could rip through me. Sever the very world around us.

Although perhaps I should unleash her and let it happen.

But no, I had one task here—for now. And for some unknown and likely devastating reason, I didn't want to do anything that might give anyone else a reason to hunt her.

She'd softened me when no one else could. Trapped me when I should've fought her lure or walked away.

Now, I couldn't imagine how I'd go on without her.

You don't have to, a tiny part of me whispered. *You can have it all.*

Could I?

Growling at myself, I focused on my task. I could dwell on that idea later—much later.

My threads of lightning scorched across my skin, but I ignored them. I needed to be infinitely delicate, not slam through her like anyone else would.

Like the old me would've.

I repaired other scorched parts in her mind, cursing the fae who'd trounced through her and left her like this. The Nullens were so naïve, believing they had nothing, that we were the only ones with power.

Instead, each was carefully—or not so carefully in this instance—masked. Locked down and suppressed with enough magic coursing through the air to make them believe they were inferior to us.

If only they knew. But it wasn't my place to tell them. If I did, all of faerie would feel their wrath—and we'd deserve it.

Finishing, I marveled at how much she glowed, how beautiful her power was. How wonderful it would be to feel it coasting across my skin.

Perhaps one day.

I tugged myself back rather than linger like I craved to do. She trusted me in this, and as wretched a being as I was, as cursed and deserving of the fury she would one day unleash on me...

... I cared about her.

Finished, I backed away, slowly returning to myself.

I lifted my fingers and tugged my hands away from her precious face. I took a step backward and watched her.

Awaken.

48

TEMPEST

I opened my eyes, feeling as if I was rousing from a deep, restful sleep, and blinked up at Vexxion.

"When will you get started?" I whispered.

"It's already done." He gave me a grim smile and examined my face. "Don't you feel any different?"

"No, I . . ." Hold on.

There.

It was subtle, but I *felt* it.

"I still can't adjust to the idea that Nullens have magic that's been suppressed for many generations," I said.

"No one wants you to know this."

"You stole it from us." Rage blasted through me.

"Not me, in particular," he said with a wry twist of his mouth.

"And no one knows because our magic isn't revealed until

we're wearing one of your collars." I clawed my neck. "Get rid of it. Now."

"I can't. You knew that already."

"Won't get rid of it, you mean."

"Can't."

"Why not?" I rose from the chair and started pacing back and forth in front of him. "I hate it. Hate it!"

"I'll remind you that unless you're collared, you won't be allowed to enter Bledmire Court." He snagged my arm as I passed, bringing me to a halt.

"*You're* going to get me inside."

"Not if it results in my death or yours."

A snarl ripped through me. "Thank you for including me in that statement."

He clutched my upper arms, making me face him. "Do you think I'll allow anyone—*anyone*—to hurt you?"

"*You* are right now." I wrenched from his grip and backed away from him. "You're going to release this collar as soon as the task is done. You implied you could do it." I wouldn't take no for an answer.

"I'll do my best."

"What does that mean?"

"I told you already. Collars generally don't leave the body until the person's dead."

"You suggested there was a way."

"There could be."

Shit. "You're saying I could have vines coiling beneath my skin, wrapping themselves around my throat forever?"

"We'll find a way around it."

"That's reassuring." My sarcastic side had taken control, and I let her rule. "And what if there isn't?"

"You, fury, agreed to be collared. No, you didn't just agree, you asked me to do it. I tried to tell you to let this go, to find a way to live, but you insisted."

"So it's like that, is it?" He'd aptly named me. I stormed back and forth in front of him, the very air around me crackling with the storm brewing inside me. I deepened my voice, mimicking his tone. "Sorry, Tempest, but that collar you want to wear so you can kill the high fae lord? I suggested we could, but now I'm not sure we *can* remove it. No, tiny one, it's going to follow you to the grave."

"It removes itself before that."

"*Not* reassuring!"

"You're powerful. More powerful than anyone I've ever—"

I stopped in front of him, glaring up at him, daring him to look me in the eye. "Ever *what*?"

"Than any I've ever felt before."

"In a Nullen." For the first time since I set myself on this trail, I truly floundered. "You're right. I'm not prepared." Just like that, my anger deflated, leaving something I couldn't define behind. Despair? No, not exactly that, though it tainted my every thought.

Disappointed. Yes, that's what it was.

I lifted my chin, hating that it trembled. "You're still keeping things from me."

"Only what I have to." His voice was as quiet as mine. In his eyes, I found a mix of sadness and resolve.

He was going to stick to this course no matter what. I couldn't let him do it alone.

I took his arm and was surprised when he let me drag him to a sofa, where we sat, our thighs brushing together. My skin flamed whenever he was around, and even my disappointment in him didn't dampen that feeling. Would I always feel this way about Vexxion? I suspected I would, yes.

Another disappointment, this time directed only at myself.

"Tell me everything about this horrible collar," I said.

"As you've discovered, the wearer bears it for life."

"There must be a way to remove it. I'm not backing out of our deal, but I want it removed as soon as the fae king's dead."

"I'm going to do everything I can to make that happen."

I liked the determination in his voice. I didn't like that he wouldn't meet my eye.

"What else can you tell me?" I asked, turning to face him and tucking up a leg beneath me. I latched onto his rock-hard jaw and made him look my way. "Tell me about access."

One corner of his lips curled up. He looked cute and boyish when he did that. That look lulled me more than his magic ever could. He made my toes curl, and my insides melt, neither of which I liked. I hated feeling vulnerable around him.

"Access means I can use your power," he said.

"And you find that cute?"

His chiseled eyebrows lifted, and his lips smoothed. He picked at his words. "Nothing about this—or the fae—is cute."

"The collar's beneath my skin. How will he know if I'm wearing one or not?"

"Trust me, he will."

"We could draw marks on my neck."

"Do you actually think this is simple? That all you need to do is stroll into the court with your blades slashing, watch his head fall on the floor, then breeze back out?"

"I'm not that stupid."

"As you agreed, you're nowhere near prepared. You need to work on your guards."

On cue, he attacked, making my brain hurt so much, it shriveled. I slammed my forest into place, finding it surprisingly easy. From practice or my newly awakened power? To be on the safe side, I added a second, thick mesh of thorns.

He winced. "As I said, excellent."

"I had a good tutor." A vicious, conniving one who was still holding things back, but I could've picked worse. "When do we start preparing me?"

"Now."

He latched onto my arm and flitted, taking us to a room with only a sofa and one window.

I tugged from his grip and strolled away from him, turning to study the simple stone walls and the high, unadorned ceiling. Smooth, slightly squishy tiles covered the floor. "What will we do here?"

He leaped, tackling me to the floor, jarring the breath from my lungs.

I bucked and snaked my legs through his, twisting hard enough to flip him onto his back. I climbed over him, straddling him, and pressed my new blade against his throat.

"Give?" I asked with a slick smile.

"You're good, but not good enough for that yet."

A flash, and I was the one lying on my back, his legs pinning my thighs. Before I could prick him with my blade, he'd latched onto my wrists and pinned my hands over my head. He leaned close to whisper by my ear. "Drop the knife, fury."

"No." I bucked, knocking him off center, but he didn't tumble to the side like anyone else would if I used the move.

His hands tightened on my wrists to the point they'd leave marks, and his taut legs crushed my hips. "Blade, Tempest. Drop it."

Seeing no way out of this situation, I did as he asked, watching his face and his eyes. He so rarely gave anything away.

"Tell me more about how this collar will give you complete control over my body." And my mind?

"I'll never try to control you, fury."

"But that's the point of the collar."

He jerked out a nod.

"Who else has access to my power and can exert control over me?"

"Only those of my blood."

His parents were dead. "You're a . . ."

"A bastard, yes." Now the curl of his lips made my insides quiver. Heat coiled low in my belly and shot downward. Who would've thought I'd be attracted to someone that literally breathed danger?

"Care to share with me how that came about?" Tilting my head, I watched. The twitch of his lips told me this was an uncomfortable subject for him, which made me soften. "Actually, you don't need to tell me anything."

He backed off me, taking me up to a stand along with him.

"I'd like to tell you everything, but some of the details aren't mine to share."

"Bastard says your parents weren't married."

"They were together only long enough to create me. My mother came here and soon discovered she was carrying me. Her family had died, though the fae don't take shame in something like this."

"Nullens do. And they usually blame the woman, though last I knew, it took two to make a child."

His lips curled up before smoothing. "You're correct. She had me and we remained here. You're standing on Weldsbane land. I'm the heir to Weldsbane Court."

On his mother's side.

Ah, it all made sense now. "The fae king took you both. He tortured her."

"It was the only way he could gain access to me."

Access? Rising onto my toes, I studied his neck. The scars made it harder to see, but when I ran a fingertip along his warm skin, I didn't feel anything beneath.

"I'm not collared," he said.

"Yet he wanted access. To your land?" I kept watching him, though he angled his head away.

He nodded.

"He annexed it like he wanted to do with Lydel."

"I was too young—too weak—to fight him."

"You were a child." Access could mean more than land. "What else did he want you to do for him?"

His steely gaze met mine. "He wanted me to be his controller."

49

TEMPEST

"Controller?" I asked. "What did he want you to control?"

"Whatever he couldn't control himself."

My breath caught. "But you were a child."

"The young are much more compliant, don't you think? Easily trained."

"What did he do to you?" I was snarling, practically frothing at the mouth.

"He tried to break me." Such bleakness in his voice. The fae king had stolen from me, from so many living in the villages, but also from Vexxion.

If someone was going to rip Vexxion apart, it would be me, thank you very much.

"All the more reason to hate him," I said. "I assume you told him no."

"I was a child."

"He kept you."

"As a pet at first, then slowly training me to be the person I am today."

"He wasn't kind to you."

His fingers shot to his scars. "He doesn't know how to be kind."

My heart wept for the small boy he'd been. I wept for the man he was now, because his wounds had sunk deep below the surface.

"How did you get away from him?" I asked.

"Like any other, I waited for my chance and left."

"What will he do when you return?"

"Now that's an interesting question."

"For which you will now give me an answer." Before he could turn away, I grabbed his wrist, holding him back.

He'd just proven he could leave if he chose with a flit. I respected that he remained with me.

"I'll have to be very careful," he said.

"Both of us. Can you wear a magical mask to hide your identity?"

He slid the borrowed blade into my sheath. "Nothing like that will fool him."

I tilted my head. "Why not?"

"You need me to get you close enough to kill him, and that won't happen if he doesn't know who I am. He'll see this as me returning, eager to beg his forgiveness. Look at this like a game of Wraithweave." A game where each piece on the board has a specific role. It took considerable strategy to win this game of war. "In this, you're the high lady."

"The strongest yet weakest piece on the board." She had incredible power, but all was lost if she died. "I assume he's the master." The deadly leader of the opposing team's guard.

"Yes."

"What's your role in this game?"

"I'm your shield." This game piece usually died near the end of the game to protect the high lady.

"Don't sacrifice yourself for me," I growled.

"I'll do what's needed."

"*Don't* be my shield."

His lips flicked up before smoothing. "I have been all along, Tempest."

"I won't do this if he's going to hurt you."

"I won't allow that to happen."

I held his face, making him meet my eyes. "Do you promise?"

"I promise." He did not blink.

WE SPENT the next few days working together, the mornings in combat training and the afternoons trying to draw out enough of my magic to reinforce my guard, our first line of defense. If I couldn't keep the king from discovering my true reason for entering his court, all would be lost the moment I arrived.

While combat came easy to me, magic did not.

"You said my guards are excellent," I said after suffering his barrage for hours.

"It is, but it's still not good enough. You won't be allowed to get close to him, not at first," he said while drilling away at my brain. "He has to trust you before we dare introduce you. As much as he trusts anyone."

"I'm trying." I flopped on the couch placed near the right wall of the training room. We'd spent our days from sunup to sundown and often even later inside this room, only leaving for short breaks or to eat.

Drask soared over and landed on the armrest. He looked up at me, tilting his head this way and that. He probably wanted to go outside, but I was nervous about that. We weren't in the Nullen realm any longer.

Something magical might hunt him.

"You're not trying hard enough." Vexxion joined me, sitting opposite Drask, stretching out his legs. His arm casually extended across the top of the sofa behind me, close enough for his warmth to sink into my bones. Close enough he was a distraction I shouldn't welcome. My control around him was shredding. Soon, everything would let loose and . . .

Would it be bad to give in if only once?

"Yeah, I get it." Irritation boiled through me, shoving aside the dreamy thought. "One of these days, I'm going to erupt. It isn't just you pressing and pressing and me trying to make magic work with only negligible success. It's—" I shut myself down before I confessed.

It was the undercurrent of heat growing between us.

We'd done sexual things together, though nothing since he killed Selitta to save me. We hadn't had full sex, and I wanted it. Craved it in a way I never had. I had no problem admitting that fact to myself.

much untapped energy inside you. You're not a tiny squall, you're a true tempest. Show me more. Show me all you have. He paused, his lips curling in a sneer. *Unless this is all you can truly offer?*

Yeah, double fuck you. I grabbed onto my power and . . . instead of blasting it at him, trying to drive him away, I . . . flitted.

I slammed into him hard enough he was driven back on the sofa.

He looked startled, but only for a heartbeat before he grinned, and his hands landed on my hips. "Now there's the fury I adore."

The mushy side of me I abhorred craved to hear whatever sweet words he cared to offer.

I was losing myself in him. Drowning in everything Vexxion. I couldn't find a way to pull myself back. "You taunted me on purpose again. You were trying to make me mad enough to slam my power around."

"It worked, didn't it?"

"Maybe I'm still mad at you." I pouted, taking too much pleasure in the look in his eyes, a mix of pride and straight-up lust. "You were turned on by our argument."

He shrugged. "Frankly, fury, you only need to exist to turn me on."

My breath caught. Electricity charged around us, heightening my awareness of everything. The warmth of his hands on my hips. His sweet breath. The way he looked at me as if I was the only one who existed.

As if he couldn't breathe unless I was with him.

Drask must've felt the heat coiling between us because he

squawked and soared out through the open doorway, leaving us alone.

The door banged shut, and the twitch of Vexxion's lips told me he'd done it.

"You can move objects with your mind," I breathed.

"There are many magical tricks, shall we say, that I can do. You've only had a taste."

"Teach me."

"Oh, I intend to." His gaze dropped to my mouth. "So many things."

I'd kill to taste his lips once more. Kill to feel his touch. I was only half alive unless I was with him.

"Maybe we should have sex and get it over with," I said.

50

VEXXION

"We will never have sex," I said.

Her breath caught, and I watched her struggle for control. Poor fury. Didn't she know?

I'd not only killed for her, but I'd also *die* to be with her. Quite willingly. She'd *always* be my sole reason for existing.

"Alright then." She squirmed until I released her and levered herself up off me, dropping onto the cushions beside me and crossing her arms on her chest. She glared at the wall. If she had a blade, she would've impaled it in my throat already.

She'd already plunged one through my heart.

"Maybe we need a break," she said sullenly.

What, no storm to thrash around me? Don't you want to blast me with your power?

Her fury was delicious. Everything about her made me long for what I'd never be able to have.

She shot me a glance, and the tears there...

I'd kill anyone who hurt her. Yet, here I was, delivering the blow. I snarled, truly hating myself for the first time in my wretched life. Everything I'd done. Everything I'd become, I'd found a way to live with.

But I couldn't live with *this*.

"I get it," she said.

"I don't believe you do."

"Then explain it to me. Don't snarl and feed me statements with double meanings. Spell it out to me as if I'm someone who has a hard time understanding you. Because I do. We . . ." She pinched her eyes closed, and when she opened them a heartbeat later, she'd snapped back into control.

So much power. Such a strong will.

She might very well shatter me when she let loose.

"If we're not . . ." She swallowed. "If we're not touching, we'll be able to maintain control."

I laughed.

She turned a startled gaze my way.

"All you have to do is look at me to make me lose control," I said.

"I don't see that."

"Then you're not looking hard enough." The time for holding back was gone. Curse me for eternity, but I couldn't deny her, even if I could find the will to deny myself. "You only need to *exist* for me to lose control."

She shook her head. "I don't—"

"You told me to be honest with you, and I am." Was that my voice cratering with every bit of the emotion churning inside? I'd penned it up. Slapped on thick guards. It found a way to

Each time I caught him looking at me when he thought I was focused on grabbing onto enough magic to actually do something with it, it was all I could do to drag my gaze away. The look in his eyes . . . As if he only saw me. As if I was the center of his world and everything he'd ever need. As if we had only one destiny—to be together.

Each time I caught the sharp, devastating longing in his eyes, it tore me open and left me bleeding. My body recognized it because the same feeling kept rising within me, as if he was all I'd ever need.

Then heat would flare inside me and plunge down between my legs. I spent half our time saturated. The rest of the time, I ran scared, because I knew I couldn't let him see the secret, aching core buried deep within me.

My blood pounded through me with the realization that there would never be anyone else for me but this man.

It terrified me.

No wonder I was distracted. No wonder I found it hard to focus.

His fingertips teased down my braid, and I swore I felt longing even in this simple touch.

"You started to say something, but you didn't finish. What's holding you back?" he finally asked, his penetrating gaze on my face.

I jerked my gaze to the side before he saw everything I was determined to hide.

"Not going to share, little storm?"

"I . . ." Naming it would make it real.

He sighed. "If you'd like, we could take a break. You've worked hard."

With so little to show for it.

"At least a billion times," I blurted, "I've wondered if I truly have what it takes to do this." There was no harm in admitting this to him again, though it felt like I'd named it almost daily. He was my teacher. He'd keep guiding me once we reached Bledmire Court. It wasn't like I'd be dumped there to figure it out on my own.

"You have what's needed to do this." The certainty in his voice stunned me.

"How can you say that when I still can't maintain my guard?"

"Because I'm one of the strongest fae lords in faerie. If you can maintain even a wavering guard for a half an hour with me, you'll find everyone else you'll encounter there easy."

"What about the fae king?"

"He'll be the biggest challenge."

"Is he stronger than you?"

"In some ways."

"You haven't tried to break the spell he cast on you yet, have you?" I turned to face him, tucking my foot beneath me.

Staring forward, he shook his head. "Only once. Never again."

"Why not?"

The silence stretched so long between us, I began to believe he wasn't going to answer. "I will. Soon."

He was *scared*.

The air in my lungs turned to frost at the thought, and I lost all control of my tongue, making it impossible to speak. The realization crushed me. I wanted to hug him, something I knew he'd scorn. He was big, strong, powerful, and . . .

And he was a person like me. He must have his own hopes and fears. Why hadn't I seen that?

I wasn't going to call him out on it. Nor would I ask him to tell me why he hadn't ripped through the spell and killed the asshole already. I sensed this was the one thing this man felt uncertain about. The fae king had devastated him, and the scars may have healed, but the wound still bled.

"I'm sure you're frightened of someone riffling through your thoughts," he said.

I was concerned about that, so I went with it. "A bit."

He snorted, and I savored his laughter, something he didn't share often. "The only reason to perfect your guards is to keep someone from manipulating you. You'll keep working on them even after we arrive at his court."

The thought of someone breaking through my barriers and exposing everything I kept hidden should be enough to make me pack up and return to the fortress.

"What's the plan once we get there?" I asked.

"You'll work in the aerie."

"Why the aerie?"

"You have more power than you can imagine, but one skill stood out when I awakened you. You've got a magical touch, literally, with beasts. The fae king will welcome that skill."

"And how will that get me close enough to kill him?"

"We'll plan for that, though it won't happen right away."

"We'll infiltrate his court, get him to trust us—me, that is—and then I'll do the deed when the time is right."

"Exactly."

I bit down on my lower lip and released it. "He has a stable of dragons?"

"Dragons are one of his few indulgences. He's there often. He'll note your skill and use it to his own advantage."

"If he wants cruelty, I'm not the right trainer. I only train with a gentle touch."

"The beasts see that." His lips curled up. "*I* see that."

And just like that, he took this conversation in another direction.

His smoldering looks made my skin tingle, and whenever we randomly touched, I pretty much exploded. If something didn't come from this soon, I was going to have to make it happen. I'd rocket all the way to the stars. If I was going to blast to the stars, I wanted him to take me there. Another realization I'd come to over the past few days.

"Guards," he said grimly, plunging into my mind.

I flung up a shield and felt him smack against it—batter it with his infinitely stronger power.

It was too much. I shrieked, scrambling to draw magic and coat the surface of my mind with it.

As he lashed at my flimsy barrier, I drew from the well deep below. That was how I'd started to think of it, as a stone well brimming with power. I could drain it like water was taken from a dug well, and it would refill over time.

I trickled more power across my forest, and then I scooped up a bucket of it and flung it at him.

He flinched, his face tightening.

I grinned.

So did he, turning my way and ripping through the shields around my heart with his flash of humor. "That's a nice trick."

I snorted. Over the past few days, we'd gotten closer, as if something deep within us both had relaxed, a thing that couldn't happen when others were around. We were friends, a relationship I never thought I'd have with one of the fae.

I enjoyed teasing him, seeing how far I could push him before his barriers dropped. So far, he hadn't even twitched, let alone cracked enough to let me fully in. I wasn't giving up easily.

"Only a *nice* trick?" I asked, tracing my fingertip down his throat to the top of his tunic.

I took in how amazing he looked in this color. The blue matched his eyes, and while I found him beyond gorgeous in black, this courtly color, plus the silver stitching that on any other man might appear silly, made him . . . approachable wasn't quite the right word, but it would do until I found the perfect one.

I, however, wore simple leathers, like usual. I wasn't sure I'd ever feel comfortable in anything else, and he must know that since he left them for me each day along with a peach-colored top I wore beneath the tunic.

His smoldering eyes watched my finger, flashing from it to my face. "*Perhaps* your trick was better than nice."

"*Perhaps*?"

He grinned. "Why did you think of reversing the spell to attack me instead of strengthening your guard?"

"It was a random thing."

"A smart move."

"Thanks." He wasn't big on praise, and I drank it up, savoring how good it made me feel.

"Again." He hammered at my shield.

I reversed his attack again, drawing more power from my well and sending it toward the forest in *his* mind.

And I slid through.

"Ah," I gasped.

His eyes widened.

I leaped from the sofa. Drask squawked, as startled as Vexxion, and flew around the top of the room before landing on the hanging light, making it rock.

"You . . ." Vexxion got up and stalked me.

Backing away with my hands lifted, I tried to block out what I've seen, hoping he wouldn't read the dismay in my mind. "Maybe you'll admit I've done more than a nice job now?"

"*Perhaps*," he purred, his gaze locked on mine.

Something else had changed over the past few days in addition to our growing friendship. Whenever we were together, which was pretty much all our waking hours, heat crackled between us as if his threads of lightning kept reaching out to . . . I wasn't sure what they did inside me, but I'd started to call it stirring my storm. My fury.

"Tell me what you did," he said. "You got through. *No one* has gotten through."

Not even the fae king?

"I like being unique." The only one who could get past his guards. "It's just a little trick I've been practicing."

He backed me against a wall and grabbed one hand, then the other, pinning them above my head. "Tell me what you did."

"I pulled some magic from my well and pictured it as a spear. Spears can travel a considerable distance inside a forest —*your* forest as well."

"I'll have to reinforce my guards."

"You will."

"Do you realize that no one—no one—has gotten past my guards since I was very small?"

I bet since he was five.

"I didn't see much," I said.

He stilled, the twitch of his smile fading. "What did you see?" he barked.

A flash of the boy he'd been. A male paying more attention to a very young Vexxion instead of the woman being sliced to pieces alive —with magic.

No one wielded the blade. It slashed through the air...

Tears streamed down Vexxion's little boy's face, and he screamed out his mother's name, over and over.

It wrecked me, and I wasn't even there. No wonder Vexxion kept his guards high.

"I didn't see much," I repeated my words carefully, suspecting he wouldn't like that I'd seen even that tiny bit of his past. This man shared a lot with me, but he kept many things back. He must guard this memory more than any other.

"Tell me," he growled, his face close to mine, his eyes trying to force me to lock on his.

I wasn't sure why I did it...

... But I lied.

"I saw *you*." I wrenched my gaze from his. "Your mother too. Gardens full of beautiful flowers." I reminded myself to keep this simple, or I'd give myself away. "She had red hair. It was long, right?"

His posture loosened. "Yes. It was prettier than the sun setting over the Barrenfall Mountains."

"You have her eyes." I couldn't block out the sight of them, wide with terror. Her face tortured with pain. So much pain ...

"I do."

Her eyes only softened when she looked at her son, and then, with complete and unending devotion. She would've done anything to protect him, to make him believe she was alright.

Even bite back her screams.

"I'm sorry." I couldn't hold back my sympathy for him.

He released me and backed away, and I hated that we'd gone from teasing and working together to him emanating sorrow. I was proud that I'd breached his walls, but the next time I did it, I'd take care where I poked.

"Teach me how to flit," I said to distract him.

"I told you that only a few can do it. Flitting also takes more power than you know how to tap."

"I can try. There's no harm in that, is there? I imagine it's a skill that would come in handy at Bledmire Court." A shiver rippled across my skin. Within a short time, I'd have to be on my guard at all times.

"I'll tell you how to do it," he said. "Don't expect much."

I pursed my lips. "Well, thanks."

He explained how I needed to draw a considerable amount of power from my well and that I had to focus on the location I wished to travel to, that I needed to have it clear in my mind.

"I can't flit to a place I haven't been before?" I asked.

"No."

"There goes my idea of flitting into the fae king's bedroom, ending it quickly, then flitting back out."

"Only travel to places you can clearly visualize it in your mind." He locked his hands on my shoulders, pressed me against the stone wall, and made me meet his eyes. "Do not—under *any* circumstances—go with him to his bedroom."

"That's the last place I'll go unless I've got blades in my hands and he's unconscious."

"Good. Remember that. *Promise me.*"

An odd request, but I nodded. "Who'd *want* to go to his bedroom?"

"Don't you know? Ladies find the fae king quite charming."

He was ruthless. Bloodthirsty. It must ooze through his skin, which in my mind would make him ugly.

My spine quivered. "I won't be able to look at him without seeing Kinart dead, knowing he's sucking the energy from people in the villages. We always said the Lieges took our energy, but the explanation was vague. It's the power they've been denied their entire lives."

"You're correct."

"Fuck him."

His lips twitched upward. "Yes, fuck him." Releasing my shoulders, he stepped backward. "See if you can flit to the sofa."

"Just like that?"

"You need to start somewhere." He strode across the room and sat, stretching his arms along the back, kicking his feet up on the table in front. "Flit like a good girl, and I'll give you a reward when you get here."

Fuck. I wanted to tell him not to say things like that, because ... Oh, how dirty my thoughts were when it came to this man. I could barely control my urges. "You said flitting would be too challenging for me."

"So is scraping through my guards to reach my mind. Yet you did it."

He watched me with so much heat in his eyes, I wanted to surprise him and flit to him right away. But no matter how I tried, pulling on my power and casting the spell, I remained where I was, and he lounged on the sofa—alone.

I wanted to do this. I needed to prove to both of us that I was closer to being prepared.

"How far can someone flit?" I asked.

"One of the fae? It varies. You? Not even one stride from where you are right now." There was that infernal sneer again, the taunt thriving in his voice, driving my irritation to a fever pitch.

I stomped my foot, a totally childish move, but I couldn't stop myself from doing it.

"When you try to kill the fae king and fail, will you fuss and stomp your foot? He'll mangle you with his magic within seconds. Unless someone discovers your ruse and mangles you for him instead."

Would they make Vexxion watch while they did it? I'd hate that. I also didn't want to implicate him in my scheme. Shakes erupted from deep inside me, and I hugged my body with my arms, my irritation sliding away as quickly as it had risen.

"I won't let that happen." I lifted my chin, hating that *it* quivered too. "It's a risk I'm willing to take."

"And what if I'm not willing to take that risk?" His jawline hardened to steel.

"You speak of yourself?"

"I speak of you," he growled.

My stupid heart fluttered, flailing behind my ribs for a completely different reason. This man was brutal; there was no denying that. Ruthless. Yet his feral need to protect me made him much, much too enticing. Heat pooled low in my belly before gliding down. A wild urge roared through me, a feeling almost beyond my control.

His nostrils flared as if he could smell my arousal.

I swallowed hard, but painful desire kept surging within me, scorching through my veins. Making me wet.

"Is there any way to pretend we're not connected?" I croaked.

"Not as long as you wear my collar."

"Maybe I can kill him from a distance. I'm good with a knife. Getting better." He'd shown me new techniques, and I'd practiced them until I'd mastered each.

"Not good enough. He's a master at this. He doesn't just throw up guards around his mind."

"I assume he also has magical guards protecting him physically from harm."

He nodded. "Plus minions who'll happily take a blade or a magical blow for him."

And I was supposed to kill him?

"I see what you're thinking," he snarled. "Don't."

"You can't control my thoughts."

Oh, no?

I sucked in a breath. "You're speaking in my mind. You've... been doing it all along." Brittle horror scraped across my bones. How had I missed it?

"It took you a long time to notice. Too long. You need to be hyperaware of everything."

"Is speaking inside someone's mind another wicked fae ability?" And could I learn how to do it?

"This is exclusive to me."

"Why only you?"

"I'm special."

"Don't be sarcastic," I snarled.

"Me, sarcastic?"

I huffed.

"Never fear, tiny storm. With work and time, *you* might discover you also have the ability."

"You just said it's exclusive to you."

"I am not alone. Not any longer."

Whatever. I concentrated fiercely, to the point my brain throbbed, but if there was a way to send him a *fuck off* or some other, equally delightful statement, I couldn't figure out how to do it. "Tell me more about his minions."

"They're as vicious as him."

Ivenrail used torture for entertainment. "How many of them are truly willing to die for him?"

"More than we'll be able to kill."

"Even you with your superior magical abilities?"

His lips twitched at *superior*.

"I'll have to avoid being caught," I said.

"Just like that, you'll avoid being snared in the spider's web? You should give up now. We can track down your pretty boy and you can tell him you've changed your mind."

"My pretty boy was claimed."

"Then we'll find you another," he said with a sneer. "They're quite common in the Nullen lands, you know."

Irritation roared through me once more, blasting through the top of my head. "Stop it."

"Stop what, *Tempest tantrum*? I believe you've misjudged me." He stared at his nails. Literally stared at his nails as if he'd dismissed me. "Do you think I'm a kind fae man, allowing you weeks to learn even the basics of magic?"

"You're the one who set the deadline. You're the one who gave me hope I could do this."

"You're special, fury, I'll give you that." Like a viper, he struck. "But you're going to be destroyed."

"Not so. I can do it." I had to hold onto my determination, or I'd fail before I entered Bledmire Court.

"When one of his minions catches you and pins you to a wall," he said. "Ivenrail will allow him to do whatever he wants with you."

I crossed my arms over my chest. "Then we'll keep that from happening."

"When they catch you, will you cross your arms on your chest and glare?" His lips twisted. "That'll make them stop."

Well, fuck you!

He sucked in a little breath. "Delightful, fury."

I'd spoken to him in my mind. I'd spoken to him in my mind! "Did you try to piss me off?"

It worked, didn't it?

Stop it. I slammed my hands against my temples as if that would hold him back. This was different than erecting guards to keep someone from reading my mind.

This was a true invasion.

"How far from you do I need to be to keep you from chattering away inside my head?" I snarled, tugging harder from my well of power.

The distance has never been tested.

"Get out!"

Make me leave.

I couldn't. *How?* The word was a wail.

Use your magic. Shove me away.

I pulled and pulled, dragging from my depleted stores and blasted it into my mind. It . . . fused around my brain, and I found silence. I could sense him poking, trying to get back inside, but he couldn't.

"Well done," he drawled. "*Very* well done."

My, oh, my, how my heart roared from hearing his praise. I was anything but a woman who'd preen or bat her eyelashes at a man. Yet I wanted to do it with Vexxion. What would it be like if we'd met as two normal people without plans for vengeance or a history that would haunt us for this life and beyond?

We could've had dinner together. Laughed. Danced, though I had no idea how to do the latter. I could've worn a pretty dress and swayed in his arms. And at the end of the evening, we'd . . .

Dreaming was going to get me killed.

Dreaming was going to shatter my heart into so many fragments, I'd never fuse them together again.

But dreaming gave me hope that one day, even if it was long in the future, things could be good for us.

Stop it, I told myself, shutting the fluttery crap down.

That left only a hint of sadness behind.

He slipped beneath my guards, showing me why I had to keep them up at all times—even with him. *What's this I see?*

I slapped barriers all over my mind. "Nothing."

"Obviously, it was something. That look on your face . . . I don't believe I've seen it before."

"It. Was. Nothing."

He snorted. "If you say so."

Had I cauterized the silly images from my mind before he broke through, or did they still linger?

Sharp vulnerability prodded my soul.

"I'd like to see you wearing my dress again," he said.

I drummed up my irritation, realizing it could become another layer of my wall. Faulty, but I'd take all the layers of protection I could get. "*Your* dress? Confessing to something, there, Vexxion?"

"I want to pick out all your clothing, then see you wear it, knowing that only *I* have touched it before it caresses your skin."

"I'm not a woman who wears dresses."

"Yet you were exquisite in the green."

Which he'd picked out. Sent to me because it matched the pendant I still wore. Because both matched my eyes.

You're even more exquisite when you wear nothing.

My skin tingled, and I sunk into an image of me drowning in the stroke of his calloused hand across my overheated flesh. My legs spreading wide. He buried his mouth there, stroking his scratchy tongue across my clit. His fingers probed deep within me, swirling through my wetness. Pumping.

Heat engorged my veins and my clit throbbed with a need only this man could . . .

He was doing it again. Invading me. Not like the fae king would. No, that would be a solitary blast of fire that would fry me to a crisp and leave nothing but dust scattered on the wind of his fury.

Get out!

He sighed. *The fae king won't obey your commands. I never will either.*

One day . . . Growling, I shook my head. I needed to stop floundering and take control, or all would be lost before I reached Bledmire Court.

You enjoy it, he said. *You crave my touch.*

I don't.

Come now. It's not like you to lie.

Stop it!

Flit over to me, and I'll leave you alone. Show me you can do it, tantrum.

Maybe I didn't want him to leave me alone. Maybe, finally, it was time we took this where it had been heading from the moment we met back at the fortress. From the moment I first felt the weight of his stare.

Once your storm is unleashed, it will be amazing. There's so break free. "One touch, and I'm lost, Tempest. Don't you know that?"

"Vexxion," she breathed.

"The way you say my name. The way you look at me as if you want to lick every part of my body."

"I do."

I laughed again, and damn, it felt good. When had I last lowered my guards enough to let someone inside?

Not since my mother was murdered in front of me.

"I adore the way you try so hard to control your power. The fact that when you flitted the first time, it was into my arms."

"I wanted to smack you."

"I'm well aware of that." I couldn't stop smiling. My face ached from it. Soon, I'd have to return to the Vexxion this world knew, but for now and with my tiny fury?

I wanted to be me, the person no one else would ever see.

"The way you snarl at me. The way your cute ass fits inside your leathers."

She snorted and swiped at her eyes.

I crawled up over her, driving her down onto the cushions, caging her with my palms on either side of her shoulders. "The way you taste. The way you come so sweetly from my touch. The way you make me crave you all the time."

"*Vexxion.*"

"I'll do anything for you," I growled. "Anything. Can't you see that?"

Her lips trembled and more tears shimmered in her eyes. These were not from pain. These expressed her joy.

The bliss slamming through me right now could crater the world.

"So, no," I said. "We will *not* have sex."

"But—"

"Sex is for releasing tension. For satisfying an itch. We'll never have sex, but I am going to claim your body completely."

"Isn't that pretty much the same thing?"

"Never for us."

"Us," she breathed.

"You are *mine*."

"This isn't about possession."

"In many ways, it is, because I'm *yours*."

Her eyes widened. "Ah."

Ah.

"How could you think I don't want everything?" I asked.

"When a man says that, he usually means sex. Maybe me sucking him off."

My laugh snorted out . . . so . . . full. Rich. When had that happened? Never other than when I was with her.

"I won't refuse an offer like that." Damn, I was still grinning.

But she was smiling, too, and seeing her happy made my insides twist into a knot then loosen. A force stronger than us both, more powerful than anything in the fae and Nullen realms combined, had drawn us together. Nothing was going to shatter the bond I'd found with her.

She didn't know, and I couldn't tell her everything. I had to hope she'd still trust me, still want me, when this game was finally put into play.

"You love me," I declared.

"Don't..." She blinked fast but didn't drag her gaze away from mine. "It hurts to love someone."

"Only if it's not shared."

"I need more than a simple fuck from you. I'm not Selitta. I won't be with you, then stand back while you're with someone else. I'll gut you if you do something like that."

"I'll hand you the blade."

"If I'm yours and you're mine, it's not just pretty words. It's real."

Lasting? Soon, I'd find out.

"Nothing between us will ever be simple," I said.

"I knew that." Her lips curled up deliciously. "And now that that's settled, I believe you owe me something."

And I knew just what it was.

I flitted us to *my* bedroom.

51

TEMPEST

Flitting was . . . A blink of an eye. A drain of my power. When he did it, he made it seem effortless.

We dropped onto my bed—our bed—and he tightened his arms around me.

His mouth captured mine like he'd already staked his claim on my heart. He hadn't outright told me he loved me, and that stung, but only for a moment. I suspected this man hadn't spoken those words to anyone since his mother.

I could be patient. He'd declare himself one day.

Lifting his head, his growl ripped up his throat. "I'm going to fuck you so deep and so hard; you won't be able to think, let alone remember being with anyone but me."

"Stop talking. Start doing."

His laugh burst out again, the sound making my insides scamper around like a chall with a ball.

He'd captured me with his darkness. Oh, how that part of

him drew me in. But his laughter? Him looking at me as if I was his everything?

This was what made me fall in love with him.

His gaze met mine, holding affection I couldn't deny, along with a touch of the vicious side of him I'd crave for a lifetime.

Back in the training room, he'd made me wet, drawing my need to the surface with a masterful touch. I was saturated, dripping for him.

And he knew it.

A flick of his finger, and I lay naked beneath him.

"Hey, I like that outfit," I said.

"I gave it to you. I'll give you another." He kissed across my jawline to my ear, where he bit down softly on the lobe. "I'll dress you in the finest of everything. I promise."

"All of it in varying shades of green."

He snorted. "If you wish."

"Show me the colors of *your* world."

"*You're* the colors of my world." He'd freed the sweet words I craved. I drank them in, and I couldn't stop grinning.

Until he crashed his mouth down on mine again.

His tongue plunged into my mouth. While I suspected he could be gentle, this wasn't the time. My craving had grown to a fever pitch.

He braced himself over me, the muscles of his forearms pinning me to the bedding. I was caught by his hardness, his strength, and I couldn't imagine being anywhere but here and now. With this man.

As his tongue expertly stroked mine, his fingertips traced down my neck, pausing to stroke across the vines trapped beneath my skin. I was always aware of them, a foreign entity coiling and releasing inside me as if they were poised to strike with the death blow of a viper.

At his touch, the vines went still. The lingering pain from the Claiming disappeared.

He was everything strong and powerful, but he *could* be gentle. I suspected only with me.

Lowering himself onto his forearms, he held my head steady and glided his fingers into my hair. The snatch of leather securing my braid broke free and my hair unraveled. I swore it reveled in his touch as much as I did. There was no part of me that didn't want this man. I always would.

His other hand cupped my breast, and he groaned, ripping his mouth away from mine, leaving me clinging to his tunic, bucking my hips up in a wanton, needy way that sent a twinge of vulnerability through me. His self-control was sharper than a newly hewn blade, as if everything we'd done and all we would ever do was orchestrated to bring about one final result.

My nipple pebbled, hard and wanton.

I tugged on his tunic, sliding it up to reach the broad expanse of smooth skin leading to his scars that I stroked with equal affection. I moved my hands lower, and his abdominal muscles rippled beneath my touch. His heady groan rang out.

"See?" He ground his leather-encased hard cock against my thigh. "You do this to me. No one else." He gripped my hair, coiling it around his palm until I couldn't move. I could only stare into his eyes that mesmerized me like everything else about Vexxion. "*No one* else. Do you see that? Can you feel it?"

Stunned by the utter devotion in his voice, I could only nod. And rip at his clothing, whimpering.

With a smile, he magicked it away.

Then he dropped down on top of my body. I could feel his long, thick cock pressing against my belly, urgent and wet at the tip.

He kissed me again, growling against my mouth. His knee spread my legs, and he shifted upward to run his cock through my wetness, coating his length. Each thrust hit my clit perfectly, and in no time, I was lost in him, a moaning wreck beneath him.

His tongue invaded my mouth, staking his claim all over again.

Feverish and blown with desire, I roamed my hands across his chest. I clung to his shoulders and jerked my hips up to meet his, wallowing in his heat, his growing possession.

My heart pounded, slamming against my ribcage as if it needed a way out, needed to wrap itself around him completely.

He stroked my face as he kissed me, his hand moving down to my breast, capturing my nipple and rolling it.

I bowed my spine, gasping into his mouth, and he swallowed my sighs like he'd soon take in everything else I had to offer.

Me. That was all I had to give. I could only pray to the fates it would be enough.

Lifting his head, his gaze locked on mine. Something flickered in his sapphire depths, a night sky full of shooting stars I could wish on.

I wished for us.

With a nod, he kissed down my neck, running his tongue across the vines embedded deeply. I swore they melted because I was melting, surrendering to Vexxion's touch, to his every desire.

He kissed across the tops of my breasts before focusing on a nipple, sucking it into his mouth while his hand teased the other, pinching it to the point it was almost painful. It felt exquisite and was almost everything I needed.

I stroked his neck, caressing his scars that had molded him into the man he was today. If I had the power, I'd take them away, though I sensed he wore them like a fancy tunic or leathers during battle. They were a tool like any other. He flaunted them at the fae who'd stood back and allowed the fae king to torture his mother.

Another reason to kill the king. Maybe I'd slice him a bit before I sent his soul to a wretched place where he could never break free.

Then, I'd hack off his head.

Nothing could be more vicious, more brutal than a woman in love.

While his fingers continued to roll my nipple, and I whimpered beneath him, he kissed across my belly.

His touch was surprisingly gentle on my thighs, urging them farther apart. He crawled between them, sending me a grin as he hitched first one leg, then the other, up onto his shoulders. "You're beautiful like this, your pupils blown from my touch. The whimpers you feed me are sweet, but I need more. You're going to give it to me."

I nodded, too far gone to speak.

"Mine," he said simply.

"Yours," I croaked.

When he drove his tongue inside me, I completely succumbed.

His mouth was hot and insistent, his tongue moving through my folds, licking everything. As if he wouldn't allow one single drop of my wetness to escape.

I sensed his control shattering, his warmth and lightning touch enveloping me. I welcomed his growls as his mouth claimed me, hard and sure, yet with a touch of the vulnerability he brought out in me.

As his tongue plunged deep, he slid in his finger, alternating the thrusts. His thumb landed on my clit and stroked, swiping across it in pace with the rapid thrust of his fingers inside me.

Growling with greed, he continued to eat me, his words mumbled as if he couldn't bear to leave me long enough to speak. "Wet. Mine."

I'd never been a woman who ached to be claimed. I was too independent for that. But as he made more demands of my flesh, of my body, I gave myself completely. I tumbled into everything he offered, my hips jerking up, my hands latching onto the ends of his hair and tugging.

He chuckled against my flesh, but when he lifted his face, he gave me a sweet smile that sent a bolt of lightning through the heart. My wetness was smeared across his face, and I should be turned off by that, right? Instead, seeing him happy about doing this for me was incredibly arousing.

"Come for me," he said, his voice shadowed with vulnerability. I was thrilled at his possession, at the way he took control and brought out everything trapped inside me.

But this Vexxion? I couldn't love anyone more than him.

"Will you?" he added. I released his hair, but he didn't chide me for pretty much yanking some out. No, his soft smile only grew wider. "I want to taste it. Feel it on my tongue and the pulsations on my fingers. It's mine, like you are, but it's about more than that. I need this right now. Fall apart for me, fury. I'm here. I'm going to catch you. I'm going to make it perfect. I'm going to hold you forever."

He didn't wait for me to speak but drove his face back between my legs, his tongue sliding inside along with his fingers. One hand still played with my nipples, sliding back and forth to make sure each found equal pleasure.

His thumb stroked my clit, and as engorged as I was, it wouldn't take long.

"I want your cock," I cried out, so far gone, I didn't care if I ever came back.

As long as Vexxion stayed with me, nothing else mattered.

"Wet," he growled. "So wet. Come," he mumbled. "Give it all. To. Me."

And just like that, I came apart, my body shuddering through a powerful orgasm, milking his fingers while his tongue swirled around, drinking in everything I had to offer and more.

52

TEMPEST

"Since the first time I tasted you," he said while his fingers continued moving inside me. It was exquisitely sweet and infinitely tender. "All I could think of was being with you again. You're . . ." He shook his head. "You give everything to whatever you do. You give yourself to me completely. I won't abuse that. I won't use you, fury. I promise."

My insides quaked and my heart melted. Could anything be better than this?

I'd never been one to come from sex more than once. It never helped that the guy would roll over and start snoring.

But as Vexxion continued to gently slide his fingers through my wetness, a spark lit inside me once more.

I was starving for him. No one else would ever give me the same satisfaction as him. I hadn't realized how deeply I could feel for someone, how those feelings would infuse everything I did with him—even this.

"I want you," he said, his voice hoarse with need. "Will you give me everything?"

"I'm already yours, so take me. I don't say this because you're sometimes a greedy prick who demands it."

He snorted, giving me another soul-melting smile, one boyish yet sly. "You like it when I claim you." He must know what he did to me—what he'd always do to me—because his fingers moved faster, driving up inside me.

And when his other hand took my clit and rolled it, my eyes flipped back in my head and my moan echoed around us.

"Keep your eyes on me, tiny fury. I need to see how my touch drives you wild."

"Can't you tell already?"

"It's a little thing. Will you do it for me?"

He sounded sweet; I couldn't do anything less. So, I let him in, let him see all the way to my soul.

"Good girl," he said.

"Show me my reward, Vexxion." This time, *I* growled. "Stop fucking teasing me. Give me your damn cock."

His laughter burst out again.

He might not realize it, but while I was giving him everything, he was also succumbing to me.

He tugged his fingers out, my body making a greedy, sucking sound, only to rise over me and glide the tip of his cock through my wetness.

He groaned, his face inflamed with tight desire, the cords on his arms standing out starkly as he braced himself over me. His sapphire eyes dove into mine, seeking all I had to offer and more, holding my soul immobile. "I'm going to give you cock, my greedy storm. Then more cock. Until you cry out that you've had enough."

"Never," I vowed.

"And that's why you're my fury."

With each swipe of his cock, I bucked up to meet him. If he didn't drive himself inside soon, I was going to flip him onto his back and do it for him. I'd had an amazingly spectacular orgasm already. How could I crave another so soon?

Leaning over me, he rubbed his chest against mine, making my nipples form hard buds, driving heat down to my core. I throbbed. I whimpered. And I needed him so much, I was going to explode before he sunk deep within me.

"Say my name," he growled in my ear. "Beg me, fury. I need this. Maybe just this once. I'll cling to it for a lifetime."

How could I give him anything less? "Take me, Vexxion. I'm yours. You're mine. I'll never want anyone but you."

"Yes," he breathed. His body rippled, shuddering, as if my words unlocked something feral inside him. His mouth found mine for one heavy kiss, before he feathered his lips along my jawline to my throat. They moved down to the sweet spot where my shoulder met my neck.

He bit down, marking me.

At the same time and with a jerk of his hips, he drove himself inside me, spearing me hard. Pulling out and doing it again while his tongue ran across the mark on my neck, soothing the slight sting.

Lifting his head, his gaze locked on mine. I wrapped my legs around him, and he pulled out and thrust into me again, this time seating himself so deeply, I groaned.

He was big. Wide. And long. Some said there was no such thing as an amazing cock, but they hadn't met Vexxion.

If I had my say, no one else ever would.

I hitched my heels on his amazing ass, urging him to keep moving. Unable to look away, I surrendered to him completely.

He whispered words in a language I couldn't understand, and I swore something snapped out of him to gather me close. It worked its way deep, just like he was doing with his cock, moving steadily within me while I bucked up to meet each thrust.

"You're beautiful," he said softly. "Your body was made for mine. Your pretty pussy was just waiting for my cock to fill it. See how you take me? No one else will ever give me the same satisfaction. I love your gorgeous, pabrilleen eyes, your thick hair that I ache to wrap around my hand only so I can arch your neck back to receive my mouth. Your strength. The way you fight me with everything you have inside. The way you shove aside my worst and bring out my best."

"Vexxion," I breathed. I wanted to say the same things, to tell him how much he meant to me, but his cock...

He started moving faster, his arms holding me in place, his eyes locked on mine. "You're going to come for me again, aren't you, my fury? You're a violent storm, and I know the exact way to diffuse you."

I clung to his arms, my nails digging in, and that seemed to drive him wild.

His silver bands of energy wrapped around me. Others dove between us, slicking across my throbbing clit.

My body crested with an orgasm like no other, my insides clenching, sucking on his cock, rippling around it.

"Yes, like that. Again," he growled, his hips jerking up to impale himself inside me again. He bucked against me, his muscles taut and his blue eyes flashing with fire. He'd gone feral.

The exquisite feel of his lightning on my clit was almost too much.

Another orgasm roared through me, slamming against the shore like the storm he'd already named me. How could I do anything else with this man? He knew exactly where to touch, where to be hard, and where to be gentle.

His body tightened. His cock stiffened even further as he thrust deep inside.

He bellowed as he came, shuddering in my arms, his gaze locked on mine. As his quivers slowed, he tipped his head down, pressing his forehead against mine, his eyes still delving within me, seeking everything that made me Tempest.

His pace slowed, though he kept moving just enough to make this last as long as possible for both of us.

Finally spent, he dropped to the side, taking me with him, keeping our bodies connected.

I lay across his chest, and he held me as if he'd never let go.

And when he kissed the top of my head, I knew there would never be anyone for me but him.

53

VEXXION

*T*wo weeks later, I stood fretting in the middle of the ballroom, something I hadn't done since . . . I'd never fretted, here or anywhere else. Complete control was the only thing that kept me from shattering.

My need for this night to be perfect was seared across my soul. It had to be.

We'd have to leave for Bledmire Court soon. At this point, we might already be too late. Yet I craved this time with her. Our entire plan could too easily fall apart and then we'd be left with nothing.

I wouldn't lose her. I was never letting her go. No one could rip her from my arms—not even her or her anger.

She was putting everything she had into her training, and her progress not only impressed me, but it also stunned me. I'd felt her potential from the moment I arrived at the fortress. But to see her power unfold like the soft petals of my favorite black and silver rose was striking.

Candles flickered around me, covering every surface except a large circle in the center of the ballroom and the path I'd left for her weaving through the flames from the door.

My hands trembled at my sides until I stilled them with a muttered curse. Nothing short of plunging my threads through my chest would slow the furious beat of my heart, however. I was—

A subtle sound drew my attention, and I lifted my head.

Tempest stood in the arched doorway wearing the black dress I'd left her adorned only with touches of silver threads that matched the silver chain holding my pendant she wore around her neck. Silver earrings winked from her lobes.

My heart came to a complete stop.

"Someone said I needed to dress in this." She pinched the skirt's fabric, pulling it away from her leg. Even this simple movement nearly sent her breasts tumbling out of the top of her bodice.

Someone?

"A man. A glorious, devastatingly beautiful fae lord left it on the bed with a note."

"I'm not only devastatingly *beautiful*, but I'm also equally malicious." My voice cratered with need. So much need only this woman could fulfill.

"I've noticed this, though you've never been malicious with me."

I'd do everything within my power to make sure she never saw that side of me.

Her scarlet painted lips curled upward. "How could I refuse your request?" Her hand lifted. "And this rose." She ran the black bloom across her lips. "I don't know where you find them. I walk through the gardens every afternoon after training, but—"

"You're supposed to be resting."

"I'm not a toddler in need of a nap." Her voice pricked as sharply as the thorns spiraling up the stem of the blossom she held like a mask in front of her face.

"Very well."

"No matter how hard I looked, and may I point out that there are many gardens surrounding your estate—"

"My mother loved flowers. She planted those gardens."

"Who tends them?"

"Me."

"I suspected you did. I haven't seen anyone here but us."

"I don't enjoy having staff puttering around."

"You've prepared all our meals. You keep this place clean, though I also assume you use magic to do that. I can't quite picture you wielding a broom."

"You should see it. I'm quite diligent."

"In everything you do."

"I don't use magic when I work with my mother's flowerbeds."

"I've looked for roses like this one, but I can't find them." She took a delicate sniff. "They say a gorgeous rosebud uses all of its energy to look pretty, leaving nothing left for a sweet scent."

Like me.

"You *are* pretty," she said with a light laugh. Her gaze traveled down my form in a caress that made my heart roar and press against my ribs. "I love that color on you. It brings out the sapphire blue of your eyes."

Which was why I'd chosen it.

She swept her eyes across the room. "It's beautiful here."

"My mother used to hold grand balls in this room. I only vaguely remember sneaking in one time, watching with big eyes until she laughingly shooed me back to my bed."

"When did your father die?"

"His soul left him long before I was born."

"I'm sorry."

I nodded.

"Do I dare walk along the path you've laid to join you?"

"I won't allow any of the candles to burn you."

"They're flames, Vexxion." Humor bubbled in her voice. "You don't control everything."

"Oh, yes, I do."

"So you say."

"So I do."

With a low laugh, she laid the rose on the polished wooden floor at the start of the trail.

She kicked off her heels. "These things are cursed. I know you wanted me to wear them, but they hurt! I'm going to have blisters I'll have you know."

"I'll kiss them until they're all better."

"Would you kiss up my legs while you're at it?"

My face ached from smiling. "You know I will."

"Maybe I should keep wearing them, then." But she left

them behind beside the rose and sauntered toward me. This woman was grace personified, though I doubted she knew it. Even when she worked with Seevar, something she'd continued to do in between combat and magical training, she moved in what I called her dance. She was the perfection of a wave gliding toward a sandy shore. A storm rumbling out at sea.

And I was so caught up in everything that made her my fury, I never wanted to break free.

She delicately walked toward me with her hair down like I'd requested, swept across her back. Her skirt swished around her ankles. Hot pain mixed with desire gouged away at my heart.

Like always, seeing her stilled the ravaging emotions I barely kept in check. I drank in the beauty of her form. How her eyes lit as they remained on me. And the flawlessness of her face. I'd memorized everything about her already, yet once again, I was struck anew.

Need was a sharp, agonizing blade in my chest. I'd feel this way for her forever. No matter what happened between us, my feelings would never change.

She stopped in front of me, looking up, reminding me all over again how tiny she was. How strong.

I'd do all I could to keep them from breaking her, but there were some things even I wouldn't be able to control.

"You put a lot of work into this." Her gaze traveled around the circle I'd left in the center of the polished marble floor. "Do you plan to seduce me here, my wicked fae lord?"

"Would I need to seduce you, or would you fall into my arms if I held them open?"

"Try it and find out."

"Only to have you bite me?"

"I do enjoy biting." She'd marked my shoulder last night, and I'd deepened it with magical ink. Now I could stare at it every single day of my life. I would do the same with her, etch magic into the subtle pink spot I'd gifted her as well.

Then everyone who saw it would know she was mine.

At the lift of my chin, lilting music soared through the room.

Her eyes widened, and she peered around. "Where's the orchestra?"

"They're hiding."

"They must be very tiny."

"This is true." I held out my arms; I could do nothing less. "Dance with me, my fury."

She flashed me a grin before her lips smoothed, though they quivered with joy. "I'd be delighted to do so, my kind sir."

When she stepped into my arms, I tugged her against my chest, savoring how warm she was. How alive.

As I swept her through the circle, her laughter trilled out.

54

TEMPEST

The next morning, Vexxion tugged off the covers and grinned down at my naked body. "Time to get up, tiny storm. You need to train."

"We've been at it for weeks."

"Perhaps I *could* give you a small reprieve."

Perhaps, huh? I blinked up at him, shading my eyes when the sunlight tried to stab them. "*Someone* kept me awake all night. He kept groaning. He wouldn't leave my body alone."

With a growl, he pounced, landing on top of me, peppering my face with kisses. His hot mouth soon moved down my neck to the top of my breast, then on to my nipple.

I clung to his shoulders, falling into his lure like every other time he touched me.

"*Who* is this man?" he snarled. His eyes sparkled as he looked up at me, watching for my reaction.

Moaning, I bucked my spine, begging for more of his heady touch. "You. It's. You." My breath hitched out with each word.

Tell me there will never be anyone else, he said. *Tell me you'll never let another man touch you.*

I don't want anyone else.

Exactly, he purred.

I drowned in the curl of his voice sliding across my mind and craved his words teasing through my body, lighting me aflame. His fingers were a gift from the fates. His tongue should be declared a lethal weapon. Yet when he spoke in my mind, growling my name or telling me how much he adored something I did for him, I lost all control.

We'd gone from our first, gritty wild sex to something I couldn't define. We'd built on our friendship over the past weeks, learning more about each other, then took it further. But he was also my lover, though it felt like so much more than that. I was connected to him in a way I'd never experienced before. We maintained our individuality, but we were one.

His fingertips slid down my side before stroking over to my breast. *These. Are. Exquisite.* He kissed one breast then the other, pausing to drag his tongue across each nipple. Forming tight buds, they throbbed, eager for more. *This. Is. Flawless.* He kissed my belly, running his tongue around my belly button. Delicious shivers erupted across my skin before diving down, sinking deep enough to make my bones dissolve.

Vexxion.

While looking up at me with the purest, most gorgeous smile, he ran his fingertips in circles on my thighs. He kissed the right one before moving his lips across my scars on the left, his touch as gentle as the drift of the finest flooferdar strands.

I winced, as self-conscious as ever about my scars.

No, he softly chided. *Never suggest that this part of you is anything but utterly perfect. This wound in particular.* He kissed the thickest scar, a bulging, twisted line gouging from one side to the other as if someone had tried to sever my leg from the hip. He ran his tongue across the patchy network spreading below, ended with kissing along the second line gouging above my knee. *Perfect.*

He moved between my legs, spreading them with a smile that stabbed through me, delivering a wound I'd never heal from.

As for your delectable pussy, you know how I feel about that.

"You adore it," I quipped.

"I do." His voice came out reverent, feverish in its intensity. "Sinking my cock into you has been the highlight of my life."

I wasn't sure about that. I suspected he'd been with many women, though I'd never ask. Surely there had been other pussies he'd enjoyed as much if not more.

He crawled up my body and held my face, staring into my eyes. "No one. I repeat, *no one* surpasses you, fury."

"Vexxion." I wasn't sure what to say. I could only feel the emotions flying through me, tugging me in all directions, dragging me up into the sky.

"Where was I?" With a smile, he moved back down my body, lingering over my scarred thigh. *You. Are. Amazing.* He kissed my scars again, growling against my overheated flesh. *I hate that they hurt you. One day, I'll learn who did this to you, and I'll make them pay.*

Let it go. I have.

"*I* have not," he huffed against my skin. While my core throbbed, aching for his touch, he kissed his way back up to my mouth and seared his lips across mine sweetly, his forearms soft along both sides of my head. His gaze locked on mine. Flames licked deep within them and the passion in his words darkened the sapphire to endless night. "There isn't anything I wouldn't do for you; anyone I wouldn't destroy if they so much as made you frown."

"Same."

He kissed me again as a reward, only to run his teeth along my jaw to my neck. His fingers slid between my thighs and through my saturated folds. He had a way of bringing everything inside me to the surface with one look. One growl. One glide of his fingertips across my quivering skin.

"I thought you wanted to train," I panted. Soon, my eyes were going to roll back in my head. I'd turn into a moaning wreck, and he'd take complete advantage of my disarray. There was no better way to fall than in this man's arms.

"Later." He leaned back and eased me toward the top of the bed, his touch infinitely gentle. While he enjoyed it rough—as did I—he could also love me in a way that made my insides melt. Whatever barriers I might think to erect, he'd shatter. "*Much* later. You're too enticing."

"It works both ways." His cock was big. Despite feeling it plunging deep within me on at least three separate occasions last night, I still craved this.

It thrust up against his abs, as eager as him.

"My, my," he said with a sly smile. "Look what I found." He pulled a clump of bright scarlet out from beneath my pillow and held it aloft, allowing parts of it to flutter down across his arm. "Could these be silken ties?"

My core throbbed. Flames licked through my veins and my heart thudded fiercely, a furious drum in my chest. "They just *happened* to be hiding under my pillow, right?"

"Isn't it funny how things happen that way?" His eyes smoldered. "What should we do with them?"

"Tie you up."

He pursed his lips, though one corner twitched. "One day, perhaps, but not this day."

"Why do you get to have all the fun?"

"Up." He urged me to sit and wrapped one of the strips of silky fabric around my head, covering my eyes. He kissed each of my eyelids before claiming my mouth in a kiss that seared through me. With a whisper of his lips, he kissed along my jaw to my ear. "This moment is for you, my precious fury. Lie back. I'll do all the work. I only want you to *feel*."

"I've been lying on my back, my belly, the side of the bed, and once lying draped across the side of the tub. I suspect I've felt all you have to offer already."

Allow me to surprise you. His words tickled through me. *I'm nowhere near done with you yet.*

"Will you ever be?" A raw edge cut through in my words. There was no denying that my need for him had grown rather than be sated. Each time he loved me, I wanted more.

Never. "You're fused to my soul," he simply said. "I'll die if you're not a part of my life."

That assuaged some of my fear. It sucked to care for someone who was only using you. I'd never been in love before him, but I no longer teetered on the edge. I'd plunged down the side because I knew he was waiting there to catch me.

A fierce need to protect him also thrashed through me, and there wasn't anything I wouldn't do, anyone I wouldn't destroy if they caused him pain.

After easing me onto my back, he took my right hand and gently coiled the silken tie around it, securing me to the headboard before doing the same with my left. "Are you with me still, fury?"

"If I wasn't?"

"While I'd be tempted to persuade you . . ." His fingers glided across my belly and slid between my legs, making me buck my hips up and moan. "If you said no, I would listen."

"I'm not saying no."

Leaning close, he slid his tongue across my earlobe. Everything inside me trembled. I was on the cusp of coming already, and he'd barely gotten started. "Then are you saying yes, my tempestuous storm?"

"I am," I breathed. "Yes." Oh, fuck, a thousand times yes.

"You're such a good girl."

My body spiraled, my mind flying apart along with it.

He lifted my hips and slid a plump pillow beneath them, making my thighs splay wide on either side. "Comfortable?"

"Yes."

"You tell me if I need to stop. Promise."

"I will."

He secured my ankles to the bottom of the bed, leaving me exposed for whatever he planned to do next.

"Where to start?" he asked in a contemplative tone.

"My breasts could use some attention."

"Ah, yes, your exquisite breasts." He traced his fingertips around each nipple, making them ache with need. "Did you know your nipples are the size of the tip of my pinky and that the color of your areolas perfectly matches the petals of a carest flower?"

"I did not know that."

"There's a large patch of them in the garden closest to the woods. Later, I'll take you to them. Show them to you. Strip you and lay you among them to prove they're exactly the same color."

"My backside might get dirty."

"Then I'll take great pleasure in lowering you into my tub and gently washing it away."

"Will you place more candles and flowers in the bathing chamber before you do it?"

His fingertips paused on my breasts. "Do you like when I leave them?"

"They're stunning. I love it."

He started stroking my breasts again, this time rolling the nipples as if this, also, was yet another reward for my words.

"Those roses . . ." I said. "You never told me where you get them from."

"They're rare and only grow in one location. I'll show you one day."

"And lay me among them naked?" Humor streaked through my voice.

"If you wish, though those flowers have thorns."

"I pricked myself on the one you left for me at Brodine's place."

"I apologize." Leaning up higher in the bed, he traced his scratchy tongue across my hand in the exact location.

"The wound has long since healed."

"Since I was the cause of your pain, I had to make sure."

"It was barely a scratch. I saw worse injury on any given day while training youngling dragons."

"I greatly admire your skill with beasts."

Heat seared across my heart. He could kiss me, climb all over me, and leave roses for me to find, but this . . . Knowing he could see how much care I took with Seevar meant a lot to me.

No more talking, my pretty one. Now is for feeling.

"Yes," I said with a laugh. "We can't take too much time from my training."

My laughter soon fled, replaced by moans as he kissed my lips, then moved downward. When he nudged my thighs farther apart and buried his face there, I pretty much shot through the roof.

He'd demanded I tell him no one else would ever do anything with my body, but how could I let them? I couldn't fathom the thought of letting anyone else close. I was his, and nothing was ever going to change that.

As he sucked on my clit and swirled his fingers inside me, soaking them in my wetness, a feral need clawed through me. I jerked my hips up as much as I could while bound to the bed and held down by his arm across my belly.

It hadn't occurred to me that our ability to communicate in our minds meant he didn't have to drag his tongue out of me long enough to speak.

I'm starving, he growled. *Feed me.*

I couldn't laugh because moans took all of my wind. As for thinking, that had flown through the roof as well. I'd melted into a puddle of pure, unadulterated passion. If he stopped now, I suspected I'd cry. Wail. Gnash my teeth and track him down, thrust him onto the floor, and impale myself on his luscious cock.

No one, and I repeat, no one will ever replace you. Burn that into your soul. The intensity of his words scorched across my mind, branding me.

When his tongue drove inside me, I gasped. He started thrusting it in and out of me, and I lost myself in the feeling, thrashing on the bed, tugging on the restraints. I begged him to finish me off. I was about to be flung off a cliff, and I welcomed it. Demanded it. Only then could I truly soar.

My body crested, then slid backward, guided by his masterful touch, only to climb once more. Each time, I spiraled higher.

Some of his fingers plunged inside me along with his tongue, while others gave my clit exquisite attention. So when something else touched my breasts, and an almost electric feeling coursed across my nipples, I stilled.

Too much? he asked in my mind.

This is your magic. Your power. If only I could see it.

My threads. They're your threads now. I and they exist only to give you pleasure.

A woman could get used to this fast.

I asked you if my threads were too much, he chided. *Do they hurt? They're . . . somewhat charged.* How could he focus on sending me thoughts while his tongue was driving me close to the edge? I was going to crash hard; the entire building would collapse around us.

It doesn't hurt. Don't stop!

Never. While his threads coiled and released around my nipples, tugging on them, he heightened his touch, his tongue and fingers driving faster within me.

I rose toward the top of the peak once more. It was too much.

It would never be enough.

Then he stopped. While I whimpered, he climbed over me and thrust his hand beneath my hips, lifting me like an offering to his own body. His other arm wrapped around my shoulders, tugging me against his chest, dragging across my nipples, while his cock probed my saturated entrance.

Perfect one. He shuddered as he thrust inside and pulled out, only to plunge back within me again. *Amazing one. You're everything to me.*

"Don't stop." I clung to the strands of silk and jerked my hips up to meet the drive of his cock.

"I won't, fury. I won't."

He continued moving within me, each jab of his hips burying his thick length deep inside me.

I was coming apart, bits of me flinging in all directions.

Only this man could do this for me, could make me feel as if I was everything.

His threads continued at my breasts while some wove between us to stroke across my clit.

"See me with your mind, fury. Know all of me," he growled in my ear.

He was beautifully flawed, each imperfection painted strokes showing me his resilience, his determination. Yet the real Vexxion hid beneath, and I knew only I saw this man as he truly was.

As he moved within me, I shot higher than I ever had before.

I crested, thrashing through an exquisite orgasm. The joy of it gripped me tight.

As I crashed on the other side, his body bucked wildly into mine.

And *he* surrendered to *me*.

55

TEMPEST

I dozed and woke suddenly, not sure why I'd been pulled from a dream of me and Vexxion happily living here at the estate. The odds of that were so low, even I wouldn't place a bet on a positive outcome. If we survived what was coming, though, I had a feeling we'd find a way to be together.

Over the past few weeks, my love for him had grown deeper. How could I do anything but love him when he gave me everything that made him Vexxion?

I still wanted to kill the fae king. That goal would never change. It was a burning need branded on my soul.

I'd only recently added "surviving to live a full life with Vexxion" to that brand.

When it was just me sacrificing everything to make sure the king paid for murdering Kinart and draining Nullens, I could accept I might die. But worry for what would happen to

Vexxion consumed me. I woke fretting deep at night and my mind was scattered when I should be focused on training during the day. My tension level was going to blast into the sky once we reached Bledmire Court.

"You'll settle into a job in the aerie," I whispered as I walked into the bathroom, finding a solitary white rose, lit candles, and steaming water waiting. My smile made my face hurt.

"You'll train dragons until the moment is ripe," I said as I sunk into the steaming, floral-scented water. Roses. I'd found the bottle on the ornate shelf beside the big tub the morning after we'd danced in the ballroom and added a few drops to the water with each bath.

"Vexxion will let you know when the path is clear to kill him." I nodded to solidify the thought in my mind.

I bathed and washed my hair, leaving it down because Vexxion liked it that way.

Wearing the leathers he'd placed on the chair, I left our bedroom and started down the three flights of stairs. When I heard voices below, I paused on the last landing.

Recognizing Zayde's voice, I flew down the rest of the stairs, leaping off the last three to land solidly in the foyer. My bare feet barely touched the wooden floorboards before I bolted into the library where Vexxion and I often sat together in the evening. He loved to read, and I did too. And if our books were tossed aside so we could read each other with our fingertips instead, so be it.

I skidded to a stop beside Zayde. "You're here!" I gave him a spontaneous hug.

His dark blue eyes widened. "Yes, I'm here. Nice to see you too, Tempest."

I peered around. "Where's Reyla. Reyla! Where are you?"

"She's not here," Vexxion said. "Zayde came alone."

"I was hoping to see her. Bro too." I needed to make sure they were alright.

"You will," Vexxion said.

My gaze caught his, but his emotions didn't shine there any longer, as if he'd pulled across shutters to hide. From Zayde? They'd been friendly while we traveled. Surely, he trusted the person he'd asked to claim Reyla.

How much of my plan had Vexxion shared with his friend? We hadn't discussed it. *Why* hadn't we talked about it? That should've been one of my first questions after he told me.

I was too easily distracted. In some ways, I was ready for this. In others, I was so unprepared, the odds were good I'd be destroyed.

"We'll leave tonight," Vexxion said. He braced Zayde's upper arms and stared into his eyes. "I'll see you soon."

Zayde nodded and flitted from the room.

"What's going on?" I asked. "Where are we going tonight?"

His grim gaze met mine, and his emotions raged in his eyes unchecked, smoldering with anger. "The fae king has moved up the wedding."

"What?"

"He's going to marry Brenna in one week." He took my hand and drew me over to the sofa, sitting and tugging me down on his lap. His arms wrapped around me should feel comforting. Instead, complete and utter dismay stormed through me.

"Why move it up?"

"He wants to solidify his power before anyone discovers his plan."

Damn. "I'm not ready."

He turned my chin, making me look up at him. "You'll have to be."

"Will one week be enough time?" I tried to think of how I might work my way inside the court while training dragons in the aerie in just a week's time, but it seemed impossible. Agitation spiked through me, panic chasing it until my heart slammed around, furious enough to break bones.

"A week is all we've got." He continued to hold my chin. "You can still back out. Let this go. I'll understand."

I traced my finger along the Claiming collar that hadn't twinged or hurt since the first time we were together. "And what would I do with this? I can't return to Nullen territory as long as it's lurking inside me."

"We could stay here."

Hide here at the estate, he meant. Why did a thread of desperation taint his voice? I must be mistaken. My anxiety kept coiling tighter and tighter until it was going to snap. I was projecting my stress onto him.

"I can't stay here. I can't let this go." I slid off his lap, moving far enough away so he couldn't tug me back, kiss me, and make me forget the real reason I was here. "I'm not backing out."

"You're sure? I won't think any less of you if you tell me you've changed your mind. As for the collar, I believe I've discovered a way around it."

Good. "We'll have to do it within the next seven days, then."

The stark bleakness scraping my insides raw told me how much I'd miss the time we'd had here. "Take me to Bledmire Court right away."

He sucked in a breath and released it before jerking out a nod. "Very well." Rising, he towered over me. "I've packed your things."

"I don't have things." Other than the bag he'd collected back at the Claiming area. My wooden dragon. Seevar. Everything I wore was laid out for me in the bathing area each morning, sometimes adorned with a solitary rose, though never a black one since the night we'd danced in the ballroom. "What about your grandfather's blade?"

"*Your* blade. I packed it as well."

"I assume I'll wear leathers like these when I work with the court's dragons."

"You'll only wear your leathers in our private suite." He lifted a strand of my hair and tugged it up to trace the end across his mouth. "You'll only wear them for *me*."

I snorted. "For about two seconds, you mean, before you magic them off."

"You love it when I do that."

Did I ever. "Otherwise, I guess I could wear simple dresses inside the castle. As your servant, no one will expect to see me in anything else."

"I won't allow you to dress simply."

"I need to blend in with everyone, not catch the king's attention." I frowned. "Wait. You said *your* suite?"

"All the upper fae echelon have suites in Bledmire Court's castle."

I braced my hands on his chest, soothed by the steady beat of his heart. Nothing else would keep me from spiraling. "I won't be assigned quarters in the aerie?"

"I never intended for you to sleep anywhere except in my bed."

While I adored how possessive he could be, I wasn't sure how this would fit with our plan. "Won't they find it odd that you're sleeping with one of the dragon trainers?"

"I'm changing the plan."

My hands froze on his chest, and I cocked my head, watching his face. Not blinking myself so I wouldn't miss *his* blink. "How have you changed it?"

"A week isn't enough time for you to start in the aerie and slowly work your way inside. Instead, I'll introduce you as my companion for the upcoming nuptials." His gaze remained steady, showing concern but nothing else.

"You mean your *mistress*."

"Collared companion if you will."

I had a feeling it was the same thing.

"You'll be safer this way," he said. His eyes remained wide open.

"Will arriving as your companion get me close to the fae king faster?"

He shrugged. "This is actually a better plan."

"Is it normal for fae lords to attend Bledmire Court events with a companion?"

"Always."

Dismay churned through me. "Not you." *Never you,* I growled in his mind.

Tempest. There was no mistaking his scolding tone. I wasn't sure how he added nuance to thoughts, but he was a master at this while I was still his apprentice in all things.

Don't ask again, he added.

Curse my stupid jealousy for jerking back its head and snarling. He'd killed his old lover, Selitta, to protect me, and if that didn't show true devotion, I wasn't sure anything else would.

I huffed, hoping it would release the squirmy feeling along with my breath. "What happened in the past stays there."

"Exactly."

My fingers loosened on his tunic. "I'm scared. I'd be stupid if I didn't name it."

"Fear's a good thing. It keeps you alert."

"And feeds my guards."

"Never let them down, not even when we're by ourselves. Don't look anyone in the eye. Make sure you're never alone with anyone but me." The urgency in his voice along with his palm pressing hard against my spine told me he was as worried about this as me. "And don't, under *any* circumstances, allow the fae king to take you to his—"

"Bedroom. Got it." My skin quivered with erupting goosebumps. "I'll stay with you or hang out in your suite in my leathers, waiting for you to join me and strip them off." I pressed for a smile, but my chattering teeth made it come out crooked. What if I—

You're losing control.

I can't help it.

"Don't worry until you have a real reason to do so."

"I think we're already at that point."

His gaze locked on mine. "You're my fury, a powerful storm billowing on the horizon. You're going to build until you're ready, then crash across the fae realm like the true tempest you've been since the day you were born."

My lips quirked up, and humor choked off my lingering fear. "I think you've got the wrong Nullen."

"You've *always* been the right person for this."

My smile came even easier. "You say the sweetest things."

"Because *you're* the sweetest thing. Never forget that." He gripped my shoulders tight. "Promise me."

"I do."

"Very well." His fingers lightened and glided along my jawline to my chin. He lifted it, and his mouth crashed down on mine.

Not pausing, he flitted us to our bedroom where he laid me gently on the bed.

He stood back and stripped off my clothing with a flick of his finger, shredding his own in seconds.

Then he crawled on top of me.

His body gave me the distraction I needed.

56

TEMPEST

I flew Seevar while Vexxion rode Glim, his sharp gaze remaining on me at all times as if he thought someone would attack and steal me away.

Drask had chosen to fly beside us, at least for now. Vexxion said we had hours of travel ahead of us. Drask would tire and could cling to my shoulder when he needed to.

Riding while dressed in a ballgown sucked, and Vexxion had insisted I could not wear my blades. He tried to insist, that is. No one would ever call me obedient. Like before the Claiming, I'd secretly strapped on a thigh sheath and slid my sharpest blade inside. I refused to enter Bledmire Court completely unarmed.

"Why not flit to the kingdom?" I asked as we flew across a vast forest with mountains looming ahead.

"We need our mounts."

"To escape after I've killed—"

He laid his finger on his lips and shook his head. "Remember. No place is safe to talk."

We could talk in our minds, I said.

That's for the best.

We haven't talked about where we'll go after we kill him. Or what might happen after I'd lobbed off his head. *Is there much chance we'll escape?*

I hope we'll be able to slip from the castle and flee in the uproar that follows. Or, even better, ensure no one suspects we were involved.

That would be a challenge if I stood with a long blade in one hand and held his head up by his hair in the other.

Will the son he's molded step into his boots and take over draining Nullens? I asked.

He frowned, staring forward. The mountains had grown closer, and we'd reach a pass we would slip through to the other side within minutes. *His youngest son knows, and he's on our side.*

I gasped. *You shared this with him?*

He nodded.

"When? Why?"

He tapped his lips.

I grumbled, but he was right. I needed to get used to hiding everything. I'd relaxed in the relative safety of his estate. I may never feel that security again.

Drask landed on my shoulder. He leaned against my neck, and if I knew him, he'd sleep while we continued to travel.

I visited with him briefly, Vexxion said in my mind. *I told him because he must be ready.*

Ready for me to murder his father? If I was speaking aloud, this would've come out as a shout.

He flinched.

Maybe I *was* able to project emotion after all. *Sorry. But you said he loves the king.*

He believes he does.

Why would he allow me to kill him, then? I asked.

It's complicated. The less you know, the better.

I'm going to make a mistake if you hold things back! I had to hand it to him. This time, he didn't wince.

I share what I have to, he said.

You should've shared this detail weeks ago.

Alright. I'll tell you more. I put this new plan in place weeks ago.

I gaped at him. "What?"

His face tightened. *Did you think I'd go along with such a simple plan? You won't be allowed to dance into the castle and stab him even if you were working at the aerie. Things need to be in place if we want this to succeed. Despite my need to see him dead, I'm not interested in sacrificing myself to make it happen.*

I flinched this time. *The original plan wasn't bad.* I huffed. *Do you think the new plan will work better?*

We don't have anything else.

What would you have done if I hadn't begged you for help? I stroked Drask's spine, taking comfort from my feathered friend.

There are many ways to do this. You're not the only one burning for vengeance. I told you what he did. I told you I was determined to make him pay.

Each word barked through my brain, making my spine jolt. *Fair enough.*

We flew in silence for a while.

Despite studying the landscape of our continent, I didn't know much about faerie, a lacking I needed to rectify.

"Tell me where the other courts are," I said.

"Bledmire Court is the largest of them all." *Ivenrail has slowly gobbled up territory from the others.* "Riftflame claims the smallest territory on the continent, to the northeast of Bledmire, plus they control an offshore island. They've held strong against him so far. Weldsbane Court is south of Bledmire, a long chunk of land spanning from the Nullen border to the sea on the east. A small section of Lydel takes up most of the southern coast below Weldsbane and they share a common border at the top." *Though the king has annexed all of this part of Lydel and Weldsbane for Bledmire. Only Riftflame remains strong.*

"Lydel's cursed. I heard the land's covered in thorns."

"Thorns only cover the island to the south of the area Ivenrail has claimed as his own. Only the island of the once great court of Lydel remains."

"What do you know about the curse?"

"Not much more than you."

The king must assume he'll be able to break the curse once he marries and collars Brenna, I said, switching to speaking in our minds. *I'm sure he'd like to claim the island as well.*

He craves it.

Is most of this motivated by his greed for more land?

Some say Lydel held incredible wealth in jewels and precious metals found below the ground and in their vast mountain range on the island, he said.

His magic should be enough. Why does he need material things?

He's greedy, as you stated.

What stops him from blasting through the thorns with his magic and claiming it all? I asked.

The thorns won't allow him to do so.

Interesting. *Is that part of the curse?*

Perhaps. Or in Lydel Court's case, a blessing.

But he placed the curse on Lydel, I said.

Is that what you were told?

Didn't he? We guided our dragons lower, and the sweep of their wings slowed as they wrangled with wind currents while soaring through the pass leading to a long stretch of plain beyond. Seevar responded beautifully to my commands, responding immediately as we angled them through the narrow gap.

I'm not vicious but—

Vexxion snorted.

I lifted my eyebrows but continued. *Will we need to kill the older brother as well?*

We might.

We have one week to figure this out.

Six days at best. We need to execute our foolproof plan before the wedding.

It's a tight timeframe. Do we stand a chance of success?

His gaze met mine, and for the first time, I saw grave concern there. *I wouldn't be here if I didn't think we'd succeed.*

I sucked in a deep breath and puffed it out.

A hiss rang out, and I jerked my head to face forward.

A bolt quivered in Seevar's chest. He screeched, blasting fire at nothing, and started tumbling, twisting as he fell toward the ground.

I clung to the saddle and leaned forward, trying to hold still, to give him the best chance of landing. Blood coursed from his wound, splattering my skirt. His ragged breathing told me the bolt had pierced his lungs.

Fear rocked through my heart. "Seevar. Hold on!"

His bellow of pain ripped across my spine.

57

VEXXION

Grabbing power, I used it to slow Seevar's plummet toward the ground. Tempest held her seat as terror crashed through me.

I wanted to flit toward the shooter, but I needed to use all the magic I had to slow Seevar's fall, or my fury would be killed when they slammed into the ground. She clung to the saddle, leaning over the dragon's neck, voicing hoarse cries to Seevar.

This woman had too much heart. Love made her vulnerable to attack. I'd yet to find the will needed to scare her as I should, like I'd done to many others without a touch of remorse.

Drask squawked and flung himself off her shoulder, fluttering toward the cliffs.

I forced Glim into a breakneck dive, determined to snatch her from Seevar's back before they made impact. My dragon was older, larger, and magically faster.

Seevar no longer spiraled but it was clear the bolt had hit

something vital. He plummeted, his wings barely flapping, his legs fluttering across his belly and tail. His head lolled. It was all I could do to reach her.

I'd flit to her if I thought I could do so safely, but my every thought and all my emotions were focused on slowing the dragon's fall so I could save her. Shifting forward in my saddle, I stretched out my arms.

Another crossbow bolt shot past me, driving through her shoulder. Her gasp stabbed through me. She reeled to the left, slipping across the saddle, starting to fall...

"No!" The ground was too far away. She wouldn't make it.

I was going to lose her.

Rage scorched through me, consuming everything worthwhile I had left inside. While using power to slow Seevar's body, I gathered the rest—and then even more—and blasted it outward, razing the world around us. A wall of blue fire seared up both sides of the cliffs. It scorched across the ground below us except for the area where Seevar would hit. I spared Drask. Seevar. And my glorious Tempest.

The wall of ice-blue flames kept going when it reached the tops of the cliff where the bolt had come from, searing across it and down the other side.

Tempest's shrill scream echoed, cauterizing my soul.

Fury!

I plucked her from the saddle before Seevar hit, pulling her against my chest, wrapping my arms and everything I had left inside me around her. "I've got you," I growled, my hands shaking and my heart a furious beast in my chest.

Seevar hit the ground, crumpling, slamming his torso along

the rocky surface. He skidded as I banked Glim up to avoid hitting the other dragon. Seevar came to a halt, no longer moving, his neck outstretched, his tail flopping. Slower. Slower. Until it remained as still as him.

"Seevar," Tempest wailed. "Seevar!" She chanted his name as if doing so would make a difference.

I reeled Glim around and flew him back to where Seevar lay, his eyes open and fixed. Leaping off Glim with Tempest in my arms, I landed not far from the dragon and gently lowered her to the ground. Holding her face, I made her look at me.

"Duck down behind him. Use his body as a shield. Wait here."

I stayed until she nodded before I flitted, landing on the cliff where the bolts had come from. I was torn between wanting to stay with her, to see if I could help Seevar, and making sure the person died. Fuck them. Fuck them all.

I found nothing but a pile of ash with bits of metal from a weapon mixed in.

With a grunt, I flitted back to where Tempest lay crumpled beside Seevar's head.

She stroked his face.

Her pain speared through my heart, slicing deeply. No one else had ever made me feel so much.

When Drask screeched, I knew.

I was too late to save Seevar.

58

TEMPEST

I stroked Seevar's face. "You're a good dragon, so brave and strong." My voice croaked, and I wasn't sure why. "Such an amazing dragon. That's why I love you so much."

Drask clung to my left shoulder. He leaned against my neck and released a mournful cheep.

My vision kept wavering, and water leaked down my face, but all I could focus on was Seevar.

"He's so still," I told Vexxion, not looking up. "I bet he's cold."

A big, fluffy blanket appeared, and he laid it across Seevar's back and neck, even covering his gorgeous, golden spiked tail.

"He wasn't an easy dragon to love," I told Vexxion as he knelt beside me and examined my right arm. It hung limply, and damn, did it hurt, but I could stroke Seevar's face with my left.

"I saw that." Vexxion grunted as he yanked something from my right shoulder.

More pain lanced through me, making my eyes lose focus.

"He didn't mean to be naughty," I said. "He was high-spirited, a truly amazing creature. He only needed someone to treat him gently, to show him the affection he craved, the affection all of us crave."

"You're right." He laid his hand on the area that burned, but that only made it worse.

Agony shot up my shoulder, through my neck, and blasted through my brain. I slumped toward Vexxion, not sure why I...

I woke held in Vexxion's arms, and snuggled deeper into his chest, sucking in his scent and savoring his warmth. He tightened his grip on me as Glim flew, and when he kissed the top of my head, I smoothed my palm across the exposed skin of his neck. This man could always make me feel good, no matter what was going on in my life.

That's when I remembered.

"Seevar," I whimpered, sucking in a breath only to wail it back out. "Seevar."

Drask screeched in sympathy. He soared in to land on me, tucking himself against my neck.

"Seevar," I whispered. "Seevar."

"I'm sorry." The words grated through Vexxion's chest like a blade grinding on stone.

I sobbed, remembering all the times I'd scolded the dragon, all the times I didn't tell him he was a good boy. I should've told him that all the time. "He was the best dragon. He had so much potential. He was going to be amazing."

"He was."

"What did you do with him?" I kept picturing him lying on the ground, predators finding his body . . . and that made me sob harder.

Drask kept cooing in my ear, rubbing his head against mine. Mourning our friend along with me.

"I made a pyre and burned him, then buried his ashes. I hope that was alright."

Because he sounded gruff and concerned, I dragged myself out of my sorrow long enough to wrap my arms around him and kiss his scars one after another. "Thank you."

He nodded, the jerk of his chin rubbing against the top of my head. "I wish I could've—"

"There was nothing you could do."

"If I'd gotten back in time . . ."

"You killed whoever hurt him, right? You ripped them apart and charred their remains, right?"

"If I could do it again, over and over, I would. There's nothing left."

"Good."

"I healed your arm. Does it hurt?" He kissed the top of my head again.

I shifted it gingerly, only vaguely remembering the bolt hitting me. "There's no pain." Only wretched, unending agony twisting through my chest. "Who . . . ?"

"Someone who hates me."

"Ivenrail Levestan." His name was poison on my tongue. "I'm going to start with his fingers, slicing them off with a delicate touch. I'll grin as his screams, then turn my attention his toes. He'll feel it when I cut off his legs at the knees and his arms at the elbows."

"I'll hold him down for you."

"And then I'm going to filet the skin off his back and chest."

"I'll enjoy watching that."

"And only when there isn't any part of him left to rip apart, I'll slice off his head."

"I'll mount it on the highest castle spire."

"Thank you." I snuggled deeper in his arms.

Glim continued flying, taking us across the great plain. We'd land in the aerie adjacent to Bledmire Castle.

"We'll arrive soon," he said. "Once we're there, I'll flit our things to our rooms."

I nodded and sucked in a breath. Turning in his arms, I stretched out my legs and wiped the infernal wetness off my face. My tears kept falling. Rain stolen from Seevar's soul.

Eventually, I saw the castle looming ahead, perched on the top of a cliff overlooking a broad, gorgeous valley spotted with clusters of tall, stately trees, the open areas covered with flowers. A pretty sight that hid the rotting carcass of the king's heart.

Eight broad, square towers jutted up from the four-story wall, each topped with a spike, as if the fae king wanted to spear the sky. The walls and entire façade of the castle had been constructed of bronze stone and each block was larger than a good-sized dragon. I couldn't imagine how they'd placed them. Likely magic.

Grand windows took up the front of the structure in a symmetrical pattern, and the view from any of them must steal the breath.

A second, equally large structure had been constructed to the right of the main building, and large, dark holes told me this was the aerie. A grand bridge made up of the same bronze stone connected the two buildings, gleaming in the setting sunlight that set the fortress aflame.

Vexxion guided Glim toward the farthest hole on the right, and the beast soared in through the opening, landing lightly in the pen beyond.

After sliding us from Glim's back, Vexxion lowered me gently to the sand-covered stone floor. He cupped my face, tilting it this way and that, examining me with concern. He must expect to find new scars.

"They're inside. I promise not to show them," I croaked. Screaming had scraped my throat raw, and the pain of my loss wracked through my body. My heart ached to the point where I wasn't sure I could bear much more.

But I'd have to. Our game was about to begin, and if I wallowed in the agony spearing through me, I'd give us away. I'd lost Kinart. Seevar. All the friends I might've made in the villages. I couldn't live through the loss of Vexxion.

He kissed me softly, his mouth gentle on mine. That made me start crying all over again.

When he lifted his head, he ran his thumbs across my tears, smearing them away.

"I'm sorry," I said. "Give me a second to regain control."

"You have every right to mourn."

"But don't let down my guards."

"Never. You need to live so you can get revenge. Promise me

you'll do everything within your power to make sure you make it through this."

"I will." I made this promise in my heart not just to Vexxion but to Kinart and Seevar and everyone else who'd been tortured by the king's greed.

With my guards high, I helped a stable hand take care of Glim, rubbing the beast down, giving him food and water, plus treats we found in abundance in the hall beyond his stall.

I told Glim he was a good dragon, the best in the world.

"There you are." Zayde slipped inside the pen, nodding to Vexxion who stood to one side, watching.

"Leave us," Vexxion told the stable hand, who jumped and fled the pen as if the dragon had shot flames in his direction.

Zayde waited before speaking in a low voice. "You arrived at the right time. The king . . ." His smile rose, though it contained no mirth. "He's in a fit, as usual. He knows you're coming and said you're to present yourself to him in the throne room immediately." His gaze fell on me. "Tempest as well."

"He knows about me?" It was all I could do not to gulp.

"Just that Vexxion picked someone at the Claiming." The grim look didn't leave Zayde's eyes.

Vexxion grunted. "We'll see him as soon as we've refreshed ourselves in my suite."

Zayde smiled for real this time. "Take care not to make him any madder than he already is. Madrood's with him."

"Who's Madrood?" I asked as we left Glim's stall, securing it behind us.

"The king's dragon," Vexxion said. "Stay away from it."

If it's anything like the king, I don't want to go near.

Promise me.

So many promises. I said I wouldn't.

A stable hand entered the aerie on the opposite end of the long hall. He took one look at us, and pure unadulterated terror took over his face. He dipped his head forward before spinning and stumbled back outside.

Zayde grunted. Vexxion said nothing, continuing to walk down the hall beside me with dragons shuffling their claws in the stalls on our left.

A slender fae woman slipped out of a pen ahead of us. When she caught us moving toward her, her breathing hitched. She dipped forward in a deep bow and after shooting a horrified look our way, she scurried back inside the pen, banging the gate closed behind her.

Zayde snorted. "I've arranged for your staff. Calm ones."

Vexxion's frown deepened. He looked my way.

What's going on? I asked.

Nothing. It's nothing.

Are they afraid of Zayde or . . . I knew. *You have a reputation here.*

Evidently.

You mentioned a suite of rooms, but I thought . . . That it was a formality, something that came with his station within the fae realm. He'd fled a long time ago. Why would they keep a suite open for him?

You thought what?

Nothing.

He stared at me for a long while before turning his gaze forward.

I swallowed hard, determined to pin him down about this later.

We exited the aerie, and I paused to gape at the beauty of this place. The setting sunlight slaked across this part of the world in gold and red, making the metal roofs gleam like jewels. Flags fluttered from each of the tall spikes jutting off the towers. And the walls glowed as if the stones had been cut in a magical world far beyond this one.

Despite the pall of sorrow hanging over me, I could still admire how magnificent the castle was. No wonder it was the seat of Bledmire Court.

Cliffs plunged all the way down to a valley on our left, and rolling green hills stretched away on my right seemingly forever before ending at a tall mountain range with white-tipped peaks. Northeast. Riftflame Court lay far in that direction.

Vexxion stopped ahead of me and looked back, waiting while Zayde continued across the enormous stone bridge arching up and gracefully swooping back down to approach the castle. A few fae walked across the expanse, some leaning against the wall to admire the view.

Are you alright? Vexxion asked.

I nodded and caught up to him, watching as Zayde continued along a path toward the castle. He must have something to do. We'd see him later.

We started up the slant. As if feral creatures were attacking them, the fae scampered away, leaving us alone.

"Why are they doing that?" I hissed.

Vexxion jerked his head back and forth. *Speak only in my mind.*

Why?

They don't like me.

I don't understand. I would've thought they'd forgotten you. Since he'd been gone for so long.

They know me all too well.

I swallowed again, unsure why it wouldn't go down, and kept pace with him. *They don't know you like I do.*

You're correct.

We walked down the other side of the bridge and crossed the stone expanse leading to the three-story carved castle doors. Five fae males stood to the right of the entrance, their gazes fixed on us, their faces universally struck by horror.

When we got closer, they rushed around the side of the castle.

No, they fled around the side of the castle.

You need to tell me what's going on, I screeched in his mind.

I will. Soon.

I bit back my questions. We could speak in our rooms soon. I'd figure this out.

We stopped in front of the doors, and I gaped at them, tipping my head back to take in the ornately carved dragons literally writhing on the dark wooden surface.

Are they trapped there? I asked, my heart on fire yet filled with a touch of terror.

You could say that.

What would you say?

"They're trapped," he ground out. *Enough.*

Tightening his grip on my hand, he flitted, and this time, he didn't stagger after. What was different now?

I found myself standing in a palatial room, the furniture very old but in exquisite condition. At least three times the size of any residence back at the fortress, the room had a wall of windows that looked out at the valley, plus a huge fireplace already lit. The dancing flames soothed me—but only a touch.

Our bags had been placed on the floor beside the enormous bed draped with thick, dark blue fabric. I'd be lost there if I slept alone, but it would work nicely for me and Vexxion.

"I'll unpack." I started toward them, but he gripped my arm, holding me back.

"The staff will take care of it. We need to change and go to the king."

"I want to wash."

"Of course." He waved to an open doorway on my right and I left him, striding into an equally large bathing chamber with a tub about half the size of the bed, plus other gilded fixtures.

After taking care of my needs, I washed my hands and stared at my face in the mirror. A few splashes of water didn't do much to improve my appearance, but I doubted the king would do more than glance my way. I used the comb in the closet to remove the worst snarls from my hair and re-braided it neatly. The gown was stained with blood. I'd don a simple dress, something that wouldn't stand out.

Hearing voices in the bedroom, I left the bathing area, finding a woman unpacking our things while another pulled down the bed for the evening. A third woman wearing a pale blue dress with her back facing me, stood at the open closet door, hanging up one of the dresses Vexxion had crafted for me.

She turned partway toward me to remove another from the bag.

I gasped.

"Reyla." I sprung across the room, barreling into her, nearly knocking her into the closet.

She said nothing. She didn't touch me. She stared at my bag blankly.

Frowning, I leaned back, my arms still snug around her waist.

Her collar writhed beneath her skin that was scarlet as if she dug at it whenever she could.

Her fingers rose and she raked across it, her face blank.

Her eyes blank.

"Reyla. Reyla!" I shook her, making her head flop like a doll's.

When I stopped, she still didn't meet my eyes.

Her milky gaze took in nothing.

59

TEMPEST

Don't. Say. Anything, Vexxion growled in my mind. *Back away from her. Come to me.* He held out his hand where he stood in the sitting area made up of three plush sofas and six tall-back chairs, all posed to face the blazing fire.

What's wrong with her? I screeched.

She was claimed.

So was I, but I'm still . . . me.

She's still your Reyla. She's just . . .

Controlled. I couldn't stop screaming, though I trapped the shrieks inside.

I told you this wouldn't be pleasant.

Had he? I couldn't remember.

Calm yourself. Come to me. His hand didn't waver.

Sucking in a breath, I made sure my guards were still strong and walked as sedately over to him as I could. He sat and tugged me onto his lap, making sure I faced the windows and not my friend. His chin dropped onto my head, further pinning me in place. *When you're ready, we'll flit to the throne room. The king is waiting.*

My body shook, and I told it to snap out of this, to find some control.

Control... It was all I could do not to laugh. It would come out hysterical. I'd never be able to stop. I knew this.

Should we change into other clothing? I asked.

He might enjoy seeing the blood, but we'll wear something else.

I didn't want to stand out.

A flick of his finger, and he wore a black tunic with only a few gold ornaments on the shoulders. Black pants. Polished boots. His hair lay smooth on his head, not in the wild disarray I adored.

I now wore a pretty green gown with a low-cut bodice, another dress that perfectly matched my eyes.

I look good in red, you know. Yellow. Blue. Other colors besides black and green.

He snorted. *You look best naked.*

If the staff wasn't still arranging things, I'd wrap myself around him and kiss him. He knew just what to say to relax me —as much as I could relax while inside Bledmire Castle and with Reyla... gone. For now. Only for now. *So do you.*

I do enjoy burying my body inside yours.

My anxiety backed down a few notches. I'd wreck this plan if I started falling apart when we'd only just arrived. So, while it pinched badly enough I could barely breath, I segmented my worry about Reyla and grief for Seevar away from my mind. I'd mourn later when Vexxion could hold me. Soothe me. Distract me.

It was time to set this game into motion.

The women left on silent feet. If I hadn't been watching them out of the corner of my eye, I would've missed their departure.

Vexxion stood and slowly released me, letting my body slide down his.

Drask cawed from where he perched on the back of a chair.

Vexxion cupped my face and studied it as intently as he had in the stable after we arrived. "You're ready?"

I sucked in a breath and nodded. *Guards up.*

A flick of a smile softened the harsh lines of his face. *Good girl.*

He held me and flitted, taking us to what must be the outer chamber of the throne room. Fae guards flanked the tall, closed doors, also made of rich dark wood and carved with writhing dragons.

Vexxion started toward the doors. *Remain behind me. Keep your eyes down. Don't say a word.*

I hear you.

As the guards gaped at Vexxion, I trotted behind him, my pulse jittery in my throat, and my breathing ragged. As I moved, I noted that the sheathed knife on my thigh was gone. *You took it.*

Keep quiet.

I wanted to huff, but I wasn't a fool. This was too important for me to give into a snit now.

Before we reached the doors, the guards swept them open,

actually sliding behind the enormous panels as if they were desperate to hide.

I wanted to ask Vexxion—again—why everyone was terrified of him, but at this point, I wasn't sure I wanted to hear his answer. He'd explain everything later. No matter what, I'd try to understand.

We walked into another huge room, this one glowing from all the gold gilt covering every surface. Paintings with unimaginable writhing creatures hung on display on the outer walls, and pillars marched on either side of the aisle, funneling us toward a broad dias with stairs mounted in the middle. A man sat in the equally huge and gilded throne, though his face remained in shadow. I couldn't make out his features, though I didn't need to.

This was the fae king—the man I was going to kill as soon as I got the chance.

A cluster of staff flanked his right side, universally staring forward.

And behind him on his left...

I'd told myself nothing could surprise me, but I'd never seen a dragon that large. His silver scales gleamed in the lights, and smoke coiled from his broad nostrils. His red eyes locked on me, and I froze for a moment, wondering if this was it. He'd sense my intention and it would be over.

Instead, he looked blandly away, his eyes landing on Vexxion next.

I swallowed hard and kept my gaze on the elaborate swirls in the stone floor underfoot.

So much wealth. A village—or three or seven—could eat heartily for multiple lifetimes with the wealth displayed here.

We reached the end of the aisle, though we still had a broad distance to cross before we'd reach the outer edge of the dias.

Vexxion stopped and dipped forward in a bow.

Should I curtsy?

Remain still. Remember the rules.

I was dragging my gaze from Vexxion's back to the floor when a subtle movement among the staff standing opposite the dragon caught my eye.

Brodine stood motionless, staring forward blankly.

Like Reyla.

Panic fluttered down my spine.

But . . . he was claimed and should be someplace else. Anywhere but here.

I couldn't help it. I slid my eyes quickly across the king, determined to imprint his image on my mind before flicking it back to the floor. He was no longer in shadow.

Images from the Claiming flashed through my mind. This was the man who collared Brodine.

Which meant . . .

The fae were only allowed to claim one person at a time. Since he intended to collar Brenna in less than a week, the king would not be allowed to do so unless the Nullen he'd bonded with was dead.

The king was going to murder Brodine before the wedding.

60

TEMPEST

*H*orror and dismay crashed through me. I swayed.

Do not move!

I wanted to snarl at Vexxion, tell him not to shout in my head, but I needed the stern warning. I was falling apart, and I couldn't maintain control of anything. I snapped my spine into position and internally growled at myself. If I wasn't careful, I'd mess this up completely.

"Please, Your Highness," someone said from ahead of us. I'd missed the person kneeling in front of the king, his torso bowed forward to press his forehead against the floor. "I told them what you required but they begged. They begged for more time. I granted them a week, until after your upcoming wedding. Surely you won't need to conclude this matter until after that."

"You're one of the most powerful lords in my Court," the king growled. "Yet, here you are, a complete failure. You disgust me." Out of the corner of my eye, I caught him lifting his left index finger.

The dragon rumbled behind him, slowly oozing forward, a silver menace bursting with rage.

"No. No!" The man scrambled to his feet and raced toward a door on his right. Before he could reach it, the dragon blasted him with fire.

Like a candle wick snuffed out, the fire cut off.

A pile of ashes smoldered on the floor as the dragon coiled back behind the king.

"Vexxion," the king said with a heavy sigh. "You misbehaved."

Vexxion remained motionless. I peered around, looking for a blade to defend him. Would the king burn him as well?

"However, I've decided to overlook that shortcoming for now," the king said. "Come forward."

Relief hissed from my lungs.

Vexxion stalked toward the dias. Should I remain here or—

"Bring your little Nullen along with you. She's quite pretty, isn't she? In a quaint kind of way. Send her up to me. I'd like to examine her."

If only I had a blade . . . He'd assume I was as passive, as blank as all the rest of those claimed.

What were the fae lords doing to us? This was much more than bonding servants.

Access . . . My gaze shot to Vexxion, but he wasn't looking my way.

The king was draining all of us, then killing us and tossing us aside. I expected to hear the guttural roar of dregs in the distance, but only the tick of silence echoed in the room tainted with the lingering stench of the scorched body.

My collar tightened, and I'd swear to the very fates themselves that my neck blazed red on the surface. Unable to hold myself back, I clawed at my skin while the vines dug their thorns deeply.

Magic churned up from my well in a rolling mass, but I found no comfort in its embrace.

My hands left my neck and flopped at my sides.

No, they'd been *pinned* at my sides. My legs were made to move forward.

I was forced to walk past Vexxion, and I was not allowed to look his way no matter how hard I tried. My deadened feet took me up to the edge of the dias. They carried my limp body up the stairs and toward the king.

The king watched Vexxion, not me.

And in that moment, I *knew* who was controlling me.

Control was the first step of a Claiming.

My heart shuddered. He was doing this to protect me.

However, I refused to allow Vexxion to magically force me onto my knees.

"Where's your cousin?" the king asked Vexxion. "He flew with you to the fortress to complete an errand for me, but he has not returned."

"I'm afraid he won't be able to make it to the castle for an indefinite length of time."

The king snarled. "What did you do?"

"Me?" Vexxion's lips twisted. "What makes you think I did anything?"

The king's glare only deepened before he turned back to where I stood a few feet away, his face coiling into another smirk.

"Interesting," he drawled, his sharp gaze gouging into me. "As I noted, she's pretty in a humble sort of way. You should dress her nicer. A lower bodice that hints at her rosy nipples. A slash up the side to reveal her legs. Tighter fabric to show off her delectable curves." His eyes raked down my form.

I couldn't move. Couldn't speak. I could barely breathe.

Out of the corner of my eye, I caught the king's hand lifting. "Leave us."

He didn't mean me. He didn't mean Vexxion. And I was certain he wished for his dragon—Madrood—to remain here as well because the beast stayed in place behind the throne, snorting fumes that clogged my throat. Clogged my mind.

Brodine and the others left the room on silent feet.

Was there anything left of my friends inside, or had it been sucked away? Despair hitched up my spine on jagged claws. My scream kept erupting up my throat only to be stomped back down. If only I could find a weapon to plunge through the king's right eye.

"You should've left things alone, Vexxion," Ivenrail said in a sultry voice. "I sent you to the fortress to handle the issue with the commander. As if I'd allow him to steal Nullen power. The fool."

The commander was part of this diabolical plan?

"I sent Farnoll to tell the commander to send this one to the Claiming. I wanted *him* to claim her," he added.

Farnoll claim *me*? "Why *me*?" I choked out.

"Some of you have more power than others," he said. "I find pleasure in seeking you out."

It all made sense now.

Farnoll would claim those with more power like me. The king would drain us. Then we'd be tossed aside and replaced.

I'd begged Vexxion to claim me. He hadn't known a thing about my plan. He wasn't involved in whatever this was.

"I supposed it no longer matters," the king said. "This will work as well." He leaned sideways to look around me. "Why are you standing down there, Vexxion? Come up. Join me. She's quite delightful, isn't she? I might even allow you to keep her. When I'm through with her, of course."

I expected Vexxion's threads of lightning to snap across the open space. Now, he would act. I'd scream with joy when they coiled around this wicked fae king's neck. I'd grin while Vexxion strangled the life from him before tossing him against the farthest wall.

He'd shove aside his fear and act.

Instead, Vexxion walked up the stairs sedately and stopped beside me. A hasty glance up showed he wasn't looking my way.

What's going on? I couldn't hold back the words.

He didn't answer, and for some reason, I sensed he hadn't *heard* me. What kind of wall could keep me out?

Ivenrail flicked his finger at me. "Come closer, rider."

"Her name's Tempest," Vexxion growled.

Yes! Now he'd tell the king I was his fury, that I meant everything to him.

That he loved me.

Although, he hadn't yet told me.

The king snorted and leaned back in his throne; his index finger slanted across his chin. His head angled so he could study my frame again. "I told you to come here, *rider.*"

I was compelled to walk closer to him and stand beside the arm of his throne. At least now, I was out of the path of Vexxion's lightning threads. Even angled away from Vexxion, I'd be able to see his face while he defended me.

"Tonight," the king said quite jovially. "I'll take a little sip of her power. Not too much. Not yet. Nullens like this are delicacies that need to be savored. I believe even a touch will go right to my head."

Vexxion's hands twitched at his sides.

I stared at him, pleading with him in my mind. I had no weapon to defend myself other than the guard I'd placed on my mind. I tried to pull up my power to flit—and it refused my command. It boiled within the well, but each time I slipped my hand into the froth to scoop it up, it coursed off my fingers.

"I know you won't be stingy." The king tipped back his head and laughed as if they were good friends out at the bar, having a drink while discussing which of the barmaids they'd take home for the night. No, which one they'd take home to share.

Vexxion's fingers coiled, forming fists, then releasing.

"I sense reluctance on your part." The king's hands smacked onto his throne, tightening to the point the metal bowed. Madrood oozed forward and sucked in a deep breath.

No . . .! Vexxion. Get back. Run!

"Zayde was quite generous, though I was disappointed that I had to persuade him as well." The steel in the king's voice told me this man would not allow anyone to refuse him. The mockery there told me he knew no one dared.

My breath caught.

Younger brother.

Zayde.

The king had two sons. A younger one who adored his father and an older one who he'd molded in his own image.

Access was the last stage of the Claiming. It could only be shared with someone of the same blood—Vexxion had clearly told me that.

At the realization of what he'd done to me, agony rocked through me, a storm blasting onto the shore. I'd . . .

I couldn't do anything.

My storm had been muted.

Controlled.

How could you? I shrieked into Vexxion's mind.

He flinched but remained stiff, his gaze looking everywhere but at me.

I gaped up at the king, taking in his piercing sapphire eyes before I wrenched my gaze away.

You fucking bastard, I hurtled Vexxion's way.

I am aptly named.

Oh, so you can speak now?

It was too late . . . for *everything.*

Farnoll was supposed to claim me. Instead, I begged Vexxion to do it, only to have him bring me to the king as an offering. He'd wrapped those wretched vines around my neck that now gave him—and the king—complete control over me.

He'd awakened my magic—for them to access whenever they pleased.

He "trained me," but that was just to give him a chance to seduce me before he brought me here as a gift for his father.

I gave that man my body. My heart. My soul. While he...

He never intended to help me. He and the king probably laughed about my silly plan to kill him.

Control. Awakening.

Access.

"I thought I was in *love* with you," I blubbered, feeling unbelievably naïve. So incredibly stupid. Tears slicked down my face. I smacked at them, hating that I showed Vexxion even this tiny bit of emotion. "All this time... You. Were. *Toying* with me."

"I was, Tempest. You're just a game piece on the board," he said in that deadly voice that used to make my heart flip over.

The voice that would make me beg him for whatever he'd deign to give me.

The voice that made me love him.

"From the moment we met, I knew the role you'd play." He said it so blandly. So... sneeringly.

I... I couldn't fathom what I should do next. There was no way out.

I was trapped.

Drask flew into the room, cawing, and I was so glad to see my only remaining friend that tears stung my eyes.

Instead of coming to me, he landed on Vexxion's shoulder. He flapped his wings and leaned into Vexxion's neck. Pecked his cheek.

"Still have that bird, do you?" Ivenrail asked. "I thought you'd disposed of it."

"Not yet." Vexxion cleared his throat. "Tempest *is* quite sweet. I'm sure you'll enjoy her as much as I have."

I'd slash his throat. I'll kill him. Then I'd do the same with the king.

But... I was completely locked down by this collar.

I could do *nothing*.

"Allow me to ready her, father," Vexxion said quite blandly. "Then I'll gladly let you have a taste of all she has to offer."

If I wasn't glaring at him with the pure, unadulterated hatred blazing across my soul...

... I would've missed it.

He blinked.

∼

Ahh. Sorry about that cliffy (maybe).

I hope you enjoyed the first book in the Kingdom of Blighted Thorns Series.

A Court of Wicked Fae is next.

While you're here,
sign up for my newsletter, & I'll send you a *steamy* cut ballroom scene from Vexxion's point of view. You know you want to read it. He's morally gray, stalker-ish, and I'm sure you're wondering what just happened, but a high heat scene between him and Tempest?

It can be yours...

Join my Facebook Group,
Romantasy Court

Follow me!
Bookbub
Facebook
Instagram

ABOUT THE AUTHOR

Alaya Wells is a romantic fantasy author who loves spinning tales about brooding heroes falling for fierce, independent heroines. Expect spicy romance, touch her and I'll hurt you heroes, and a guaranteed happily ever after.

A romantic at heart, Alaya loves walking on the beach and sipping expensive tequila, sometimes at the same time!

BOOKS BY ALAYA

Kingdom of Blighted Thorns Series

A Kingdom of Bitter Magic

A Court of Wicked Fae

A Crown of Cursed Hearts

Printed in Dunstable, United Kingdom